C2103

CW01430047

Jessica Meats is a graduate of the University of York and works in the IT industry. She draws on her experiences as a technology specialist and martial arts student to create a unique and interesting fictional community of combat experts and computer geeks.

Shadows of Tomorrow

Jessica Meats

Shadows of Tomorrow

Vanguard Press

VANGUARD PAPERBACK

A CIP catalogue record for this title is
available from the British Library.

ISBN: 978-1-84386-769-2

*Vanguard Press is an imprint of
Pegasus Elliot MacKenzie Publishers Ltd.*
www.pegasuspublishers.com

First Published in 2013

**Vanguard Press
Sheraton House Castle Park
Cambridge England**

Printed & Bound in Great Britain

To Jen and Nicci for the loan of a torch when the light at the end of the tunnel went out.

Part One

One

Arrivals

Five coffins lay on trestle tables at the front of the large training hall. Five occupants, their bodies shredded and wrecked, were dressed in neat uniforms and swathed in flowers to mask the extent of their wounds.

There would be an official funeral later, with TV cameras and diplomats, streamed live over the internet so that the planet could mourn the passing of these heroes. But that would be later. Here and now was a private moment. This was the time for Defenders to say farewell to their own. Almost three hundred souls stood together in neat lines, looking towards the coffins and their fallen brothers.

Gareth stood by the coffins at the front of the room, looking at each body in turn. He'd known these men. They'd laughed together, eaten together, trained together, fought together. Then Gareth had let these five men go through the portal to die on the Norwegian coast, their bodies torn to shreds by Outsiders and smashed against rocks by the violent sea. What lay in the coffins now were jig sawed fragments of fallen warriors.

Gareth had let them die.

He stared at the faces, seeing them branded into his memories, the image carried in perfect clarity to past and future.

A hand rested on Gareth's shoulder, a warm attempt at comfort that couldn't quite reach through the grief. Adrian Boron, second in command, stood beside Gareth, looking at the coffins.

"We're ready," Boron said. Ready to hear the supposed wisdom of the Defence Master. Ready to be told that the world wasn't as terrible as it seemed at that moment. Ready for Gareth to speak.

Gareth had rarely felt less ready but he did what he must. He turned to face the gathered Defenders, lines of men and the occasional woman, almost all of them older than him, yet looking to him to lead. Their faces were grave and serious, each with their memories of the departed, their pain and anger. Gareth took a breath, trying to swallow down his own pain, bury it inside so that he could speak with clarity.

"We all know the risks," he said. "We know what might be asked of us. We stand as warriors and protectors, knowing how high the cost might be. We stand between this world and the Outsiders, between the innocent and the death that would take them. Is there a more selfless act than to stand between a monster and a complete stranger? To put yourself in harm's way to save people you've never even met? These five men made that sacrifice. These five chose the selfless path. I have spoken to each of them about being a Defender, about the dangers of the life we lead. I believe Pip summed it up best."

Gareth had been slowly walking along the line of coffins. Now he stood by the smallest, bearing the young Chinese Defender who'd been known, almost at an official level, as Pipsqueak or Pip because of his height.

"Pip told me," Gareth continued, "that if his death meant just one more person living who would otherwise have died, it would be worth it. I don't know how many people are alive today because of these five, but it is far more than one. Thank you, Pip, for your sacrifice. Farewell."

Gareth touched his hand to his heart and then to Pip's forehead, his fingertips brushing the dead flesh. He moved along the line, repeating the final words and the gesture, bidding goodbye to their teammates.

Boron was a step behind him, looking down at the coffins and saying his own words of parting. Then came the others, moving from their places in a slow procession, senior Defenders first with the others following one-by-one. Each wanted to say something, each knowing that one day it could be them lying in this place.

Gareth slipped from the hall while the others were still gathered around the coffins. He moved quietly down the corridor to one of the smaller training rooms. He left the door open a crack, an implicit invitation to Karl, who'd followed him out. This room was one of many along the hall, little but well-equipped for private practice. Gareth headed straight for the punch bag hanging in the back corner.

He didn't bother with gloves or padding; sometimes it was good to feel the sting of skin against leather because the physical pain helped deal with the guilt.

He'd known the portal would open. He'd known those five would be the first response team. He'd known they'd be coming home corpses.

In the first days after his accident, against Master Amiron's advice, he'd tried to change the events he remembered. There had been another memorial service with a single coffin. Gareth had remembered that day and fought to keep it from happening, shifting the duty rosters to everyone's annoyance, trying to keep the coffin from becoming filled.

The unfortunate young man in question had been in the control room arguing about the fact that he'd been apparently pulled from active duty. Which meant, when the next attack started, he'd been perfectly positioned to respond to the call and to lay down his life. He'd only been there because Gareth had tried to keep him away. So, this time, when he'd remembered the upcoming funeral he'd stood by and done nothing when these five answered the call.

He pounded his fists against the bag, pummelling pure rage into its weight. Behind him, the door opened and shut again with a click. Gareth didn't pause, letting a flow of punches fill the quiet room. It took Karl a while to speak, sifting through silence to find the right words.

"Hey," Karl said.

Gareth gave a grunt of greeting between heavy breaths. His fists were stinging now, his heart racing, his lungs heaving from the effort. But he didn't slow. Anger poured out, anger at the Outsiders who had killed his friends, anger at the world that had put them in the position to die, anger at the abilities that let him see their deaths coming but not prevent them.

"Good speech," said Karl. "Nice and… respectful."

Gareth delivered a final punch that set the bag swinging on its hook. He held on to it, partly to still it, partly to hold himself up as he fought for breath.

"Pip was nineteen!" he burst out. "He was younger than I am."

"He was a Defender," Karl replied. "He did his duty, just like any of us would."

Karl didn't know, none of them did, about Gareth's ability to remember things that hadn't happened yet. He couldn't understand what it felt like to stand on the edge of the flow of time, seeing those caught in the currents, but being unable to haul them out before they were pulled under. Karl and Boron and the others were all trying to make him feel better, telling him that he shouldn't feel guilty for the passing of those who'd served here. But how could he not? How had Master Amiron coped with this?

Gareth wanted to believe things could improve but he couldn't remember a better time. His future lay before him, portals and Outsiders and fighting. This was his life now. For every Defender who had retired or quit or stepped aside, a hundred more had given their lives in the fight. And now it was Gareth's duty to send them out there, knowing that they would die.

Gareth wasn't sure he could do that. He wasn't Master Amiron.

"The world doesn't revolve around you, Gary," Karl said suddenly. "You can't control what people choose to do. Those guys knew what they signed up for. Stop beating yourself up."

Gareth took a breath. He took another, trying to hold the tempest of emotions in check.

"You're right," he said.

"I'm always right," Karl said.

Gareth chuckled. It was the first laugh he'd had for a while, a pitiful sound that barely qualified as humour. But it was a start. Gareth forced a smile and then headed back to the main room, where the others were still gathered, talking quietly and mournfully around the coffins. Gareth straightened his uniform as he entered, offering nods and quiet words to those that he passed.

He found Adrian Boron standing with some of the seniors, sharing an anecdote that brought sad smiles to those listening. Funeral humour, trying to find a bright memory to shed light on the gloomy present. Gareth waited politely for Boron to finish before breaking him from the group.

"We've got some planning to do," said Gareth, quietly. "We need to go over the recent applications."

"You want to hire new Defenders?" Boron asked.

"Not immediately. Certainly not today, but soon. There are too many empty rooms here and we've just added five more."

"Of course. I'll fish out the most recent ones and give them a preliminary scan for the more promising candidates."

"Thanks."

"And, Gareth, good speech."

Gareth stayed a little while longer, talking with the assembled Defenders, sharing memories and stories, letting companionship soften the sting of grief. Then he stole away, catching Karl's eye and nodding towards the door as he went. Karl hated funerals too. They moved in silence to the lifts, through the security doors and up towards the control room. Karl didn't try to make conversation; he was built for brooding and, right now, Gareth was glad of it.

As always, there were two Defenders on duty in the control room, watching over instruments and screens for some sign of danger. It was virtually unheard of these days to have two attacks so close together, but they were still watchful and attentive at their posts. Losing friends had the effect of making people more diligent.

Gareth nodded a greeting before telling them to head down to join the others.

"Are you sure, sir?" one asked.

"Yes. Karl and I will take over watch, but there won't be an attack today."

No one asked him if he was sure or how he knew. As usual, they just accepted a statement from Gareth as certain fact and signed over the change of staff on the computers. Gareth slid into place behind one of the consoles, pressing his thumb to the reader to activate the controls. Before him, screens shone with energy readings, magnetic fluctuations and global positioning data. Their machinery was ever-alert for the next attack, the next portal that brought the Outsiders here from some other world, some other dimension that existed alongside their own.

All this technology at their disposal, all this equipment custom-made to Master Amiron's specifications, and they could still fall so easily to creatures of claws and teeth.

Gareth looked down at his hands over the controls, his knuckles reddened by his earlier exertions. He would stop them. He'd find some way to stop these Outsiders from their continued assaults, to prevent the portals that brought these incursions from a parallel universe.

Despite his future memories, he didn't know everything that would happen to him, which meant there was still a chance to shape the events to come. He would shape them. He would take these brave men and women, these people who would lay down their lives for their mission, and he would find a way to stop things once and for all.

In the silence of the control room, his friends' deaths so recently on his conscience, he made a vow to himself to do whatever it took to stop simply reacting to attacks and to craft a conclusion to the conflict.

* * *

A few days later, Gareth emerged from a lift on a floor only slightly subterranean, a level built early on, before the base had begun its underground sprawl. He started heading towards the main control room, but a voice called him towards one of the other doors.

"Gareth, I was going to call you," said Adrian Boron from behind a desk. "We've got some paperwork to tackle."

Boron sat in the office like he owned it. The chair was adjusted to his height, the computer screen angled as he liked it, the paper filed in his system. It didn't matter that every piece of official documentation stated that this room was Gareth's office. At least, it had the last time Gareth had bothered checking. Since Boron handled all the paperwork, it could say anything now.

Gareth took the papers Boron offered him, the legal documents regarding the recruitment process, the bill payments that needed signing off and the monthly requisitions. Gareth scanned each document with a cursory glance and then signed where Boron pointed. He probably wouldn't spot any abnormalities even if he read these things more closely. Boron knew better than anyone what the Defenders needed to keep operations running. He'd been here since the beginning, since Master Amiron had first given warnings of the Outsiders and the attacks that were imminent. Boron had stood beside the Defence Master during those frantic years of the first invasion and then the years that had followed when the war calmed enough to gain routines. Boron was no longer as young and strong as he'd been, but he was a Defender through to the core and he knew this place better than anyone.

"Have you given yourself a pay rise lately?" Gareth asked, still working his way down the pile of papers.

"What would I spend it on?" Boron countered.

He had a point. The wages of the Defenders weren't high, but everything they needed was paid for out of their funding. They had food and lodging, electricity and hot water. A person could live here for years and, aside from an occasional holiday, never spend a penny of their earnings.

Next came a pile of cardboard folders, each with a photo paper-clipped to the front. The papers within held CVs and application letters, test scores and interview assessments. Gareth gave a cursory glance at the materials within, more interested in the photos. He hunted the images for signs of familiarity, hints that these people would be known to him. Many were total blanks. He laid these aside somewhat reluctantly; it wasn't really fair to reject someone because he didn't remember accepting them. When Boron questioned a couple of the dismissals, Gareth shrugged and said that they could trial any Boron thought promising.

Then Gareth picked up the next file. Cassie Forester, according to the name printed on the front. A twenty-one-year-old athlete who'd applied two months earlier and whose physical test scores were rated highly, sometimes higher than a few of the current Defenders. It was the photo that caught Gareth's eye, a plain passport-style picture that he knew instantly.

"Her," Gareth said, with absolute certainty.

"The Olympic superstar," commented Boron, taking the folder and flicking through.

Gareth had a moment of doubt. Perhaps he recognised her face because he'd seen her on TV during the Olympics? He closed his eyes for a moment, holding onto that image of her face, seeing the young woman dressed in Defender black, a dark metal sword in her hand. He recalled fragments of conversations that were yet to be.

"She'll be a Defender," Gareth said.

Boron nodded, "I've learned not to argue when you use your Master tone."

Gareth smiled. The Master tone was the description they'd used whenever Master Amiron had said something with such conviction it left no room for doubt. He would make some declaration, without proof or explanation, and those that heard it would find themselves believing, despite all logic. When Master Amiron said something in his Master tone, he was inevitably right. It seemed that Gareth had acquired something of Master Amiron's style as well as his job.

Gareth finished with the rest of the admin, handing the papers back to Boron and asking if he was needed for anything else. He was almost asking permission to go. Hard to believe that Gareth was the one in charge. Gareth might have been the one Master Amiron had named as his successor, but Adrian Boron was the man who'd been here since the beginning, trusted by the Defenders and by the government reps. Gareth knew that his takeover of the Defence Master role had been approved so smoothly by the various governments funding the Defenders, largely because Boron had accepted it without question.

Out of the office, Gareth made it about three steps before being waylaid yet again. This time it was Richard. Gareth had been expecting this conversation and dreading it. He knew he couldn't stop the things he remembered happening but that didn't mean he had to welcome them, so he'd been steering clear of places Richard might be, prolonging the inevitable.

"I want to talk to you," Richard said.

"About?" asked Gareth, feigning ignorance.

"I want to train with the new recruits. I want to be taken seriously round here. Let me try out as a Defender."

"Richard, you are a great many things but you are no Defender."

"No one thought you could do it when Master Amiron took a chance on you."

"That was different."

"Why?"

It had been different because Gareth had at least been in decent shape when he'd argued his way into being considered a recruit. Richard spent every minute in front of a computer screen and had the physique to prove it. The closest he got to exercise was walking to the canteen for his meals. There was no way to say that tactfully though. When Gareth had asked to be trained as a Defender, Master Amiron had known he had it in him, just as Gareth knew now that Richard didn't. Richard was the smartest person Gareth knew but he was as likely to dance the lead in 'Swan Lake' as he was to be a Defender.

It wasn't simple doubt. Gareth knew that Richard would never be a Defender. He could remember it, remember the pain it would cause Richard to try and fail. But Richard wanted this and he wouldn't take no for an answer. He would try again and again, ask over and over. He would argue and demand and pester. He was of the unshakable belief that he could do anything he wanted. Learning that lesson would be an agonising truth but it was one that had to come. Gareth remembered the pain that would come but there was no way to convince Richard to heed his advice, no way to shield him from his own ambitions. Maybe the simplest way was to let Richard try. It felt like a terrible thing to do to a friend, but Gareth yielded.

"Fine. Join in with the training when the new recruits arrive. But no complaining. If you want this, you'll be treated like everyone else."

"I'll show you what I'm capable of," Richard said.

Gareth knew otherwise. His warped view of the world let him remember the events of the next few weeks as he did the last few. He knew the problems Richard would face. But telling him that wouldn't help.

Master Amiron had told Gareth that his memories would happen. Whatever he remembered of the future became fixed. Trying to evade a painful future would simply drive the path towards that future. All he could do was accept it.

* * *

Cassie struggled to sit still as the taxi wound its way through wooded lanes towards its destination. She was bubbling over with a stew pot of emotions. Everything was in the mix. She was excited, nervous, proud to be one of the few to make it this far, worried about what might happen if she failed, thrilled to be so close to achieving her goals, sad to be leaving her old life behind, but delighted to be offered this new one. So much was going on inside her that she felt like she might burst.

It was exactly the way she'd felt before her first Olympic race. Everything she'd worked for her entire life had been right in front of her in that moment and it had been overwhelming. It was strange, given that she'd worked for years to earn that place, that she felt now that this, not the podium, was what her life had been building towards. The Olympics had been the triumph of years of training but the decision to become a Defender had been almost made on a whim. Some reporter, microphone shoved in Cassie's face, had asked her what she was going to do now that she'd achieved her dreams and she'd realised that she didn't know. What came next after the happy ending to her story?

She'd decided in that heartbeat that it was time to put her skills into helping others. She had such speed, let it be her gift to the world.

The taxi made its final turnings, revealing a massive wall of grey concrete along the side of the road, a structure topped with barbed wire and jagged glass. It was a wall with very definite ideas about inside and outside. The driver pulled in beside the only feature in its length, a looming gate of solid metal about twice Cassie's height.

Cassie took a moment to use one of the breathing exercises her coach had taught her. Slow calming breaths letting her push her raging emotions to one side. Then she paid the taxi driver and stepped from the car with all the appearance of a calm young woman. The emotions were still in there, but they weren't controlling her now. She collected her bag and went to a small panel beside the gate. There was an intercom set into the concrete, along with the dark lens of a camera. Cassie pressed the button.

"Yes?" demanded a suspicious voice from inside.

"I'm Cassie Forester," she said. "I've applied to be a Defender."

She wished her voice sounded more confident; she'd proven what she was capable of when she set her mind to it and she'd prove it again. There was a long pause, during which a few, heavy spots of rain began to fall. She shifted her bag on her shoulder and pulled the edges of her fleece together. She'd just started fumbling with the zip when there was a heavy clunk of something shifting inside the gate and the metal started to swing open.

"Proceed to the front door," the voice through the intercom informed her. "Don't deviate."

She got her first view of the Defender base. It managed to be intimidating and disappointing at the same time, a construction of metal and concrete perhaps three storeys high. It was as if someone had dumped a grey box in the centre of the wide, paved area within the wall. She'd expected something bigger, at least a building that looked like someone had put thought into the design. The only feature she could see was a metal door as imposing as the one in the outer wall. Cassie walked quickly to it. She passed beneath another security camera and stepped inside.

The entrance was as utilitarian as the outside. There was an x-ray machine and metal detector that reminded Cassie of an airport. Beyond them was a desk with a bored-looking attendant. At his instructions, she dumped her belongings on the x-ray machine and watched the conveyor suck them inside. She walked through the scanner to the desk.

Cassie found it almost insulting that this guy could act as though this massive turning point in her life was a tedious inconvenience. He turned his semi-vacant expression to her and demanded her ID and invitation letter, sticking them into slots of some machine in front of him. He wasn't wearing the uniform of the Defenders, just shapeless, grey overalls. He had an ID badge hanging round his neck. Cassie made out the word "worker" printed below a fairly bad photo.

"Stand there," he waved to a point which was the focus of another camera lens. "Don't smile."

A moment later, one of the machines on the desk was printing out an ID badge similar to his own. It had the word "temporary" plastered on the bottom along with her name and a picture that made her look like a brainless moron. A brainless moron with flyaway hair. Couldn't he have given her a moment's notice to sort it out before taking the photo that would probably be stuck with her forever?

She was handed piles of paper with security procedures and legal disclaimers that she was expected to read. She was expected to sign off statements that the funding governments and the Defenders were in no way responsible if she were injured, and fill out fields regarding next of kin if she was killed. The nervous part of her was gaining ground on the excited part by the time she handed the finished paperwork back to the guy, who told her that someone would come to collect her. He retrieved a battered paperback and proceeded to act as though she was no longer there.

After several long minutes, a pair of doors slid open to reveal a large lift. Inside stood a man in the familiar black uniform of the Defenders. He was almost as forbidding as the building and Cassie felt a flutter of butterflies at the thought of being in the presence of one of the great heroes who protected the planet.

"I'm Defender Karl Edinct," he said. "Welcome on board."

His tone and expression were nowhere near as welcoming as the words. His face was a serious mask as he appraised Cassie. She wondered how she appeared to him, a young woman dressed in jeans and a worn fleece. She'd gone through a month of testing to get here to prove she was more than just a fast pair of legs. She'd earned a trial here, yet still she felt that she should have dressed for another interview.

She followed Edinct into the lift, watching him press a thumb to a scanner and enter a code before the doors would even close. Now that she was standing close to him, she noticed that the logo stitched into the left breast of his shirt had an extra word sewn in, declaring him a senior Defender. She was surprised. She would have guessed him to be mid-twenties, certainly no older than thirty, which was very young to be senior. She also noted a little icon of a sword stitched into the collar and wondered what that might signify.

"You're here on a trial basis," Edinct said as the lift plunged downwards. "Your pass will give you access to the main training areas, bedrooms, canteen and the recreation rooms. You want to go anywhere else, you'll need an escort. All new recruits are expected to train with the Defenders but you won't be put in the duty rotation until the Defence Master has determined you're ready. That means if the alarm sounds, you get the hell out of the way. Got it?"

He fixed his gaze on her with those last words, his eyes drilling into hers with fierce intensity.

"Got it," Cassie replied.

"The alarms mean an open portal and, nine times out of ten, that means Outsiders are coming through. Even a few seconds' delay can cost lives. If you get in the way of the responding team or interfere with anyone while the portal is open, you'll be out of here faster than you can blink. Break any other rule and you can argue your case to the Defence Master, but if you delay us doing our job, it's over."

"I understand."

Cassie's stomach lurched again as the lift came to a stop and the doors slid open. She followed Edinct out into a white corridor lined with doors. They were identical in form, but some stood wide open, some sealed shut, some ajar. There were people in the corridor, Defenders casually talking or striding past on unknown business. There were a few others, dressed in the same baggy grey overalls as the guy at the entrance, carrying piles of linen from the bedrooms. Cassie was left with the impression of calm busyness, populated by people who could leap into action at a moment's notice. Most of the people looked at her as she passed, some with warm friendliness, others with undisguised curiosity.

Cassie felt a surge of excitement at the thought that she could belong here, be one of these people, standing on the front line in defence of the planet.

Edinct led her to a door that looked no different from all the others, except that it had her name printed on a piece of card that was slotted into a holder on the wall outside. There was something disturbingly temporary about it. It would be so easy to slip her name out and put someone else's in its place.

And then Cassie was left alone in her new room. She dumped her bag on the narrow bed and took stock of her situation. The room was a windowless cell, furnished practically but sparsely. Everything was compact and useful, giving the impression that the whole place could have come moulded off an assembly line. Only a rectangular patch on the wall where the paint was slightly miscoloured gave any indication that the room had ever been inhabited by a person. From the blue-tack stains in the corners, that patch had once had a poster covering it.

Cassie wished she'd packed some personal items, some photos or decorations, so that she could make this room feel more like a home. As it was, she pulled out various t-shirts and tracksuits, folding them neatly in the narrow cupboard. The act of unpacking took mere minutes and the room looked just as barren when she'd finished.

There came a quiet tap on the door. Cassie turned to see another Defender standing in the corridor outside. He gave a smile of greeting.

"Hi. Welcome to the Defenders. I'm Gareth."

He offered a hand to Cassie to shake as she introduced herself. He was a young man who looked barely into his twenties, the brown hair flopping scruffily around his face giving an impression of youth. He was in the black uniform of a full Defender but she would put money on him only recently having earned it.

"You're an athlete?" he asked

Cassie was almost surprised that he had to ask. She was used to aspiring runners stopping her in the street for autographs after her Olympic win. Even before that, she'd been a bit of a celebrity in certain circles. But still she managed to smile and answer calmly.

"A sprinter."

"You'll have a bit of a disadvantage then. No fighter training?"

Cassie had never thought that being a gold medallist could be a disadvantage but she supposed he had a point. Running away from Outsiders was hardly the point of being a Defender.

"I'm a quick learner." She was no stranger to training. She could do this too.

"Glad to hear it. Anyway, I've got things to be getting on with. Good luck."

Then Cassie was left alone again.

She left her door propped open as an invitation and, sure enough, several Defenders took the opportunity to say hello. They introduced themselves in a blur of names and faces that she struggled to keep straight in her head. A woman in grey overalls asked her if the room was in a satisfactory condition without bothering with any pleasantries.

A little before seven came another tap on her door and a cheerful young man. He gave her a wide grin and introduced himself as, "Just call me Jerry."

"I'm here to take you to the most important room in this whole place," Jerry said, "the canteen."

The canteen proved to be as functional and dull as the rest she'd seen of the base, but it was bustling with black-uniformed Defenders, queuing for food or sitting at the long tables, creating a cacophony of clanging cutlery and chattering voices. Cassie picked up a wealth of accents, some of which she could barely interpret. Thankfully, they were mostly speaking English. She should be grateful for the random chance that had caused the first major Outsider attack to take place in London. She wouldn't have stood a chance of getting in here if she'd had to work in another language.

Cassie had known that this was a male-dominated job but she wasn't quite prepared for the sea of men she saw before her. Her eyes automatically sought out the female and she spotted a blond ponytail among those seated at the table. A young woman was laughing at something someone said.

"That's Lizzie," said Jerry, following Cassie's gaze. "As good as just about anyone with a sword but you might want to keep your distance or you'll be caught up in wedding planning."

"Wedding?" The word caught Cassie by surprise.

"Karl proposed a few months ago and they've not talked about anything else since."

The name was familiar and Cassie looked closer at the man Lizzie was sitting beside. It was Karl Edinct, the man who'd shown her to her room earlier. Now though, the cold expression had disappeared and he was smiling warmly at the woman beside him.

Jerry led Cassie past them and she had to stop staring to avoid bumping into someone. There was a serving area at one end of the canteen, separated from the dining area by a thin partition wall. Cassie was struck by the similarity to a school canteen, with its long line of heat lamps above huge dishes. Figures in grey overalls and hairnets doled out large portions of stew and vegetables onto plates for the line of Defenders. Cassie noted a strange metal bracelet around the wrist of the worker who handed it over. There was no payment system, so she simply followed Jerry back to the tables and took a seat.

"What's with the bracelets?" she asked.

Jerry looked at her in puzzlement for a long moment, before realisation crossed his face and he glanced back towards the servers. "Oh, some of the workers aren't exactly model members of society. They get the choice to work here to avoid a jail sentence."

Jerry glanced past Cassie and muttered, "Speaking of."

Someone slid into the seat beside Cassie. She looked at him in surprise. An overweight young man, a scruffy t-shirt taut across his stomach, smiled a greeting at Jerry that wasn't entirely pleasant. He wasn't massively fat but he appeared incongruous next to the lean and muscled Defenders who filled the rest of the tables. Cassie noted the bracelet on the young man's wrist.

"Worker shift is after us," Jerry said.

"Today, I'm not a worker. The Defence Master agreed that I should be trained as a recruit."

"He's finally lost his mind," said Jerry.

Two

Day One

The alarm clock's frantic beeping was like a laser drilling into Cassie's skull. She was up and out of bed before she was fully awake. She pulled on the clothes on top of the pile in the cupboard, sports gear suitable for whatever training with the Defenders might entail. She emerged from her room into a river of people all heading in the same direction. The Defenders, all neatly dressed in their black uniforms, were heading down the corridor. Cassie noticed a handful of people who, like her, were dressed in ordinary sports kit. There was Richard, looking half-dead and wearing trainers that appeared to have never seen a speck of mud.

The recruits were gathered together by Lizzie, the young woman Cassie had seen in the canteen the day before. She was so chirpy that Cassie half wanted to slap her. Lizzie smiled at them all, counting up arrivals to make sure they were all assembled, while the rest of the Defenders kept on their way. Once all the recruits were together, Lizzie took them after the others, through a door which had a heavy security pad beside it.

Lizzie took them along another of the white corridors to a space that was practically empty. Then Cassie saw it for the first time. The portal. A series of metal objects were fixed to a perfectly ordinary patch of wall making a circle. That circle was filled with shimmering, golden light. It hung there, a few millimetres off the wall, a glimmering pool of energy. Cassie had seen pictures of portals but she'd never been this close to one before. She'd never imagined the radiance, the power held in such a small space.

Of course Cassie had heard of portals. They were the way the Defenders managed to protect the planet from this one base. According to the stories, the Defence Master had given them to his team, but no story would agree as to whether he'd found them or created them. The portals were also what the Outsiders used to get here from wherever they came from. Some said the Defence Master had stolen their technology, using against them the very means they'd devised to invade the planet. All Cassie knew now was that she was standing in front of a circle of light that could zap her into another dimension.

She watched the Defenders walk through the portal like it was no big deal, stepping into the light and vanishing. Her rational mind knew that the Defenders had been using this technology since the first invasion ten years earlier. They used it on a regular basis without mishap, but there were still fears dancing around her mind. What if the portal cut off while she was half-way through? What it she tripped and left a foot behind? What if that thing sent her to some crazy other dimension or even to the homeworld of the Outsiders? What if it killed her?

She watched others step through and vanish, each one bringing her closer to the shimmering surface. Now or never. If she couldn't step through the portal now, she'd have to give up any thought of being a Defender. One step forwards or she'd have to leave and spend the rest of her life wondering what it was she'd missed. A flutter of excitement filled her, like the slow climb of the first rise of a roller-coaster.

In a rush of adrenaline, Cassie took that step.

She wasn't sure what she'd expected. She didn't really feel anything. She saw bright, golden light for an instant and then she was emerging into a damp woodland. It was still dark beneath the trees, the first glimmerings of dawn visible in glimpses through the tree branches. Cassie turned to look behind her. There was another portal, this one made by devices stuck to the wall of a derelict building that looked like it had been deserted for years. Cassie could just make out the brickwork through the portal.

The portal blinked out, the light vanishing into nothing. Most of the Defenders stood expectantly as a voice cut across the general chatter. It was a senior Defender, a man with a glimmer of silver at his temples. His face was vaguely familiar; Cassie had seen him before on TV when there were reports about the Defenders, acting as a spokesman for the organisation.

"For those of you who are new," he said, "I'm Adrian Boron, second in command to the Defence Master. For the morning run, we follow that path. There are a couple of junctions. Our route is the most well-trodden but in case of confusion, we've tied some red markers to the trees down the correct path. Everyone does two laps. Just remember, this isn't a race. Run at your own pace."

He started jogging down the route he'd indicated, the other Defenders following in his wake. Cassie set off with the crowd. Five miles was nothing to her but she knew she'd have a morning of training following this and she didn't know what that might entail. She settled into a steady-paced jog that she knew she could maintain for miles. She saw a couple of other recruits set off too quickly trying to keep up with the leaders. Cassie kept on, step by steady step. Unsurprisingly, as the path wound through the trees, she found herself passing one of those who'd been racing. The guy had now slowed to a walk to get his breath back. That continued for the first few hundred metres, with Cassie playing tortoise and hare, overtaking those that had started too quickly.

Cassie saw another figure ahead of her, a black-uniformed back. She instinctively started using him as a pace-setter, keeping stride behind him as their feet slapped against the damp earth. It was Gareth, she realised after a while. Cassie stayed patiently behind him, feeling the steady rhythm of her feet against the beaten dirt. There was a sense of timelessness beneath the trees, the cool air damp with the promise of rain, the light growing gradually brighter as they ran into the dawn. She wasn't sure where in the world they were; that portal could have taken them anywhere. There was no sound of cars or machinery, just the rustle of the wind through the leaves and the beat of her heart in her ears.

After a while, she reached the clearing where they started, passing the crumbling building. The second half of the run seemed somehow easier as she recognised things she'd noticed on the first lap, odd shaped tree stumps and patches of mud to be avoided. It felt like she was on the home stretch of a race, the finish line drawing gradually closer with each breath.

She could still see Gareth's back a little way in front of her. She pulled up the pace slightly. She knew this wasn't a race, knew that she had to be prepared for whatever came later, but still she couldn't allow herself to just follow someone to the end of a run. She closed off the distance, falling into a place beside Gareth and creeping slightly ahead.

He sped up.

So Cassie pushed a little harder. As she caught the first glimpse of the building through the trees, she was bringing up the pace. Gareth didn't let up. As they rounded the final bend, they were as close to sprinting as could be managed after five miles. They pelted the final metres into the clearing neck and neck.

Cassie was panting and yet fighting down the urge to laugh as she saw Gareth beside her gasping. They exchanged grins. There were other Defenders scattered around the clearing but Cassie didn't think any of them had been there long. More were arriving, all at a more sedate pace than she'd managed.

"I think that was a photo finish," said Karl Edinct, holding out a bottle of water to her. She gulped it down gratefully. When she'd recovered her breath, she went to Gareth, congratulating him on the final push.

"You too," said Gareth. "I guess you didn't hear the bit about it not being a race."

Cassie laughed, "So why didn't you let me pass you?"

The portal was open against the wall of the building, some of the Defenders already moving through it. Cassie wondered if she was meant to do the same, but the other recruits all seemed to be lingering. It had been a while since anyone had arrived in the clearing but there was still a sense of waiting. Defenders were talking worriedly, looking often at the path along which they'd arrived.

"Did anyone pass Richard?" Edinct asked, his voice quieting the general chatter. Only murmuring met the question. Cassie didn't remember seeing Richard since they'd started. The remaining Defenders went back to talking quietly to each other, definitely worried now. Cassie heard one of them saying something about running back along the route to look for Richard.

Then the missing recruit came round the final bend. His face was almost crimson, his t-shirt soaked through and his pace barely above a snail's. He was panting like crazy, desperately fighting to keep jogging.

"Come on, Richard!" Gareth called out. "You've nearly done it. Come on!"

As Richard stumbled the last few steps, Lizzie went to him. With gentle hands, she guided him to sit down against one of the trees. He started to slump forwards, but she stopped him.

"No, no. Put your hands behind your head and sit back. It opens up your chest. Now breathe, just breathe."

Richard had gone from a bright red to being so pale he looked almost green.

"I think I'm going to throw up."

"Breathe slowly." Lizzie grabbed a water bottle from one of the other Defenders, unscrewing the lid. "Now drink. Slowly. Just a little at a time. And breathe."

"He thinks he can be a Defender?" Cassie heard someone ask.

She felt so sorry for Richard. She could only imagine how humiliating this must feel. Even though everyone said there was no race, it must feel awful to end the run so decidedly last. Hopefully he'd get in shape quickly and be able to hold his own against the others. After all, the Defenders wouldn't have let him train to be one of them if they didn't think he could do it.

Since everyone was now accounted for, the rest of the group headed back through the portal to the base. Cassie went with the flow, following the black uniforms to the canteen. She loaded up her plate with toast and eggs and then stared around the tables for a face she recognised.

She spotted Jerry and slid into an empty seat across from him. He was sitting beside another Defender, who introduced himself as Enrico. This man had Italian colouring but spoke without a trace of an accent. According to the logo on his shirt, he was a senior Defender.

Cassie started eating in silence before her curiosity got the better of her.

"What's the story with Richard?" she asked.

"He's a genius," said Enrico at the same moment that Jerry said, "He's a sociopath."

Enrico shot a glance sideways at Jerry that was an unmistakable instruction to be quiet.

"Richard has a brilliant mind," Enrico said. "He's amazing with computers and he has an intuitive grasp of the portal technology which no one can match."

"Which puts him in a perfect position to abuse said technology," Jerry muttered.

"He just gets bored easily. He's not a bad person."

"You found him in jail."

Cassie blinked between the pair of them, suddenly regretting that she'd asked. Richard had just seemed such an enigma, a figure who didn't fit with the rest of them. She felt she understood even less now what he was doing there. Whether a sociopath or a technical genius, she wasn't sure he was the right person to be wielding a weapon in defence of the planet.

Conversation turned to less contentious topics, with Enrico and Jerry making polite enquiries into Cassie's background and reasons for joining. She gave the reply that was becoming her standard now, about wanting to do something to help others now that she'd achieved her racing goals.

They didn't spend long at breakfast. Pretty soon, there was a steady flow of people towards the door and Cassie let herself be carried by the stream. She followed Jerry and the others past small training rooms and gyms into a large hall. There was equipment stacked against the wall, pads and mats and wooden weapons, but the majority of the floor stood bare. There was no chatter now. The Defenders entered in a cathedral hush that filled the huge room more than any noise. They might have talked and laughed in the canteen, but here they were serious, focused.

Adrian Boron strode through the room, parting the crowds like a saint through a sea. The Defenders were all watching him intently as he moved. Cassie watched the Defenders forming neat lines, moving orderly and by instinct. There was no argument or jostling for place. They all knew exactly where they were meant to be. Cassie saw the lines form and took a place at the back of the room, behind the sea of black uniforms. Around her were the other recruits. In front of her was a neat line of heads up the front of the room. She wondered if the order signified anything or if people just stood where there was a space.

She didn't have much time to wonder because Boron began the training. He gave curt orders and the room obeyed in unison, running through basic warm up exercises that quickly became more vigorous. Soon the training progressed to martial arts. Boron gave clear orders of moves, simple punches and blocks, which the Defenders executed instantly in precise motion. Cassie had never done anything like this and just tried to copy those in front of her.

Boron moved through the hall, the movements progressing to a steady count that was taken up by Defenders in turn. He paused to make minor corrections occasionally on his route to the back. Then he got to the recruits. Cassie found herself staring at the Defender diagonally in front of her, trying to make her every move identical to his. Yet, when Boron got to her, he seemed to want to correct everything. Her feet weren't angled correctly. They weren't the right distance apart. Her legs weren't bent evenly. Her hips were misaligned. It seemed he'd made a hundred changes before he'd even got to the fists that were punching the air in time to the count.

It felt humiliating to be doing so much wrong. She wasn't used to being new to something. She tried to remember every little correction so that she could be certain not to make the same mistakes again but there were so many. Were her hips right now? Was her elbow in tightly enough when she punched? What had he said was the correct position for her feet?

The only consolation was that he seemed to be making a lot of corrections for all of the recruits.

On the surface, the start of the training seemed remarkably simple. Cassie found, however, that her arms were quickly aching from the repetitive movements. Her legs, usually her greatest strength, began to tire from holding the bent-legged position. She wasn't sure how long they'd been in here but the training was so completely different from what she was used to that her body was reacting badly.

She was overwhelmed with relief when Boron instructed them to change, simply because it meant she could straighten her legs for a bit and get some blood flowing as she walked over to the racks of neatly ordered equipment. At Boron's order, she took a wooden sword from the rack along with everyone else. But here there was a clear difference. Boron separated out the Defenders from the recruits. Cassie wasn't sure what the majority of the Defenders were doing, but it looked fast and complicated, wooden swords moving in a whirl around their bodies.

The recruits were gathered in a small corner of the hall and given much simpler movements to accustom them to the use of the sword. Cassie felt the weight of it in her hands, the first weapon she'd wielded. It was little more than a stick with a hilt but it still lent her a sense of power. Boron didn't seem to bother with the recruits, focusing his attention on the Defenders. Instead, a couple of senior Defenders were assigned to work with them. One was Karl Edinct.

He looked as cold and serious as he had when he'd brought Cassie into the base. He watched them with a critical eye, correcting every wavering movement, every inaccurate stance, every weak gesture. Every fibre of Cassie's being was focused on the wooden sword, on making each movement what Edinct ordered. She was a gold medal athlete and she'd damn well prove she could be the best here too, however much effort it took.

A clattering sound cut through her attention. Cassie looked sideways and saw Richard looking flustered and embarrassed. It seemed he'd dropped his sword on his foot, the wooden blade bashing against the floor of the hall.

"What have I told you about your grip?" Edinct demanded.

The sword training continued for some time, giving Cassie a whole new set of aches. Then things got difficult. They put aside the wooden blades and gathered again in their neat rows. Boron ordered them through a series of gruelling exercises. Cassie could understand the point of them, the squats and the sit-ups, the dips and the press-ups. These exercises were designed for strength. But they hurt. Over and over Boron pushed them through the rigorous calisthenics.

Some of them, Cassie did alright. She held her own through the twisted variations of sit-ups, even though her stomach protested and her whole body was slick with sweat. But the press-ups were a killer after the hours of unfamiliar exercises with the sword. Her arms trembled and her shoulders didn't want to support her. After the first couple of sets, she struggled to hold it together. Not after the hours of training her arms and shoulders had been put through.

About the only person doing worse than her at press-ups was Richard. He couldn't even manage one. Cassie didn't want to be considered unfavourably to him of all people, so she forced herself to keep going, to keep trying, even when she didn't think her body would take it anymore. She wasn't going to let them see her as weak.

When Boron called a halt, Cassie wanted nothing more than to just collapse. Somehow, she managed to get to her feet and take her position in the lines with the others. She bowed to Boron with the rest and then slumped her way out of the hall.

She was used to physical training so she'd never imagined that the Defender training would feel so much harder. Maybe it was just that it was such a different style of training, muscles being used in different ways. Maybe she'd get used to it and everything would feel easier soon.

* * *

There was an attack coming soon, Gareth knew as he headed from the canteen to the upper levels of the base. Gareth could tell because his memories of the coming afternoon were hazy. It was frustrating that the thing it would be most useful to remember about the future was the very thing that was never easy to see. He knew from experience that trying to focus too hard on an upcoming Outsider attack would just give him a headache. All he could do was wait and be prepared for it. The future would be the past soon enough. At least he could see with some clarity that none of his people would die in this attack.

He hated those fights more than anything else in existence. Master Amiron had told him that he couldn't prevent his future memories from coming to pass. Anything he remembered would happen. Of course, all memories were imperfect and subjective. Still, if Gareth remembered that a teammate, a friend, was going to die in a battle with the Outsiders, Gareth still had to give the orders that would send that person into death.

He loathed that part of his supposed gift.

Master Amiron had been little comfort when they'd discussed it. He'd just sighed and said that he knew exactly how Gareth felt. That was the Defence Master's burden. That was the price that came with this power.

"Hey, Gareth, you look a million miles away."

Gareth had reached the door leading to the lift. In the time it had taken to unlock it, Karl had come up behind him. Karl had obviously cleaned himself up after the morning's training. His hair was still damp from the shower, almost black with the water, and his uniform was clean and perfectly pressed as always. Gareth held the door for him and tried not to show his nervousness concerning the coming attack. Karl would be the senior Defender on the first response team this afternoon.

"I was just thinking," Gareth said, "about our new recruits. What's your opinion?"

They got into the lift side by side and Gareth authorised it to take them up.

"It's too early to say. Most of them have no real combat training. They seem capable enough. With one exception. What possessed you to let Richard join in the training?"

"I wanted to shut him up," Gareth admitted. "He's been on at me for weeks about wanting to be treated like a Defender, not a second-class citizen. I figured that this way, he wouldn't be able to say we didn't give him a fair chance. Besides, there's always a possibility he'll surprise us."

Karl laughed, "You don't honestly believe he could survive a week of training do you?"

Gareth knew exactly how long it would take for Richard to concede that he wasn't cut out for Defender training, but he couldn't admit that.

"I don't expect him to," Gareth said. "But, I owe him a chance. After all, Master Amiron gave me a chance to train."

That had been a slightly different situation. Master Amiron had been able to remember that Gareth would make it through the training to become a Defender. More than that, Master Amiron had known that one day Gareth would acquire this gift and become his successor. Gareth knew exactly the opposite about Richard. But without revealing his abilities, he couldn't put that argument out there whenever Richard protested that he deserved the same chances Gareth had been given. So Gareth would let Richard take his place with the recruits. He'd let Richard try and he'd let him fail without interference.

"Richard just isn't right to be a Defender," said Karl.

Gareth smiled as the lift pinged their arrival and the doors slid open, "I distinctly remember you saying the same thing about me."

"Yes, but that was mainly because I hated you."

"Trust me, the feeling was mutual."

They shared a grin as they walked along the corridor. They reached the door to the ready room. This room was rare in that it had no locks or even a handle. It opened at a push from either direction so that it wouldn't slow people down should they be needed. Karl walked in, Gareth trailing behind. It was obvious Karl was slightly surprised by this, as were those already in the room. Lizzie was sitting at a table, colourful magazines and catalogues spread out on a table in front of her, buried in wedding plans again. Gareth took in at a glance the others in the room. Aiden and Wyatt were sprawled on beanbags with video game controllers in their hands. Rafael was sitting on the sofa with a book. To all appearances, they could have just been relaxing here, but Gareth knew that it would take mere seconds for them to grab their weapons from beside the door and be ready for action.

Jakob had been the senior Defender on duty this morning. He crossed the room at their arrival and began the official process of signing over shifts to Karl. Gareth walked past them both and went to a small cupboard tucked unobtrusively in the corner. He tapped in his code to the keypad and pulled the door open, taking out a small tube of mirus from its slot. He was aware of the others watching him curiously. He made no disguise about his actions. After all, the store recorded all accesses and there were sensors to detect the removal of items. This would all be logged. It was a logical precaution to prevent people stealing and selling the paste in the tubes which, in the right circumstances, was more precious than anything else in the world. Even Gareth couldn't get round it.

Gareth left the others in the room, where they were ready for either an afternoon of relaxation or a lethal attack. His destination was the door across the hall. Though it could be incredibly secure if needed, it was rarely locked, another design feature that allowed the response team to be as close to instantaneous as possible.

For that reason, the consoles and controls were all down the sides of the room, giving a clear path between the door and the circle on the opposite wall where the portal would form. On either side of the room were the status screens and controls, as well as banks of computers. Officially, this room should always be manned by two Defenders, who were responsible for monitoring the status readings. Harjeet and Kenji glanced up at Gareth's arrival, before turning their attention back to their screens.

The other three in the room weren't here officially and none of them were paying much attention to Gareth. Richard was sitting at one of the computers, Enrico looking over his shoulder. Meg, a young worker in Richard's team, was standing beside them. Her pale face was flushed with anger, her arms folded across her grey-overalled chest. Unsurprisingly, there appeared to be an argument going on.

"That program you sent me could have been anything," she was saying. "There was no explanation, no comments in the code, nothing to explain what it was meant to do."

"I would have thought the purpose should have been obvious to anyone with a basic understanding of programming and ETL functions," Richard replied, not bothering to look up.

"You really think we've got nothing better to do than trawl through three thousand lines of code to figure out what you've been playing around with this time?"

"Since the only reason you're here is to support my work," Richard said, "yes."

"You arrogant," she began. Enrico stepped between them, ready to intervene. Fortunately for Richard, the alarms went off before Meg could slap him.

Three

The Outsiders

The automated systems were already pulling up details of the latest portal, Harjeet and Kenji responding immediately. Kenji was refining the location information while Harjeet fed that into the systems here for creating the portal to respond.

"China," Gareth muttered, the instant before the marker had appeared on the map

"China," Kenji agreed. "Looks like a subway station in Beijing. Local time, 9:32pm."

Damn! Urban locations were always tough and a subway had way too many bottlenecks for civilians to get out of the way. At least it wasn't rush hour there.

Gareth took a spare sword from a rack against the wall, buckling its belt around his waist. The door was already open, Karl and the others hurrying in as Harjeet fired up the portal. A bright point of golden light formed at the centre of the circle of devices on the wall, energy shooting out like lightning to form a perfect circle of radiant gold. There was no time to admire it. The first response team were hurrying through it. Gareth ran after them, certain that he'd be helpful. He yelled out to Kenji to get the second response team through the portal as soon as possible.

Gareth took a single step from the control room of the Defender base and was standing in a Chinese subway station. He took in the scene at a glance, noting the clear walls and doors that separated the platform from the tracks, the staircases that were a flow of people, thankfully not too many, running up the stairs in terror. People were pushing and panicking, tripping over their feet and the steps, knocking each other down in the rush to get out of the way.

And there, hanging in the air in the middle of the platform, was a circle of light that mirrored their own.

The first Outsider had already come through, a tall figure that looked almost human except for its vicious claws and slavering teeth, sickly pale skin taut over a skeletal frame. It had grabbed hold of the nearest person, an old man who'd been too slow to run. The Outsider had pierced the man's clothes and skin with its sharp claws, its mouth open to reveal the row of razor teeth, ready to tear open flesh.

It took only an instant to review the scene and, in that time, Lizzie had run across the platform and sliced off the Outsider's head with one stroke of her sword. The creature fell, black blood spilling across the tiles.

With an efficient order, Karl had the five members of the first response team in a semi-circle around the active side of the Outsider portal. He glanced at Gareth but left him to what needed to be done. Gareth pulled out of his pocket the little tube he'd taken earlier and hurried to the old man's side. The man was babbling in Chinese that was utterly incomprehensible to Gareth. He focused on squeezing out small portions of green paste from the tube, applying it on the cuts caused by the Outsider's claws. At least the man hadn't been bitten.

Once Gareth was sure that every cut had been covered in the green paste, he shoved the tube back into his pocket and pointed up the stairs, yelling at the man to go. If the word wasn't understood, the gesture was. The man stumbled away, slow and faltering, hurrying as well as he was able after the last of those fleeing the platform. Gareth didn't bother to watch him escape.

Instead, he drew his sword, the black blade glinting dully in the golden light of the portal and the glare of the fluorescents. He took his place in the circle. In the time it had taken him to deal with the old man, three more Outsiders had come through. Their bodies now lay as severed pieces on the platform. Another one emerged, a thin, pale figure coming through the circle of energy, looking with large, hungry eyes on the world it had entered. Its body appeared deceptively frail, bones showing through the pale skin like those of a starving child, a wraith of death stepping into a world of life. Its claws were out, its teeth bared, slathering like a hairless wolf. It had already set its gaze on the Defenders around it, not with fear, but with a drooling desire to eat.

Karl stepped briefly from his place in the circle as the Outsider approached him. With one stroke his sword severed the creature's grasping arm and went on to slice through its chest.

More were emerging, the Outsiders coming through in twos or threes. These creatures were stupid. They had no plan or strategy and didn't seem aware of what the dark metal blades could do to them. A couple even stopped to devour their fallen brothers, eating the spilled guts that flowed free of the impossibly tough skin, while Wyatt dispatched them with his sword.

For a fraction of a second, Gareth dared to hope that this afternoon would be an easy one. Then he had a flash of future memory in the instant before the event happened. He turned to the rush of noise and the flash of movement in the tunnel, the flowing metal of the arriving train. As doors opened, people stepped onto the platform before they'd realised what was happening. Most people rushed back again, trying to get out of the way. But it was too late.

In the moment of distraction, an opening had formed between the Defenders. One of the Outsiders ran at the open door of the train carriage, seeing the people within.

Gareth was running almost before he saw the creature move. Let the others deal with the ones on the platform. He was through the doors of the carriage just before they slammed shut and a sudden movement took him off his feet. His sword clanged against the floor. The driver must be panicking, trying to get away from that station.

Gareth scrambled to his feet, grabbing for his sword. The Outsider was in front of him, its teeth already sunk into a woman's shoulder.

He slashed a wild and unbalanced stroke, but it was all that was needed. The Outsider fell dead.

The woman was in one of the seats of the carriage, pressing her hand against the wound in a desperate attempt to stop the flow of blood. Now that the moment of terror was over, the other passengers approached, talking rapidly in Chinese, probably trying to help.

Gareth shoved them away and reached again for his pocket and the small tube. This stuff could work miracles and a miracle was what was needed after an Outsider bite. He unscrewed the top of the tube and smeared a generous helping of mirus over the bleeding shoulder, the paste going on skin and blood and clothing. The woman was pale and crying, but Gareth kept working.

He looked about him at the passengers, all staring at him. One of those who'd tried to help earlier was a young woman grasping shopping bags. Gareth gestured at her bags.

"I need that," he said. Whether or not she understood, she let him reach inside and pull out a shirt, still with the tag attached. Gareth wrapped it around the injured shoulder as a makeshift bandage, pulling it tight around the wound.

He gave what he hoped was a comforting smile to the injured woman and reached out to touch her cheek, which was relatively cool to the touch. Her skin was still pale, no trace of the flush of fever. His smile came more genuinely now.

The train came to a grinding halt at the next station, the doors opening. People poured out in a frantic torrent. Gareth grabbed two men who looked strong enough, gesturing towards the injured woman.

"She needs a doctor," he said. "Doctor. Hospital."

He hadn't the faintest idea if they understood his words, but the two men put their arms around the woman, helping her up, half carrying her from the train. Gareth stepped out of the carriage, watching them head for the stairs.

He'd have to get back to the other station somehow. The screen on the opposite side of the platform was flashing up something in Chinese characters, probably a warning that the train was delayed. Getting back was going to be interesting but there was no rush now. The others would take care of the rest of the Outsiders until the portal closed. The second response team was probably there already.

He felt the flood of relief. That woman would be fine. He was almost certain of that. His gift might be vague and disturbing at times, downright misleading at others, but there were days it had its perks. He'd known to be in the control room, with the mirus, the paste that was the only known antidote to the poison of Outsider bites. His future memories regarding portals were always fuzzy but he'd remembered the injured. He'd remembered that he could save them and so he had.

***

Cassie had been exploring the public areas of the base when the alarms went off. She was walking through the floor of training rooms to see what facilities were available. She'd made it past three big halls and an array of smaller ones when she picked up the scent of chlorine and was led by her nose to a swimming pool. It felt peaceful inside, the only sound, the faint splash of a lone swimmer doing steady strokes along the length, the water making tiny waves at his passage.

Cassie was somewhat overwhelmed by the size of it all. She felt like she'd barely scratched the surface with the floors that she was able to wander. She had no idea how large this place really was. All she had to go on was how long it had taken for the lift to get down to this level when she'd first arrived. Then, once lunch was over, Defenders had disappeared. She'd seen some of them in the training rooms. A handful had been in the bedroom corridor or enjoying the recreation spaces, but not many. This lone guy, swimming lengths in a pool that could take a dozen easily, summed up the strange sense of emptiness in this area. It seemed most of the Defenders had vanished somewhere else in the base and Cassie hadn't the faintest idea where. When she tried to go through the doors that led to the rest of the base, the lights blinked red at her.

She wasn't sure what she was meant to do in the afternoons. It was obvious that the Defenders generally had somewhere to be, something to do, but no one had given her anything. Cassie wondered about retrieving her swimming costume from her room and joining this guy in the pool. Or maybe she could use one of the smaller rooms and work on the things she'd been shown that morning.

Then the alarms went off. A blaring noise filled her ears, lights she'd not noticed before now flashing red in the corner of the room. The lone swimmer changed direction mid-stroke and was, in moments, hauling himself out at the edge of the pool.

Cassie stood there, like a rabbit caught in the headlights, beneath the flashing red.

Was this a portal? Was it an emergency? What was she meant to do? No one had told her.

She watched the swimmer grab a towel off a hook and disappear through a door that presumably led to changing rooms. She headed back to the corridor, remembering Edinct's words on her arrival, the only instruction she'd had on these circumstances. She wasn't to get in the way of the Defenders.

Back in the corridor, the lights were still flashing, the alarm still blaring. The noise pounded at Cassie's ears. Along the corridor, a couple of doors open, Defenders emerging at a jog. They weren't racing, but they obviously had somewhere to be. Cassie pressed herself against the wall as they passed to prevent herself being mown down. After Edinct's warning, she couldn't interrupt them to ask what was going on.

It was so frustrating. Here she was, in the heart of action, with something important going on, and she hadn't the faintest idea where she should be or what she should do. She couldn't remember ever feeling so lost before. She wanted to do something, to help; this was why she'd come here.

The alarms stopped as suddenly as they had begun, but red lights were still flashing along the length of the corridor. A voice came over the PA.

"First team deployed. Second team to control room."

It felt like seconds since the alarms had started. The first team's response must have been instantaneous but that shouldn't be surprising. This was what the training was for.

Cassie headed along the corridor, looking for Defenders or the stairs back to the living corridor. She saw a few more coming from the training rooms. None of them seemed to be racing but they all moved with purpose. So Cassie followed.

Some left through a door she knew wouldn't open for her, but the others made their way to one of the larger recreation rooms. No one seemed to be relaxing now. The room was packed with people, crammed in front of a massive screen that would have served a small cinema. The screen showed a map of the world, a little red dot somewhere over Asia. Down the side of the screen were numbers, a timer, various statuses listed. Even as Cassie arrived, a red icon changed to green and the PA voice came again.

"Second team deployed."

The timer in the top of the screen was showing less than five minutes. Since the portal had opened? Edinct hadn't been exaggerating when he'd talked about fast response being important.

This room full of people were anxiously waiting. They were watching the status board and Cassie watched them. A number of them were carrying weapons and she wondered where they'd got them from. There was a faint murmur of voices but it wasn't relaxed chatter. She stood just outside the door, not wanting to press into that crowd. She wasn't one of them yet. So she just waited and watched them waiting, aware of their anxiety like it was a wall blocking her out.

She watched the counter ticking down, seeing seconds slowly turn into minutes. The status board didn't seem to change. The tension in the room built with each passing moment until it was an almost physical force.

After what felt like forever but which, according to the board, was a little over twenty minutes, the red light over Asia disappeared. The flashing red lights along the corridor vanished with it.

"Outsider portal is closed," the PA voice told them.

The room of Defenders breathed a sigh of relief almost as one. Cassie found herself joining in, tension she'd been barely aware of suddenly released.

The Defenders began to talk more freely, but there was still a layer of tension there. Cassie couldn't think what it was until the voice came on the PA again.

"Situation contained. Initial assessment, two civilians injured. No fatalities."

That was the cue for everyone to relax.

Gareth's Story

Part One

The apartment they lived in was far too small for a family of six. Gareth grew up with an elder sister and two younger brothers, crammed into four little rooms along with their parents. The two younger boys shared a bed because there wasn't enough space for one each in the bedroom the three boys occupied. Mel got the cramped space in the back of the apartment all to herself by virtue of being a girl. Mum and Dad's bedroom was no bigger than the boys' and the main living area hosted a couple of tired kitchen appliances and, more importantly, the TV. The walls were so thin that Gareth could lie in his bed and he'd hear in perfect clarity the music coming from Mel's room, the blare of the TV from the other side and, of course, every word uttered between his parents.

The place never seemed smaller than when the arguments started. Even a mansion would have felt too small. Dad would call Mum a lazy, alcoholic hag. She'd call him a heartless thug. Then it would build. Gareth learned all he could wish to know about insults lying with his head under his pillow trying to drown out the sounds of swearing. On those nights, Gareth wished he could be anywhere else.

Mel did manage a partial escape. When she got a boyfriend and started spending nights with him, Dad called her a whore and told Mum she'd raised Mel badly. But at least Mel didn't have to hear the fights.

Then, when Gareth was fourteen, Dad finally walked out. The first night, as Gareth lay grinning at the peaceful silence, he felt that they could finally make something good out of the family. Mel spent more time there for the first few weeks but she was practically moved in with her boyfriend so Gareth got the back bedroom. Even the faded floral pattern on the wallpaper couldn't dampen his hope. They were free of the pain that Dad had brought.

It was maybe a week before that hope started to tarnish. About a month before the rust really set in. Even with Dad gone, Mum barely

46

moved from the sofa except to get herself another drink. Without Dad to yell at her, the drinking got worse. And there was no money coming in except Mum's benefits, which vanished into the off license practically as soon as it arrived. Gareth tried to sober her up. He tried to get her to go down to the job centre. He circled vacancies in the free paper that came round twice a week but she didn't even call up for an interview.

So Gareth got a job, working evenings and weekends waiting tables and scrubbing dishes. He hated it. He hated his Mum as much as he'd ever hated his Dad. He carried other people's food and then scraped away their grime for pitiful wages and lousy tips. But the restaurant let him take home leftovers at the end of the night, so at least his brothers got something decent to eat.

That kept them going for a while. Gareth came home each night with enough food to last them through the next day and his wages would deal with whatever bill had the biggest red letters. Pretty soon, he was paying off bills the first time they came instead of when the final reminders arrived. There even seemed to be enough money to go down to the charity shop and buy clothes that actually fit him, his cast-offs being given to Chris, the older of his two brothers, to grow into.

Just when Gareth thought they might be able to manage, disaster hit them again. This time it was in the shape of a pre-approved credit card. A piece of junk mail had arrived while the boys were at school and Mum, in a surprising bout of energy, had filled out the form. She'd started using that in the off-license. Gareth had noticed the fact they had a little money after the bills but never put two and two together. He actually dared to hope that it meant his Mum was drinking less.

But she'd ticked the box on the form for the card to automatically take minimum payment each month. And each month she kept spending. The combined work of interest and alcohol purchases meant that it took little time for the minimum payments to take dangerous chunks of Gareth's hard-earned money.

When he realised the truth, he almost burst into tears. After everything he'd done for the family, they were worse off than ever. He actually slapped his mother and he screamed all the things he'd hated his dad for screaming.

For the first time in his life, Gareth wished for his dad. He wished for a phone number to call up and beg for help, or to take Chris and Davy away from this woman who was passively destroying their chances.

He went to Mel. She gave him a twenty and suggested he just take the boys and leave Mum to rot. She was actually apologetic of the fact that the place she was currently living in with her boyfriend was even smaller than that apartment but she did say, somewhat reluctantly, that she could make a camp bed on the floor for Davy if things got desperate. Gareth tried to be grateful. He knew that really there was little else Mel could do. It wasn't as though she had money lying around to pay off their Mum's debts.

Gareth thought frantically about what he could do. Loans and cards just added up to more debt and more trouble. They needed money and Mum seemed oblivious in her alcoholic stupor. Chris suggested he try to get a job as well. Gareth didn't want to allow his little brother to put himself through the misery he was enduring but he didn't see a better option, unless he called child services and told them that their Mum wasn't fit to look after them. The option was very tempting.

Chris managed to find a job, working Saturday and Sunday afternoons in a shop. Gareth was grateful to his brother for trying to help and hoped it wasn't too obvious how miserable he still felt. Chris's wages would barely make a dent into the credit card bills, let alone the rent, electricity, gas and water demands that were turning up again with glaring red lettering. When the gas got cut off, they made fires out of the free newspapers and junk mail to keep the place warm. Gareth almost wished that the electricity would go. Maybe if there were no TV, Mum could be persuaded to get out of the house and actually do something useful.

The weight of desperation was sitting squarely on Gareth's shoulders. At least when Dad had been there, he'd dealt with these worries. A part of Gareth wanted to track down his dad and apologise for hating him all those years. Now he knew what it was like to feel responsible for a family and to watch the person who should be responsible just drowning herself in beer and cheap wine.

The landlord had been pounding on the door demanding rent. He said he'd throw them out if he didn't get payment by the end of the week. Gareth felt that it would be fair to leave Mum sitting in a doorway begging for her booze money and Mel had made her reluctant offer to Davy, but there would be nowhere for Gareth and Chris to go.

That was when Gareth had made the decision that would change his life so completely.

He stepped into a jewellers shop. He knew his appearance was scruffy and poor, so he made a point of heading for the costume and second hand displays. When the snooty shopkeeper asked if he could help, Gareth said that he was looking for something for his mum's birthday. He stared at the displays for about a minute then left the shop, sneaking some watches into his pocket when he thought the shopkeeper was occupied with another customer.

He made it about three strides out the door before a hand clamped onto his shoulder and Gareth found himself looking round at a security guard about three times his size.

Gareth actually cried at the police station and he hated himself for it. It turned out that the watches had been worth over five hundred pounds and that the shop had a policy of always prosecuting thieves. There was camera footage and eye witness reports that would damn Gareth for his reckless actions. Gareth knew he was doomed. If he was sent to jail or a juvenile centre or whatever the hell they did with fifteen year olds, Chris and Davy would be out in the street with no one to support them. And there was no way in hell Gareth could afford to pay a fine. His act of desperation had just ruined them all.

In a little interview room at the station, Gareth spilled everything. The arguments, the alcohol, working so many hours to feed his family that his homework lay ignored, the bills and demands, the landlord, everything.

When Gareth was done, the officer fetched him a cup of tea and left him with a box of tissues to compose himself again. Gareth felt like he sat there forever, wondering what would become of him and whether anyone would look after the boys.

The officer eventually returned and he smiled. He said he had an offer to make. Social services could look into the situation with Chris and Davy, but they still had to deal with the charges against Gareth. There was an alternative Gareth might be interested in. He could work off the fine.

The man explained that the Defenders had people work for them, doing the basic, menial tasks. Gareth could become one of them. His food and accommodation would be taken care of, his wages would go towards paying the fine or, if he chose, a portion could be sent each week to his brothers. That would mean he'd have to work longer, but at least he could be sure his family was taken care of. If he worked the full period, then he would end up with no mark on his permanent record, no indication of criminal offence. They would even give him a reference for his CV.

Of course he said yes. He'd have been stupid not to.

He was taken to the Defenders' base. They gave him the grey overalls, took his thumbprint for the door scanners and locked the tracker bracelet on his wrist. That was the first moment that Gareth wondered if he might have been better off going to jail. He was as much a prisoner here as he would have been there.

Still, he started off with good intentions, determined to work hard and show his worth. After all, the work was no worse than the restaurant. Gareth swept floors and scrubbed dishes, piled sheets and uniforms into the huge washing machines, even took a hand at cooking meals. There was also schoolwork. He was given assignments and reading to get through. Without money frets, for the first time he was able to focus on studying. Away from the classmates at the comp, where showing brains was equivalent to social suicide, Gareth found he actually did well, even enjoyed learning things. And there was one major perk here. He saw the Defenders.

He saw these heroes of the world, even got to talk to them from time to time. Sure, most of the time they acted as though he were invisible, but it was amazing enough just to watch them.

Gareth made a point of trading duties for anything that might let him see them practice. He cleaned the mats in the training rooms and polished the practice weapons. He took his time with those tasks so he could watch them sparring and training. He admired their form and tried to memorise their moves, experimenting in the privacy of his own room.

Now that he had a full stomach each night and wasn't just fretting from one bill to the next, Gareth had time to develop dreams of his own. He wanted to be like them. He wanted to trade these grey overalls for the neat black uniform of the Defenders. He wanted to train with them, to fight beside them, to be all that these strong and powerful young men were. Gareth watched carefully and practiced solo, all the while imagining schemes that might allow him to become one of them.

Four

Doubts

Gareth's first stop on his return to base was the shower room. He left Karl doing the official mission sign-off in the control room with Boron. Delegation was certainly one of the perks of being technically the boss. So Gareth headed straight for the lifts and down several levels to get rid of two people's blood and the mass of Outsider gunk that was all over his hands, his uniform and, for some inexplicable reason, in his hair.

The shower rooms were designed with this scenario in mind. Gareth walked along the line of cubicles and picked one at random, nudging the door open with a relatively guts-free elbow. Inside the large cubicle, Gareth stripped off the disgusting uniform and dumped it into a plastic laundry bin that was there for just such a purpose. There was still half a tube of mirus in the pocket, which he retrieved before it ended up in the laundry cycle too.

There was a clean towel hung on the inside of the cubicle door ready for when he was finished, since Defenders often came back from missions in such a state that the act of picking up a clean towel would render it unclean. Therefore everything they needed was ready and waiting.

Gareth stood under the shower head and let the grime of battle wash away in a stream of hot water. His worries were less easily cleared. His thoughts turned, as they so often did, to the Outsiders.

They just didn't make sense.

The Outsiders were stupid. They were fixated on eating to such an extent that they didn't even seem to care for self-preservation. They had no tactics, no thought of strategy. They would stream through the portals and all they cared about was eating whatever happened to be handy. They would devour anything organic regardless, according to the biologists who'd spent the last ten years dissecting and studying the Outsiders' corpses, of whether there was any nutritional benefit. Outsiders would eat animals while they were still alive, munch on fruits and vegetables if they were handy, or, with just as much enthusiasm, eat a bed sheet that was hanging on a washing line in front of where a portal opened.

In the early days, the Defenders had tried capturing Outsiders alive to study them, to try and reason with them. Reason had proved impossible. The things had no desire except eating, even when it was proved they could live weeks at least with no food. Gareth had seen footage of one trying to gnaw its own arm, blunting its teeth against skin only dark metal could pierce. It had tried to eat itself in its hunger and failed, still surviving against its apparent starvation until one of those studying it could bear it no longer and killed it out of pity. The beast had been virtually immortal and yet always hungry, hungry enough that any trace of other thought was impossible.

They were animals, with less intelligence than the average dog.

Yet the portal technology given to this world by Master Amiron was more advanced than anything else on the planet. Richard, Enrico and a whole team of technical geniuses were employed to work on the portals and even they didn't really know how all of it worked.

There was absolutely no chance that the Outsiders could create portals.

But someone did. For a while, back before Gareth had joined the team, the Defenders had considered the possibility that the Outsiders' portals opened randomly but the evidence just didn't fit. Maybe one portal in a hundred opened over an ocean or in some spot so remote that it was impossible to get to without another portal. When that happened, no Outsiders emerged. Most of the time, the portals opened in or near populated areas. The longer that pattern continued, the more unrealistic it became that the portals' locations could be random. By now, the statistics showed it to be virtually impossible.

One of the multiple tasks Richard's team was meant to be working on was figuring out if there was any sort of pattern behind the portals so that they could predict when and where the next portal would show up. Gareth's screwed up memories could help with the when but he didn't do so well on where. The details of future Outsider attacks were always fuzzy. It was frustrating. He sometimes got muddled regarding whether day to day events had happened yet thanks to his broken brain but he couldn't remember things that would actually be useful to the team.

Memories aside, it was a clear fact that the Outsiders couldn't be causing the portals that they came through. Which led to the inevitable question. Who was?

Gareth always came back to this point. For ten years, this world had been under attack by creatures from another dimension. For ten years, the Defenders had used the portal technology to protect the civilian population. For ten years, they'd responded to every attack, dealt with every incursion, but they'd never been able to fight back. They'd never been able to figure out who was responsible for the portals opening in the first place. There was a reason this team was called the Defenders and not the Attackers.

Would they always be one step behind? Always reacting and never acting?

Gareth tried to search his memories. He closed his eyes and tried to think through what he knew of future events, looking for traces that could answer his questions. His mind sank into a state that was cut off from his physical position, like his consciousness sinking into a deep well where his memories could be clearer. His breath came slow and deep.

And he breathed in a mouthful of shower water.

Coughing and choking, all of the calm vanished instantly. Gareth was left clinging to the cubicle wall as he tried to get rid of the liquid that had gone down the wrong pipe.

This wasn't the best place to explore the depths of his screwed up brain.

"Are you OK?" came Karl's voice through the thin partitions of cubical walls.

"I'm fine," Gareth said, once he'd recovered enough to be able to breathe properly. "It's not a good idea to breathe while your face is covered in water."

"You're just figuring that out?" Karl chuckled.

Gareth turned off the shower and grabbed the towel. He'd find somewhere better to think about the paradox of the Outsiders. He scrubbed himself dry quickly and emerged from the cubical with the towel around his waist. He headed for the rows of lockers against the back wall. He punched the combination on the keypad for his own and opened it to reveal the mass of clothes he'd shoved inside. He yanked things out of the crumpled mass until he'd acquired something of everything. This required digging around for a second sock. He shoved the tube of mirus inside; he'd return it at a more convenient time. He felt something at the edge of his awareness, a memory trying to break through the fog of confusion, a quiet premonition that this tube was important here.

He could still hear the flow of water from Karl's shower as Gareth started to get dressed. He then reached into the locker for his deodorant and already knew what he would find. The can was empty. He'd known this morning that he'd needed to get a new one but it had slipped his mind with everything else going on. It was embarrassing that he could be forgetful when his memory went in both directions. So Gareth stood there, half-dressed, with an empty deodorant in his hands.

"Hey, Karl," he called out. "Can I borrow your deodorant?"

"Sure. There's some in my locker. Just give me a minute."

Gareth didn't bother with waiting. He went to Karl's locker and remembered. This was something he liked about his gift. He only needed to remember the next few seconds to bring to mind the buttons he was about to press. Then he did what he remembered, pushed the right numbers on the keypad and opened Karl's locker to reveal immaculately folded piles of clothes, each precisely placed.

"How did you do that?" Karl asked. He'd emerged from his shower now, wrapped in a towel, staring at the open locker. Gareth just shrugged.

"There's no way you could know the code," Karl went on. "I changed the combination three days ago."

"I've told you that that won't work," Gareth said.

"No you haven't."

"Haven't I?"

Gareth frowned. He was sure he'd talked to Karl about his trick with codes. Maybe he'd just been thinking of this conversation, assuming it had already happened. He'd done that before, remembering future conversations as though they were past, being utterly confident that people knew things he hadn't told them yet.

"How did you know my locker combination?" Karl asked.

"I knew it was the right code because it opened it."

"Yes, but how did you know?"

Gareth just shrugged and said, "I just knew."

Karl blinked at the statement and, like a haze passing across his face, the look of bewilderment changed to one of acceptance simply because Gareth said it was alright. Gareth got on with using the deodorant that had caused all this confusion. The truth was, the whole thing bewildered him even more than it did Karl. He could remember the combination to open the locker because he remembered opening it. The act of knowing his future made it possible. Master Amiron had never managed to explain that in a way that didn't give him a headache trying to understand.

Gareth was putting on his shirt when the shower room door opened and the conversation was, at least for now, forgotten. Lizzie walked in, still covered in mess from the battle, the Outsider blood sliming her hands and arms. She grinned appreciatively at the sight of Karl wearing nothing but a towel as she crossed the room to them.

"Looks like I got here just in time," she said. She moved to kiss Karl, but he stepped back.

"You're filthy," he said, "and I've just had a shower."

She made a show of putting her hands behind her back and kissing Karl without any other part of her body touching him. She was giggling through the kiss.

Gareth turned away and put on his shirt.

"I'm going to need to make a rule about shameless public displays of affection," he said. The pair broke the kiss, Lizzie still grinning.

"Gareth," said Lizzie, "we're going to have to set a date for you to get fitted for your suit."

"My suit?" he asked. "Can't I just wear jeans?"

"That's what I said," put in Karl.

"No one is wearing jeans to my wedding."

"I thought it was Karl's wedding too."

"I gave up on that delusion about a week after I proposed," said Karl.

"Hey." Lizzie gave him a playful slap on the chest.

"Hey!" Karl protested at the smudge of Outsider guts that was now in the middle of his bare chest.

"Well you'll just have to come back in the shower with me then," Lizzie said.

Gareth slammed his locker shut and walked out of the shower room. The two were always impossible after a mission. The rest of the time, they could be perfectly calm and professional but, in the few hours straight after a battle, their need took over. They had to prove to themselves that they were both alive and safe. Master Amiron had apparently, when the relationship just became official, experimented with putting them onto separate teams. But that had just made them worse and whoever was left behind during a mission was impossible to deal with. So they'd learned to live with it.

***

Karl decided to take advantage of his unexpectedly free afternoon by putting in a few reps on the weights. He was heading that direction, finally clean despite Lizzie's best efforts, when he saw Adrian Boron standing outside one of the small practice rooms. Boron glanced at Karl, with a silent nod of greeting, before turning his attention back to whatever was happening inside. Curious, Karl approached the door and looked within.

Gareth was standing in the middle of the empty floor. All equipment was stacked away neatly at the edge of the room, giving Gareth as wide a space as possible in which to move. His eyes were shut, his body flowing through a series of slow motions that could have been a form of tai chi.

"A new training pattern?" Karl asked quietly, unsure why this would merit such rapt attention from Boron. Gareth's eyes were shut, his body gliding through the movements like a dance. He seemed oblivious to the two at the door, but Karl didn't want to break his concentration.

"Look deeper," Boron said. That was something Master Amiron always used to say. Portals left scars on this world, the press of one dimension against another could have an impact. With the right frame of mind and enough practice, it was possible to see those traces. It wasn't an easy skill but Karl had been practicing at it since he'd first come to work with Master Amiron. He tried now, bringing himself into an almost meditative trance. He let his eyes become unfocused; it was easier to see the invisible when the visible was less distinct.

Once he caught the first glimpse, the rest followed more easily. With this new layer of sight, Gareth stood in a haze of gold. All around him were lines of energy where this universe rested against another.

The radiance flowed around him, brightening or dimming in time, the lines shifting around him like swirls of colour within a pool of water.

Karl watched Gareth's movement, flowing with the lines, around them. The light and the man were part of a greater pattern, each a complement to the other. Gareth seemed almost mystical, a wizard figure weaving some great magic. At moments like this, it was hard to see the boy he'd been and easy to see the Master whose role he had stepped into.

"Is he moving the lights?" Karl asked. "Or is he moving because of the way they're moving?"

"I saw Master Amiron like this once," Boron replied, "and asked him that question. He said yes."

Karl laughed, "Of course a Defence Master wouldn't give a straight answer."

* * *

Cassie soon fell into a pattern in the Defender base. The mornings were spent in group training and she found herself quickly picking up the fighting moves, the practice sword feeling less awkward in her hand. Richard was having no such luck. He still finished the runs looking like he was about to die. He still battled through the sessions in the large training room with all the grace of a drunken hippo. The Defenders, so patient with Cassie and the other new recruits, showed obvious frustration with Richard. She was left frequently wondering why he was putting himself through this.

Cassie's afternoons were spent either making use of the varied training facilities to try and catch up with the others, or exploring the areas of the base she had access to. She was limited to the training and living areas, aware that so much must lie beyond those boundaries. She couldn't even get through to the kitchen beside the dining room.

What she did find was sometimes intriguing. There was a long corridor on the floor below her allocated bedroom. This one was almost identical to the hall where it seemed the majority of Defenders lived. The big difference though was that this one was deserted. Door after door led to empty bedrooms, each one neat yet with a somewhat forlorn feel. The rooms felt musty and still, with no trace of life or personality. Bed after bed had a perfectly placed pillow and smoothed covers. Cupboard after cupboard stood open and bare. In many ways, this corridor looked smarter than other parts of the base. Certainly, the paint was less scuffed, the floors less trodden, but still there was a melancholy air about the place.

Near those deserted rooms, a door led through into a dining room, eerily silent. In design, it was identical to the one in which she'd now eaten several times. But the chairs were stacked on the tables. The serving area was polished and cold. Cassie's footsteps seemed echoingly loud in the large room, her presence merely emphasising the emptiness.

She asked about it one dinner, as she sat with Enrico and Jerry in the other dining room, this one packed and crowded.

"The Defenders are less than half the size we used to be," Enrico answered. "This place was built at the height of the first invasion. Portals were opening a couple of times a day and staying open for hours. More Outsiders came through each portal."

"And they walked uphill both ways," grinned Jerry. Cassie stared at him blankly for a moment, before glancing at Enrico for explanation. He just shrugged away the attempted joke. Jerry looked almost hurt that neither of them had understood, let alone laughed.

"The point is," said Enrico, "that we were constantly on alert. At any given time, just about everyone was either out on a mission, on an active response team or recovering from having just been out on a mission. We had three shifts so that there were always people awake and each shift was in a different area so that they weren't kept awake by the alarms during their off-shift."

"But now everyone's in one shift?"

"Basically. There are always at least two teams alert as the first and second response teams and there are always people in the control room, but there's no need to split us into shifts anymore."

"Why are there less attacks?" Cassie asked.

All Enrico could do was shrug, "We're still trying to figure that out. If we do, we might be able to stop them once and for all."

There was another Outsider attack three days after the first, another two days after that. Each time, Cassie went to watch the screen with the others, hearing the alerts and updates broadcast on the PA system. The first of these attacks was in rural France, dealt with by a single response team. The next came in the middle of New York. Three teams went through on that mission because there was a high risk to the local population. Cassie listened to the reports of twelve injuries, one of which was serious and one of which was a Defender.

All she could do was stand there, feeling utterly helpless. A part of her wished that she could do something, anything, to be useful; she'd come here to help people, to save lives, not wave a wooden sword around in a training room. How long would it be until they decided she was ready?

It was hard to keep track of the passing days since, aside from the interruptions of attacks, the days were each the same. She wasn't in the cycle of days off because she wasn't yet on the duty schedule, so one day flowed into another. Cassie had to stop and count to realise how long she'd been there.

About mid-way through her second week, she was making her way to the training rooms for an afternoon of private practice. She was improving rapidly with the sword but still felt miles behind where she needed to be. She couldn't lose the sense that she would be killed if she came face to face with an Outsider at her current level of skill. She was determined not to stay behind for long, so she was planning on spending a couple of hours going through some of the exercises Boron had demonstrated that morning.

She went to the door of the nearest of the small training rooms. She opened in, to be met by annoyed looks of the two men who'd been sparring inside.

"What?" one demanded.

"Sorry." Cassie hastily shut the door again. She heard a chuckle and looked along the corridor to see Lizzie. She was smiling but not unkindly.

"Rookie mistake," Lizzie said.

"What do you mean?"

"There's almost no privacy in this place. And, as someone engaged to another Defender, you can trust that I know what I'm talking about on this. So we've got to be careful of what privacy we can get. If a door's shut in any of the public areas, you don't go in. Not unless you really, really have to."

Lizzie was walking along the corridor as she talked, passing Cassie and walking onwards. She indicated a door that was nearly closed but still ajar.

"Someone's in there," Lizzie said, "but whoever it is doesn't mind being disturbed."

They reached a door that was wide open, revealing the small room within to be deserted. Lizzie gestured for Cassie to go inside and then made a point of pushing the door until it was nearly, but not completely, closed. Cassie realised that she still had so much to learn about the Defenders, beyond the obvious martial arts training. This base was a society in its own right, with its own rules and customs. She'd violated one without thinking about it. How many other unwritten rules might she be ignorant of?

This training room was like so many others along this corridor. It was a mostly-empty rectangle, designed to allow people to practice in the space in the middle. Along one wall was equipment that might be useful. A few mats leaned out of the way; there was a pile of pads in the corner. Most of the wall was taken up by a rack of training weapons. Lizzie had already crossed to this rack so Cassie went too. There were the swords they trained with in the large group but other things as well. Cassie picked out a wooden axe and gave it an experimental swing.

"Stick with the sword," Lizzie advised. "Don't get me wrong, it's good to be able to use all the weapons but we've only got two dark metal axes and we've got two Defenders who've made a point of being extremely good with them. The weapons we've got spare of are the swords."

"How many are there?" Cassie asked.

"Swords? About a hundred. The other weapons, maybe one or two of each. That's why there's always been an upper limit on the size of the Defenders. Even at the height of the first invasion, we could only be so big before we started running out of dark metal weapons."

"Couldn't you make more?"

"No one knows how. Master Amiron brought the dark metal weapons here when he brought us the portal technology but he couldn't teach us how to make more. That's why we've got to be so careful with the bullets; once they're gone, they're gone."

Lizzie handed Cassie a wooden sword from the rack. She took it and moved to the centre of the room, Lizzie coming to join her, her own hands empty.

"Aren't you going to get a sword?" Cassie asked.

"Outsiders don't use swords. I'm going to try and eat you. You've got to stop me."

Lizzie approached, arms out and grasping. Cassie brought the sword round and tapped Lizzie's arm, not wanting to actually hurt her. Lizzie kept coming, grabbed her with the other arm and then brought her head forward, mouth open, as though she was about to tear open Cassie's jugular. Then she stepped back.

"You chopped off my arm," Lizzie said, "but I'd have still killed you. Outsiders don't stop until they're dead. Let's try again."

Again and again, they practiced. Lizzie kept attacking and Cassie kept trying to stop her. The moves that had been drilled into her in the morning training sessions were beginning to flow now. She brought the sword round, striking at arms, at Lizzie's torso, towards the neck. Her strikes were slow, not wanting to hurt, but the pace increased. Lizzie came in running and it was all Cassie could do to avoid getting bowled over.

"Use your feet!" Lizzie said. "Don't just stand there and wait to get eaten."

So Cassie practiced movement, tried to evade as much as strike. Over and over again, they danced round the training room floor. Both of them were breathless and sweaty but Lizzie kept insisting they try things yet another time.

Cassie was almost enjoying it. It was like some strange game of tag, a competition to see who could be quicker. She was grinning, despite the exertion. But behind it all, behind the smiles and the cheerful advice, lay the knowledge that this was just preparation for the real fight. Sooner or later, Cassie would have to face the real thing. She'd face creatures who wouldn't walk away and point out her mistakes.

* * *

Karl was heading up to the main meeting room after dinner. Gareth had summoned the senior Defenders. There had been no explanation as to the purpose of the meeting, but where their Master summoned, they obeyed. Karl met Grigory in the lift. The burly Russian was obviously heading to the same meeting.

"Do you know what this is about?" Karl asked.

Grigory shrugged a giant shoulder, "Training schedules?"

It seemed Grigory had got it right. When they were in the conference room, each of the senior Defenders in their customary place around the circular table, aside from Jakob who was on alert in the ready room, Gareth started the meeting, talking about additional training that some of the less experienced Defenders might require. The discussion wasn't purely focused on the new recruits, though they were a key component. Gareth had his list, clearly outlined, with his own thoughts, but he made sure to check with the assembled seniors for their opinions.

Gareth kept the conversation to the point, moving on to plan a schedule of training, asking each of the seniors to fit in private coaching for one or two of those discussed. Karl had Cassie on his list, but only for a couple of hours a week. He queried this.

"Cassie is doing some private training with Lizzie," Gareth said. "If that's working for her, there's no reason to change it, but I want to have a senior checking on her just in case."

The meeting wrapped up promptly, their plans organised after perhaps half an hour of talk, Gareth's plan neatly divided into individual actions.

Karl, with the others, was getting up from the table to go downstairs. He was planning to find Cassie and tell her of their newly scheduled classes, then to find Lizzie and ask how well things were progressing. His thoughts were entirely on the new training plan when the alarms sounded.

Outside the conference room, Karl was nearly bowled over by Jakob and the first response team charging across the hall and into the control room. Gareth was a step behind them, Karl immediately behind him. The assembled seniors all piled into the control room as Gareth surveyed the information appearing on the screen. It looked like somewhere in America, one of the southern states.

Gareth had the information digested in a heartbeat, even as the first response team were heading through the portal. Karl had reached for the sword racks automatically, before Gareth gave the order for them to follow.

"Send the second and third teams," Gareth ordered as he ran for the portal.

Karl didn't hesitate. He followed Gareth into a chaos of screams and sounds, rock music still playing, lights swinging in automated patterns that blinded and dimmed and added a new layer to the madness.

It was a sports arena, set up for a conference or show, a stage at one end, seats across the floor and then rising in tiers up to a ceiling high above. Beneath strobing lights, a hoard of people were panicking, screaming, trying to run, trampling each other in a scramble up steps and away from the arena floor in a mad rush for the exits.

In the arena floor, among scattered chairs and scattered corpses, the portal glowed. It could have been just another special effect from the light show above, were it not for the sea of death around it.

Gareth was giving orders as Karl drank in the horror of the scene, the cramped setting and the Outsiders mad with a frenzy at the buffet of bodies in front of them. Gareth spoke with calm urgency, directing the Defenders with short words.

"Guard the stairs," Gareth yelled above the noise. "Make sure these people have room to get out."

Karl rushed to a cluster at the base of one set of stairs. Perhaps three dozen people were trying to force their way up a gap designed for two, with a barrier of backs all pressing away before them. An Outsider was there, tearing at them as they tried to flee. It had gored open a young man, its face dripping with blood and scraps of skin.

Karl shut away his disgust for later, severing the creature's head so its blood mingled black with the red it had spilled.

The rest of the crowd were still screaming and trying to run, scrambling over seats and each other, pushing and yelling and forcing their way up.

Karl positioned himself at their back, near the base of the stairs. Another Outsider was heading his direction, its jaws already bloody, in its eyes a strange delight at the carnage all about. Karl cut it down before it got close to the fleeing civilians.

He had a moment now to look about, seeing the other seniors like him, trying to guard the over-crowded escape routes. The first response team, now joined by the second, were in a tight line around the Outsider portal, stopping any invaders before they could get their bearings. The third team was there, Gareth directing them among the injured scattered on the arena floor. Some had been hurt by the Outsiders, others simply tripped and trampled by humans who would at other times have been friends.

Gareth was at the heart of it all, directing the Defenders like a choreographer of a dance. He sent them where they were needed, holding back the tide of death.

He'd never hesitated, never doubted.

The portal light winked out. There was still a mad press for the exits, but it grew less frantic when the people realised there wasn't an army of monsters still pouring through behind them. Karl guessed the portal had been open less than five minutes, one of the shortest he'd seen, but the injured and the dead lay scattered among the seats. Karl moved slowly in, looking for any he could help while they waited for the ambulances to arrive.

Among those who could be helped, there lay those who couldn't. Karl found a woman, barely recognisable as human. One arm had been ripped clean off, her face was mangled with teeth marks, her torso ripped from crotch to neck and her insides gnawed out of her. Beside this gruesome mass of blood and flesh, lay the remains of the Outsider who'd killed her. Its eyes were still open, staring up at Karl with a strange sadness, now that death had robbed it of its insatiable hunger. The face, pale and miserable beneath the congealing blood, had regained a human quality in its demise.

There were surprisingly few dead, given the carnage they'd arrived to. Perhaps five people in total. More were injured on the arena floor. It was impossible to tell how many had been hurt trying to escape. Those bodies were a tragedy but Karl couldn't help thinking how much worse it could have been. If they'd been a few seconds slower, if the seniors hadn't been right there when the portal opened, ready to support the first response team, five might have been fifty.

A situation like this was about as bad as it could get, a mass of people in a confined space, a feast for the Outsiders and a lethal trap for those who'd gathered here. Karl had acted on instinct, training taking over to guide his actions, but it was Gareth who had to give the orders, who'd sent them where they were needed.

At moments like this, when he spoke with quiet certainty in the midst of death, Karl could see why Master Amiron had chosen him. Gareth did exactly what was needed without a moment's doubt. He made the right call and gave the right orders. He'd even had them once again, whether by luck or some strange instinct, in exactly the right place to deal with this catastrophe before a handful of deaths became hundreds. However strangely he might act sometimes, Karl knew that when the portals opened and ravenous death charged through, Gareth would make the right decisions.

Five

Richard

The computer lab was Richard's domain, a sprawling mass of electronics cobwebbed in cables. Servers blinked away along the far wall. The bulk of the space was filled with tables pushed together to make a single flat surface that was now swamped in screens and laptops, peripherals and paraphernalia. In this space, the techies worked, bathed in the pale glow of their computers. Enrico came here sometimes, but mostly it was inhabited by a team of workers recruited to understand the technology behind the portals.

In this world, Richard was king. Unfortunately, he was a king often beset by revolutions.

Gareth went to the lab one afternoon after yet another portal. This time it had been in Melbourne. The alarms had woken the Defenders in the middle of the night but the two response teams had contained the situation and everyone had been able to return to bed promptly. Gareth had lain awake for hours, his mind still swirling with the problem of the Outsiders. Three of the last four portals had been in cities. There was no way in hell that it could be just a coincidence.

He wished, as he so often did, that Master Amiron had left them with a bit more information regarding the Outsiders. This team held the line against those creatures but they still knew so little about their origins, their methods, or even how the hell they opened the portals into this world. Gareth had asked, of course, but Master Amiron had always deflected the questions. From talking to the others, it seemed that he'd been that way with everyone. Even Adrian Boron, who'd been at his side since the very beginning, knew no more about the Outsiders than Gareth did.

Why had Master Amiron always needed secrets?

Gareth couldn't ask him that question or any other, but he could ask questions of the people who were hired here to find answers. So he walked into the computer lab. There was Meg, as usual, pouring over two screens at once with a look of intense concentration on her face and what looked to Gareth like gibberish on the screen. Around the other side of the table was Richard. He was still in the clothes he'd worn for training that morning. The distinct aroma of sweat might have something to do with the frown on Meg's face.

"How are things going?" Gareth asked. "I wondered if you'd made any progress with working out a pattern to predict portal openings?"

"It would be going better," said Meg, "if our supposed leader would actually do something."

She glared across the table at Richard, who kept on staring at his computer screen. He appeared oblivious to the tone.

"It's just number crunching," he said. "Feeding numbers into data mining tools and watching it spit out zippedy squat. It's boring."

"It's also what will let us prepare for Outsider attacks in advance, instead of just reacting," pointed out Gareth.

"And maybe, if you'd help us, we'd actually find something," Meg added. When Richard ignored her, she sighed and turned to Gareth, "We haven't found anything we didn't already know. Frequency of attacks decreasing for the last ten years. Duration of portals, ditto. Probability of an attack, higher in more densely populated areas or regions with heavy industry. But, aside from saying that we're quite likely to have another portal open in a city somewhere in two to four days, I can't help you."

Richard didn't say anything. Gareth tried to hold back his frustration and speak calmly.

"Richard, Master Amiron brought you here because you're supposed to be brilliant. You're supposed to be amazing at finding patterns. Instead, you're insisting on trying to be a Defender and when you're not doing that, you're also not working on the project you're paid to complete."

"I am brilliant," Richard said. "I am amazing at spotting patterns. And I am going to be a Defender."

Gareth knew otherwise. He knew with the absolute certainty of a remembered future.

"You have the same natural talent for martial arts as a slug," Gareth said. So much for remaining calm. At least it got a reaction.

Richard turned away from his computer and stood, glaring up at Gareth.

"I will be a Defender. I will show you all what I'm capable of. And I'm not going to waste my time on that stupid global prediction project because it's utterly pointless. We are never going to find a reliable model for anticipating the location of the next portal because there are random factors in the location and those factors which could be used to determine causal links are all in whatever world the Outsiders come from. That's where the portals are opening and it's stupid for us to try and use things in our world to make guesses. It will never work."

Gareth blinked at the long stream of words. He got the overall drift even if pieces of the explanation had passed him by.

"Is he right?" he asked Meg.

"I don't know," she answered, even as Richard muttered an indignant, "Of course I'm right," under his breath as he turned back to his computer.

"We've not found any factors we can use to make a reliable model," Meg went on, "and every time we think we're onto something, we find that a couple of the portals just don't fit the pattern at all. I'm sorry."

"Not your fault." Gareth wished he could remember whether or not this project was going to work. He could save them a lot of trouble now if he knew. But that was all hazy. Whenever he tried to focus too hard on specifics of portals, things got hazy.

"So," he looked back at Richard, "what are you working on that's more interesting than doing your job?"

"I'm working on upgrading our tracking system," he said. He then spewed out a stream of syllables, talking about resonance frequencies, harmonics, spectrum analysis, vocal points and dimensional coordinates. He could have been speaking a foreign language for all the sense it made to Gareth.

"Why?"

Richard employed his most patronising tone, as though talking to a particularly stupid three-year-old. "Because if I can work that out, I can mirror it. We can open portals the other way. You want to be on the offensive instead of always reacting? This is what will do it. Not that stupid global analysis project."

There was something familiar about this, some trace of importance fighting through the confusion of Gareth's mind. This mattered. This project, this interesting diversion for Richard, was a golden thread travelling through Gareth's future to some significant event. He couldn't see the end of the road, but he could see this thought like a path through the fog. Even without his broken memories, he could understand the significance. If they could open portals to the Outsiders' world, they could attack instead of defending. They could finally get the upper hand.

Gareth might actually get some answers.

"Do it then," Gareth said.

* * *

Cassie was, according to the Defenders who were teaching her, making considerable progress. She'd been given some exercises to increase strength and flexibility in her wrists to make the sword work easier. She was getting faster and more precise with the blade. And Lizzie was continuing their private sessions to prepare her for facing an enemy in combat. Despite all the work, she still felt woefully inadequate.

She watched one of the other recruits drop out. She'd barely spoken to him, a man from Sweden who'd been recruited in from the army. He just disappeared one day, leaving only the whisper of rumour. No one was sure whether he'd left or been pushed out.

She watched one of the others take the uniform. Jayden had been a New York police officer who practiced martial arts in his spare time. He came to the Defenders already knowing what Cassie was trying desperately hard to learn. In his third week, he was taken aside by Defender Boron. He disappeared for a day or so, leaving Cassie wondering if he too had left. Then the portal opened and it seemed he'd been sent to face it. The next morning, Boron called him to the front of the assembled Defenders and handed over a neatly folded pile of black cloth. Jayden's first Defender uniform.

Cassie had congratulated him afterwards with all the others, fighting back the twinge of jealousy that she was still just practicing. It could have been worse. Richard seemed to be making no progress whatsoever. He ran with the rest of them before breakfast, limping in last every time. In the training in the large hall, most of the Defenders had taken to ignoring him. They were happy to help the other recruits, but Richard was left to fend for himself when it became apparent that all the demonstrations in the world weren't going to help him master the techniques.

One morning, Jerry just snapped. It was clear he'd barely tolerated Richard's presence from the beginning. As Richard fumbled a basic move yet again, Jerry turned from his own exercises to ask, "Why don't you just stop fooling yourself?"

"Excuse me?" said Richard.

"You're not a Defender," Jerry said. "You never will be. You're a computer geek. When will you get it through your genius skull that you don't belong here?"

There was silence across the hall. Every pair of eyes was fixed on the two glaring at each other towards the back.

"I make this place happen," Richard said. Every word was slow and careful, every syllable dripping with anger. "You think yourself superior to me because of your muscles and your sword but compared to me you have the intellectual capacity of a lemming. You're a weapon against the Outsiders because I can deploy you. I control the portals. You're just a jumped up caveman with a metal stick."

Richard dropped the training sword and stalked from the room.

* * *

Richard fumed his way back to his bedroom. Not a room on the same floor as the Defenders, like every other recruit, of course. No, he was still stuck in his worker room, a tiny space that could be unfavourably compared to a cupboard.

None of the Defenders had taken him seriously. None of them had treated him like the other recruits. Every other recruit got help, guidance, coaching, advice, even just kind words of encouragement. But Richard? No. Richard, they looked at like he was some disgusting slime that had no right to be in their presence.

Of course he hadn't improved! Who could? They'd barely put up with him being in the room. They were never going to actually teach him enough to make him succeed. They'd wanted him gone. They'd wanted him to fail.

Computer geek. That's what Jerry had called him. And he was, there was no denying it. But did Jerry have to say it like he was referring to some sub-species? Homo Nerdus?

Jerry thought himself so great because he could shoot a hole in the centre of a target. So what? Trained monkeys could be given a gun and shown how to pull the trigger. The Defenders looked down on him because he couldn't use a sword but most of them hadn't the faintest idea about the portals they used every day. Did any of them understand string theory or dimensional harmonics or the Everett many world interpretation of quantum mechanics? Of course not. As far as they were concerned, the portals were just a magic door that could take them wherever they wanted.

Or wherever Richard wanted, since it was Richard who'd programmed the targeting system that let them lock their own portals onto the Outsider ones geographically. Before Richard came along, it took five minutes of manual calculation to get the portal fixed on the right point. How many people would get hurt or killed in that time? Richard had probably saved more lives than some of the Defenders with that little program. But did he get thanks? Of course not. They were the heroes and he was just the computer geek.

This internal rant had carried him up four floors to the row of cramped rooms where the workers resided. Richard reached his microscopic accommodations and slammed the door, but he was still full of restless energy fuelled by his rage. He wanted to pace but he could make it about three steps before bashing his shin on the bedframe. He wanted to hit something, but there was nothing here. All those punch bags down in the training rooms but Richard wasn't going to go back there. He wasn't going to give Jerry the satisfaction of seeing how much his words had affected him.

So Richard lay back on the narrow bed, thumping the mattress with his right hand. His mind was still racing in furious circles.

He spent some time dreaming up petty ways to get revenge on Jerry. Something in the food would be easy, since the Defenders ate separately from the workers, but there'd be too much collateral damage. He could hijack the alert lights, isolating Jerry's room from the rest of the base. That could be fun. He could make the red attack light come on in Jerry's room, just for a fraction of a second. Enough to disturb his sleep but not enough for that Neanderthal to work out what was actually going on. But the lights along that corridor were on the same circuit. Richard would have to physically interfere with the wiring and that was risky, tedious and ran the risk of getting caught.

How about a security glitch? Richard could put a gremlin in the system to randomly reject Jerry's password on the doors. Not every time, but just once in a while. He could write it so that the program watched for alarm conditions; he wouldn't want to slow Jerry down if there was an actual attack. But the rest of the time, Jerry would walk up to doors never sure that it would open for him.

Richard grinned at the ceiling. Jerry might suspect the computer geek, but he'd never be able to stop him.

Six

Reflecting on the Accident

Gareth went to see Richard as soon as training officially ended. He hadn't caught all of the exchange with Jerry but he'd seen most of it. Enough to know that Richard was probably very upset right now. So he left the crowds heading towards food and made his own way up to the computer lab near the control room. Someone had stuck a hastily-written sign on the door, warning potential visitors to stay out if they valued their lives. Meg's handwriting.

The door was very firmly shut, but Gareth ignored the sign and the privacy protocols. He opened the door with the air of someone stepping into a lion's den.

Richard was sat at one of the computers. He didn't even look up to the sound of the door.

"Go away."

"I just wanted to check that you're alright."

"Sure you don't just want to be smug? You've got me out of the training. That was what you wanted all along."

Gareth hesitated over the best way to soothe the damaged ego. For all his brilliance, Richard was fragile.

"You could have stayed in training. You could have practiced for months or even years. You could have trained harder than anyone else in the base and learned to use the sword like a master. But answer me one thing, Richard. Would you have ever liked it?"

There was a confusion that crossed Richard's face, briefly obscuring the anger.

"Richard, you are brilliant. You're brilliant *here*. I've seen you buried up to your neck in computer code and grinning like a maniac when you solve some problem. Would being a Defender have ever made you feel as alive as the work you're doing here?"

There was a long silence, then the whispered admission: "No."

"This is where you belong, Richard. You know it as well as I do."

"I also know that I deserve more respect than those thugs give me."

"Those thugs are highly trained, highly skilled and also intelligent."

Richard's derisive snort was very eloquent. He tended not to think of anyone with an IQ below a hundred and sixty as being anything close to intelligent.

"Richard, please don't do anything that I'll have to deal with officially," Gareth said.

The look of guilt was quickly smothered in a look of fake innocence that was just as incriminating.

"I don't know what you mean," Richard said.

"I may not be a genius but I'm not an idiot. I know you're planning something but don't. Just let it go. Get on with whatever project takes your interest this week and forget about what Jerry said."

The advice was pointless. He could remember the arguments. But at least this way, he could honestly say that he'd tried to warn Richard. And it wouldn't hurt their relationship if Richard thought that Gareth was smart enough to figure this out. He needn't know that he had broken memories giving him a helping hand.

"Jerry's got nothing to worry about," Richard said, "if he apologises for being rude to me."

Gareth already knew that was hopeless.

* * *

Gareth was lecturing him about behaving properly. This from the guy who'd had Richard hack his tracker bracelet so he could stalk the Defenders. Richard might have laughed if he weren't so infuriated. Gareth was acting like a teacher scolding a naughty child. They were practically the same age!

Ever since Master Amiron had named Gareth as his successor, Gareth had been acting like he ruled the world. Stalking about this base as though he knew better than everyone else. He never gave a straight answer anymore, just said things that he probably meant to sound enigmatic. From Master Amiron, they probably would have done. But Gareth was a former thief promoted above his level.

Why the hell had Master Amiron chosen Gareth?

That was a decision that no one really understood. Sure, Gareth had become a decent enough Defender under Master Amiron's guidance and with Karl's training, but practically every other Defender was senior to him. When Master Amiron had announced that he was leaving, everyone knew that Adrian Boron was the logical choice of successor. Boron was a fantastic fighter, a senior Defender who'd served since the first days of the first invasion and who knew the organisation by heart. Even if, for whatever inexplicable reason, Master Amiron hadn't wanted to give the job to Boron, there were a dozen senior Defenders. Any one of them would have proudly taken on the duty of Defence Master.

But Master Amiron had stood there, before the assembled Defenders, before the workers and everyone else, and announced that Gareth Walker would be the new Defence Master. Why?

The decision hadn't bothered Richard at the time. He'd thought it odd, but he'd been pleased for his friend. And a little pleased to see some of the other Defenders so upset at the choice. Since that day though, Gareth had stopped acting like a friend.

A thought niggled away at the back of Richard's mind.

It wasn't since that day. It was since the day of the accident. Ever since then, Gareth had been different. Sometimes, he'd behave as he always had but at others, he would look through people as if they weren't there. He'd stare off into the distance for ages and then say things that didn't make sense, state as pure fact things he couldn't possibly know. He stopped giving straight answers and, sometimes, would look at Richard like he was looking straight through him. Sometimes, Gareth would say something impossible, but he'd say it with such conviction that anyone who heard would instantly believe. When he got in that mood, speaking in his Master tone, the entire assembled body of Defenders would believe him if Gareth said the sky was green.

Richard stared around the empty room.

The whirring of computer fans laid a background hum over the desolation. He'd always been alone, surrounding himself with computers because they were easier than people. Until Gareth. A random guy, put in the room next to his purely by chance, equally alone. They should never have been friends but somehow they had become so. Richard wasn't sure how or when it had happened. The boy who sat at the same table as him because they had no one else, had somehow transformed into someone whose opinion Richard actually cared about.

On the day of the accident, Richard had seen Gareth, lying in the blackened ruins left by an exploding portal generator, and he'd been sure his only friend was dead.

And then the miracle.

Richard had no idea what had really happened, what Master Amiron had done. Gareth had survived. But he'd changed, more than he'd changed the day he'd exchanged the grey worker clothes for the black uniform of a Defender.

In some intangible way, it was as though a piece of Gareth had gone and some stranger was looking out through Gareth's eyes. A stranger who looked at the world with a strange sense of knowing and who seemed to stand apart from those around him.

It was that stranger who denied Richard now. Gareth, the old Gareth, believed everyone should have a chance to change, to prove that they could become whatever they wanted to be. When Karl and the others told Gareth that he couldn't be a Defender, he'd argued. He'd fought. He'd faced anyone who'd tell him he couldn't and he'd proved them wrong. Richard remembered those rants up in Gareth's pokey room as a worker, every word Gareth had uttered about demanding the opportunity to show what he was capable of. He'd fought against the grey worker uniform, fought to gain Karl's trust, fought to gain the respect of those who'd overlooked him. He'd made his own opportunity out of the fire of his determination.

But now he denied that opportunity to Richard. The hideous hypocrisy stung more than the failure itself. Of all people on this base, he'd expected Gareth to support him in his attempt, not to push him aside, scolding like a child for getting revenge on Jerry. He hadn't done anything to Jerry! Not yet, anyway.

Richard wasn't used to failing. He couldn't remember the last time he'd tried to do something and not managed it. Certainly not something that mattered to him as much as this. The failure burned like a brand in his heart and he couldn't shrug it off like it was nothing. It wasn't just Jerry he was angry at now. He was furious with Gareth. The anger he felt for Jerry was a blazing fire, hot and deadly but quickly burned out. The anger he felt for Gareth had a different feel to it, a cold, hard sensation that settled inside him like a core of iron.

He wasn't going to let this go. He was going to figure out what had happened to Gareth. The accident was something no one really talked about, a subject glossed over and shied away from. But no more. Richard wasn't going to be just shoved aside, cast back into the worker grey, without at least knowing why.

Richard hated mysteries but he thrived on puzzles. This puzzle wouldn't elude him. Somewhere, in this mess of equipment, in their portal research and their archived records, was the answer. Richard would figure out exactly what had happened to Gareth on the day of the accident. He'd find out why his one friend had changed.

**

Cassie went through another training session with Lizzie, practicing how to defend herself against the grasping claws of an Outsider. Cassie thought she was getting better. At least, she felt the need to apologise for the accidental bruises that were beginning to form on Lizzie's arms from blows with the training sword. Lizzie dismissed the bruises casually.

"Thanks for helping me," said Cassie as she put away her training sword in the rack, ready to get cleaned up for dinner. They were still standing in the little training room, door shut so that no one would walk in on Cassie experimenting with new tactics.

"No problem. Us girls have got to stick together."

Cassie hesitated over her next question, uncertain of how best to phrase it.

"Is it difficult," she asked, "being a woman in the Defenders?"

"Yes," the answer came without hesitation. "Don't let anyone tell you differently. Oh, the HR people will talk about equal opportunities and most of them will even believe it, but the fact is that we're in a minority. Maybe ten percent of applicants are female and as long as we keep recruiting from police and military forces, we'll never have balance. You've got to be tough. You've got to force them to see you as an equal, not just as 'the girl'."

"Does it make that big a difference?"

"Absolutely. It probably didn't help me that I came here young. I signed up as a recruit on my sixteenth birthday. That was in the early days when the first invasion was only just beginning to slack off, so the process was quick. I got through the initial tests and was here on the base a few weeks after turning sixteen. I was a kid. I was a girl. And I'd never fought for my life before."

"That must have been terrifying."

"Yeah. It was. But I was surrounded by these tough, macho guys, all keen to prove how manly they were. If I showed how scared I was, even for a moment, I would have lost all chance of getting their respect."

"But surely they were scared too?"

Lizzie laughed, "God, yes! But you take a good look at them during training and ask yourself if they'd ever admit it."

"So that's how I've got to do it?" Cassie asked. "I've got to be as tough as they are?"

"No. You've got to be tougher. Being good enough isn't good enough. You've got to prove to them that you've got as much right to be here as they have. More. You've got to show that you're better than them." Lizzie tapped her collar, where a little symbol of a sword was stitched into the fabric in gold thread.

"What is that?" Cassie asked. "What does it mean?"

She'd spotted them before on some of the uniforms. Lizzie and Karl both had the sword. Jerry had a gun stitched into his collar. One of the others, a burly Russian whose name Cassie didn't know yet, had something that looked like an axe sewn into his.

"The Defenders have a competition," Lizzie explained, "every year. Just amongst ourselves and theoretically friendly. We compete against each other with the various practice weapons that we have at least two dark metal equivalents of. If you win the competition in any category, you get to wear the mark."

"But you and Karl both have the sword. You can't both have won?"

"Different years. I've won twice. He's won four times. Before that, it was Adrian Boron, but he stopped wearing the symbol the second year that he didn't even make it to the semi-finals. He said he didn't feel right wearing it anymore when he knew for a fact that he'd stopped being one of the best. He stopped competing after that."

Cassie could almost understand that. She thought of the gold medal, sitting with pride in a glass case specially made on her parents' mantelpiece. She'd walked away. She'd proved herself the best, won her medal and made her point to the world. Then she'd backed off. Oh, she could have gone back, run again in four years' time at the next Olympics and maybe added another medal to the first. But by then, someone younger would have come along. She couldn't imagine going through all that, after her great glory, and coming out with a silver or a bronze. Or worse, not getting a medal at all. Better to step aside gracefully than to wait to be cast aside by time.

She'd fought for her glory once before and won it. She'd do the same again. She was learning quickly, catching up with the others. Cassie eyed the stitched sword and had her new challenge set in her mind. She'd never backed down from a challenge before. She'd prove herself worthy as a Defender and earn the mark in the competition. Whatever it took.

"Come on," said Lizzie. "We'd better hurry up if we want time to clean up for dinner."

Cassie nodded. The pair headed back out into the base, these areas bustling with people thinking similar thoughts, heading for the shower room or lingering around the bedrooms, waiting for the food.

Cassie was still uneasy about the shower rooms. She was used to communal changing rooms. She'd been to enough gyms, sports centres and stadiums, that changing kit and showering in front of other women was perfectly normal to her. She just kept her eyes on her own stuff and trusted the others to do the same. A shower room full of guys though was different. Sure, she could stay inside the cubical as she changed, but it was slightly cramped and she inevitably got something damp getting dressed where she'd just showered. Besides, the guys didn't bother about that, wandering about calmly between showers and lockers.

So Cassie had taken to going to the deserted corridor. It was a bit out of the way, but she could walk past the empty bedrooms to a shower room all to herself. So she cleaned up in perfect privacy, wondering if she should have asked Lizzie about this as well.

A long shower and a change of clothes later, Cassie was heading into the dining room with everyone else. She joined Lizzie sitting with Enrico and Jerry near the middle of one of the long tables. Around them, the buzz of chatter filled the air. Enrico and Jerry were discussing something but, having walked in on the middle of it, Cassie wasn't sure what. Before she could figure it out, Karl came to join them, sitting beside Lizzie.

"Hey," Lizzie greeted. "Have you had a chance to look over those centre piece designs?"

"No wedding talk!" Jerry said, before Karl could utter a word. "I mean it. I don't want to hear a single word about the wedding."

He was pointing his fork across the table menacingly, first at Lizzie then at Karl. Lizzie held up her hands in a gesture of surrender.

"Fine. I won't talk about the wedding. But you guys both need to get measured up for suits."

"Suits?" Jerry sounded sceptical. "Why the hell did I agree to be an usher anyway?"

"If you figure it out, maybe you could help me figure out why the hell we thought it was a good idea to ask you."

Cassie concentrated on her food, feeling rather left out. She hadn't even had an invitation to the wedding. Not that that was surprising, since she barely knew Lizzie or Karl. It was just that she was starting to feel like Lizzie might be a friend when things like this reminded her that she didn't quite fit in yet. These guys had all been friends for ages. Cassie was still on the outside, not yet in Defender black, not yet one of the team.

She was grateful for the interruption when Gareth sat down across from her, taking the place beside Jerry. With no preamble or polite greetings, he addressed Jerry: "You need to apologise to Richard."

"What?"

"You were extremely rude earlier and you should apologise."

"For what? Saying what everyone was thinking? Richard was never going to be a Defender and it was ridiculous for him to be there. Frankly, I don't know why you let him stay as long as you did."

"Look, Jerry, whether he should be a Defender isn't the issue. The fact is, you were deliberately mean and you've hurt his feelings. You should apologise."

"He doesn't have feelings. He's practically a robot."

"Of course he has feelings. How would you like it if you were trying really hard at something and someone just shot you down?"

"I'm not going to apologise for saying what needed to be said."

"Fine then," said Gareth. Cassie could just hear him mutter, "Don't say that I didn't warn you."

Richard's Story

Richard always found it easier to talk to machines than people. Some of his earliest memories were playing with the old BBC computer his Dad had cast off. He'd learned about disks and programs and memories and hard drives before he'd even started school. They'd just made sense to him.

When school came and Richard got older, he found himself retreating more and more to the comforts of computers. He hated school. The other students called him a geek and the teachers didn't know what to do with him. He had no interest in history or modern languages or geography or English literature and so he didn't bother. On the other hand, the work set in maths and sciences seemed so ridiculously easy to Richard that he didn't bother there either. His parents knew him to be extremely intelligent and so couldn't understand the reports that seemed to imply the teachers thought he was incompetent or lazy.

Only with bribes of new computer components did his parents get him to turn up to his classes and hand in his homework. At last, as he began senior school, he started getting some good reports, though he still couldn't be bothered with languages or humanities. His parents were called into the school and, after a long discussion, it was decided that Richard should be put into maths and science classes with the A-level students. In computer science, he was allowed to ignore the assignments about making spreadsheets and just do whatever he felt like. That worked well enough for a couple of terms. But by then Richard had grasped the A-level syllabus. He couldn't keep doing the same course each year until he graduated. He got his A-level maths at the age of twelve, physics and chemistry at thirteen and then discussions restarted about what on Earth they were going to do with him.

Richard seemed oblivious to much of the debate. As long as he had his computers, he didn't care.

In the end, it was decided that he would share the majority of his classes with his year, dozing through the subjects that bored him. When the others did maths or the other subjects where Richard was miles ahead, he was allowed to sit in the library with his laptop and do whatever he felt like. He'd enjoyed the more challenging work of the A-Level courses but now he had to find his own challenges. Like breaking into the school's computer system to get a look at everyone's grades. When that proved to be too easy, he worked out several modifications that would improve their data security.

At the age of thirteen, Richard was fascinated by internet security and, more importantly, how to break it. Things started innocently enough. He tried to find ways to fool password checkers or even ways to bypass log-ins altogether and get to the data within. Generally, after spending hours or days working on breaking into something, he didn't actually care what it was he was reaching. Quite often he'd send an anonymous message to whomever's system he'd cracked explaining what he'd done and what they needed to do to fix it. Then he moved onto the next challenge.

His anonymous messages had given him something of a reputation online but no one could be sure whether the encrypted emails they received, apparently from their own accounts, were from the same person. He didn't really start attracting official attention until he figured out how to break into his internet banking site. The people working to identify him were, at first, unsure whether this was just another layer of clever deception. After all, why would a teenager hack into his own bank account just to check his balance when he obviously knew the password?

By that point, Richard was getting bored and complacent. A lethal combination.

He wanted something more challenging and this stuff hadn't felt dangerous in years. Unfortunately, an attempt to access the Prime Minister's account on the Downing Street computer network apparently counted as treason.

Richard never knew how the Defenders found out about him and what he was capable of. The first he knew about it was when he was pulled into a grey interview room and sat across a table from two men in the black uniform of the Defenders. One of the men stood in the corner, watching Richard with a stern expression that seemed somewhere between hate and contempt. At the time, Richard wouldn't have been surprised if he'd been informed that Karl Edinct was incapable of smiling. The other guy, with Italian colouring but a perfect English accent, sat at the table and slid a computer across the surface at Richard.

"In this folder, we have recordings of energy readings. Identify the pattern in these readings from the background interference and write an algorithm to identify similar but non-identical patterns in other samples. You have six hours."

That was all the help or instruction Richard was given. He looked at the samples. When he opened the files, they were displayed in a manner similar to audio files, but the program he was given allowed him to filter by various factors, overlay samples and do various automatic pattern recognition. It took him a few minutes to familiarise himself with the capabilities of the software and then he dove right into the problem. Across the table, the Italian guy had got out another laptop and begun working on something else, but Richard couldn't care less.

He'd finally been given a challenge. The looming deadline caused adrenaline to surge, giving him a sense of excitement he hadn't felt in an age. The problem itself was immensely complex. He could apply various filters and believe he'd found a pattern but trying the same techniques on other samples for corroboration would give garbage.

And he had to find a way to make this reusable!

His algorithm had to be generic, not tainted by the sample he'd been given. Richard used everything he knew about genetic algorithms and pattern recognition, writing a program that would apply filters to a subset of the samples to find similarities, then test those filters to the rest of the samples. The program was recursive and those filter groups that worked best would be combined to give new groups. He added random variance to the breeding of the filter groups and heuristic checks to determine the best results of each round. At last, he thought he had his answer.

Just to be sure, he ran the program on small random subsets of the sample group, delighted to get perfect results each time. He'd still want to check them against another sample set because there was a slim chance his algorithm was biased by this set, but he thought it was based on sound principles.

With almost twenty minutes to spare, he announced he was done.

"What?" asked the Italian guy. Richard recognised the expression on his face. It was the one his old teachers used to have when he announced he was done with his classwork an hour before everyone else.

The guy took the computer back, frowning at the screen. He stared at it for what seemed to be an age. Richard wasn't sure why it should take so long; he'd documented his code and the test cases that demonstrated the fit of the pattern identified.

"Well?" asked Edinct.

"Hmm," was all the response he got.

It was only later than Richard learned that the reason Enrico spent so long pouring over the algorithm was because his code was marginally more efficient than the program Enrico had spent a week working on. No one had expected him to solve the problem in six hours. They'd intended to test him to see if he was on the right lines.

The two men left the room. Weeks later, while doing some unofficial digging in the communications records of the Defenders, Richard found the recording of the call between Enrico and Master Amiron. Enrico had simply said, "We need him."

That excitement, even desperation, wasn't obvious in Edinct's expression when he returned to the room alone and took the seat across from Richard. Richard still didn't know what this was about or what pattern he'd be hunting for. He just knew he'd had to exercise his brain to its limits for the first time in so long and he loved that feeling.

"Work for us," Edinct said, "or spend the rest of your life in jail without access to a computer."

Richard would have said yes even without the threat. He wanted more challenges like that.

Somehow, the truth of what he faced wasn't nearly as exciting and interesting as he'd hope. At least at first. He was taken to the Defenders' base, shown a tiny room that was no better than the prison cell. He was given a stack of grey overalls that he was apparently to wear from now on. The grey t-shirt and shorts beneath, even the underwear, were all standard- issue. He was fitted with a tracker bracelet that would monitor his every movement. If he attempted to access a part of the base he wasn't meant to be in, or his movements seemed suspicious, or if he tried to leave, everything would be over.

A lot of the Defenders seemed to assume that the grey overalls meant Richard was their skivvy. Many of the other workers thought so as well. It took a couple of weeks for most of them to get it into their heads that Richard was there to do more than just scrub toilets and make sure the Defenders had clean clothes. That caused more than a little resentment, but Richard was used to feeling different and so he accepted it.

At first, Richard was put into a quiet workroom with an unnetworked laptop that had the day's assignments on. Before long though, Enrico started coming into the room, asking Richard's opinion, running ideas past him, offering ideas and support of his own. Richard was used to feeling contempt for everyone else and so he was surprised to find he respected, even liked Enrico. Stranger still, Richard found himself becoming friends with another worker. Intellectually, Gareth would never be even close to his level, but Richard found he could look past that.

After about a month, Enrico asked Master Amiron for permission to let Richard into the control room. The permission was granted. Richard was meant to be escorted but since Enrico and Master Amiron were the only people who fully understood what Richard was meant to be doing, he more or less had free reign whenever someone else was set to monitor him. That meant he could peek into files that were supposed to be off-limits. In them, he glimpsed technology way beyond anything he could currently comprehend.

Richard had challenges equal to his mind. He had people he could talk to about highly complex concepts without feeling he had to dumb everything down. He was making friends. Better than anything, there was a sense that there were things he had yet to learn, things people could teach him about the universe and he was in the perfect place to learn. An alien feeling was beginning to make itself known.

Richard was happy.

Seven

On the Edge of Knowledge

Richard had three projects to worry about at once. Four, technically, but he didn't count the location analysis because he'd decided working on that was pointless. The first project was easy. Messing with Jerry's security permissions had been a fun little logic problem but nothing that pushed his limits. The hardest part was making sure no evidence pointed to him. In the end, he'd managed to bypass Gareth's password and use the Defence Master's own credentials to play with the authentication system. Gareth would know exactly who to blame, but he wouldn't have a single shred of proof. In fact, if he tried to make anything formal, he'd be the one in the spotlight. It was a neat little solution.

Richard had designed the program in an evening and pushed it live the following day while the Defenders were at breakfast. He'd meant to give the code one last check, but Meg was in the room, trying to get Richard's input on something and generally being annoying. When she'd come over to see what he was doing that was more interesting, he pushed the code live and brought his next project on the screen, just in case she managed to figure out that he was playing with security protocols.

The second of his projects was the real challenge. No one could reverse the path of a portal. They had the ability to open portals to anywhere on earth in this reality. In theory, they could open portals to parallel worlds in the same way that the Outsiders came through to theirs. But the theory and the practice were two different things. They needed coordinates. They needed specific frequencies. He knew that Master Amiron had been able to open portals to other worlds; that was where he'd gone after all and where he'd come from. But Richard didn't have the data necessary to be confident of a destination and this was too dangerous to try if he wasn't confident. If something went wrong with opening a portal to another reality, it could do more than just kill someone. It could scatter their atoms across a billion universes, or trap them outside of reality, or strand them in a universe where the laws of physics were different. There were so many possibilities, each of which would make Gareth's accident look like a grazed knee.

That was the third of Richard's projects. That had challenges of its own. He didn't want Gareth to realise what he was working on. Unfortunately, Gareth had taken to coming to visit Richard in the computer lab. Maybe he was feeling guilty for betraying him over the issue of becoming a Defender.

It just complicated things for Richard. He had to make sure he was only working on uncovering the truth of Gareth's accident when he could be absolutely sure that Gareth wasn't going to walk in. That restricted him to mornings, since all the Defenders would be in training. Unfortunately, mornings were when the rest of Richard's team tended to be in the lab getting on with their official work. In the afternoons, people were all over the place, working with the Defenders on private issues or acting as an informal helpdesk to random people who were having email issues, sorting out the computers of dumb thugs who didn't know the different between an Ethernet switch and their bum.

A lot of what Richard needed to do involved pouring through the archive footage from the security system and the portal controls. He couldn't do that when Meg or the others might be looking over his shoulder. He definitely couldn't do that when Gareth might come barging in, attempting to be friendly. So that project was squeezed into little gaps between his work on portal reversal.

It was made harder by the fact that the explosion had been in the control room, frying several systems, taking out one of the security cameras entirely and damaging the other. Most of what he needed to know had either been destroyed or had never been recorded because of the blast. But he had found something interesting in the accounts of those who'd been in the control room that day. Jakob and Enrico had seen it happen, had seen Karl rush to Gareth's side and seen Karl declare Gareth dead. Both their accounts were identical on that point.

Karl's own report stated that he must have been mistaken because of panic. But there was still something in the wording, some little hint of doubt. Karl hadn't found a pulse.

The picture from the surviving security camera was lousy, half the image whited-out by damage. But it was enough to show Gareth lying there, burned and still, caught stepping out of the portal in the moment that the generator blew. His face was a mess of blood and burns.

So how come the medical reports showed no damage? Not so much as a bruise. Gareth had been hurt. If Karl could be believed, Gareth had been dead. Yet when the medical staff got him down to the infirmary, he'd been perfectly fine.

The impossibility of it worried away at Richard's mind while he got on with other things. It was always there. Whenever he had a quiet moment, whenever his mind went still, the problem returned to the surface, always without an answer. How could a man go from being dead to being in the picture of health within ten minutes?

He wanted to ask Enrico. After all, he'd been on duty in the control room when it had all happened. But how could he ask without raising suspicions?

He had to find some other way to start a conversation and then lead the topic round to Gareth. Richard grinned to himself. He had the perfect topic.

He headed down from the lab to the Defenders' living quarters as the Defenders were pouring out of the canteen after lunch. Richard lurked against the wall of the corridor, watching the faces of those who walked past. Most ignored him completely. In the worker grey, he became invisible. Or almost.

"What the hell are you doing here?" demanded Jerry. "Come to smirk about messing up my security pass?"

Richard gave a slow, knowing smile, and said sweetly, "I don't know what you're talking about."

Richard met Jerry's angry glare quietly, suppressing the urge to grin like a maniac. His calm demeanour just made things worse for Jerry, who closed the distance, looming in Richard's face.

"I could punch you in the face so hard you'll be seeing out your ass," Jerry growled.

It was considerably harder to remain calm with that furious glare inches in front of Richard's face. He knew Jerry could do it. Richard might have called Jerry a caveman, but cavemen knew how to hit people and, judging by the recent attempts at training, there wouldn't be a damn thing Richard could do about it. A faint smile touched the corners of Jerry's mouth and Richard knew that the trace of fear had been spotted.

"What's going on here?" Another voice cut across the angry showdown. Richard had never been so grateful to see Enrico in his life.

"We've got a worker hanging around where he shouldn't be," said Jerry.

"We've got Defenders threatening physical violence against innocent bystanders," said Richard.

Enrico sighed, "It's like dealing with toddlers. Jerry, just go... shoot something. Richard, what are you doing down here?"

"I'm working on a tricky problem and want to bounce some ideas off someone."

Jerry broke into a grin, "Is the great genius asking for help?"

"Of course not. It can just sometimes help my thought process to run through the problem verbally and the only person round here whose probability of comprehension is greater than zero happens to be Enrico. Unless you want to listen to me talk about measuring harmonic resonances of multi-dimensional constructs?"

Jerry stared at Richard for a moment before turning to Enrico, "Did he just call me thick?"

"He called everyone thick. It's what he does."

They left Jerry before he had an apoplectic fit. Up in the computer lab, Richard pulled up the work he'd done so far, using every screen available to display his data. He didn't waste time asking before disconnecting one screen from the laptop Meg was currently working on and carrying it round the table to where Enrico was waiting to be told about Richard's work.

"Hey!" Meg protested.

"I've told you, that project's pointless," Richard said.

"The people who give us our funding don't agree with you. If you can't be bothered, then I'm the one who'll have to present our findings to the Defence Review Committee next week."

"Those pencil-pushing morons wouldn't realise if you put your slides on the screen upside-down," Richard said. "It doesn't matter how much work you put into presenting it, they won't have a clue what you're taking about. Just tell them that any kind of accurate prediction method is impossible with the data we have available and that they should leave the decisions on research topics to people who have more brains than the inhabitants of the monkey cage at London Zoo."

"It's probably a good job you're presenting to the DRC, Meg," said Enrico.

"There are a few fundamental facts of life you've yet to grasp, Richard. One of them: don't insult the guys who write the cheques. Now, if you excuse me, I'm going to go work somewhere that I don't have to deal with raging sociopaths."

Meg unplugged her laptop from its various connections and stalked out of the room, computer under one arm.

"You could be a bit nicer to her," suggested Enrico.

"Why?"

Enrico gave him the exasperated look that Richard had long since given up trying to understand.

"Let's just see what you're trying to do," Enrico said.

Richard started with the basics, explaining about trying to calculate the factors needed to reverse a portal, allowing them to track an inbound portal and create one of their own to go in the opposite direction. Enrico nodded along with the look of one who actually understood and had grasped the significance. That made a pleasant change from all the people who would nod along because they didn't want to show their stupidity by speaking.

Enrico listened. When he spoke, it was to clarify minor points or to ask questions. Not stupid questions. Insightful ones. Mostly questions that Richard had already asked himself, but occasionally a question phrased in a new way or looking at the problem from a new angle would spark off an idea. Enrico was the perfect sounding board, letting Richard's thoughts bounce off him and come back tingling with new and bright ideas.

Half an hour after they'd started, Richard was picking up speed, talking rapidly, his mind fizzing with plans for measuring portals. Enrico had stopped talking and was frantically typing notes, scribbling diagrams on a tablet and just trying desperately to keep up with the flow of words.

Two hours after they'd started, they had a plan. It was a plan filled with typos and probably unintelligible to anyone but the two of them, but still it was a plan.

Richard had been so caught up in solving one problem that he'd almost forgotten that he'd had another purpose in bringing Enrico here. It was as they were discussing the practicalities of hooking into the control room's systems that it came back to him.

"We'll have to be careful," Richard said. "We don't want to cause another accident."

Enrico fumbled the pile of scribbled scraps he was tidying up. Richard pretended not to see.

"After all, we don't have Master Amiron around anymore if someone gets hurt like Gareth was."

"True," Enrico muttered, not looking in his direction.

"I never did get what happened to Gareth," Richard hoped he sounded casual. "I remember when it happened that people had said he'd died."

"Yeah, well, Karl made a mistake. He was scared and he felt in the wrong place for a pulse. Nothing mysterious about it."

Richard decided to throw subtlety out the window.

"Everyone says there's nothing mysterious about it. If there was nothing mysterious, they wouldn't need to keep saying it. What happened to Gareth?"

"I don't know."

"Was Gareth dead?"

"OK. Fine. Gareth was dead. Then Master Amiron was there and there was all this golden light. And then Gareth wasn't dead. I don't know what happened. No one does."

* * *

So much for urban centres being likely targets. The next portal opened in rural Finland. The nearest town was Levi, a place that could gather a handful of tourists for the tiny ski resort in winter or the midnight sun in summer. On a dismal, grey day in late autumn, the town was half deserted. The portal opened amid the trees and ponds, golden light bringing a bright pool of colour to the grey mist.

The only victim of the Outsider attack was an unfortunate reindeer that had happened to be nearby. The first response team dealt with the Outsiders and then returned home without so much as a scratch, squelching mud onto the base's floors.

Gareth sat in his office and signed off the reports as usual, frowning at his computer screen. Something about this portal bothered him. Usually, he fretted about the attacks where things went wrong. This time, everything had been ridiculously easy, yet still he fretted. Maybe it was just because it struck home how unpredictable it all was. Even when they thought they had the Outsiders figured out, something like this came up and threw all their theories out the window. Richard was right that they couldn't possibly predict where future attacks would come.

He hated always being reactive. They were called Defenders because that was all they could do. They waited for an attack and they defended against it. They couldn't strike back. They couldn't hurt the Outsiders the way the Defenders were hurt by them. They were stranded here while the Outsiders moved between worlds, killing wherever they wanted.

Master Amiron had travelled between parallel worlds, crossing the dimensions. It was how he'd come here, bringing the portal technology with him just when they needed it most. It was how he'd left, saying that there were other worlds he had to see, other things he had to do.

Always so mysterious.

If he'd known how to cross to other universes, why the hell hadn't he left them with instructions to do the same? If they could get to the Outsiders' home, maybe the Defenders could actually do something to stop the attacks once and for all.

Gareth knew Richard and Enrico were working on it. He hadn't a clue about the science behind it but he'd seen them talking excitedly about the possibilities. They were in the control room now, making changes to the machines that were used to scan for incoming portals. Enrico had tried to explain and Gareth had tried to understand. Then he'd just let them get on with it. Working out how to trace and reverse a portal was the most important thing that anyone on this base could be doing right now.

He just didn't know why.

Gareth could feel something urgent about it, something sitting right on the edge of awareness, trying to break through, but he couldn't focus on it. When he tried, he just got a jumble of memory fragments. There was a skyscraper in the wind, a bloody handprint on a white wall, a dark-haired woman, an echo of a song and the scent of jasmine. Nothing that he could piece into sense.

It was important.

Master Amiron had warned him about this, after the accident. He'd said that Gareth would know things without knowing why he knew them. The simplest thing to do was to just accept it and wait for time to fill in the gaps.

That was why Gareth had agreed to let Richard and Enrico tear half the control room apart in their quest for a reverse portal. That was why there was still half a tube of mirus in his locker in the shower room, even though he knew he ought to return it. That was why he'd changed his locker combination on a whim.

Something was lurking on the edge of Gareth's awareness, some future event that held importance he couldn't quite grasp. Master Amiron had told Gareth to trust his instincts on these matters and, no matter what, Gareth had always trusted Master Amiron. They all did.

Eight

Blood

Cassie had calculated days, counting backwards the passing time. She'd been on the Defender base a month. It felt like a lifetime. The routine of training was normal to her now. She was used to the random alarms that could stir them all, day or night, whenever a portal opened. It seemed that the person she'd been before was another person in another world. The base, despite being connected to the entire planet, felt cut off from it.

Yet she was starting to feel like she fitted. There was Lizzie, mentoring and coaching her. There was Jerry, a grin on his lips and a joke on his tongue, unless of course someone brought up the subject of Richard. Cassie still felt a little on the outside. Karl was still a distant, imposing figure who offered advice but only seemed to smile if Lizzie or Gareth was nearby. Gareth was just weird. He would say things that made no sense sometimes, but she found herself automatically believing them. It was only later, when he'd gone away, that she would think about it and try to figure out why. But she was settling in. She recognised most of the faces and could even remember several names now.

That morning, she got dressed and joined the others through the portal for the morning run. It was beginning to get chilly, a cold wind reminded her that autumn was fading to winter. There was no sign of Lizzie on the other side of the portal, but she found Jerry stretching in the clearing.

"Lizzie's on duty in the control room," Jerry said. "Enrico's there too. He's helping that maniac rig up some science experiment on the portal equipment."

"You think Lizzie's a maniac?"

"No, Richard. He's got some mad scheme about tracking portals that's apparently more important than fixing whatever he's done to mess up my security pass."

"Why do you two hate each other?"

"I hate him because he's an arrogant sod who thinks he's cleverer than everyone else in the universe put together. I was given the job of security escort for him when he first arrived and, frankly, I think I should have got a medal for not punching the guy."

So there was no mystery, no hidden story, it had just grown from the fact that Richard was irritating. As they set off for the run, the conversation ended. She was a little disappointed that there wasn't more to the conflict. Maybe some part of her had been hoping for soap opera drama among the Defenders.

There was still so much she was just figuring out about the members of the team. Friendships and allegiances, the official team structures and the unofficial rivalries. A whole complex world of emotion crammed into that base. OK, so the place was huge, but it was still a pressure cooker of rumours and personal relation problems. There were so many questions.

Cassie found herself jogging along behind Gareth as she so often did. He was at the heart of the questions. He was younger than most of the other Defenders. She would have guessed that he had only recently been recruited, but he fit with the others. He'd be the best man at Lizzie and Karl's wedding. People talked to him and about him with a slightly nervous air at times, as though even they weren't sure what to make of him. They listened to him when he spoke, automatically agreeing with his suggestions as though they were gospel and Cassie found herself agreeing too, without ever knowing why.

Her thoughts had drifted in these patterns for a while until she was almost oblivious to the woods passing by on either side, the damp earth beneath her trainers. She could see a fallen tree up ahead, recognising that she was close to the clearing now, nearing the half-way point of the run.

Then Gareth stumbled. For an instant, Cassie wondered if he'd tripped on something, but Gareth had come to a complete halt in the middle of the path. He clutched at his head and blindly stumbled towards the trees, using a sturdy trunk to hold himself upright. His face was pale and his whole body trembling slightly, the expression on his features one of shock and fear.

"Are you alright?" Cassie asked.

"We've got to get back."

The moment had passed and Gareth looked perfectly well again, but there was a determined look to his face. The fear hadn't vanished completely, just been hidden behind this mask. Gareth ran starting along their jogging route but not continuing through the clearing. He went to the wall of the lodge where the portal-generating devices were still stuck. They were deactivated of course, but Gareth pressed a series of buttons on one of them and the golden light of the portal burst force.

"What's going on?" Cassie asked.

"Come on!"

It didn't occur to her to question or disobey. Something in his tone compelled her to follow.

She had questions all lined up to ask Gareth but those questions evaporated when they emerged on the other side. They were replaced by a whole host of new ones, mainly about the blood. The normally gleaming white walls and the tiled floor were smeared with deep red. An obvious handprint was on the wall, just beside one of the portal controls. The whole place was lit by flashing warning lights and there, lying motionless in a pool of her own gore, was Lizzie.

"Oh God," murmured Gareth. Cassie was too concerned with fighting down the urge to vomit to be able to say anything. The smell of blood was overpowering. Cassie just stood there, frozen in place by the vision in front of her. Her mind couldn't summon a rational thought. There was just the sight of the blood and the memory of Lizzie smiling yesterday during training, perfectly alive and healthy. How could things fall apart so quickly?

Lizzie was lying face-down on the floor, arm outstretched towards the portal. She must have been reaching for the controls and collapsed. Her blond hair was matted with dark red, her uniform slashed along with the skin beneath. It seemed just about every part of her was scratched and cut. All around her was a puddle of crimson.

For a long moment, Cassie thought she was dead. The rising panic threatened to consume her entirely, but Gareth never lost control. He crouched beside Lizzie, checking for a pulse, then he turned to Cassie, urgent but not frantic.

"In the shower room, in my locker, there's a tube of paste. Mirus. Bring it to me right now. And anything we can use for bandages. Locker 127. The combination's all zeroes."

Cassie ran, repeating the locker number in her head over and over. She found it quickly enough and there was the tube, sitting on a pile of crumpled shirts as though waiting for her. She grabbed it and then pulled an armful of towels from a shelf. She was back with Gareth in moments.

Gareth opened up the tube and a delicious scent managed to almost drown out the smell of blood. Gareth started with the gash on Lizzie's head that was the cause of the mess in her hair. He rubbed the green stuff over the cut and then began moving down the rest of her body, touching the gunk against any place that was still bleeding.

The towels weren't much use as bandages. They were too big and Cassie stood no chance of tearing them with her bare hands. Still, Gareth shoved them against the deeper cuts, holding them in place as well as he was able. The lack of bandages enabled Cassie to see the effect of the green paste. There was still a mess of dried and drying blood all over her but the cuts that had been anointed were stopping bleeding. They even looked like they were healing.

"What is that stuff?" Cassie asked, looking at the tube which had been squeezed of every last drop.

"Mirus. A miracle in a tube," Gareth said. "Master Amiron gave us the formula. Come on. She'll be OK for now and we need to find the others."

"But whoever did this might still be around."

There was a pause. Gareth shut his eyes. His head tilted slightly as though listening. But there was no sound but their own breathing.

"No. It's gone now."

"How the hell could you know that?"

"I just know."

Again came that tone that broached no argument. Cassie found herself automatically accepting the statement. Gareth hurried down the corridor and Cassie almost ran to keep up. There was a door at the end, locked and sealed, but Gareth entered a code, pressed his thumb to the panel and waved his security pass at the reader. The door slid open. The corridor on the other side was lit by the glaring red warning lights, but at least there was no sign of anything else red.

Gareth headed straight for a lift, again using the security panel beside it without hesitation. This time, the doors remained firmly shut. A tiny screen above the keypad flashed up the message: Lockdown.

Gareth muttered something under his breath that was probably a swear word.

"We've got to take the stairs," he said. "Someone's initiated full lockdown and the lifts won't work."

Cassie followed again, her brain racing to try and make sense of this, the questions his certainty had dismissed were creeping back. Gareth had known. There in the woods, he'd reacted somehow.

Gareth took them through a door by the lifts into a stairwell and he headed up the stairs at a pace close to a run. Cassie followed. The pace inevitably slowed but Gareth never paused the ascent. Cassie lost track of the number of floors they'd passed. The base had never felt as large as it did now, passing door after door as they headed right for the top of the building.

There was another corridor and another door. Cassie felt that there should be a better word for it than that, something to sum up the weight of it. It was metal and looked so solid that it would take an army to break through. The keypad to the side had a scanner for the whole palm as well as a strange round scanner which Gareth looked into after entering a ridiculously long code. A retinal scanner then.

Cassie wondered what they'd do if this door locked them out but the scanner beeped and a little light turned green. The door opened surprisingly easily to Gareth's push and once more Cassie was overwhelmed by the smell of blood.

The room was undoubtedly some kind of control room. At least it had been. There were computers and consoles and strange devices running down either side of the rectangular room. On the wall opposite the door was a ring of portal generators; the circle they formed was twice the size of a man. This place had probably been amazing once.

Now the computers were toppled, chairs upended, monitors were dark and machines silent. A huge glass screen that had once hung in clear view was now a mass of glittering shards on the floor in the middle of the room. Pieces of equipment were scattered on the ground, trampled and smashed. And over everything were splatters of blood. There were sticky puddles on the floor, smears up the once-white walls, drops on just about everywhere else. Judging by the mess of crimson under the broken screen, Cassie guessed the reason for the broken glass was that someone had been thrown through it.

But, despite the blood that was everywhere, there was no sign of the person it had come from.

The room was deserted.

Cassie looked around, barely able to breathe from the fear. What could cause this? What could take down trained Defenders and leave such chaos? And what the hell did she think she was doing trying to investigate? She wasn't ready for this!

A faint noise caused her heart to leap in her chest.

The sound had come from behind a door Cassie had failed to notice earlier. It was small and white, almost the same shade as the wall. A table had fallen or been shoved against it. Cassie spotted a fallen rack of swords, seizing one for the comfort of a weapon in her hand, while Gareth hauled the table aside. When he opened the door, someone came out, flailing ungainly, striking whatever was in front of him.

"Richard! Richard, it's me!"

It had been Richard trapped in what was obviously a supply cupboard. He didn't look too badly hurt. One shirt sleeve was torn to shreds and the skin beneath it marred with crimson lines, but otherwise he looked uninjured. Certainly, the blood all over the room couldn't possibly have come from him. Richard stared around now, looking as pale and scared as Cassie felt.

"Oh God," he breathed. "Enrico?"

"He's not here," Gareth said.

"That thing must have got him. He shoved me in the cupboard. The last thing I saw was that thing cutting Enrico's back as he saved me. I could hear him screaming but I couldn't get out. I tried. I really did. Oh God, I think it killed Lizzie. Oh God, Gary, I'm sorry. I did try."

Richard was still talking, rambling and muttering in clear terror. Cassie couldn't follow. She couldn't understand what thing he was talking about. She didn't understand any of this. All she knew was that she shouldn't be here. She'd thought she'd wanted adventure but she hadn't been prepared for what it was really like to be a Defender.

"What happened here?" Gareth asked Richard. "What attacked you?"

"It was black, humanish-shaped. But it had claws like razors. Lizzie and Enrico tried to fight it, but the weapons did nothing. It slashed Lizzie to pieces and threw her through the portal. Enrico kept trying with the dark metal dagger but he couldn't even scratch the thing. If the Outsiders have found a way to block dark metal, we're done for."

"No need for doom saying. We'll figure this out. One hand doesn't make the game, as Master Amiron would say."

"But it's taken Enrico. It's probably killed him or eaten him or something."

Gareth closed his eyes. Again, there was that strange expression on his face, as though listening to the silence.

"No," he said quietly. "Enrico's still alive. But we've got work to do, Richard. I need you to get the main system online and then pull out whatever you and Enrico have managed to get on reversing portals. We'll need to go after him."

"But we're not ready. We've only just implemented the scanner. We haven't had a chance to test it out to see if the results we get are valid. And what happens if I make a mistake? If we open a portal to the wrong place, it will clear the cached coordinates from the generator and we could lose any chance of finding Enrico."

"So don't make a mistake. You wanted to be part of this team, Richard. That doesn't just mean joining in when things are going well. You know more about these systems than anyone else and this was your pet project. So do what you're best at and find your teammate."

Richard swallowed visibly, but he righted a chair and sat down in front of one of the computers:

"Yes, sir."

* * *

How had he not remembered this? Gareth tried to push that thought aside so he could worry about it later but it was rather a big thought to avoid. He remembered his future yet this whole thing had been missing. He hadn't even noticed that there was a gap. Not until the portal opened and it was like a fog had been lifted.

He didn't usually waste his time wishing, not anymore, but right now he was wishing that Master Amiron was here to take charge. At the very least, he wished Master Amiron had explained a way to make his messed up memories make sense so he could remember if he was going to find a way out of this. Why couldn't Master Amiron have explained how to deal with these gaps? What use was remembering the future if he forgot that his friends were about to be ripped to shreds? And the future was no clearer now. Everything was a fog of half-remembered fragments, moments that wouldn't coalesce into certainty. It felt like he'd forgotten something important, something lurking just out of reach but he couldn't quite grasp it. Gareth knew, deep in the back of his mind, that they were standing on the verge of something monumental. He just didn't know how it would end, whether it would be the greatest thing since Master Amiron had handed over the first dark metal sword, or the bloody end of the Defenders.

He knew though, with absolute certainty, that this was more than just another Outsider attack. He'd known it the minute he'd sensed the first portal opening. He hadn't felt a portal like that since they'd lost Master Amiron.

There was so much that needed doing and Gareth was fighting to prioritise the tasks. First off, he needed to get the communications system up and running again so he could contact the others and let them know what was going on. They would have been alerted to the lockdown that Enrico must have initiated. Fortunately, the system appeared undamaged. It had come disconnected but once plugged in, it started to boot up as usual. While he waited for the machine, Gareth thought of the other things that needed doing.

They had to do a sweep of the base to be sure that he was right in his initial thought that the attacker was gone since apparently he couldn't trust his memories right now. They had to go over the security footage to get a clue about whoever or whatever had done this. They needed to account for all the workers, let them know what was happening and make sure none of them were hurt or missing. They needed to get Lizzie to the infirmary. She might be stabilised and the mirus would help but she'd almost certainly need a blood transfusion. Karl should probably take her; he'd be no use to anyone until she woke up. Gareth could at least be sure she would pull through; he had a very vivid memory of her yelling at him for there being a stripper at Karl's stag party. Master Amiron had told him that his memories of the future were certain to happen and Gareth's own experiments with influencing causality had backed that up.

The minute the communications server came online, Boron's signal came in.

"Status report!" he snapped, almost before Gareth could put on the headset to answer the call.

"We've had an incursion," Gareth stated. "Unknown hostile. Lizzie is injured but stable. Richard has minor injuries, nothing dangerous. Enrico is missing, known to be injured but we don't know how badly. We have considerable damage to the control room. Enrico initiated lockdown. We should leave it active until we've done a full sweep of the base and checked for further hostiles or weaponry."

"Outsiders?" Boron asked.

"No. Richard says that dark metal was ineffective. Plus, the portal was different."

"Richard thought it was different or you did?"

"I did."

"OK."

Those two syllables filled Gareth with a sense of relief that surprised him. Boron trusted him. This was the biggest emergency since the accident that had screwed up Gareth's brain and led to Master Amiron leaving them, yet Boron accepted Gareth's judgement without question. That was the first moment when Gareth thought he might actually manage to get them through this in one piece.

Gareth took a deep breath, then spoke calmly, quickly and with as much authority as he could summon:

"First order of business, assign someone to watch over the recruits. Cassie's here with me but keep the others out of the base until things are sorted. Karl and one other should take Lizzie to the infirmary; she's in the corridor off the main living quarters, by the portal. Everyone else, full sweep of the base. Once you've got them organised, you're going to be needed in the control room."

"Yes, sir."

Nine

The Creature

Cassie was more than a little unsure what she was doing in the control room. Everyone else seemed to have some purpose or task. Richard was working at something complicated-looking on one of the computers. Cassie wasn't about to interrupt him in the middle of important work just to ask what all the squiggly lines and numbers meant.

Gareth, to Cassie's astonishment, was giving orders. Even more astonishingly, people were listening. Boron, second-in-command only to the Defence Master, was listening to what Gareth said and translating it into deployments of the Defenders. He was stood in the control room, dealing with the issues of which team member should go to exactly which part of the base, gathering their data and following progress on the reactivated security monitors. Yes, Boron was giving the detailed commands, but it was Gareth who had told him that the team should sweep the base looking for any sign the intruder had left anything.

Meanwhile, two other Defenders who had come to the control room with Boron were following Gareth's instructions about resurrecting the computers and machines that had been disrupted by the fight. When things seemed to be broken, they were sent out in search of new cables, spare fuses, even a projector that could display on the wall whatever used to be on the now-shattered screen in the middle of the room. Cassie tried to help them out with the tidy up but she didn't know what anything was or where it was meant to go. She hated the sense of helplessness and wanted to do something, anything to help. All she could do was try to clear away the mess, sweeping up shards of glass into a pile with her foot, moving broken furniture and equipment away from the repairs. When that was done, she stood to one side and let them all get on with things. The Defenders didn't argue or question. They seemed to accept that Gareth had a right to tell them what to do. They even called him sir.

She could see why. His whole demeanour projected a calm authority. When he spoke, she listened. He had a quiet confidence in his voice, even when the whole world was falling to pieces. Where he pointed, they followed, as if it was the most natural thing in the world. Cassie found herself listening to him, taking in that composed tone and borrowing some of his calm. When he said that things would be alright, she believed him instantly, right down to her core.

A crazy notion came into Cassie's head as she watched from the edge of the room. She tried to dismiss the thought as insane. After all, the Defence Master had been a grown man during the first invasion. He'd supplied weapons and training, formed this team out of nothing and fought off the wave of Outsiders that had threatened to destroy the world. Gareth couldn't be more than a couple of years older than Cassie was. But Cassie remembered the rumours that the Defence Master had come from some other place, some other dimension. Many people said that he wasn't human.

Cassie looked again at Gareth. Could he be some alien who didn't age at the same rate as human beings?

She almost laughed. No. Gareth was just a guy like anyone else. There'd be some other explanation for this that she was currently too confused to see; she'd ask for it when there weren't lives at stake.

"I've got the security footage, sir," one Defender said.

Boron nodded, "Hook into the projector. We should all see this."

The man did just that and soon an image of the control room was displayed on the wall, Richard and Enrico calmly working at different consoles, Lizzie sat across the room, bent over a console of her own. The room looked so completely different that it was hard to believe it had become the mess that surrounded them now. The people on the screen were cheerfully conducting their business, oblivious to what was to come.

The circle of devices on the wall lit up. Lizzie and Enrico got to their feet, clearly puzzled. Enrico turned to say something to Richard, but the projector didn't have sound so they could only guess now what it was. Probably a question, wondering if Richard was the reason for the portal opening. Richard shook his head as he answered. No one looked worried. Cassie had an irrational urge to yell at the screen, to warn them to get out of there.

Then the thing came through the portal.

It was black, gleaming like polished jet. Every limb, every piece of torso seemed solid, like some sort of exoskeleton. It was humanoid, probably no taller than Cassie was. It moved with slow, cautious steps, looking around with a face as dark as the rest of it, except for two gleaming red eyes. There was no sign of white or pupil, just the malevolent glare of crimson as deep as the blood that was about to be shed. Those eyes fixed on Lizzie.

She took a sword from a stand against the wall, not looking scared yet. Enrico said something, his expression still calm, even as he reached into a drawer and pulled out a glistening black dagger.

The creature raised its limbs and bared vicious claws.

Enrico said something again and Richard stumbled backwards, eager to get out of the way. Enrico and Lizzie raised their weapons, Enrico addressing the creature again. There was no change in its face to register understanding. Its mouth was just a black line beneath the eyes, offering a glimpse of fangs.

The creature leapt. It placed a hand on the console between it and Lizzie to vault over. She swung her sword but the blow glanced off its side. Lizzie's surprise was visible on her face, then the look of pain as the thing raked its claws down her torso letting loose a fountain of crimson. Then Enrico was there behind it, slashing with his dagger with as little effect as the sword. The creature was between the two Defenders, moving in a blur of bloody claws.

Lizzie was still trying to attack, despite the blood pouring out of her. She got in, stabbing again with the sword. The creature took hold of Lizzie's arm, claws digging into the flesh, and it moved in a fluid motion that sent Lizzie tripping forwards past it, stumbling through the still-open portal.

Then there were just the three of them on the screen and the creature's focus snapped to Enrico.

Enrico tried again with the dagger and again. He discarded it after the third useless attempt and concentrated on trying to avoid those deadly talons.

The creature seemed almost oblivious to Richard. Despite his failures in training, Richard wasn't about to let his friend get shredded.

Richard lifted the only weapon he could find, the chair he'd been sitting on, and he swung it as a club.

He caught the creature with the full force of his weight behind it. The creature stumbled. In that moment, Richard dealt an appallingly ineffective roundhouse that barely came above the thing's knee. The chair might have done something, but the kick did little more than irritate it. It spun round, those eyes glaring now at Richard. A claw struck out and Richard barely managed to get his arm up in front of his face. Deep lines were gouged into his flesh.

Enrico hit the creature again, yelling something to Richard. But Richard seemed frozen, pale as a ghost in front of this nightmarish creature. So Enrico took charge. He dodged past the creature, grabbed Richard by the shoulder and shoved him backwards into the supply cupboard. It took moments but that was all the creature needed. It came at Enrico again, claws cutting down his back. His face was away from the camera so they couldn't see his expression, but they saw him grab hold of the doorframe for support, clearly in agony.

Still, he turned and fought. Shutting the door between himself and Richard.

With careful blocks, he made it to one of the consoles with barely more than grazes. He slammed his hand against a huge button. He turned back to the creature, saying something. There may have been a trace of satisfaction on his face along with the pain. Was that the button that activated lockdown and alerted the other Defenders?

The monster didn't seem to care. It was interested only in Enrico. The two fought across the room. There was nothing showy in their moves, none of the choreography Cassie was used to seeing when she watched old martial arts movies. There was just speed and skill and, increasingly, a trace of desperation in Enrico's moves. The creature could hurt him, had hurt him, but it didn't seem to feel anything much.

Its expression remained stony, its mouth locked in that grimace of fangs, but there was a moment when it seemed to feel pain. Enrico managed to get a leg hooked around the creatures as he dealt a series of punches. The thing stumbled over his foot and fell. Enrico helped it to the floor with a kick to the chest. The creature slammed into the corner of a table hard enough that the table slid across the floor, ending up in front of the door to the cupboard where Richard was now trapped.

That was the one victory Enrico managed in the whole fight. With every moment that passed, he was struggling more. He was losing blood rapidly from cuts all over his body. His arms were cut to shreds as he tried to block. His torso was weeping crimson. Enrico was using his legs more, using the distance they offered to keep the thing at bay. But then it got its claws into Enrico's calf and he was barely able to stand on his right leg after that.

The creature was still attacking viciously. The room was becoming more and more like it had been when Cassie and Gareth had found it. Enrico's blood was just about everywhere. Equipment was being upset. At one point, Enrico went flying through the glass screen. He landed on his back among the shards. They didn't need sound on the projector for the watchers to recognise the scream that tore out of his mouth.

The creature was over him. It raised its right arm. It would take a moment to deliver the killing blow. A slash across Enrico's exposed throat and it would all be over.

But the claws were tucked away. The hand that came down struck Enrico on the forehead, slamming his head back against the hard floor. Enrico slumped, unconscious.

The creature looked around the room. Its gaze lingered a moment on the cupboard but it turned aside. When it spotted the discarded dagger, it crossed the room and picked the weapon up. It was strange that a monster bestowed with a deadly weapon on each digit would be interested in a dagger, but apparently it was, staring with strange curiosity for some seconds. It grasped the hilt as it returned to Enrico. With obvious effort, the creature heaved the unconscious man up over its shoulder.

Then the monster walked calmly through the portal, Defender over one shoulder, dagger in the opposite hand. On the projected image, the portal winked out.

There was silence in the control room for several long moments as the Defenders took in what they'd just witnessed. A monster with skin impenetrable even to a dark metal blade. A Defender, injured and helpless in the clutches of the enemy.

"I'm sorry," Richard broke the silence at last. "I was useless."

"You tried," Boron said. "For that at least, you are a Defender."

"At least we know that thing wanted him alive," one of the others said. "That means there's a chance."

"I know he's alive," Gareth stated.

"It threw Lizzie through the portal," Cassie muttered. She hadn't meant to speak aloud but now she found herself with everyone looking at her and she felt she had to continue, "How did Lizzie end up in the corridor? Why didn't she end up wherever it was that creature came from?"

Richard answered, "It created a portal to the corridor in the living quarters where our security is not so tight, then it managed to use our internal portal system to create a link between the corridor and here. We're not just dealing with a random attack. Even I'd take days to figure how to do what it just did if I didn't have the passcodes. It would probably take me a few hours even with the passcodes."

"Bring up the security footage from the corridor just to be sure," Boron told one of the Defenders, then he turned back to Richard. "Can you track the portal? Can you take us after it?"

"It won't be easy. The cache was cleared by you guys coming in, half of the equipment is damaged and our program for analysing and reversing portals is still unfinished."

"I didn't ask if it would be easy. I asked if you could do it."

Richard swallowed. Cassie was so glad right then that she wasn't the person on whom everyone was relying. Finding an injured teammate was down to Richard and Richard alone doing something immensely complicated with a computer system that wasn't finished.

"Yes," Richard said at last.

"Then get on with it. The rest of us will be in the conference room. See if Karl can be dragged away from Lizzie's bedside; we want every senior Defender to be part of the conversation. And where the hell's Gareth?"

It was only then that Cassie realised that Gareth was no longer in the room.

* * *

Gareth needed a moment of peace to gather his thoughts together. He'd recognised the creature. He'd known it the instant he'd seen it step through the portal in the security footage; he just didn't know where he knew it from. He remembered what Master Amiron had told him, when Gareth was piecing his mind back together after the accident. He'd said that he'd experience hunches and insights based on future memories. He'd do things knowing they were the right thing to do, but even he wouldn't be sure why that was the case. He'd done just that with the mirus, leaving the tube right where he could get at it when Lizzie's life was in danger. Now Gareth knew that this creature was somehow linked to the future of the Defenders. He just didn't know how. He needed to. Guesses and intuition weren't enough.

He didn't go far. He just headed to the stairwell. The lifts would be working now that the lockdown was lifted so it was unlikely he'd be disturbed.

He shut his eyes and, despite the frantic racing of his mind, he reached for that quiet state where everything slipped into place. He let his breathing slow, he let his senses reach out. He sank into another state of being. This was what Master Amiron had called looking deeper, seeing beyond the surface of things until the flow of dimensions became clear.

There were more dimensions than the standard four everyone dealt with. Infinitely more. In some of those dimensions, their universe twisted around on itself like a screwed up piece of paper. The portal technology could use those dimensions to turn a distance of a thousand miles into mere millimetres, allowing the Defenders to move around the world in moments. But there were other dimensions. To step in those directions would be to step into another universe, lying parallel to the one they knew. Some of those universes would be so similar to their own that a man might live a lifetime there and never know things were changed. But some universes were vastly different.

Most people would never see more than the three spatial dimensions they knew, experience the fourth as the uniform passing of time. But some, a lucky few, those who'd stepped outside their normal bounds with the aid of the portals, could be made aware of the others, of the ripples in the world they lived in.

Master Amiron had worked to teach all the Defenders. Some had grasped the concept better than others. Gareth had been hopeless up until the moment of the accident. Now he didn't even have to work at it.

He opened his eyes to the light of the universe. Golden energy floated around him, but Gareth was looking for something in particular. He hunted for the thread of the recent portals, for the echo of what had come through them. Hands moving in gentle patterns, he stirred through the touching dimensions, reaching for the sense of that creature, following it through the flow of time.

He reached out a hand, moving slowly through this shining vision and saw the effect he was having. He moved again, everything careful and cautious, pulling on tendrils of that energy, catching glimpses of the wonders of the multiverse.

He found a memory like a glimmering point in the distance, it was a moment in time so monumental in significance that it pierced through the fog of vague confusion. He stepped gently, moving towards it with care not to cause ripples and lose sight of his target. All around it was a dark uncertainty, a shadow in his thoughts, but that instant mattered enough to glint like a beacon. He guided the soft movements of the dimensions with infinite care until he was able to sweep his arms round and draw the memory into himself.

It was as vivid as if he were living the moment, fuelled with emotion powerful enough to reach his waiting mind, through the fog and confusion and all that lay between. A moment that defined destinies, echoing back through time. He felt the strong arm around his torso and the five points of death against his throat as razor-sharp claws held him millimetres from death. Five more were at his side at the end of the arm that held him motionless. If he tried to escape or fight, the monster that held him could kill him in under a second.

Standing in front of him was the creature that had been in the control room. Claws tucked away now, it held a blanket-wrapped bundle gently in the crook of an arm. Those red eyes were staring directly into Gareth's.

"Give me the Abomination," snarled a voice close to Gareth's ear, "and I'll let this one live."

The creature before him, not an it, but a she, held closer the child in her arms, a baby not entirely human. She gave Gareth a last, lingering look, before lowering her gaze. The arms that were such lethal weapons now held her child tenderly. She wouldn't sacrifice that infant for anything or anyone. Gareth heard the faint sound of a sob.

"I forgive you," he said.

"Gareth?" The voice snapped him out of the memory and back into the present. Disorientated for a moment, Gareth reached up and touched his throat where he knew claws would rest. It was a memory of his future, already fading into the fog of uncertainty, out of place and devoid of context like much of what came to him. Yet he knew that creature was not just a monster to be destroyed.

"Gary, are you feeling alright?"

Gareth was called once more to the present and he saw Karl standing in the stairway a few steps down from him. He must have decided to walk up from the infirmary, which was only a couple of floors below this. He was staring with concern now.

"Yeah, I'm fine," Gareth said. "Are you? How's Lizzie?"

"They say Lizzie will be fine. She may not even have scars thanks to your quick work with the mirus. She woke up a couple of minutes ago and yelled at me for fussing over her instead of getting on with fighting the thing that did this."

Despite the light tone, Gareth knew how worried Karl had been. He might act cold a lot of the time, but Lizzie meant so much to him. It would kill him if anything happened to her. He must have been so scared.

"We should re-join the others," Gareth said, "to discuss tactics."

"Just so long as you give me my turn. I want to rip the heart out of the thing that did this to Lizzie."

Gareth knew that wasn't going to happen, but how the hell was he meant to convince the others that this creature wasn't the enemy they all thought she was?

Ten

The Council of War

The conference room had a large circular table in the centre of it. Cassie's first thought was that it seemed a faintly Arthurian concept, even if the clean white décor was far from Camelot. As the Defenders sat down, Cassie realised that they each had a specific place. She wondered if there was some sort of hierarchy despite the round layout of the seating. Boron and Gareth took the seats furthest from the door, the others positioning themselves from there. Karl Edinct, the youngest in the room aside from Cassie and Gareth, was sat a few places around from the two in charge.

There was one seat left. Presumably it was meant to be Enrico's. Cassie didn't feel she had a right to take it. She stood awkwardly against the wall near the door. One Defender, a man whose name Cassie had yet to learn, looked at her and asked what she was doing there.

Cassie shrugged, "I've got nowhere else to go."

"Cassie can stay," Boron said. "You handled yourself well when Lizzie needed help. Consider yourself a provisional Defender."

Cassie supposed that this was a step up from recruit but she didn't even finish saying thanks when Gareth called the meeting to order.

They started talking and Cassie found it hard to follow all the trails of conversation. Occasionally, a couple of people would break off from the main discussion to quietly talk with neighbours, before rejoining the talk that flowed across the table. They'd all seen the footage from the security camera. They'd seen the dark metal weapons have no effect on the creature. The greatest weapon they had against the Outsiders and it was useless against this new beast.

Someone suggested authorising the guns. Cassie knew how serious a step that was. Dark metal was a precious resource. From what Lizzie had told her, they had no way in this universe to create more of it. So every bullet was an irreplaceable treasure.

"If a dark metal blade does nothing, what makes you think the bullets will work?"

"That thing can be hurt. Even if the bullets don't penetrate its hide, they'll pack a punch. If you shoot a guy in a bulletproof vest, you can still break a few ribs."

"But the amount of bullets we'd need would eat into our supply way too much."

"So we use ordinary ones."

The discussion crossed the table, with Boron and Gareth listening to it all. Cassie stood out of the way at the back, feeling incapable of offering any useful insight. She wondered if she'd be better off with the other Defenders, or even the recruits who must surely be feeling as lost as she was. She didn't belong at a council of war.

As the discussion raged, without much fruitfulness, Boron raised a hand and the room fell silent.

"Your thoughts, Gareth?"

"It's more important to work out what this creature wants and why she attacked us."

"Who cares why?" someone asked. "It's taken one of us. We've got to stop this thing and get Enrico back."

"It could have killed Lizzie!" Karl said, his first contribution to the discussion.

"Could have but didn't," Gareth said. "She had opportunity to kill three people and chose not to. Lizzie will be fine, Enrico is still alive and she ignored Richard as soon as he was out the way. She took one of us hostage; that implies purpose. If we can figure out the reason, we might be able to get Enrico back without bloodshed."

No one spoke at first. Eventually, despite still feeling completely out of place, Cassie asked the question that was no doubt lingering in several minds.

"Why do you keep calling the creature 'she'?"

"Because she is."

Which really wasn't much of an answer.

Karl asked, "How certain are you that it... she hasn't killed Enrico?"

"Certain."

"Good enough for me."

"That brings us to the next problem," Boron said. "How do we figure out what she wants?"

That question was answered by the door opening and Richard walking in. He clutched something dark in his hands.

"That was quick," Gareth commented.

"The good news is: I think I may have enough information to reverse the portal. The bad news is: we're screwed. Another portal opened long enough for this to come through."

Richard laid his burden on the table. It was a blood-stained shirt, part of Enrico's uniform. Richard took his time spreading it out and the reason became obvious. Someone had cut crude letters into the cloth, spelling out an ominous message:

AMIRON COME.

* * *

Gareth stared at the shirt. The message was so clear and yet so beyond their abilities. It had been months since they'd lost Master Amiron, away through a portal to some other world. The last time Gareth had seen him, Amiron had embraced him exactly the way his dad never had. Amiron had smiled and said, with such a tone of certainty that Gareth could have perfect faith in it, that this would not be farewell forever.

That wasn't much use now.

"Can you contact Master Amiron?" Boron asked him.

The hopeful looks of those round the table were almost more than Gareth could bear. He shook his head.

"No."

"I can't believe this," that came from Nigel Corron, a Defender who'd objected to Gareth's initial training almost as much as Karl had. When Master Amiron had announced he was leaving, Nigel had argued more than most about the appointment of Gareth as successor. Nigel had been a Defender since the beginning. He'd signed up when the entire team, including Amiron and Boron, could be counted using the fingers on one hand. He resented Gareth for having come from nowhere as a worker and been placed in authority; he'd been eyeing up

Boron's spot as second-in-command. That resentment was obvious in his tone now.

"I can't believe that we're stuck with you. You're just a kid and you expect us to follow you. We've already lost a Defender because of your supposed leadership. We nearly lost two!"

"Enough!" snapped Boron. "If you trusted Master Amiron, you should trust his judgement in choosing Gareth."

"Gary," Karl said, "what were you doing in the stairwell before we came in here?"

Gareth was slightly puzzled by the question and not entirely certain the best way to answer it. He couldn't explain the change that had taken place inside him on the day of the accident. He couldn't describe what he was now able to do. In the end, Gareth decided to take an approach that was close to honesty.

"I was looking through the dimensions," he said, "searching for the creature."

"And did you find it?"

"I just saw a glimpse."

"Even so, you go into some sort of trance and you can see things that are happening in other dimensions." Karl turned to Nigel, "If that doesn't make his opinion worth listening to, I don't know what would."

"All that makes him is a freak."

"Then so was Master Amiron! They are the same."

There was a short silence. Gareth stared at the bloody shirt, Karl's words echoing around his thoughts. Gareth and Amiron were the same. Amiron had passed the leadership of the team over to Gareth because of the changes in his brain after the accident, because the two of them had the same abilities, the same curse.

"Maybe that's the answer," he said. "This creature wants the Defence Master. So let's give him to her."

"You can't be serious," said Karl.

A couple of the others were frowning, but realisation slowly dawned across their faces. Gareth was suggesting he face the creature.

"We can all go," Boron said. "If Richard's right, we have the coordinates now. We can create a portal and all of us go together."

"What if this thing kills Enrico?" Richard asked.

Gareth gave him a brief nod, "Richard's right. We can't take that risk."

"What if this thing kills you?" Karl asked. "You can't just walk in there alone."

Gareth knew that the creature wouldn't kill him but he couldn't tell the others that because he couldn't predict the events that would lead up to that future memory. Perhaps the only reason he'd live to experience that moment would be because he'd let the others talk him into going through with the rest of the team. He couldn't second-guess fate. Master Amiron had said that it was sometimes harder glimpsing the future than going in blind because it was so easy to fixate on that point that he could miss everything else.

"We need a better plan than you just going in," Boron agreed. "This is obviously a trap."

"The armoury," said Jakob, a French guy who'd been one of the earliest recruits after the first invasion started. "We still have the assault gear. If a group of us put on the gear, including the helmets, it will be difficult for the creature to distinguish us. It won't know if Master Amiron is there or not."

Gareth nodded. The assault gear was probably a good idea anyway. There were some stab vests stored away in there that would be a great help against the creature's claws. The helmets were bulky uncomfortable things that no one generally bothered with against Outsiders because the benefits were minimal. Right now though, they could be immensely useful. They were a bit like standard army helmets, round and thick enough to shield the skull against damage, but the ones in the armoury also had a visor that covered the face. The visor served partly instead of sunglasses in bright lights, partly to shield the eyes from dirt or shrapnel, but they were dark enough that they could be pretty effective as a mask. If Gareth went through the portal wearing one of them, maybe he could fool the creature long enough for him to get close to Enrico and get him out.

"The helmets are a good plan," Gareth said. "But we've got to be careful that this isn't a trick to lure us out. Whatever you may say about my safety, we have to leave this base defended. We have to leave some of the team here prepared for another attack. We don't know how many of these creatures there are."

No one could argue with that logic. The debate raged a little longer but they were all painfully aware that Enrico might not have much time. Gareth had already made up his mind that he was going to go and offer himself in exchange. The others could argue in circles but he wouldn't shake from that belief. He wouldn't let one of his team suffer and Master Amiron wasn't here. Gareth was the only logical choice.

Eventually, it was agreed that the majority of the team should remain behind. Gareth would go through the portal with only two others. They would report back on their situation through the open portal and have a scheduled check-in. Boron would remain behind. He would defend the base in case of further attack and he would be the one to decide the appropriate course of action should Gareth's group fail to make the check-in.

Gareth could tell that Boron was still unhappy with the situation and he didn't feel much more confident, though he made sure his doubts didn't show. Only Karl was even close to satisfied because he'd argued his way into being one of those who would accompany Gareth through the portal. Gareth had tried to convince him that his place was with Lizzie. Karl's response had been that Lizzie would never forgive him if he let Gareth go alone and something happened to him. Gareth had to smile at that. Lizzie could be as fierce as anything when she had to be and she was as protective of Gareth as anyone else on the base. That was exactly what she would say.

So now it was decided. They still had preparations to make and Gareth wanted to leave as soon as possible. Every minute they hesitated left Enrico in enormous danger.

* * *

Richard had work to do. He'd told the senior Defenders that he could reverse the portal and take them through after the thing that had taken Enrico. He wished he was slightly more certain though. They'd not had a chance to test their theories, even within this world, to be sure that they could accurately reverse a portal. Fortunately, Richard had the information on the portal the creature had used to leave by. The cache had been wiped by first Gareth then the other Defenders coming back to the base, but there was still enough information in the system about the outgoing portal.

When the portal had opened again for the shirt, Richard had fed the information through the program he'd been working on with Enrico. The answers that emerged matched what remained of the information that had been recorded on the portal the creature had left by. That implied that their theory worked. That implied that Richard could open a portal which would follow the creature.

But he kept thinking of Enrico, one of the few kind voices in this place, one of the few people he could interact with intellectually. Richard didn't want to lose Enrico. He knew it was a possibility. He knew that a single miscalculation here could cost them their only shot at getting him back.

But there was something else bothering him.

How had the creature got onto their base in first place? Their security should have prevented it. Any incoming portal within half a mile would automatically be drawn to their portal generators, like lightning to a rod. Their security systems should detect the incoming signals that their own technology created. Without the code of a known Defender, it should signal an automatic security alert and send an electrical charge across the portal's surface to incapacitate whoever came through.

There had been no code transmitted when this creature's portal opened but no alert had sounded.

There was a hole somewhere in their security systems and Richard didn't like holes.

While he waited for Gareth and the others to prepare for the rescue mission, Richard pulled up the code for the security protocols.

Eleven

Through the Portal

The preparations were simple enough. Gareth had given instructions to Boron to take care of the defence of the base and went instead to the armoury. Karl was already there, fastening a vest over his uniform shirt. Jerry, by virtue of being the best shot in the team, had drawn the duty of being the other to go through the portal with Gareth and he too was getting his equipment from the cupboards.

The armoury was an impressive word for quite a small room. They had training weapons by the hundred but the dark metal stocks were limited. Most of the team's weapons were elsewhere in the base in places protected by security codes but easily accessible in times of need. This room just stored the bits and pieces that weren't used regularly, like the guns and the armour.

"These things need sleeves," said Jerry as he fastened on his stab vest.

"They'd hamper your movement," Karl pointed out.

"Yeah, but did you see the state of Richard's arm?"

"No one is forcing you to come!" Karl snapped with uncharacteristic force. This whole business with Lizzie must have seriously messed him up, no matter how he might try to hide it.

Gareth busied himself with his own gear. He strapped on the stab vest, attached a groin guard inside his trousers and tried a few helmets until he found one his size. Then he placed a hand on the lock to the gun case, his palm print giving him access to the neat row of guns and the boxes of bullets beneath. Gareth lifted one of the boxes, hesitated, then carefully counted out the bullets.

"One clip each," he said, "and I hope to come back with any many as we take."

He handed the box to Karl, who counted out his own bullets before easing them into the clip of the gun. Gareth remembered the rush the first time he'd fired a gun in the practice range, the thrill of adrenaline and the way his heart had jumped in shock at the sound of the shot. Now he was just terrified. The lives of his friends, maybe even his entire world, could rest in a little bullet and the choice he would make of whether or not to fire.

"I'm going to stop by and check on Lizzie before we go," Karl said.

"I should do the same," Gareth said. "You go ahead. I'll join you in a minute. We'll meet in the control room in twenty minutes."

So, once Gareth had finished his preparations, he went to the little hospital wing, where Lizzie lay in a white bed, Karl sitting at her side. Karl's hand gently clasped Lizzie's and a look of gentle affection rested between them. The doctors waited nearby, crisp white uniforms marking them apart from the Defenders and the workers. They nodded to Gareth and left him to have a moment alone with Lizzie. Karl too looked up. Without a word, he leant over to kiss Lizzie's forehead, then he strode from the room.

"You're insane," she said.

"Probably," Gareth answered. "But I will be back."

"Always over-confident."

"No, just certain of some things."

Gareth saw her there, surrounded by white. White hospital gown on, white sheets covering her, blond hair fanning out across the white pillow. So different from the usual black uniform, it reminded him of another time he would see her all in white. He could bring that image to the front of his mind and see it with perfect clarity.

"What things?"

"I will be at your wedding," Gareth said.

Lizzie gave a small laugh, the sound followed immediately by a sob. Her emotions cracked through the shell she had built, her fear tempered by her faith in Gareth's words.

"You'll keep him safe?" she asked. "You'll make sure he comes back to me."

"I promise."

She smiled again, taking her faith from Gareth's. Gareth returned it, then he walked slowly from the room. It was time.

Gareth and the others were geared up and as ready as they were going to be. The little group assembled in the control room. There were others there, those officially on duty and some that just didn't want to miss the possibility of major action. Richard was at one of the computers, working at something as usual. Gareth recognised the targeting program for the portal system.

"I've set the co-ordinates," Richard said. "The portal should open within a couple of hundred metres of the one that they used to send back Enrico's shirt. Hopefully you won't walk into an ambush."

"Couldn't you get the portal to open a little further away than that?" Karl asked.

"Possibly. But I could also get the portal to open in entirely the wrong universe or in the void between worlds. You want to risk that?"

There was no need for an answer. If Richard thought it was too dangerous to risk moving the target site, then it would be. Richard pressed a couple more buttons on his computer and checked the status read-outs. He nodded to Gareth that he was ready.

"Is Rover prepped?" Gareth asked. One of the other Defenders got out the little machine and positioned it before the space on the wall where the portal would open.

Rover had been around since before Gareth had been sent to work for the Defenders. It had started off as a camera duct taped to a remote control car but over various iterations it had been augmented with more equipment. It was no longer held together with tape, but there was still something chaotic about it. Bits and pieces had been jammed in wherever there was space, its equipment forced in wherever possible following no grand plan. Gareth wasn't sure quite how or when Rover had acquired its name but he suspected Jerry had something to do with it.

Gareth nodded to Richard and he fired up the system. Golden light erupted from the portal generators on the wall, the streams of energy colliding in the centre and flowing outwards. It took moments for the gleaming circle to form. It was a sight that still inspired awe in Gareth no matter how many times he saw it. The others got blasé about it after a while but Gareth could almost feel the power of the universes gathering in that window between worlds.

Rover trundled slowly towards the portal, guided by a Defender's hand on the remote controls that had never changed from its earliest incarnation. The little machine reached the edge of the circle of light and was swallowed inside, moving forwards into what had been a solid wall less than a minute earlier.

Gareth gathered round the screens that were displaying the read-out. Rover's camera was picking up a long, empty room. The miniature radar corroborated this with no evidence of movement in the vicinity. Pressure was normal and the atmosphere apparently contained enough oxygen. They hadn't come up with a particularly effective way of detecting poisons or toxins but what they did have suggested that Rover's location was similar to home in its air composition. The Geiger counter showed the radiation levels to be well into the safe zone. Best of all, there was absolutely no indication of people or that creature.

"OK," Gareth said. "Let's go."

"Are you sure you don't want a bigger team?" Boron asked.

"I'm sure. Keep an eye on everything until I get back."

Now that he was so close to the events, the memories were bubbling close to the surface. Gareth could almost glimpse fragmented images from his own thoughts, as close as the other side of a portal, but they were too jumbled to be certain of anything. He clung to a few certainties that he could glean from the mess. He would be there for Karl and Lizzie's wedding, as would Enrico. He would see Master Amiron again. That creature would one day care enough about him that he would be effective as a hostage against her.

He held tight to those thoughts, those fragments of memory, and wished once again that his ability to recall future events came with some guidance.

Gareth went to the portal, the other two immediately behind him. He heard multiple voices wishing them luck and then he stepped into the golden light. For a fraction of a second, Gareth felt as though he saw all possible universes spread out in front of him. He drank in the sight, like a man surveying the scenery from the top of a tall mountain. In that instant in the void, everything made sense, the twisting lines of dimensions formed clear patterns that connected past to future.

Then he emerged. He felt the loss as a physical pang. He could glimpse some of that beautiful clarity when he got his mind-set right but nothing to equal the perfect vision when he was inside the void. He sometimes wondered what it would be like to stay there forever.

He mentally shook himself. He was in a strange world in a potentially dangerous situation. Now was not the time for such things. Karl and Jerry had emerged from the portal behind him so Gareth focused his attention on the here and now, looking about at the place they found themselves in. They stood in a long room, something between a gallery and a corridor. It looked like it could belong in the country houses Gareth had been towed around on school trips, albeit somewhat decrepit now. One wall was lined with tall windows, the glass broken in places to let in a chill wind. The other wall was hung with paintings, massive portraits that stared down out of their frames.

As Karl found Rover and carried it back to the portal to be steered home, Gareth looked up at the paintings. Most were of serious-looking men in formal dress. There were a couple of ladies or family pictures up there. One massive painting held life-size images of a group of people. A beautiful young woman sat in a plush armchair, smiling as she cradled a young baby. In front of the chair was a small girl; the painter had captured the look of mischievous intelligence in her dark eyes. Behind the chair stood two men. At least, they had stood. The painted image of one looked out as serenely as ever, but the second man's face had been brutally vandalised. Someone or something had torn at the face, cutting not just the painting but scarring the wall behind. Now tattered scraps of canvas hung from around the jagged hole.

She'd wanted to remove him from the painting because she couldn't remove him from her family's history.

The thought had finished before Gareth caught himself and noticed the pronoun he'd used. Some part of his mind was ahead of his conscious thought. Somewhere inside his confusion of past and future recollections, he knew who had sabotaged this painting. He also had a suspicion whose face had been erased.

"This place is a dump," Jerry said. He was looking out one of the windows. Gareth went to join him and looked out.

The building they were in was either very tall or had been built on a cliff. The window afforded a vista of a city spread beneath them. Although perhaps city was too kind a description. The place had a feel of a shanty town. There were old buildings, some mostly standing, some just fragments of wall. Over time, people had built new constructions that borrowed shelter from what remained. A mishmash of materials had been piled up to form crude shelters nestling in the rubble.

It wasn't all chaotic. There were some buildings that were newer and stood intact, but they were ugly, rectangular blocks, built with no thought of aesthetic. They'd been constructed hurriedly and cheaply, intent only on function. As Gareth's eyes wandered over this wreck of a city, he realised he could identify those newer buildings as easily as he could name London's landmarks. That was the hospital. Those were the housing projects. That one, with the two great chimneys, was the power station. That low building was the school. Government projects to restore some semblance of civilisation to a world that had crumbled.

"We should be looking for Enrico," Karl said, recalling them to the present danger. "Which way, do you think?"

Gareth closed his eyes for a moment, trusting the instincts that told him this place was as familiar as the Defenders' base.

"This way."

"You're sure?"

"Mostly."

Gareth led the way through a door at one end of the long gallery. The gloomy drawing room beyond was as familiar as the view outside the windows. They walked a trail in the dust as they moved through the disused spaces in a once-great house. Much of the furniture was missing; that which remained was more decorative than functional. Anything useful had been taken to where it would be of more use.

They reached a passageway that didn't seem as deserted. The floor wasn't so dusty and there were fewer cobwebs. Gareth knew they were getting close to the parts of the palace that were still in common use. A young man stepped from a doorway and stared at the three armoured Defenders. The man was skinny, dressed in a badly-fitting uniform that had been inexpertly repaired in places. He stood in frozen fear for a moment, then held out his arms in a gesture that was unmistakably a surrender.

"One of our comrades is a prisoner here," Gareth said. "Take us to him."

The young man nodded once, slowly. He turned, every movement slow and careful as if to ensure no possibility of misinterpretation. The three Defenders followed. Each had a hand on their weapons, though Gareth couldn't conceive being scared of this frightened and half-starved figure.

"This could be a trap," Karl muttered.

"You two keep behind me," Gareth said. "I'll go into the room and you stay behind. That way you can get me out if things go badly."

"Are you sure you know what you're doing?" Jerry asked.

"Yes."

"OK then."

This whole exchange passed in whispers so that their frightened hostage didn't hear. He was leading them through the building, glancing over his shoulder nervously on a frequent basis, as though he expected a bullet between his shoulder blades at any moment. The man's uniform was of dark blue material that had faded to grey in places. A symbol was sewn into the front above the heart. The white thread had dirtied while the cloth had faded so the symbol wasn't as clear as it would once have been, but Gareth recognised it. The same sign was etched into the once-glorious decorations of this building. It was the same crest that was set in the hilt of the dagger the creature had taken, as well as several of the other dark metal weapons Master Amiron had brought with him when he first came to Earth.

The conclusion had settled in Gareth's mind without him even having to consider the subject: this place was Master Amiron's home. That thought carried with it traces of emotions, of anger and pain. The memory was built on a foundation of feelings that Gareth hadn't experienced yet.

Their destination was obvious as they rounded the final corner. Two guards stood outside a striking pair of doors. The ornately-carved, dark wood loomed oppressively over the hallway, impressing approachers with the importance of the room within. The doors were, in fact, rather more intimidating than the guards, whose uniforms were scruffy. Like the group's unwilling guide, the guards looked like they could have done with a few more good meals. They were armed though and they raised their guns towards Gareth's little team.

Gareth wondered what getting shot would feel like through the armour. He wasn't in a hurry to try it out; dying once was enough for one lifetime. He stopped a little way from the door, hearing the other two stop just behind him. He looked through the helmet's visor at the guards, trying to portray an aura of confidence with his stance.

"I believe we're expected," he said.

They looked at each other then, without either lowering their weapons, one touched a panel on the wall. The doors swung majestically open. At least, that was probably the intention. The effect was spoiled by one door sticking slightly near the end before jerking into its open position. Still, it had probably been very impressive once.

No doubt visitors would have been awed by the grace of the opening as well as by the majesty of the building.

Gareth walked forwards. The servant, or whoever it was they had followed, stood to one side. He obviously wanted to see what happened next but he was keen to stay out of the way of any weapons. Gareth knew one of the guns was still trained on him but there were three of them and only two weapons that he'd seen so far. Besides, it wasn't the guns he was worried about.

He walked through the doors and into a hall that still clung to a little ancient majesty, now shrouded in decay. Tall pillars rose to an arched ceiling, decorated with figures in tarnished metal. Windows, high in the wall, let through shafts of light that lit the dust in the air. The fact that many of the windows were broken and boarded and those that survived were dirty, meant that the light seemed more to highlight the gloom. The once-great hall was filled with shadows. Shadows that moved and shifted with hidden enemies.

In the middle of the room was Enrico. Heavy chains were manacled to his limbs and his bare torso showed wounds that were still bleeding in places. He tried to sit up when he saw Gareth, but it was obvious the man had very little strength left to him.

"Do not move," a voice came from the darkness at the other end of the long room. "If you value this man's life, you will not take another step."

Gareth stopped. He knew the voice, as well as he knew Karl's or Lizzie's. Yet he knew that this was the first time he'd heard it. She spoke in a tone that was firm and commanding, used to control but also feeling the need to remind everyone with each word that she did have that control. That voice seemed harsh now, challenging and laced with hate. It hurt that she could hate him like that. Gareth remembered what it had been like when things had happened in the proper order. It was so much simpler when he'd lived in the same straight line as everyone else.

"You're not Amiron?" she said, her tone not quite certain.

Gareth tried to make her out, but that end of the room was shrouded in gloom and so she was just a black shape in the shadows. The chandelier that had once bathed the throne in golden light hadn't worked in years. She preferred the darkness in many respects.

"No. I am Gareth, Defence Master for the world you attacked. That man's life is my responsibility."

"That man's life will be ended unless Amiron surrenders himself to me."

"Enrico is not your enemy. I think if you wanted him dead, he would be so already. You spared him, just as you spared Lizzie and Richard. You can't afford to start a war."

"I don't want a war. I want justice!" He could see her moving slightly in the shadows, a black figure with the stalking stance of a predator.

"You want vengeance. You won't get that by killing Enrico. Let him return home so that his injuries can be tended to. If you want a hostage, you can have me."

Gareth was immensely grateful that Karl and Jerry had enough control not to speak in surprise at that statement. Their helmets would hide any shock that they might be feeling right now. He could picture the look that must be on Karl's face. Enrico reacted, starting to protest. Gareth ignored him and continued to stare at the dark shape.

"If Amiron wouldn't come for him, why should I believe he'd come for you?"

"Amiron left our world. He doesn't know that Enrico is here but if he learns that I am in danger, he will come for me."

There was a sound that might have been an amused chuckle or a derisive laugh, "You have such faith in him."

"Because he has faith in me. I don't believe this because he entrusted his team and his technology to me. I believe this because I know his secrets. I know who you are, Mira daughter of Janon. I know why you want to kill him."

Gareth's voice stayed perfectly calm through this little speech. He couldn't afford to let on the faint bluff in what he was saying. Yes, he did know some of Master Amiron's secrets but only because he was now remembering things he would learn here and discussions that would come later because of what he would know. Cause and effect were circular. He knew what he knew because he remembered knowing it later. The fact remained though, that he knew the truth of what had happened here. Some of it anyway. A lot was still hidden in the fog of distant thought, memories too painful for his mind to fix on clearly.

Mira stalked out of the shadows towards him, her stride firm. Her entire form gleamed darkly. Gareth forced himself to stand still as she reached out, claws extending on her fingers. She stood before him and reached one deadly tip to touch the weak point at his neck, below his helmet but above the armoured torso.

"I could slit your throat right now for being his ally," she said.

Now that she was out of the shadows, it was easy to spot the fakeness. Her mouth moved when she spoke, but not correctly. It opened and shut but it didn't shape the words. The eyes that had shone redly in the security footage were orbs of coloured glass that let her see but concealed the real eyes beneath. The overall effect was like a monster in a low-budget horror movie. Richard and Lizzie hadn't spotted it because they'd been too busy fighting for their lives. It hadn't been obvious on camera because she'd been moving quickly and not in particularly good resolution. But Gareth could see it now. He could see the way the joints of her armour didn't move as smoothly as if this really was the skin of a menacing creature.

"You won't kill me," Gareth said, having to be careful he didn't slit his own throat with his words. "I will stay as your hostage until either Master Amiron comes or you choose to release me."

"Or I kill you," she said. "You will have one month. If Amiron hasn't come for you in twenty-eight days, you die."

She withdrew the claw. Gareth turned to Karl and Jerry.

"Help Enrico," he said. "Get him home. Tell Boron not to mount a rescue or try anything stupid. I will stay here for twenty-eight days or until you manage to contact Master Amiron."

The two men entered the room and crossed to the prone Defender. As they passed Gareth, Karl quietly muttered the question, "Are you sure?"

"Take care of him," Gareth said. "Wait for Master Amiron."

They helped Enrico to his feet and he stood with one arm draped over each of their shoulders. Gareth reached for his belt and took the sword and gun. He heard, almost felt, the movement as Mira's guards reacted, but he handed his weapons over to Karl, who took both with his free hand. Gareth knew the pleading look that must be behind that helmet, begging Gareth not to do anything too stupid.

"I will see you again soon," Gareth said. "I'll be at the wedding."

There was a moment of hesitation that seemed to last minutes, then Karl started moving and the three Defenders left the room, heading back towards their portal and home.

"Are you brave or stupid?" Mira asked.

"Neither," Gareth answered. "I'm trusting."

"Take off your helmet. Let me look at my prize."

Gareth did so, actually glad to be rid of the uncomfortable thing.

"Will you let me see you?" he asked.

To her credit, she barely hesitated. She reached up to her neck, triggering some hidden switch, and the monstrous face cracked, a slit appearing along the side of her head. The creature's head, part mask, part helmet, came easily into two pieces that she lifted clear. She shook out a long train of black hair that floated down her back in dishevelled waves. Dark, intelligent eyes gleamed out of a face that could have been sculpted in porcelain. There was a sadness that didn't belong in a face so young and Gareth wished he could wipe that pain away. He wanted to bend those soft lips into a smile and make it stay there forever. He wanted to close the short distance between them and kiss her.

"What are you smiling at?" she asked.

"You. You're beautiful."

She punched him.

Karl's Story

Karl had been studying martial arts for as long as he could remember. His mum had worked at the local sports centre. In the evenings, after playgroup or kindergarten, she put Karl in with various classes to keep him occupied. Karl took aerobics almost as soon as he could walk and played badminton with a racquet nearly as tall as he was, but it was karate he loved.

He trained and took classes and practiced. He went into tournaments and competitions. By the time he was ten, his sensei put him in with the adult classes. One wall of his bedroom was lined with trophies and ribbons. His parents called him their little champion.

Karl didn't really care about being a professional athlete. Sure, he liked winning and, as careers went, it would beat being an accountant or shop assistant. What he really wanted was to save people. His room was full of comic books, with heroes fighting monsters and villains, defending the innocent from all dangers. Karl never admitted this out loud but what he wanted more than anything else was to be one of them.

He didn't honestly believe he'd get his chance. Not until the first invasion began. There had been a few isolated incidents, dismissed as ordinary murders or grisly pranks gone wrong. Karl was there the day that the world learned the truth and the war really began.

He was sixteen, walking home from another competition with a tall trophy under one arm and his uniform slung over his shoulder in a kit bag. He was passing Saturday shoppers on a drizzly grey afternoon. Everything seemed perfectly normal and Karl had nothing more pressing on his mind than an English essay he'd been putting off that was due on Monday.

The portal formed in the middle of the pedestrianized zone. Bright light sparked from empty air, glittering out to form a perfect circle of golden radiance.

Karl just stared at this unbelievable sight. Around him, shoppers were staring too, some dropping their purchases as they were overwhelmed by the beauty of this gleaming vision.

How quickly awe turned to terror.

The Outsiders poured from the circle of light. Hairless beasts of vaguely human shape, twisted and warped into something hideous. These foul mutations swarmed through the portal and looked with desire at the world they saw. Some people screamed and ran, others stood frozen in shock. Karl stared at the beasts, seeing the misshapen growths on their skin and their emaciated bodies. Bones showed beneath pale skin and they had the distorted bulge of a stomach that was reminiscent of charity ads. The monsters were starving and now they salivated at the feast around them.

Long seconds seemed to linger on forever in frozen surprise. Then the tableau was broken by gore. An unfortunate woman had been standing too close. The creatures leapt. She screamed as they tore into her flesh, already devouring her.

More people fled but Karl ran in the opposite direction. He threw his kit bag at one creature, using his karate trophy as a club against another. He struck the beast hard enough that the gold-plated fighter fell off the top of the trophy but the thing, despite its appearance of frailty, seemed barely hurt.

Then the Outsiders were on him like a hoard of zombies in a horror movie.

Karl fought with all the skill he could muster but the Outsiders were all around him. His training hadn't included how to handle a crowd of monsters trying to eat him.

Afterwards, Karl could barely remember the first part of the fight. Adrenaline and terror drove him, instinct alone helping him keep the monsters at bay.

Inevitably, the Outsiders overwhelmed him. Teeth tore into his left arm and the weight of their bodies drove him down. Karl would always remember, far too vividly, the sight of one of the beasts, eyes frantic with hunger, mouth dripping in anticipation, leaning over to tear out Karl's throat.

The bang was thunderous. Karl found himself staring at the new spot between the creature's eyes. The hole oozed black gore, a drip of viscous blood. The other creatures started tearing it apart almost before its body fell.

Karl was so terrified his brain seemed to have stopped working. It took him several seconds to realise that the thing had been shot. By then, a young man in dark uniform was at his side, hacking through the Outsiders with a sword as black as the blood he was spilling. Fortunately, the creatures seemed immensely stupid. They were more interested in eating those that died than they were about stopping the people killing them.

In those early days, Master Amiron's team consisted of only four people. All four were there now, armed with guns and swords, slaughtering the Outsiders that swarmed out of the portal. Karl stood beside them. His left arm was dripping blood but otherwise he was unhurt and he wasn't about to run.

"Here, kid," his saviour, who he would later come to know as Adrian Boron, gave him a short knife.

Karl wasn't used to fighting with knives but he used what he did know and sliced into the creatures as they came at him. The fight was a blur that seemed to last forever, with Karl hitting and slicing and desperately struggling not to get eaten.

He didn't notice when the portal vanished. He only realised when he looked around and saw the mass of motionless corpses. The four armed men moved through the piles, looking for Outsiders that weren't quite dead or any humans that could still be saved. Boron came over to Karl, who was clutching the knife so hard his fingers seemed to be welded to the hilt.

"You did well, kid," Boron said.

"Is it over?"

"Yeah. It's over."

That seemed to be the cue for the knot of tension in Karl's stomach to release. He bent over and threw up on his trainers. Boron chuckled and patted Karl on the shoulder.

"Happens to the best of us, kid."

Twelve

Earthside

When Karl and Jerry had returned home, nearly carrying Enrico through, Richard had watched with relief he hadn't known he could feel. Then the portal had closed and Karl explained what had happened. Gareth had given himself in exchange. All the tension came back and Richard's guts tied themselves in worried knots with unfamiliar concern. What if Gareth didn't come back?

His arm throbbed with dull pain in time to the beat of his heart, a constant reminder of what that thing was capable of. It had taken down Enrico and Lizzie like they were kids playing at soldiers. What chance did Gareth have in its own territory? Richard thought of those glaring red eyes and his imagination furnished him with visions of the creature ripping Gareth to shreds just for the fun of it.

He left the control room, sick with apprehension. He didn't want to be around people, all asking questions no one could answer, all exuding the same fear. So Richard retreated to the computer lab and pulled up the security files, thinking to lose himself in solving a problem. He would figure out why the security protocols hadn't activated. He'd get to the bottom of that to distract himself from this strange sensation of anxiety. So he pushed aside the worries about what that creature might be doing to Gareth and he buried himself in code.

What he found just made the sick sensation in his stomach worse.

The answer was easily uncovered, staring out at him from the screen, black text on a white background. A few simple functions in a computer program.

"Are you OK?"

Richard looked up from the screen. Meg was sitting across the room. He hadn't noticed her come in. She was looking at him now, her voice soft and slow, as though speaking to a hurt child.

"You haven't called anyone an idiot for a few hours," Meg went on. "Are you alright?"

Richard didn't know how to answer that. Enrico, one of very few people round here that seemed to respect him, was badly hurt, Gareth, his only friend, was trapped in another universe with a monster and now Richard knew exactly who was to blame. He felt physically ill.

Richard closed the file before she could see it, before she could work out the hideous truth. The authorisation procedure, making a call to check someone's ID against their security permissions. The flaw was so obvious even a bog standard programmer could spot it within two minutes of looking at the code. The amended security file would treat a call with no associated user ID as though it was being authenticated by the Defence Master. The implication was horrifying. The creature, or whoever had sent it, had created a portal that had locked onto their systems. This little function, hidden in the main security protocols file, had allowed it to bypass all of the precautions they had against unauthorised actions.

Richard swallowed against the sickness he felt, disgusted at such blinding stupidity.

He'd put it there.

He'd put it there while playing his childish prank on Jerry. He'd thought it funny to make it seem that the authorisation was coming from Gareth's own account. But in doing so, he'd left a hole in their security, a gaping chasm that the creature had simply walked through.

He'd been so convinced of his own cleverness he hadn't even bothered to check the code properly. He could see the fault now so clearly that it might have been lit up with neon lights, but he'd been so sure of himself he hadn't even looked for problems. If he'd bothered to spend five minutes checking this over, Gareth would be safe now.

If Gareth died, it would be Richard's fault.

He could see Meg still watching him, looking at him with concern in her eyes. She stayed with him no matter how often they'd argued. She wouldn't stay with him if she knew this. She'd hate him.

Everyone would hate him.

* * *

Karl had been furious with Gareth more times than he could count. At first he'd hated the boy, believing him to have some ulterior motive for asking to be trained. Later, when he'd come to care about him, Karl had been angry every time he'd run rashly into danger. The day of the accident, when Karl had thought they'd lost Gareth forever, the anger and pain had filled him up to the point where he thought he might burst from the grief.

But he'd never been more furious than he was now.

Gareth had gone through that portal knowing more than he'd let on. He'd known who the creature was, known her name even. He'd spoken of secrets, of the reasons why that beast wanted Master Amiron to die. Yet he'd never breathed a word of it. He'd not even hinted to the Defenders at the council of war that he might know what this was all about.

It wasn't fear for his friend that fuelled this fury, though that was a part of it. Karl fumed because it felt as though Gareth had betrayed him. He should have said something. He should have spoken before they went through the portal. He definitely should have warned them that his plan involved trading himself for Enrico. Karl just didn't know what was going on inside Gareth's head anymore. He couldn't even guess the reasons why he'd acted as he had. Did he have some plan? Was he acting based on some greater knowledge? Or was he just rushing in recklessly as usual?

Gareth wasn't the same kid that had been dumped on Karl for training by Master Amiron. He wasn't a kid at all now. Karl wasn't even sure he was the same person. Since the accident, his whole demeanour had changed. Sometimes he looked at Karl but seemed to look straight through him. Or he'd say something that could only be a guess but he'd state it as fact. When he'd speak with his Master tone, it could have been Master Amiron talking and it was easy to believe. When he did that, he was invariably right.

Karl just had to hope that Gareth was right about this choice too.

Karl was in one of the training rooms, this one filled with pads and equipment. He stood at a punch bag, pounding his rage into the leather. He needed to vent. Pummelling the bag was only marginally satisfying though. He almost wished for an alarm so he could fight something real. He wanted to smash something just to see it break. He kept on punching despite the soreness in his hands, a slight graze where

134

he'd caught a bare knuckle on the seam in the leather, the racing of his heart and the fact that his breath was now coming in gasps.

Damn it, Gary! Why the hell couldn't he have explained his plan to anyone?

It was just like him!

Except it wasn't, Karl realised. At least, it hadn't been. But it was exactly like Master Amiron. The first Defence Master had never felt the need to explain himself. He expected the team to trust him absolutely and do whatever was asked without hesitation. They would have done it too. Every word Master Amiron spoke seemed to carry the weight of truth itself. Since the accident, Gareth had gained the same sense of certainty. He would speak or act and just assume that they would go along with him.

Master Amiron had made Gareth Defence Master in his place. That had to mean something. That had to mean that this apparent assurance Gareth showed was based on something solid. Didn't it?

Damn it!

He dealt the bag one more blow that sent it swinging so much it nearly flew off the hook. He grabbed the bag, as much for support as to stop it swaying, and he stood there gasping for breath. It wasn't that long ago that he'd watched Gareth do the same after the funeral.

Gareth had said he'd see them again. He'd said it in such a way that, at the time, Karl had been able to believe it. Now he was less sure. What if he never saw his friend again? They had no idea how to contact Master Amiron. What if that creature got bored of waiting and killed him anyway? Karl would never forgive himself for leaving Gareth there if that happened. Not for the first time, Karl found himself wishing that Master Amiron were still here. He'd have known what to do.

Karl wondered if there was some way to contact Master Amiron. He'd always said that all the dimensions were connected so there ought to be some way to communicate with him. The difficulty would be finding him. They had an infinite number of universes to choose from.

Karl's memory surfaced a recent moment. Before the council of war, he'd found Gareth running through some focusing exercise, apparently trying to locate Enrico. He said he'd done it, at least to some extent. Maybe that meant that there was a way to reach Master Amiron. Maybe if he focused enough, Karl could see through the fabric of the universes to the place where his teacher stood.

At any rate, trying to do something would certainly beat standing here fretting.

* * *

Cassie had thought the training was tough before. Now she'd been provisionally accepted onto the team, everything was scaled up. She still trained with the Defenders in the mornings but now Defender Boron would accept no weakness. In the afternoons, she had to learn everything else that went with being a Defender.

Her weapons training increased. She ran through drills with the practice swords until she felt her arms might drop off. She fought against the others, gaining bruise after bruise as encouragement to go faster. Karl in particular seemed determined to rap the wooden sword against her ribs at least a hundred times a lesson, but Lizzie said that was just because Karl was worried about Gareth. She was improving though. After about a week, Cassie was allowed to try a drill with a dark metal sword.

Cassie also had to learn to fight the Outsiders, expanding on the lessons Lizzie had begun. She studied video files of them so she could see how they moved, how they attacked. There were simulated fights where a dozen Defenders grabbed at her while she tried to hold them off with a practice sword. Those exercises would have been fun if it weren't for Boron summarising them afterwards by explaining how many minutes she would have lasted before getting eaten.

Jerry took Cassie to the gun range and they spent hours there, firing practice rounds at paper targets. Jerry, always cheerful and smiling in the canteen, became terrifying when he had a gun in his hands. His grin vanished and he could empty a clip in seconds, with every bullet going through the centre of even moving targets. Cassie still felt a sense of achievement when she got the hole anywhere on the target. The first time she'd tried firing a gun, one of the empty bullet cases had flown backwards and gone down the neck of her shirt. She'd had to put the gun down and frantically try to get the hot bit of metal out of her bra, while Jerry stood beside her laughing hysterically.

Along with the fighting skills, Cassie was expected to understand the portal technology. She sat for hours in the control room, trying to grasp not just how the equipment functioned but also the physics behind it. Cassie had always considered herself to be smart. Sitting with Richard, and Enrico when he was allowed back on duty, Cassie felt like a simpleton. Richard proved an impatient teacher. Occasionally, those in Richard's team would step in and translate Richard's condescending remarks into useful explanations. Enrico, on the other hand, explained things carefully until they could be understood

Despite Richard's attitude, Cassie gained new respect for him. His mind raced well above the normal speed and, when he talked about portals, he could have been speaking a different language. Even the most senior Defenders deferred to him about technical subjects. He might have failed as a candidate but there could be no doubt that he belonged here.

Cassie had been given permission to call her parents but Boron had been very clear that some things weren't to be said. The general public weren't to be told about this new danger at this time. So she'd been forced to endure the excited congratulations of her family without any way of explaining her concerns. That creature had nearly killed two trained Defenders.

Meanwhile, Boron and the senior Defenders kept heading off for meetings with leaders around the world. No one really told Cassie about them but she gathered that various governments and military groups wanted to have their say in the situation. After all, there was a new enemy their weapons couldn't touch, the base's security had been breached and the Defence Master was missing. It seemed a large number of people felt that they had a right to call the shots. Poor Boron was buffeted between them, having to fight to keep control as well as worrying about mysterious enemies.

So much was going on that Cassie wasn't involved in. There were discussions she wasn't invited to and whispers that quieted when she passed. Several times, alarms blared and groups of Defenders ran off to fight Outsiders but Cassie hadn't been put on the duty rota yet. She was left, gathering bits and pieces of understanding that wouldn't coalesce into a clear picture, and everyone was too busy to sit down and explain it all to her.

Cassie had been accepted, but she wasn't one of them.

***

Richard was sitting in the computer lab. He'd fixed the security file, removing the changes he'd made. The gaping hole was patched up as if it had never been and Jerry's badge would act like it should. He'd even added a layer to the code that would flag an alert if someone attempted to do what he'd inadvertently done.

"We need to talk."

Richard looked up to see Meg at the door of the room. She had a hard expression on her face that he'd never seen before.

"I was trying to figure out how that creature got in here," Meg said, "and I spotted some irregularities in the code logs for the security system."

That sick sensation was back in the pit of Richard's stomach. She knew. Of course she knew. She was in these systems every day. Richard tried to find some response, some answer, some excuse that could dismiss the heinous nature of his mistake.

"I didn't," he began. "I just... I didn't know this would happen."

"You tampered with the security files!"

"I wanted to punish Jerry," Richard said. It sounded so childish when he said it aloud.

"You screwed up our security and nearly got two people killed."

"I know." The words came out quickly, but he spoke again, his tone filled with grief he hadn't known he was capable of. "I know," he repeated.

For a moment, it seemed that Meg's hardness melted, but only for a moment.

"Have you told Defender Boron?" she asked.

"No. No! He'll send me back to jail or confine me to my room or... or let Jerry pummel me to death."

"And why the hell should I care about that? You think you can do something like this and just get away with it?"

"We need to find Master Amiron," Richard said. "He's involved in this somehow, he can get Gareth back. We've got to figure out where he went that's only going to be possible if I'm here doing my job. If Boron locks me away, I won't be able to help Gareth."

He tried to pour everything he felt into his words, the shame, the sick guilty feeling, the desperate fear of what might happen to Gareth. He had to make her understand. If he was sent back to jail, there wasn't a chance in hell that anyone else here could fix this mess. He had to stay. He had to solve the problem he caused.

Meg took a breath.

"Tell Boron," she said, "and tell him that too. If it comes from you, he might go easy."

So Richard went to the office and quietly admitted to Boron about the prank he'd played on Jerry and the unexpected consequence. Once Boron had grasped the full implications of the confession, Richard had thought Boron might hit him. Instead, Boron went very quiet.

Normally, Richard was perfectly happy with silence. This time, standing in front of the desk in what was technically Gareth's office, it felt like torture.

At last, Boron spoke. He said that he didn't have the authority to discipline Richard for his breaches in the rules or his behaviour towards a Defender. Only the Defence Master could do that, so Richard would have to help them get Gareth back. But there would be consequences. Boron reached out for Richard's wrist and the tracker bracelet that was locked around it. The bracelet had been idle for a long time, but Boron went into the systems and reactivated the alerts. Richard could go to the canteen during the worker meal shifts. He could go to his room and the showers on the worker floor. He was allowed in the computer lab. If he stepped beyond those bounds, Boron would be alerted and Richard would be locked up in the darkest pit that could be found.

It was clear, even to Richard, that Boron was furious. But everyone knew that Richard knew more about the portals than anyone. They all knew that he was the only one who stood a chance of figuring out where Master Amiron had gone.

It was as he was walking away from the office that Richard realised he'd wanted reassurance. He'd wanted Boron to say that it was OK, that Richard couldn't have known what his actions would do. He'd wanted Meg to say that. But neither of them had. No one had and no one would. Because Richard should have known. He was so much cleverer than every other person in the base. He should have thought through what he was doing. Even if no one else could have realised, he should have at least considered this possibility.

Except...

Maybe Gareth had known. Gareth had advised Richard not to play this prank. He'd known that Richard would go through with his plan to get petty revenge on Jerry. If Richard had listened, none of this would be happening now.

Richard cast his mind back over their strange friendship. How many times had Gareth seemed to know something before he could? How many times had he just assumed things that had later turned out to be right?

Richard tried to dismiss the thought but it nagged away at the back of his mind. He turned once again to the reports of Gareth's accident. He'd been dead. Then he'd been alive again.

A crazy notion lodged itself in Richard's thoughts and refused to shift. What if Master Amiron had somehow manipulated time? What if the portals could do that? If Master Amiron could move someone through time and change them from dead to alive, maybe Richard could go back and fix his mistake.

Since Richard hadn't the faintest idea where or how to start looking for Master Amiron, this was worth a shot.

Part Two

Thirteen

In the Darkness

When Mira's guards hauled Gareth from the throne room, he expected to be taken to a cell. What happened next was almost worse. He was taken down servant passages and pokey stairways until they reached the cellars. These stone rooms with their vaulted ceilings had been used for food storage back when the Outsider invasion had been at its height. No wonder the locks and walls down here were so secure. Now, the far rooms were dark and deserted.

Gareth was shoved into a small store furnished only with empty crates and old sacks. The low ceiling had a small light that shed a weak, dirty glow. As the heavy door trapped him, Gareth peered around the room. Maybe it was a good sign that this place was empty. Maybe that meant there was no longer such need to ration food supplies.

The information was at the surface of his mind without him needing to focus on it. He knew without thinking that this place had been attacked by Outsiders just as his world had. He'd recognised this room just as he'd known the throne room upstairs. His memories were furnishing him with facts that hadn't been in his brain on the other side of the portal. The act of stepping through to this world had allowed his memories of it to form. But while he could recall random facts on seeing the architecture of his impromptu cell, his recollections of future events here were still blurred.

He sat down on an upturned crate and pulled off the bulky armour that had proved to be utterly pointless. He would be here a while so there was no reason to be uncomfortable. He didn't have anything to do. If he'd planned ahead, he could have put a puzzle book in his pocket or something. But he hadn't known until he'd stood in the same room as Mira what was the right thing to do.

He rubbed at the sore patch on his jaw where she'd hit him.

Mira didn't know him yet. Gareth couldn't act based on how he knew he would know her. Master Amiron hadn't warned him about this. When they'd talked about the dangers of remembering the future, they'd never discussed what would happen if he met someone with whom he'd yet to fall in love.

Gareth sat there and shut his eyes, trying to picture Mira and their future. Most of it was foggy and vague, resistant to being clearly recalled. He let his mind sink into the relaxed state when dimensions began to show through. That made it easier. Moments in time danced across his recollections. Just glimpses, like the fragments of images seen in a shattered mirror. There was no complete picture, just an impression. A sense of love and happiness associated with this person whom he had only just met, music on the edge of hearing and the scent of jasmine.

The door opened.

Gareth had to force himself to come back to the present, startled to see the very person he'd been thinking of. Mira had left off the helmet but she still wore the armour. It was impressive stuff, sleek and form-fitting so that it appeared to be a part of her, no doubt custom made specifically to fit her body. No wonder Richard had been fooled. The gloves were made of hundreds of tiny scales, hinged so she had freedom of movement. Those lethal claws were set on the tip of each finger, shaped so that they could be swivelled around to lie against the digit, the vicious points stopping just short of the first joint. She had those claws folded away now but she could easily be armed in an instant. The whole thing was shaped from dark metal, a wealth of protection beyond the dreams of his world.

She stared at him, taking in the casual pose and discarded armour.

"Aren't you afraid of me?" Mira asked.

Gareth almost laughed. He stopped himself. That would probably just get him hit again.

"No."

"If Amiron doesn't come for you, I have twenty eight days to do what I like to you. Then I will kill you."

"You'll never kill me, Mira, because you're a good person. You wouldn't be able to hate Master Amiron so much if you weren't."

"What makes you think you know anything about me?"

That flush of anger gave her cheeks a delightful rosy tint. In her armour, she stood a fierce and powerful warrior but there was something of the innocent girl in that childish temper. Gareth caught his thoughts before they went too far down that road and instead focused on the memories that were gradually surfacing through the murk.

"You are Mira, daughter of Janon, who was Master Amiron's cousin. It was your throne and your father's that Master Amiron tried to steal."

"You know Amiron's crime?"

Gareth thought he did. He'd not known this morning but the instant he'd looked out across the ruined city, the truth had surfaced from the distant recesses of his mind. The thought was sickening, chilling him to the core. Master Amiron had been a hero back home. He'd been the one to accept Gareth for training instead of punishing him for being out of bounds. Master Amiron had been a supportive father figure who had smiled kindly and presented Gareth with his first Defender uniform and, with it, his entire reason for being. Gareth owed his life and his purpose to this noble warrior who'd come to his world as a saviour.

Gareth wanted desperately to cling to that image. He wanted to believe in the man who had believed in him.

But the future was invading the present, pushing out childish hero-worship with the bitter tang of truth.

"He released the Outsiders," Gareth said. "He destroyed your world and nearly destroyed mine."

The words tasted foul in his mouth. Each one felt like a betrayal, a dagger in the heart of the great man who had risked his life for a people who weren't even his. But, even as he said them, Gareth knew that they were true.

"So why do you follow him? Why do you use his title like he deserves it?"

"Because he does deserve it. He destroyed your world by accident but he saved mine by choice. He saved me."

"That man is a monster."

"You don't know him. Whoever he once was, whatever he once did, he's now the greatest man I've ever known. He's loyal and brave and kind. I trust him with my soul."

"You'd better hope he deserves your trust. Otherwise, you'll bleed."

Gareth watched her stalk out of the room, the door closing with a heavy clang behind her and sealing him away. He hoped he was right. It felt like there were two forces at war inside him. In his past was a teenage boy, desperate to prove himself, begging to be trained. Back before the accident, Gareth had looked on Master Amiron as an idol, the perfect man, a brave fighter, a noble leader and someone who would risk life and limb to protect the innocent. Some spark of that old belief hung on, like a fortress in Gareth's soul. All about it were the invading armies of doubt, bearing their weapons of future knowledge.

Master Amiron had saved Gareth's whole world, saved Gareth. That had to count for something. Shut away in the dark, Gareth clung to that thought like a drowning man clinging to a rope. Master Amiron was a hero.

Right?

***

For the first couple of days, time drifted past in a tedious fashion. Gareth sat in the gloom of the storeroom, going stir crazy from lack of activity. He worked out as best he could, practicing martial arts forms in the confined space. Sometimes he dosed, using the old sacks as a rough mattress. He used the quiet to try and meditate, reaching that state of awareness where he could see everything.

He focused on Master Amiron. The realisation of his past hurt but it was a dull ache, like an old wound almost healed. The pain of the realisation was somewhat distant but Gareth could feel it growing as the moments passed, drawing him closer to the moment of truth and the source of this bitter sense of betrayal.

In the quiet of his mind, Gareth heard whispers of future conversations. They would discuss this world at length.

There was something else in his future. Amid the golden trails of timelines, it stood like a black hole. He'd not felt it before coming into this world and it hung there, distant and vague, no matter how he looked for it. Some event, huge and powerful, was blocked from Gareth's vision. Was it his death? Was that why it seemed to swallow his future memories?

The door opened and Gareth once more saw Mira standing there, shattering his future visions.

"I want to see how you fight," she said.

Gareth had cleared most of what space there was for his own practice. He just had to push aside the crate he had been using as a seat. Then he was ready to face Mira. She'd left off the armour today and wore a dark outfit that provided free movement but which was tight enough not to get in the way. Gareth had to remind himself not to get distracted by the way it highlighted the curves of her young body.

They bowed to each other, Mira barely nodding her head. Then the fight began. Gareth had a major advantage. He remembered future fights and sparring sessions. He knew her style almost by instinct. He could recognise the subtle movements that hinted at her attacks. He could predict her but she didn't know him yet.

He quickly noticed how much she relied on the gloves. Her attacks largely consisted of sweeping blows that would cause lethal damage when her fingers were tipped with those claws. Now though, they just left her open and vulnerable. Gareth made it inside her defences repeatedly, but he was careful enough to barely touch her with his own attacks.

If anything, that made her more angry than if he'd just hit her hard. She didn't hide her emotion at all well. She glared at Gareth as they sparred. She was a good fighter, but she was used to the Outsiders, not a practiced opponent.

At last, she stepped back.

"Enough! Amiron has taught you well."

"Actually, most of that I learned from Karl. He's one of the Defenders who came with me to get Enrico."

"Why should I care who taught you?"

"So you're just curious about my fighting, not who I am as a person?" Gareth's tone was lightly teasing. In another time, she might laugh back. Now though, it fuelled her anger. He needed to learn to control himself better. He wanted her to love him back, not to go on hating him.

* * *

Mira returned to her study, angry at herself almost as much as the man in the cellar. She couldn't afford to let herself be so distracted. Of course, hunting the murderer responsible for the Outsiders was a worthy task, but she couldn't allow herself to be blinded to other matters.

The man in the cellar was convinced that Amiron would come. Mira hoped that was true. She would see him regret every drop of blood that had been spilled because of his treachery. Every man, woman and child who had suffered for the past decade could finally see justice done.

But she had other duties to attend, other tasks that needed to be done. In her study, there waited, as always, a mountain of information to be digested and decisions to be made. Her advisors all had their points to make and agendas to drive and she couldn't deliver everything she wanted. All her visions for the future and plans for her world had to be carefully considered because moving forward with one grand scheme usually meant that another had to be set aside.

Someone always wanted to make changes to hospital budgets or education policies. There were procedures to decide for defence and policies to lay down for food distribution. A million and one things required her attention at any given time.

So she needed to get on with them and stop thinking about the young man in the cellar. He'd just stood there, so calm and collected. He didn't seem to understand how much danger he was in. Mira was used to being underestimated, but she was seriously unnerved by the way this man would just look at her like he was seeing right through her. He spoke with an almost hypnotic confidence that made her want to believe him despite her hate.

Mira reached her spacious study, positioned herself behind her desk and reached for the first of the files that covered the expansive surface. She would work. She would stop thinking about that infuriating young man and get on with more important things. She looked at the file. Renovation plans for the major sewage treatment plant on the west coast. She flipped through pages of technical diagrams, chemical formulae and, inevitably, the budget breakdown. Why couldn't her ministers deal with more of this trivia for her?

He'd called her beautiful! The angry thought cut through the banality of the paperwork in front of her. He'd looked at her and that was the first thing it had occurred to him to say. Did it matter that she was intelligent or a leader who thought about her people's well-being? Of course not. He just thought she was pretty.

Like that mattered.

Like that had anything to do with him.

He should be more concerned about the fact that she was dutifully following her own regulations about prisoner well-being instead of stuffing him into a tiny box and letting him starve.

Why did it matter if she was pretty? It didn't. Just like it didn't matter that he had a nice body under that armour he'd come here in. It didn't matter in the slightest.

She'd teach him that. He might be a strong fighter but she would show him that she was stronger in her own way. She would make him see what really mattered about her and to her. She would show this young man her true strengths.

But right now, that strength was getting on with the task that needed to be done. Even if it did mean reading about sewage treatment plants.

Fourteen

The City

On the morning of his third day in captivity, Mira told Gareth she would show him the world Amiron had wrought. Gareth's hands were cuffed and he found himself surrounded by half a dozen guards. He inspected them as he was taken from the cellar, taking in the ragged uniforms over scrawny bodies. He felt he'd be able to take any one of them easily, even with the cuffs. But each was armed with both a gun and a dark metal blade. He wasn't stupid enough to try taking on the lot of them but Mira must have seen something of his thoughts in his face.

"If you try to run," Mira said, "you will spend the rest of your stay here in pain."

She held out a hand and extended a single claw on one of the gloved fingers. She wasn't wearing the rest of her armour, but she would be armed to face him.

"I gave you my word," Gareth said. "I won't run."

The little group moved up staircases to the main rooms of the palace, Gareth kept always in the middle of the guards. Mira walked in front, striding ahead with confidence. How much of that was an act? How much was a show to diminish that apparent weakness of her age?

They moved through passages that, like everything else round here, struck Gareth as hauntingly familiar. The group emerged from a small doorway beneath the looming wall of the palace. Ornate stonework reached to the heavens, carved faces peering down from alcoves, stone flowers arching over graceful windows. The majestic image of a glorious past.

"Come on," Mira snapped.

They walked down a narrow road that clung to the face of the cliff, hair-pinning down to the city below. Gareth wondered why they were walking and the answer came almost at once: fuel supplies were precious.

The walk down was easy enough but Gareth wasn't looking forward to the climb back up. Still, it was a relief to get movement after those cramped days in the cellar. He wanted to break into a run just to stretch his legs but he suspected the contingent of guards wouldn't take it the right way. So he walked calmly down the steep slope in the midst of those who thought him an enemy.

The houses of the city were nestled right against the base of the cliff, sheltering under the protection of the palace above. In the stone here, Gareth could see the same evidence of a rich past. Fragments of architectural brilliance lurked beneath the present chaos. On an ornate facing above an ancient doorway, the front half of a deer pranced in a meadow of stone flowers, as though trying to escape the smears of rough plaster that were holding the rest of the fronting together, already engulfing the creature's hind-quarters. Repairs had been made crudely with any material available. Wood, brick and stone were crammed together in a patchwork mess. But most of the repair work already showed evidence of age. The bulk of the damage had been done years ago.

There were people in the streets and looking out from the buildings. They kept away but peered curiously at Mira and Gareth. Gareth saw shoppers and workers. He saw children ushered along by parents and friends chatting by their homes. He saw evidence of life continuing all around him. These people had jobs and families and homes, however makeshift they might all be.

They reached a square that centred on a cracked fountain, long since dry. The paved area stretched around them, almost every one of the large stones broken or damaged. The buildings surrounding the square were shattered, worse than the rest of the city, fragments of broken masonry too insubstantial to try repairing. There were market stalls around the edges of the square, but Mira ignored these, walking straight to the fountain, at the heart of which stood a statue of a tall and regal man.

"This is where my father was crowned," Mira said. "Here, before the city, with the entire world watching the broadcast. The festival lasted for three days, with this site filled with food and music and joy.

This place was known as Royal Square. Do you know what people call it now? Blood Square! Amiron chose this point to open the portal and let the first Outsiders into our world."

The heart of the capital city and the heart of symbolism for Janon's reign. A location chosen to maximise the panic while undermining his cousin's image. No wonder Mira hated him.

"Three Outsiders came through that first portal," Mira went on. "Just three, but it was enough. Innocent civilians fell in the first minutes so my father sent in the law enforcement, then the army."

Gareth had heard the stories of the Paris massacre. The authorities had refused to listen to Master Amiron, insisting that regular forces would be enough. Gareth could easily guess the next part of Mira's story.

"Our people came with guns. When those failed, they brought in the heavy artillery and then the bombs. One hundred and fifty-seven people died that day before Amiron got there. He made some speech about the nobility of sacrifice before leading the charge. He killed the Outsiders. My father proclaimed him a hero for his apparent willingness to give his life for his people. But he planned the whole thing!"

He saw the rage and pain on her face and felt the ache in his own heart as an echo. He wanted to scream at her to shut up, that Amiron really was a hero. But a piece of him knew the truth. He knew that his mentor had let those people die. Master Amiron was guilty of everything Mira accused him of. That burned inside Gareth, destroying another piece of the boy who'd looked to Amiron as a mentor and role model. But Mira was still talking, her words eroding the pedestal in Gareth's mind on which this man had been placed.

"He claimed not to understand why he'd been able to kill the Outsiders. As he opened new portals and let the death toll rise, he led the fight against them. He used his knowledge of my father's plans to make him look a fool at every turn, but Amiron's team were always prepared, able to defeat the Outsiders and save the people, responding with perfect preparedness to every surprise attack. He was a global champion."

She spat the last word as though it were poison in her mouth. Her eyes were damp but she wasn't crying.

"For two months, portals continued to open. People died. Livestock was eaten by the Outsiders. People panicked. There were riots and food shortages. Businesses collapsed. Then Amiron announced he'd made a discovery. He claimed that he'd discovered it was the dark metal in his sword that was the key and he authorised the building of a new arsenal. He stated that they'd uncovered a way to detect the portals as they were forming, so that his team would be able to evacuate civilians and stop the Outsiders as they came through. He seemed to have all the answers and the people rallied around him. They cheered him and celebrated him, while ignoring the fact that my father had been working himself sick trying to solve the problem of the Outsider attacks."

"That was what he wanted," Gareth said. "He wanted your father's throne but didn't want to take it. He wanted the people to give it to him."

"Then why did he abandon us? If he wanted the throne so badly that he would cause the death of so many, why did he leave just when we needed him most?"

Every word Mira uttered stirred up future memories, bringing to the surface knowledge that he hadn't quite gained yet. Gareth knew the answer and he knew it would do nothing to lessen Mira's hate.

"He abandoned your world," Gareth said, "because he knew mine needed him more."

Mira glared at Gareth with cold fury in her eyes. In that instant, she hated him as much as Amiron, just because he was closer. He was a target for all the rage that had filled her since she'd learned the truth about her father's cousin.

"He let those monsters into my world! He destroyed my father's reputation as a leader. He caused chaos in our society and wrecked the economy. He caused food shortages and riots and uprisings. Then, at the moment when we most needed a strong leader to take charge, he left us. The portals became more frequent and completely unpredictable, and the great Master Amiron had vanished. We thought him a martyr! We thought he'd died trying to stop the attacks. Instead, I learn that he fled. He left us to suffer the ravages of the Outsiders so he could play the hero to another world. So he could convince people like you to follow him."

In that sweet face that should have been innocent, Gareth saw the heart of her pain. She'd believed in him. She'd grown up with the stories of his nobility and courage and his great sacrifice. And then she'd had that image of a hero stripped away, leaving only the bare bones of his betrayal. A schemer and would-be usurper.

Gareth felt that same sting of betrayal. Master Amiron had been his mentor and his friend, a leader he would have followed into any danger. The knowledge of these past atrocities tore at his heart as they did Mira's. For them both, the knowledge was recent and so cut new pain with every moment.

Gareth longed to hold her, to take her in his arms and promise her that it would all be alright. But she didn't know him yet. It was hard to just stand there, caring for her so much but knowing that any such action would be seen as an inappropriate intrusion. They were surrounded by her guards, who would defend her against what would appear to be an attempt against her honour. So Gareth just stood there, wondering what he could say to her that might take some of her pain away.

An alarm blared across the city, a siren rising in a wail that pierced the ears and summoned the attention of all. Mira's demeanour changed in a flash. Her anger was still there, but it was covered over by a determination and purpose. She reached into her pocket and pulled out a small device, a flat rectangle, the size of a smartphone, that sat in the palm of her hand. She looked at it, reading something off the screen. Her argument with Gareth had vanished from the forefront of her mind as she focused on the cause of this sound.

"The portal's less than three streets from here," she said. "We're the nearest group." She looked at Gareth, hesitating a moment. "If this is your friends, I'll see that they're all dead before this day is over. If it's Outsiders, try to stay out of the way."

A hand grabbed Gareth's arm and he found himself half-towed as the little group ran towards the new portal. The guards all had their weapons out. No doubt this was one of their main duties, otherwise they wouldn't need the dark metal swords. Gareth wished for a weapon now, but he was still cuffed, clearly a prisoner. At least he was certain he wasn't about to die today but he couldn't afford to be overconfident. He couldn't just go through his life assuming that he'd be alright. Still, he supposed he had Mira's promise too. She'd agreed he'd be kept alive for a month and she considered her honour to be vital. She wouldn't let him die.

There were no other people in sight as they reached the portal, which was at a slight angle on one of the streets of the city. A handful of Outsiders were already on this side of the portal, spreading through the streets in search of food. Mira gave her orders clearly and concisely, much as he might have on his world. She sent four of the guards out to stop those Outsiders that had been first through and were now spreading into the city. She and the other two were going straight to the portal, stopping the wave of creatures as they came through. Gareth was left standing there, aware of the cuffs on his wrists and his helplessness should the things come near him.

He wasn't used to being a witness to a fight instead of a participant. He had nothing with which to hurt these things, which were still stepping from the portal and staring around with hungry eyes at this poor city. They looked at Gareth with longing, some heading straight for him while the three fighters tried to stem the tide.

"Give me a weapon!" Gareth yelled, dodging a clawed hand and using his legs to divert their assaults. His heart was beating frantically, natural fear rising despite the knowledge that he would survive this day. He could keep the things at bay for a time but he would tire quickly and he knew that no amount of fighting skill could make up for the lack of a dark metal weapon.

"Hey!" The short yell cut across the sound of battle and Gareth turned to Mira. She tossed something, the arc of the throw going across the melee. Gareth raised his cuffed hands and snatched the thrown dagger from the air. He didn't have time to stop and think about how lucky he'd been not to catch it by the blade. He now had the weapon he'd demanded.

One of the Outsiders grabbed at him and he sliced through its guts, dark blood splashing sticky on his hands. Gareth kicked the thing away before it was even dead and turned to the next, hacking at the limbs that tried to grab him. He was used to the reach of the sword but he was glad of any dark metal in this throng. His mind was a blur of movements, no time to think. He just acted on instinct. Dodging, kicking, slicing.

One by one, the creatures fell away.

Gareth heard a cry of pain, the sound drowned out by the loud crack of a gun. An Outsider fell back, a bullet hole through its skull, its mouth still crimson with the human flesh it had tasted. And there was Mira, still fighting, the clawed glove on her left hand still cutting through the Outsiders that wanted to feast on her. But her right arm was held close, her dark shirt torn near the shoulder by the creature's teeth. Her face showed only the pain and determination, but she'd fought these things half her life. She must know what the bite meant.

At last, Gareth found himself standing in a sea of corpses, the portal closed and no trace of anymore Outsiders. He turned to Mira, her guards already at her side, helping her to sit on a patch of ground that wasn't stained with the marks of battle. Her white face was a stark contrast to her dark hair and clothes, even her lips looking colourless as she looked down at her arm. One of her men was cleaning the Outsider blood from his sword.

"Make it quick," she said.

She held out her right arm, turning her face away. Her left arm grasped desperately at the hand of the guard who knelt beside her. Gareth saw the guard before her raise the sword and in a moment he knew what was about to happen.

"What are you doing?" Gareth demanded, putting himself between the sword and the woman.

"It bit me," Mira said. As though it was so simple. As though losing a limb was ordinary.

Gareth knew what she was thinking. In the early days of the fight back home, people had died from infected bites. Karl had nearly been one of them. But back home there were treatments, ways to prevent the death that would come if the bite was left alone. Amiron had brought the secret of healing with him, but did these people not know it?

"There's another way," Gareth said. "You don't have to lose the arm." He poured everything he could into those words, the Master tone the others made jokes about, needing her to believe. He yanked up his shirt as proof, revealing the pale scar that was so obviously a bite mark on his side. Mira stared. A flicker of hope crossed her face.

Fifteen

The Miracle

"How?" she asked.

"We have a machine," Gareth said, "back home, that monitors the dimensions around our world. It's what alerts us to new portals. You have one too?" It was barely a question, but Mira nodded. "There's a grate on the back of ours and a green substance builds up." She nodded again. "I need the substance. A lot of it."

Mira looked to one of her men, giving a nod that was as good as an order. The man ran off. Gareth yelled a, "Quickly!" after him, but it was probably unnecessary. Gareth then turned to one of the others, who waited nervously nearby with a look of anxious helplessness on his face.

"Give me your belt," Gareth instructed. Again, the man looked to Mira before obeying. Gareth took the belt and wrapped it round Mira's arm right at the shoulder, above the wound. He pulled it as tight as possible. He didn't have time to wonder when it was he'd learn how to do this.

"That won't stop the poison," Mira said.

"No, but it will slow it down. Keep your arm raised." He lifted it high for her. She was, if anything, even paler now. With the combination of the poisonous bite and the adrenaline leaving her system, she could pass out at any moment. Gareth knew she would survive this, his memories were filled with her, but still he couldn't quell the rising terror. The woman he loved was before him with poison racing through her veins. He had to fight with every breath to stay calm, to keep from panicking, because if he panicked he'd be able to do no good for her. She needed him.

"We need to get you somewhere you can lie down," he said.

One of the guards stood and went to a nearby door. Gareth would have to find out their names; he couldn't just keep on thinking of them as a collective entity anymore. The man beat a fist against the sturdy wood of the door.

"Open in the name of the queen!"

From the scrapings and scratchings on the other side, opening the door was a difficult task. No doubt, whoever was inside had barricaded themselves against the Outsider attack. By now though, there were people at upstairs windows, faces drinking in the sight of the young queen bleeding on the street, surrounded by the bodies of the beasts she had defeated. At last, the door opened and Mira's men lifted her up, carrying her as gently as a mother nursing a sick child. Gareth stayed at her side, his cuffed hands around Mira's forearm, lifting it aloft. In the few steps it took to get her inside, she slipped quietly into the realm of unconsciousness.

The building turned out to be a shop, fresh fruit and vegetables locked in glass-fronted cabinets. No wonder they'd taken such precautions when barring the door. An anxious shopkeeper and a couple of men who looked like bouncers guided them in, clearing the long counter so that Mira could be laid down. The shopkeeper removed his own jumper and folded it beneath her head as a pillow.

"I need a lot of water and some clean cloth," Gareth instructed, still holding Mira's arm and feeling desperately for the faint flutter of her pulse. The shopkeeper gave instructions regarding a neighbour who had pharmacy supplies, going himself to fill a large basin with water at a sink behind the counter.

There was no room beside Mira's still form for the basin. So the shopkeeper just stood there holding it. Gareth looked about, seeing some crockery beside the sink. He asked to be passed the cup and told the nearest man to hold Mira's arm. It was astonishing how easily they obeyed now. Perhaps it was simply the act of speaking with authority when they didn't know how to help their beloved queen. Gareth took the cup and, after a cursory glance to check its cleanliness, he used it to pour some water over the wound. Water splashed on the counter and floor, coloured pink with the flow of blood, but he had other things to worry about. It had been mere minutes since Mira had been bitten, but already she was as white as a ghost.

There were people crowded round the door now. They'd come from the other buildings nearby, desperate to see the scene, whether through concern or curiosity or simply the need to be able to say that they'd been there when it happened, should it come that their queen would die. A woman was fighting her way through the crowd. One of the bouncers spotted her and forced a path for her. She held a plastic box in her arms from which Gareth saw a trailing end of bandage.

With a brief mutter of thanks, Gareth dived into the box, pulling out a square of cloth that was probably intended as a sling. Whatever it was meant to be, Gareth used it to wipe away the area around the wound, which was still bleeding freely.

Over the murmur of voices, he heard an unexpected noise. A roar of a motor cut through the quiet of the city. Once again, the bouncers were forced to step in to make people move aside. White-uniformed men came into the building, obviously doctors. They took one look at Mira and Gareth recognised the look of dismay on their faces. They didn't believe there was a chance.

"You should have removed the limb at once," one said. "We might be able to save her if we do it now."

"No," Gareth said. "I can save her."

He stood between Mira and the doctors, glaring at them. One looked down, seeing the cuffs that were still around Gareth's wrists. Gareth had no authority here except what he'd claimed. If they started to argue with him, he'd have no chance. But the doctor just looked at Mira, seeing the pale face and the bitten arm. It was written across his face; he knew that he wouldn't be able to save her.

"You may as well try," was all he said.

Another engine roared across the murmuring voices. The people must know how serious the situation was, for two motor vehicles to be driving through the same part of the city in one day. Gareth looked eagerly to the door. The man who had left earlier was pushing through the crowds, a plastic container clutched in one hand. The box was plain white, about the size of the lunchbox Gareth had used to carry to school, its lid held down by clasps. The man reached Gareth's side and began undoing the clasps, showing the pale green substance within. This was fresher than the stuff Gareth was used to, more liquid, but it carried the same delicious aroma into the room. This green substance was the main ingredient in the mirus that was used all over his world as the antidote to Outsider bites.

"Is this right?" the man asked.

"Perfect," Gareth answered. Still giving orders, he had the doctor hold up Mira's arm. Then he reached into the medicine box for a coil of bandage, dumping the whole thing into the green goo. He didn't care about getting the stuff on his hand as he ensured that every point of the bandage was soaked green. This wasn't as refined as what he was used to and he wasn't sure how much he'd need. He lifted the mass of fabric out, shaking off drips, before turning to the wound.

"That stuff's the run-off from some machine!" someone protested. Gareth began wrapping the bandage around the bleeding bite. Every part of the wound must be seeped in the liquid.

"Back home," Gareth said, "we call this the miracle liquid and it's used to make our most precious medicine. It can heal Outsider bites."

Gareth knew that it had to be used quickly. They might have already taken too long. If Mira died because he'd told them not to remove the arm, he would be executed as though he were her assassin. They would have their revenge for the loss of their beloved queen. But Gareth knew that she couldn't die today. He knew that she would live long enough for him to love her. So he reached for another bandage, this time wrapping pure white over the soaked one to make sure the precious substance was held where it was needed most.

He scraped his hands on the edge of the plastic container, letting the goo drip back to join what still lingered at the bottom. There was no sense wasting a drop by washing it into the drains. Finally, he wiped his hands on a third bandage, handing this one to the doctor along with the box with its small residue of green.

"Use this on someone else who's faced the Outsiders," Gareth told him.

Mira's face was already regaining some trace of colour. She was still paler than she should be and showing no sign of waking, but there was a hint of rose again in her cheeks. He touched a hand to her skin and felt the returning warmth. He felt the heartbeat beneath. The doctor almost pushed Gareth to one side to do his own inspection. He was staring wide-eyed at the signs of life in the young queen.

"That's impossible!"

"That's why we call this stuff a miracle," Gareth responded.

He stepped backwards now, letting the doctors fuss around Mira. Someone was already at the door, calling to the crowds that the queen would live. Her guard were smiling as they led Gareth from the shop. Some of those people who'd been close enough to the door to see were clapping Gareth on the shoulder as he was walked past. There were cheers and yells of thanks. Embarrassment burned its way through his body as this crowd of strangers applauded his saving of Mira.

Gareth was acutely aware of the cuffs around his wrists, the fact that Mira had yet to open her eyes. He was still a prisoner here, still an enemy in the eyes of Mira's guard.

Gareth found himself taken to a vehicle that reminded him more of a go kart than a car. It was a minimal frame over four wheels. There was the driver's seat, with controls that looked straight-forward enough, along with two seats behind. Gareth was put into one of the back seats, while the guard took the one at the controls. Either they didn't feel he needed so many guards now, or the others simply didn't want to leave their queen's side while she was still so close to death. Either way, Gareth had just the one man as escort on the drive back up the cliff road to the palace. In a short time, Gareth was back in the cellar, hidden away in darkness. He sat there, with nothing to do but wait for word.

Strangely, he felt more worried now than he had been in the shop. He supposed it was just because, back there, he'd been doing something. He'd been actively working towards protecting Mira. Now all he could do was fret. He tried to tell himself that Mira must survive, otherwise he would not have remembered her so clearly. But it was harder to remember her when she wasn't beside him. It was harder to feel the certainty that their futures were bound together.

Gareth paced the small room, wishing he knew how long it had been. Mirus usually worked quickly but Mira had been very close to the end when he'd used it on her. Naturally, it would take time to recover. Besides, her doctors would want to check her out carefully, and they probably weren't concerned over telling a mere prisoner about her state. The fact he hadn't heard anything in no way implied that there was a problem.

He forced himself to stop pacing and took a deep breath. He gathered himself, turning his thoughts inwards, trying to sink into the right state of mind. He would not be calm until he knew Mira would be safe. The easiest way to do that was to walk the boundaries of dimensions and find the memories of her echoing back through time. He slowed his breathing, feeling the world slip away. He would find her somewhere, there in the coming times.

When he opened his eyes, it was to a room blazing in golden radiance. He saw the trailing lines drifting off through the walls of dimensions, curving their way through countless universes. He let his mind flow free and tried to spot the thread he wanted, the light that would carry him into the future. He felt more than saw the effect his breath had on the lights, causing ripples along the shimmering lines. The right one tugged at his attention and he turned to it, his movements cautious so as not to disturb the peace. Everything was so careful. A hand, a step, guiding himself along the lines of time, guiding his thoughts back to him from however far away.

He heard voices whispering in his thoughts from days to come, saw glimpses of memories that had not come to pass. He saw Lizzie in her wedding dress, smiling as she turned towards him. He heard Master Amiron's voice, laced with both humour and pain, saying, "You're a braver man than I am."

Then Gareth saw the darkness. The lines trailed into it, fading into blackness. It was an emptiness across the dimensions, swallowing up the lines that reached into the future, a shadow lying across his tomorrows. The fear was a cold force inside Gareth's gut as the golden light diminished on the boundary of this darkness. What lay beyond it? Gareth mentally grasped for more lines, something to follow, something that would let him see what lay beyond.

Was there anything?

Was there any future beyond this dark barrier in his memories?

The door to the cellar brought Gareth back to the present. He snapped around, frightened beyond reason by so simple an act. He forced himself to calm, reminding himself that there was no point getting panicked over events that hadn't happened yet.

It was one of the guards standing at the door, a smile on his face.

"Queen Mira is awake," the man said. "She's asked to see you."

This time, there were no cuffs. The man was more of an escort than a guard as he led Gareth up into the more habitable parts of the palace. Gareth followed eagerly, longing to look on Mira's face to erase the fear which lingered still.

The door they reached was of carved wood, elegant and dark. Flowers wound their way around the frame. Jasmine flowers, which sent a smile to Gareth's face without him knowing quite why. The guard knocked, opening the door at an invitation and then closing it firmly behind Gareth.

Gareth was standing in Mira's bedroom.

He knew he ought to feel embarrassed, but instead he felt like there was something deeply familiar about being in a room alone with Mira. It felt like he had a right to be standing here, looking at the wide bed on which Mira lay. Her colour was back now, her arm bandaged more neatly than Gareth had managed it. She was propped up by pillows, the covers down by her waist revealing an elegant nightgown. Once again the thought danced through Gareth's mind of how beautiful she looked. He wanted to rush across to her bedside and kiss her.

"I owe you my life," Mira said.

Gareth shook his head.

"No. Your guards would have saved your life. You just owe me your arm."

She moved her arm in a slight wave, a smile creeping across her face.

"It's still quite a debt. Thank you."

"You're welcome."

"How did you discover about what that liquid could do?" she asked.

"Master Amiron taught us. I don't know how he found out about it." Gareth had occasionally wondered if it was more circular causality. Perhaps Amiron had known what that run off could do because he had seen it in his future memories and so had led to them developing the mirus. Whatever the source of the knowledge, Mira didn't look at all happy to know that she owed something so immense to the man she despised.

"I owe you something in return for what you've given me," Mira said. "You gave me your word that you would stay with me until I release you or the deadline is up. I will trust your word. You will be moved to more comfortable accommodation and you may move about the palace as you wish."

"Thank you."

"Do not leave the palace without my permission. There are limits to my trust and if you try to escape or to contact your allies, I will make sure you suffer for it."

"I won't betray your trust, Mira. I would never betray your trust."

Mira's eyes narrowed, a trace of her earlier anger returning.

"Yet you serve my enemy gladly."

Gareth didn't push it. She'd taken a great step in offering him the freedom she had. He wasn't going to press his luck so soon.

* * *

Mira was under strict instructions to remain in bed but she felt perfectly fine. Her arm hurt a little, but no more than a dull ache as though the wound were days old. She'd been conscious the second time her arm had been bandaged, the doctors using that strange, green liquid because they were told it was the cure. She'd looked down and seen the skin already healing. Gareth had been right.

She told herself that this could all still be a trick. He could have helped her purely to try and gain her trust. It was hard to believe that though. He'd fought the Outsiders by instinct, killing the beasts with skill she'd be glad of in any of her guards. He'd protected her to the end and when he spoke, her heart wanted to believe him even if all the logic in the world said it was crazy.

Maybe it had been the delirium but she'd seen something in his face, as though losing her would be the end of the world.

She almost laughed at herself for that thought. She had too much to do to get all mushy about some man from another world who just happened to know something her doctors hadn't. Childish fantasies were for people who didn't have duties.

She needed to do something. Sitting in bed daydreaming about men from other worlds was a waste of time that could be better spent elsewhere. Her doctors had told her to stay, but she was feeling stronger by the second. Right now, she felt that she could run for miles or fight an army of Outsiders. The sensible part of her mind suggested that the feeling was just the influence of that strange, green stuff but she could still do something useful. The doctors had told her to stay in bed, but they hadn't told her not to do anything.

She rang for assistance and told the boy who answered that she wanted to speak to Corlion, one of her ministers and an old friend. Several years older than her, Corlion had looked after her sometimes when she'd been a child. As the youngest of the ministers when she'd become queen, he'd been the one she'd felt most comfortable turning to for guidance about her duties. He'd always been there at her side throughout her reign but, Mira smiled at the thought, this was the first time she'd invited him to see her in bed.

When he arrived, Corlion stared at her for a few moments then started fussing like a worried parent. Mira had to snap at him to regain control. She sent him hurrying to her study to fetch various files that needed to be worked through. He returned shortly, arms full of work.

"I'm not sure, majesty," he said. "Surely you should regain your strength."

"If anyone else says I need to regain strength, I'll show them how strong I am by punching them in the jaw."

The worry didn't disappear completely, but Corlion acquiesced. He pulled a chair up to sit beside Mira's bed as he handed over the files as she wanted them. Mira started to bring her thoughts to bear on the problems of rule, but Corlion obviously had something on his mind. He was staring everywhere but at Mira, inspecting the bed covers or the ceiling or the carpet.

"You shouldn't fight the Outsiders yourself, Mira," he said. "We nearly lost you today. We need you. I..."

He broke off, cleared his throat and then the moment had passed. He turned to Mira and was completely focused on the business at hand. Mira wondered what he might have said if he'd carried on.

Amiron's Story

Part One

Amiron was born the first son to a second son. In the early years of his life, he was told he would be king and was trained accordingly. When the king married and dared to conceive an heir of his own, Amiron's father was furious. At Janon's birth, the lesson became that Amiron should be king. This was drilled into him for so long that Amiron never doubted it. He was older, stronger and more intelligent than his young cousin. Of course he deserved the throne.

The boy grew to a man, still bearing the certainty of his right to rule.

After the accident that claimed both their parents, Janon was crowned king. Amiron burned with a sense of injustice as he was forced to stand beside his cousin and wish him well. Amiron was appointed Master of Military Research, a prestigious position. With his quick mind and determined nature, Amiron thrived. He even began to enjoy his work.

Then Janon announced his engagement. A marriage would likely mean an heir. Another obstacle to the throne.

Janon was weak. He had no will to hold control, no stomach for the difficult decisions. He would not make the hard choices that could ultimately lead to the benefit of their world. So Amiron would have to take action. At the birth of Janon's daughter, named Mira in Amiron's honour, Amiron resolved to take the crown from his cousin.

It would not be easy. Janon was soft and, for that weakness, many people loved him. If Amiron took the throne by force, he would have to use further force to subdue a rioting population. He had no desire to cause unnecessary suffering in his bid for control. He had to gain the support of the masses.

Some time was needed to conceive a plan but Amiron was a patient man. Rushing could bring about the ruin of all. So Amiron waited and plotted but did not act. He still felt a piece was missing. It was as Mira toddled her first steps that Amiron's research team discovered the portal technology.

The discovery was kept secret even from Janon. Amiron developed the devices and his plans, carefully exploring the multiverse that was opened up to him. It never occurred to him to stay in any of those worlds. His people and his duty were here. When Janon announced that his queen was once more with child, Amiron knew his work must accelerate.

That was when he found the dying world.

Whatever name its inhabitants had once known it by, Amiron never learned. The portals opened into mighty cities whose towering buildings pierced the sky. The air burned from the heat of old technology, still churning away beneath the ground. Each breath carried a taste of poison. The initial quiet was emphasised rather than interrupted by the hum of distant machinery. The society that had created such a mighty metropolis was gone.

But something had replaced them, twisted monsters emerging from a once-proud people.

As the first team explored, armoured and masked against the radiation, scuffling sounds of life broke the background quiet. The creature appeared, seeming timid and frail. Its pallid skin gave it a sickly quality and its flesh was withered to the point of starvation across its lanky frame. It hardly seemed a threat, this pitiful thing distorted by mutations and constant hunger. It sniffed the air, perhaps trying to decide what these intruders were. Amiron's team studied the pale thing in return. Unfortunately for them, the creature concluded they were food.

Without radiation armour, none of them would have survived. As it was, the creature's teeth and claws struggled to find a purchase.

One of the researchers fired a shot and Amiron was amazed. The creature was obviously sore, but the bullet had failed to pierce its hide. Perhaps some mutation that had allowed its species to survive the radiation. More shots were fired. These slowed the creature but attracted others, the thunderous sounds bringing the beasts in astonishing numbers. Amiron yelled at his team to get back to the portal but he was a fighter. He would at least try to put the closest things down to give his people a chance.

He fired a series of bullets into the faces of those that were nearest. It caused them to falter momentarily but the pain just seemed to make them angry. As his gun ran out of ammunition, Amiron reached for a small dagger, forged of dark metal, kept as an heirloom more than a weapon. Still, it was something. With the dagger in hand, he slashed at one of the creatures, astonished to see the blade slicing through the skin as if it was nothing. Black blood spilled on the ground and the creature fell back.

In his astonishment, Amiron hesitated and that nearly cost him his life, but his long years of training took over. He slashed and stabbed and cleared a path through the creatures, running back towards the portal. He reached it just before his team gave him up for dead and he stumbled through into his own world, covered with the blood of the creatures he'd killed.

He'd found an enemy that only he knew how to stop. He'd found his way onto the throne.

Sixteen

The Dance

Since Mira and her people seemed to have grasped that Gareth wasn't about to run away or attack anyone, they gave him remarkable freedom to move around the palace as he chose. Sometimes he was glared at for his presence, on other occasions he was specifically asked to move away, but usually that was when he drew too close to conversations that might be important to the world's security or government. It was clear that the palace was also the hub of the politics of this planet. Mira had an office on one of the upper floors, alongside conference rooms of various sizes, meeting areas and a debate floor. It was the only part of the palace that seemed completely free of dirt and decay.

Those that spent their time in that area treated Gareth in a range of ways, from curiosity, through indifference, to outright hostility. Gareth was surprised to find that several of them were more familiar than the politicians back home.

He spent a little time in there, enough to get a feel for Mira as a leader. As the ruler of the world, she obviously worked very hard. She was surrounded by a mixture of advisors and representatives, all of whom had their own agendas and aims. Mira was sat in the middle of a whirlwind of information and intentions, striving to make sense of it all and drive her planet forwards in the right direction. Despite her age, she managed to hold the meetings to order and drive her views across.

Watching her, Gareth felt a sense of admiration for her achievements. He tended to leave much of the administration of leadership to Boron, and that was in a team of less than three hundred. Mira had to deal with budget requests and project approvals and legal disputes for an entire world. No wonder she liked going to fight the Outsiders; she must need the stress relief.

Most of those who worked in that area made it clear that they didn't want Gareth around during their discussions and meetings. They obviously suspected him of being some sort of spy. Mira spoke to him with politeness but she was always busy and it was clear she resented any interruptions. Gareth had no intention of making her any more hostile towards him than she already was.

After a while, he took to wandering the disused parts of the palace. A lot of the rooms stood empty or furnished with only useless items. Anything useful had been donated to those whose homes were destroyed by the weapons employed to fight the Outsiders in the early days, or in the riots when business closed. Some rooms had lingering hints as to their prior purpose. Gareth found one where each wall was lined with shelves, though the books were long-since gone. There was a bathroom that had aspirations to being a swimming pool, the gilded tub now dry and the huge mirrors spotted with age. This place had once been a showcase for extravagance, but Mira focused on the sufferings of her people rather than the splendour of her home.

In his wanderings, Gareth came across a massive hall. It was larger than the throne room in which he'd first met Mira. Marble floor stretched away into the distance, with marble pillars arching up to the high roof. A viewing gallery ran around the walls and a host of chandeliers hung in the gloom overhead. Huge doors lined one wall, once used to let guests enjoy the gardens and evening air, now sealed and shut, locked by the passage of time.

Gareth's footsteps raised up little clouds of dust. When was the last time feet had glided across this floor in dance?

A small stage was set up in one corner, with stands for music and instruments. Now the only sound was his own breathing.

Something about this place resonated in Gareth's mind. He didn't even have to try. He saw the hall through a haze of golden light and a memory stirred, finding him without effort. Distant music echoed in his thoughts, the sound of laughter and swish of silken skirts. A moment of his future, so pivotal it would shape realities around it, flowed backwards to embrace his consciousness. As he stared about him, Gareth saw the room shining in the radiance from the chandeliers, brilliant with the outfits of those who danced beneath. He saw Mira, a bright smile rendering her breath-taking.

The vision vanished and Gareth found himself staring at Mira, dressed in her customary black from her day's meetings. She was looking at Gareth with a slight frown.

"So here you are," she said.

"Here I am," Gareth replied.

"Why are you here?"

He shrugged, "Just looking around the place."

Mira didn't seem to hear him. She was looking at the room, a melancholic look on her face. When she spoke, it was in a quiet, distant voice, more to herself than to him.

"I haven't been here in years. One of my earliest memories was of this room, the celebration ball after my brother was born."

"There will be balls here again," Gareth said.

"We haven't had much to celebrate in a long time."

"What about the hospital? The housing projects? The power station? What about the fact that the people have a queen willing to work so hard to help them and to fight to protect them? What about the way the government is funding new businesses to boost the economy?"

"That's just... day to day stuff."

"It's still work to be proud of. You've done so much for this world that you should celebrate it."

"What do you know about it?"

"An outsider's perspective," he smiled. "Things are improving. You're making them improve. It won't be long before this room can be put to its proper use again."

She looked doubtful.

Gareth's smile grew to a grin and he held out a hand to Mira. She looked puzzled for several seconds. Then she held out her own hand and placed it into his. Gareth stepped towards her, a hand at her waist, and he began to hum. It was a slow and gentle tune, one he knew he'd never heard before. It just sprang to the forefront of his mind and seemed to flow so naturally.

Mira gave a surprised laugh as their feet started to move, their steps uniting in a slow waltz to the melody Gareth provided. Future and present melted into one. After a few steps across the dusty floor, Mira began to sing, adding the lyrics to the music. She obviously recognised the song Gareth was humming.

171

"Sweetest flower that blooms by night, Gives beauty 'til return of light. My love, through gloom of deep despair, I'll hold the jasmine's flower fair."

Mira's voice faded to nothing and Gareth's tune fell too. Their feet came to a halt on the dusty floor, the faint echoes of their impromptu music disappearing into the silence of the old hall. It seemed quieter now than before they had started, the sounds of their momentary happiness swallowed by the deserted air.

Gareth became acutely aware of Mira's hand on his hip, her body so close to his own. Her face was tilted up towards his, the smile on her lips making her dark eyes sparkle. He could so easily lean in and kiss her.

A trace of common sense reminded him that she'd punched him for calling her beautiful. She wasn't in love with him yet.

They stood there for a moment that became an eternity. Gareth wondered what was running through her mind. Was she thinking about how slight the distance was between them?

The moment shattered. Mira stepped back, snatching her hand from his as though burned. Even in the dim light, he could see the rosy hint of a blush on her cheeks.

"I... I have work to do."

She fled.

Gareth was left standing in the middle of the old hall with only the lingering warmth of her touch. And the memories.

He could picture Mira clearly. She would wear a dress of pale silk, glittering with pearls and diamonds. Her eyes would shine like jewels as she laughed. She would weave through the crowds, her subtle grace turned to the art of dance. A single white bloom would decorate her dark hair, adding its perfume to the night. The musicians would start and he would offer Mira his hand. Together, they would dance to the song of the jasmine flower.

On that night, she would love him.

Gareth closed his eyes and danced in time to music that was only in his thoughts.

"What are you up to?"

The voice was harsh, driving away the phantoms of distant memories. Gareth realised how strange he must look. He stopped, suddenly awkward, and looked for the owner of the voice. A man stood in the doorway. The angry look on the guy's face reminded

Gareth of Karl back at the start of his training. He glowered with undisguised hostility. A feeling of antagonism rose in Gareth, stirred up by some future sense. A name emerged from his jumbled memories: Corlion.

"Are you trying to seduce Mira?" Corlion asked, his dark brows knotted with anger.

Gareth couldn't really deny it.

"She's been through so much in her young life," said Corlion. "She's lost so much and taken on so much responsibility, she hasn't much innocence left. I'm not going to let you steal what remains."

"I'm not planning on stealing anything."

"You have no right to be here, no right to her."

"Rights? It's her choice who she spends time with."

"You're just some boy from another world, some upstart who works with her enemies and wants to sleep his way into the queen's authority."

Behind those words, he heard the echoes of a dozen future arguments. The anger would turn to hatred over time. Corlion would never forgive Gareth for daring to love his Mira. He felt the hatred reflecting back through the years and matched Corlion glare for glare.

"You know nothing about me. You don't get to say any of that. You don't get to decide what I should or shouldn't do."

"I know that some fighter from another universe shouldn't be worming his way in with the only royalty left here. You shouldn't be taking advantage of her kind heart."

"I'm not taking advantage!"

"So all that twirling was what?"

"That was... that was a bit of fun."

"Well, while you're having fun, some of us have a planet to govern."

The tension was a solid force between them, anger linking the pair. Was this circular causality again? Was he causing the hatred in the future because of his anger today? All he knew was a surging fury disproportionate to Corlion's words.

"You think I don't understand responsibilities? I have a world's survival resting on my actions."

"Which is why you chose to come here?"

"To save the life of a teammate! Perhaps you've forgotten what Mira did to Enrico?"

But the truth was, Gareth had almost forgotten it. The pain she had caused his friends was all but overwhelmed by the intoxication of her presence. In this moment, it all rushed back: Lizzie bleeding on the floor, Richard's panic, Enrico in the throne room. Gareth had been so concerned with wooing Mira that he had disregarded the fact that his friends were probably terrified for him.

"Mira is acting in the interests of justice," said Corlion.

"She wants revenge."

"And so you're manipulating her into thinking Amiron isn't so bad?"

"I'm not manipulating anyone!"

"But you're not denying your connection to the greatest enemy this world has ever known."

"Master Amiron is a hero to my world."

"He's a greedy, ambitious monster and you are just like him."

Gareth moved without thinking. He wasn't sure when his hands had formed into fists but now one shot out under the volition of his rage. His punch landed square on Corlion's jaw with enough force to knock him flat on his ass. He skidded across the floor, leaving a streak in the dust. Perhaps it was his own recent doubts that added fuel to the rage, but Gareth couldn't bear the thought of this man saying such things about his former mentor.

"You can insult me," Gareth said, "but I won't let you insult Master Amiron."

Gareth strode to the door. Corlion's voice chased him out.

"I won't let you have Mira! You hear me, boy? I won't let you win!"

Gareth knew that voice, just as he'd known the man's name. When he'd tranced to find the memory of Mira's armour, he'd heard that voice threatening him and the baby in her arms. They would be enemies and it had all started today, with that single punch.

He'd just endangered that unborn child.

Seventeen

First Date

The day after their dance, Gareth was invited to dine with Mira. He wasn't sure what to expect, knowing that he would be sharing a meal with royalty. Was it going to be a formal affair? Was he expected to observe any specific customs? In the end, a servant brought Gareth a much-needed change of clothes. The silky shirt smelt slightly musty at first. No doubt it had been pulled from an old supply, too impractical to be in regular use. Still, he enjoyed a hot bath and changed into what had been provided. His Defender uniform was taken away for cleaning.

Darkness fell outside and Gareth was led through the palace corridors to a small dining room. Everything was smoothly polished wood, clean and elegant. Gareth wondered if the room was more frequently used than other areas or if effort had been put into cleaning up for this date.

If it was a date. The word kept creeping into his mind but he couldn't be sure. There was one detail of the room's preparation that had Gareth leaning towards the conclusion that it was; a small vase of jasmine decorated the table.

Gareth stood alone in the room for some minutes, wondering about the etiquette of the situation. Then Mira swept in and he lost all capacity for rational thought. She wore a black dress decorated with red stitching. The sleek fabric clung to every curve. Her hair was twisted into a complicated knot and held to her head by a red clip. She caught the dazed look on Gareth's face and smiled, the expression lighting up her whole face.

"Do you approve?" she teased.

"I... yes."

"Tonight," she said, "we won't discuss politics or wars or Amiron. Tonight, I'd like us to get to know each other better."

So this was a date. Gareth agreed to her terms and they sat across from each other at one end of the rectangular table. When the food came, it was simple enough fare and by no means a feast. They ate a pleasant stew but Gareth noted that there was very little meat. Gareth asked why, careful of his phrasing so as not to cause offense.

"Meat is strictly rationed," Mira explained. "We can only kill livestock once it's past breeding."

She didn't explain further but Gareth could infer the rest. When the Outsiders burst through, all they'd want to do was eat. Crops, animals or people, they didn't care. If they emerged in farmland, they would eat whatever was slowest to run away. Civilians were evacuated as a priority, livestock could be sacrificed. Except that the losses would build up. Over time, there would be fewer animals to spare and the hunger would follow.

The conversation turned to less sensitive topics. Mira asked about Gareth's childhood and he found himself revealing everything. He hadn't spoken so openly about his family in a long time. Mira returned the favour, telling anecdotes of her father and brother. They shared distant hopes and bittersweet memories across the dinner table.

At one point, as Mira spoke of her brother, Gareth lay a comforting hand on hers. She didn't pull away.

"You miss him a lot?" Gareth asked.

She nodded, "Every day."

"I sometimes miss my brothers and sister, but my family was never that close. Karl and Lizzie mean more to me than my real siblings ever did."

"You miss them?"

"A little. But I know I'll see them again."

"So confident?"

"Yes."

Mira laughed at that, a merry, musical sound. She didn't get to laugh nearly often enough.

The door opened to admit a servant carrying their dessert. Mira snatched her hand from under Gareth's. Her pale cheeks were touched with pink at being caught with her guard down.

They ate their dessert, a fruity soup, in awkward silence. As they set their spoons aside, Mira started to hum. It was a slow, sweet tune that immediately danced across his memory and penetrated his heart. She was humming the song of the jasmine flower.

"Did he teach you that song?" Mira asked. It took Gareth a moment to realise that there was only one person she could mean: Amiron.

"He never taught me songs."

"Then how did you know it?"

"You taught me."

Mira looked angry at that simple statement, "I hadn't sung it in years until yesterday. I certainly never sang in front of you."

"That song's written across your heart."

Mira was rendered speechless by her confusion for several seconds. Gareth had to resist the urge to laugh at her expression.

"You are the strangest person I've ever known," Mira said. "You talk nonsense but the way you look sometimes, it's like you're looking at something that isn't there."

"Or something that is. I knew your heart from the moment I first saw you."

"How exactly did you do that?"

Gareth wasn't sure the right way to answer that. It wasn't the first time he'd been asked and it wouldn't be the last but he wasn't sure he'd ever figure out the best way to respond. He couldn't explain the change that had come over him but he couldn't stop acting on that change. He just had to help her accept that sometimes he knew things he shouldn't be able to.

"The portals changed me. They made me a different person, let me see things." He hesitated before continuing, "The portals changed Master Amiron in the same way."

"We agreed not to talk about him."

"I know but you have to understand. Whatever Master Amiron is now, he's not the same person who betrayed your father, any more than I'm the same boy who agreed to work for the Defenders out of desperation."

Gareth was trying to convince himself as much as he was Mira. Gareth knew first-hand how much a portal accident could alter a person. Was it really so incredible to believe that Master Amiron's change had been as dramatic, if not more? Every moment that Gareth had known him, Master Amiron had been focused on helping people, protecting others, defending the world against the Outsiders. Why shouldn't Gareth put faith in that?

"I suppose you've seen his heart too?" Mira asked.

"I know Master Amiron for the man he is now; you know him only from distant memories and records of a man who was since reborn."

"No one can change that much. Once a traitor, always a traitor!"

"He died inside the portal! I'm not talking metaphors here. He literally died somewhere in the nothingness between our worlds. He fell through into my world and was resurrected a new man, a new person. I know what it was like for him because I've been through the same. I died!"

That was the first time Gareth had really spoken about the accident except to Amiron. The Defenders shied away from the subject. No one else knew at all. It was strange to acknowledge his death in words, as though saying it made the event somehow more real and put another brick in the wall between who he was and who he had been.

"You... died?"

"Yes. Master Amiron brought me back, he used the energy of the exploded portal to twist time around me. Since then I've been... different. Different from every other person on my whole planet."

This time, as silence settled over the table, it was Mira who reached out a comforting hand. Her soft, warm fingers rested gently on his arm, as if they belonged there.

"I was born different," she said. "I was raised knowing that I would rule this planet and that set me apart."

Her words stirred the murky waters of his memory, bringing to the surface a fragment of another conversation, a future piece of advice from his master.

"He will be born different," Master Amiron would say. "You and I were born human. We remember what it was like and so we can pretend, even to ourselves, that we still are. He will have no such luxury."

Gareth would have loved to have tracked that moment of memory through the dimensions, to figure out who Amiron was talking about. But there was Mira's hand on his arm, holding him firmly in the present. He couldn't drift into future recollections during his first date with the girl he would love. He'd learned, or would learn, that people thought it rude when he started staring into space, focusing on past or future.

"At least you're still human," Gareth said. "I'm not so sure I am anymore."

"Then what are you?"

"I don't know."

* * *

Trust was dangerous. Mira knew that. Her father had trusted Amiron and he'd betrayed their entire world. Mira's father and brother had both perished because of the Outsiders, because of the war Amiron started. Thousands of others had died and millions had suffered. An act of trust could crumble an empire.

Yet she wanted to trust.

As she'd looked across the table at Gareth, hearing him talk about Amiron and accidents, she'd wanted to believe him. Despite the hard lessons taught by Amiron's betrayal, she wanted to trust that Gareth meant everything he said. When he'd looked at her, she'd seen tenderness, seen kindness and seen something buried deep in those dark eyes.

When he'd spoken of his family, she'd wanted to erase the pain of his past and she'd felt the echoes of her own suffering in her heart. The two of them, cut off from the rest of their worlds, sought out the comfort of a familiar soul.

As she returned to her rooms, she had to remind herself that he was an enemy, a prisoner here. Yet her pulse had quickened at his reaction to her dress. She'd wanted him to be impressed and she'd seen the effect she'd had. She'd heard him talking about songs and hearts and she'd dared imagine what else he might say.

This was foolish!

She reached her suite and shut the door firmly behind her. She caught sight of her reflection and felt a rush of anger. Quickly, she pulled the clip from her hair and let the strands fall around her shoulders. She was acting like a lovesick schoolgirl, dressing up for some handsome boy who knew the right words to say.

She was a queen. She couldn't afford to go dizzy over anyone, let alone someone she barely knew. There were a million reasons why it was ridiculous that she should ever feel anything towards Gareth,

Amiron being first and foremost of those reasons. But she couldn't help her mind returning to him. Her breath caught when he walked in the room and she felt the flutter of butterflies in her stomach when she thought about him.

She paced the room. At least, that was the idea. The skirt of her dress was too tight about her legs for her to get a good stride. It was a ridiculous outfit. Why had she even considered wearing it?

She'd worn it for Gareth. She'd worn it because he'd called her beautiful with a look in his eyes that said he meant it. She'd been called beautiful before, but she'd always felt that they'd only said it because she was the queen and it was expected. When Gareth had said it, he'd breathed the word like something precious. Mira had basked in the glow of his stare for a minute and wanted to feel that again.

The best thing to do was to avoid him. He was only here a couple more weeks. Then either Amiron would come and Gareth would go home or Mira would...

Could she kill him? After he'd saved her life, danced with her and shared her table?

She felt another flush of anger.

He was manipulating her! He must be. It was the only explanation for the way she was feeling. He knew his life was in danger so he was trying to get inside her head. He was playing with her emotions so that, when the time came, she wouldn't be able to go through with it.

Well, she'd prove him wrong. If, when the deadline came, Amiron hadn't come to make the exchange, Mira would kill Gareth. She'd make it quick, as painless as possible, but she would do it.

No matter what seductive games Gareth might play, Mira would still end his life.

Eighteen

Where it all Began

One room Gareth found in his wanderings about the palace was obviously a training room of sorts. It had a smooth, empty floor, like in one of the small training rooms back home, but with high windows overlooking the city. The windows were glazed with stained glass, spilling rainbows onto the polished floor when the sun was at the right angle. A rack of ornate metal held training weapons. Gareth ran his hand along a row of hilts of wooden swords and knives. There were no claws among the training weapons; perhaps it was just Mira who favoured the clawed gloves.

He picked up a wooden sword and ran through some practice sequences. Once his heart was beating hard and his skin pricked with sweat, he put the blade back and went to the centre of the room, slowing everything down again.

His friends were out there somewhere, separated by the walls of dimensions. He was sure they were worried about him, especially Karl and Lizzie. Gareth had promised to be there for the wedding, clinging to the memory of Lizzie in her wedding dress. He knew, with all the faith he was capable of, that he would be there on the wedding day. He could also picture Cassie in her Defender uniform, despite the young woman being a long way from ready for his test. He could picture Enrico, showing off his scars to some random girl in a bar in Vegas, the scars he'd received from Mira. Gareth summoned these images to the front of his mind, knowing that they had to come to pass. Every future memory he'd ever experienced had come to be; these must too. He would be going back home. He would be with his friends again soon enough.

He held those thoughts as he let his mind sink deeper, seeking the radiance that would guide him forward. His breathing slowed, his heart beats sounding loud in his ears, cutting him off from the rest of the world. He gathered his soul in on himself, opening his eyes to a universe of light.

He moved through the web of connected energies, reaching for his friends. He felt them so close, a shadow's breadth away. He could almost see Karl beside him. If he could pick the right direction, Gareth felt that he could just step and be back where he belonged. The portals were just a door, but the way was there.

Gareth could see Karl, so close now. He was sitting in one of the small practice rooms, his legs folded on the floor. Gareth knew Karl was trying to do one of the relaxation exercises that he'd never been particularly good at. Karl must be trying to see the flow of dimensions as Master Amiron had taught them.

Gareth had a strange feeling that Karl was trying to look for him. A whole world away, Karl was hunting with his mind because he couldn't with his body.

Gareth reached out, his hand moving glacially slowly. He hardly dared breathe until his hand touched a shoulder. He could feel the fabric of Karl's shirt, just barely, beneath his fingers.

"It's alright," Gareth murmured. "I'm alright."

Karl's eyes snapped open. For a fraction of a second, their eyes met.

"What are you doing?"

Gareth was completely back in the palace, the force of his return painful on a nearly physical level. He gasped for a moment, regaining his composure and his sense of place. Then he looked to the door and saw Mira standing there. She was dressed in her armour, her helmet under one arm, as she looked at Gareth in confusion. For some reason, the thought of lying didn't even occur to him.

"I was trying to talk to my friends," Gareth said, "to let them know that I'm OK. I don't want them to worry too much."

"Can you do that? Can you talk to them?"

"Not easily. I'm not sure if Karl heard me or not."

"How is that possible? You need portals to get through to other worlds."

Gareth took a deep breath, trying to form words into an order that could make sense of things most humans couldn't comprehend. They were three-dimensional beings, not meant to wander beyond their bounds.

"There are ways," he said slowly, "to see where other worlds press against this one. Your world and mine are close. I was… trying to peer through the cracks."

"You were sort of… glowing," Mira said. Gareth thought of the light he saw, brighter where other worlds were pressed against the surface of his own. He must truly have been pushing through a crack between worlds, a part of him inside the boundaries.

"The human brain can't quite process it so our minds interpret it in a way we can. That's what you saw."

"Could you teach me? Or is this a side-effect of your change?"

"Yes and yes. It is possible to be taught but it became so much easier because of what happened to me."

"Will you show me?"

There was an eagerness, almost hunger in her voice. Gareth wouldn't have been able to deny her anything she so obviously wanted. He gave a smile and nodded.

"It's easiest in a place where lots of portals have opened. The boundaries become weaker."

Mira hesitated before saying, "I know just the place."

One arm still clutched the helmet of her armour, but the other hand she held out to him. Gareth took it. He wondered if this was just a difference in the cultures of their worlds. Perhaps holding hands was something that meant nothing here, beyond a guide to help him find his way to an unfamiliar place. Or perhaps it meant the same to her as it did to him. He felt the sleek metal scales of her glove, warmed by the heat beneath it. He wished he could tear the glove off and touch skin but, for now, he was content to have this trace of contact.

The practice room was forgotten, Mira leading him down through dark passages. He saw a dusty stairway, a path cleaned through the middle by the frequent passage of someone who'd found their way here recently and returned often. Someone came this way often, so why had no one attempted to clear the dust which must have lain here ages? The staircase wound downwards, stone walls pressing in around, lit by dim bulbs, infrequent and occasionally dead. The ornate decorations of the rest of the palace had vanished, leaving only chill rock that seemed to sap the warmth from the blood. Gareth kept his hand in Mira's, even as they were forced to go single file by the narrowing stairs.

At last, they emerged into a long hallway that stretched away into darkness. Mira let go of his hand to open a small cupboard, pulling out a light that dangled from a handle. It reminded Gareth of old-fashioned oil lamps, but Mira illuminated it with the flick of a switch and spilled a powerful white light into the hallway. Again, Gareth saw the path through the dust, wide enough to be just one person, but the ground was scuffed enough to evidence more than one passage. Mira came down here alone and often.

Gareth suspected he was the first person she had allowed to come with her.

He walked beside her, their feet cutting a new pathway through the dust. He considered taking her hand again, but didn't want her to think it was because he was afraid of this dark and abandoned passageway.

It didn't take long to reach their destination. Gareth saw their route written in the disturbed dirt. How many years had this place lain undisturbed until Mira had chanced on it? He suspected he knew the answer but he didn't search his memories because he knew he wouldn't like the truth. Future knowledge hung just in front of him, laced with bitter pain.

Mira leaned heavily on a metal door, it swinging slowly in its frame to reveal a dark room beyond. The gloom was filled with shapes, most dulled with dust and cobwebs. Mira reached along one wall for a switch and soon Gareth was blinking in unexpected brightness while she deactivated her lamp.

As his eyes adjusted, Gareth saw machines which were painfully familiar. The differences seemed to make the similarities more obvious. There was a circle of devices stuck to one wall. There was a screen bearing a map of the world, virtually identical to his geographically, ready to light up with a location when a portal opened. There were consoles and controls that powered the machines which could pierce holes in the universe. Even the layout was similar. Master Amiron had designed the control room of their base to mirror the design of this room.

"This is where your master destroyed my world," Mira said.

Gareth didn't try to argue or deny it. He moved past her, past the silent machines, to the wide circle of the wall. The portal generators were still there, perhaps drained of power, perhaps rusted to uselessness. Or perhaps they functioned perfectly. He ignored them, laying his hand in the centre of the circle, the point on the wall where the lines of energy would meet and explode outwards. His skin tingled with a contact that wasn't physical.

He barely had to shift focus to see the fracture in this world.

"Never open a portal here!" he said.

"Why?" Mira asked. She was standing close to the wall so that she could see Gareth's face as he stared at what must look, to her, like just a patch of tired paint.

"The other worlds are pressed too closely here," he answered. "The boundary's weak. Too many portals, too much power has been through this point in space and it's fragile. Another portal could shatter the walls between this world and the others."

A portal was like poking a hole through a sheet. It could be done to allow a little passage. Afterwards, the sheet could heal itself so that the wound was barely noticeable except to one who knew the dimensions well. This fracture could become something else entirely, not a small hole but a massive gash. This could tear apart the walls around an entire world, leaving them exposed to everything that lay beyond it.

Gareth knew, deep in his soul, that this had happened before. This was exactly what had happened on the Outsiders' world. One portal too many had opened in a place where the barriers were weak. The walls had torn apart. The Outsiders' world had begun to bleed into those nearby. That was when the portals had gone out of control. That was when the attacks had become random and caused this civilisation to spiral into the dust.

Gareth also knew, somehow, that the force of that gash opening had been what had changed Master Amiron. He'd been caught up in it, flung through the nothingness into a whole new universe and a whole new life.

He'd had no idea what would happen.

Tears pricked at Gareth's eyelids as the knowledge rose to the surface of his mind. Master Amiron hadn't known enough about the portals, not then, to realise the consequences of what he was doing. He'd known enough to create the portals but hadn't understood properly the physics behind it, the dangers involved. The random portals, the unpredictable attacks, the Outsiders charging through into more worlds than just his own. He could never have guessed any of that was possible.

"What's wrong, Gareth?" Mira asked.

Gareth shook his head. He couldn't explain the sensation of understanding rising from his mingled past and future memories. He couldn't explain the pain of knowing exactly how Master Amiron had caused so much suffering.

"Are we in danger?" she asked.

Gareth shook his head again, "Not as long as this stuff stays switched off."

"The portal tech's been off since Amiron vanished. He locked the systems to his DNA print. The only time it's been used since he left was when I went through to your world."

"Coming through alone into a hostile world," Gareth commented.

Mira went to one of the machines, touching a console that had been swept of most of its dusty coating.

"The computer stored the coordinates of the last portal opened here," she said, "the one Amiron left through, but it wouldn't make a lock. Something was interfering. Then one day, I came in and the screen was saying that the interference was gone. I didn't know why or how or how long it would last, I just knew I couldn't waste what might be my only chance to find Amiron and make him pay."

Gareth could have laughed. Brave to the point of foolishness, desperate for justice for so many lost lives. He would have done the same, in her place.

But however foolish she might have been then, she was listening to him now. She reached behind the machine and yanked out the cable connecting it to the power supply. No automatic alerts now. The portal would stay dead.

"What else have you switched on?" Gareth asked.

Mira crossed to a small rectangle of black that sat on one of the tables, the surface scuffed and smeared where hands had manipulated the device through the dust. She swiped a point that looked, to Gareth, just like the rest, but lights flickered on along the front of the device. An image rose up from the top, like a projection onto a screen, but without any visible surface to hold the picture. Puzzled and slightly amused, Gareth waved a hand through the air above the device, his fingers passing right through the projected picture of his mentor.

"The bastard kept records," Mira said. "He recorded everything he did. Opening the portals, letting in the Outsiders, every single piece of treachery! He left it here to taunt us."

"No. He left it as a warning." Again, the knowledge came from the depths of Gareth's mind where he hadn't been aware of it moments before.

"Master Amiron left the recordings here in case something happened to him, in case the Outsiders killed him. He left it tied into the family's DNA so that your father would be able to learn the truth and know how to defend against any remaining Outsiders Amiron's team hadn't stopped. But the accident changed everything. Amiron never imagined the random portals. He never suspected that the dimensions were beyond his control."

"His pride destroyed my world."

Gareth's Story

Part Two

Gareth enjoyed his time with the Defenders. He didn't enjoy the chores he was forced to do, but he was learning more than just his official lessons. He was learning about fighting and about the organisation of this team. Rank among the Defenders was fairly informal. Boron was undisputedly the second-in-command to Master Amiron and there were some who, through skill and experience, had earned the right to be called senior Defenders. Beyond that, there was nothing official, though it was clear to Gareth, even as a menial worker, that there was a hierarchy. In the field, some had authority over others.

Gareth became curious how this order was established. That was how he learned of the tournament. Every Defender took part. It was a way for them to showcase their skill to each other. No one outside of the team would be a witness, the results would never be published, but showing skill in the tournament was a way of demonstrating worth. Receiving praise from Master Amiron or those most senior was worth more than a medal and, among the newer team members, could be almost a promotion.

Training increased in intensity as the tournament approached. The most skilled strove for a chance at the winning spot. Those who'd joined the team most recently were determined to show their abilities at their finest. The whole base, from the most senior Defenders to the most menial of workers, was engaged in speculation over who would win. Among those who knew they were nowhere near the front running, surreptitious gambling emerged over who would take first place.

Gareth had to see the tournament. It wasn't just that he wanted to, he knew he had to be there, somehow, to witness the immense skill of these great warriors.

Richard found him trying to force the tracker bracelet over his wrist and he was forced to explain what he was trying to do. Richard, who had never understood his obsession with watching the Defenders fight, sighed and agreed to help. He was able to hack into the main computer systems in a moment and set up a fake report that would pronounce Gareth safely inside his room, regardless of his real location.

So Gareth was able to sneak down into the large training hall where the tournament would take place. He positioned himself in the store cupboard, his eye to the crack to get a view of the centre of the room.

As the Defenders filed in, chatting or warming up, Gareth found his view rapidly obscured. As the tournament started, Gareth was staring at the uniformed backs of the Defenders more often than he could even glimpse the fighting within. But he hadn't come this far to give up so easily. He used the equipment in the cupboard, shifting the mats and building a pile of training weapons on top. His cautious noises were drowned out by the cheers and shouts of the Defenders as another pair took their turn.

Gareth stood on his pile of gear, pressed against the roof of the cupboard. Now he looked through the crack and saw over the sea of heads to the wide circle where two men sparred with lightning speed.

To Gareth, whose training consisted of experimenting in the privacy of his room, the strength and skill of those fighting was incredible. Their limbs were blurs that could shift direction half-way through a move and strike out from unexpected angles. They leapt and dodged, avoiding the rapid attacks, blocking with moves so fast their reflexes seemed almost precognition. Gareth had his eye pressed to the crack, drinking up every instant of the sight.

Pair after pair faced each other across the training hall. Even to Gareth's untrained eye, some clearly had more skill than others. He watched Lizzie's speed and grace. He watched Karl's precision. He watched Enrico's strength. He saw them all and longed to be like them.

Tension rose as matches were concluded and more and more of the Defenders were eliminated from the tournament. Even the senior Defenders, despite their experience, were forced to bow to victors in their turns. As the final match began, Karl against Lizzie, anticipation was a solid force. Everyone was caught up in the excitement. Even Gareth, shut in the darkness of the cupboard, couldn't avoid being part of it. He watched Lizzie and Karl bow to each. He watched the first testing blows, then the fight began in earnest.

His heart beat frantically as the pair danced across the smooth floor. Strikes and blocks, kicks and dodges. The pair seemed to move as one, each responding as though to the other's thoughts. Gareth didn't know then that the two were a couple and practiced together regularly. All he knew was that they seemed to be flowing around each other. The match was so finely balanced that it seemed it would take just a breath to tilt it in the favour of one or the other. Gareth could hardly breathe for the pumping adrenaline, scarcely blinking in case he missed a crucial instant.

When Karl dealt the final blow, half the room yelled, each in triumph or commiseration. Gareth felt himself such a part of the fight that he punched the air.

The movement sent him off-balance. His precarious perch was lost and he tumbled onto the stacked mats, the practice weapons clattering around him.

Then the cupboard doors opened and Gareth was blinking up into the faces of the Defenders, first confused, then angry.

Gareth found himself hauled to a smaller room with Master Amiron. Karl was there as well, arms folded, a fierce glare locked on Gareth. Gareth hadn't felt so small since he'd sat in the police interview room.

"I'm sorry," he said. "I just wanted to watch the tournament."

"He's obviously a spy," Karl said.

"I'm not. I just wanted to watch. I just wanted..." He fell silent.

"Wanted what?" Master Amiron asked.

"To be like you. To fight like you."

There was a long silence, broken only by Karl's disdainful humph. Master Amiron was looking at Gareth, his eyes fixed on his so strongly that it seemed he was looking through into Gareth's soul. Gareth suspected later that Amiron had been hunting out traces of future memories.

"Very well," Master Amiron said. "If you want to fight like a Defender, you shall have your chance. Karl will train you."

"What?" two voices chorused, Karl's furious, Gareth's thrilled.

Karl hated Gareth passionately from the first moment. He would obey any order given to him by Master Amiron, so he arrived each afternoon in the small training room to teach the basics of fighting. But Master Amiron had been unspecific as to methods. Karl couldn't refuse to teach, but he could try to make Gareth choose to quit.

The training sessions were a step away from torture. Karl would assign Gareth the most painful strengthening exercises he could think of, ostensibly to build up the required muscles. When stretching, he pushed Gareth to the point it felt like his joints would snap out of place, all in the name of increasing his flexibility. When they sparred together, he held nothing back, dealing harsh blows for the slightest mistakes, stating that it was more mercy than he could expect from the Outsiders.

Gareth learned later that there had been spies. People had accepted the role of workers to try to steal the secrets of the portal technology for monetary gain. Karl believed that Gareth was one of them. After all, he was a known thief. The simplest explanation for him sneaking about was that someone was paying him to find out information on the Defender's technology. Karl was certain that Gareth's claim about wanting to learn was a lie and he wanted to end the charade as quickly as possible.

But Gareth wasn't going to give up. He had been given this one chance to do something he was passionate about. This was the first time someone had offered him an opportunity like this in his life. Nothing in the world would stop him from seizing it, no matter how many bruises he ended up with after the training sessions.

Gareth thought that Karl would become easier once he got over his annoyance at having to teach. But days went by and still the pain continued. Now though, Gareth could see that he was learning. He was improving rapidly under the brutal training. He was even working on techniques in his room when he should have been doing his real work, just to try and prevent Karl getting in so many blows in the training.

At last, nearly a month after these daily sessions had begun, Gareth was waiting in the small training room. The door opened and Karl came in.

"Here." Karl threw something which Gareth caught by reflex, nearly squashing it in the process. It was a cupcake.

"Is this some sort of test?" he asked.

"I heard today was your birthday," Karl answered. "People should get cake on their birthday."

Gareth had to do a mental calculation to realise that Karl was probably right. He hadn't needed to look at the date in a while. He wasn't even sure what day of the week it was. But the length of time he'd been here would be about right for today to be his seventeenth birthday. He looked at the cupcake for a while, surprised that Karl could offer this hint of kindness.

"It's not poisoned," Karl said. "I thought you'd quit after two days. I never imagined you'd keep training this long and I can think of only three possible explanations. One: you're incredibly stubborn. Two: you're a masochist. Three: you genuinely want to be a Defender."

"Or all three?" suggested Gareth. There was a slight trace of a smile touching Karl's lips for a fraction of a second. Then he was serious again.

"I have been very harsh on you," Karl said, "because I doubted your commitment. I was wrong. And if you are still crazy enough to want to be a Defender and if you deserve it, I'll make sure you get it."

"Thank you," Gareth replied.

"Don't thank me yet. This doesn't mean I'm going to start going easy on you."

But things did get easier. The exercises were as painful as ever, the sparring as brutal, but Karl's demeanour had changed. He'd offer praise when Gareth did well. He gave encouragement. He hinted, on multiple occasions, that Gareth might have the skills needed after all.

Then, one training session, Master Amiron came to watch. He stood at the side of the room in silence as Karl and Gareth went through their usual routine. When they were done, Karl looked to him for approval and got a quiet nod.

"I think it's time Gareth faces the test."

Nineteen

Opening Eyes

Gareth was spending a great deal of time in Amiron's old lab, Mira apparently unconcerned about the risk of him opening a portal home. No doubt, she recognised how truly scared he was of the dangers of a portal opening here. He didn't touch most of the equipment but he watched the records. Each word sounded familiar as he heard it, each account sifting through his memories to the surface, bringing with them the sense of pain and betrayal. He'd known what Master Amiron had done since the moment he'd recognised Mira but he hadn't really felt it until now. Watching the recordings, listening to his mentor talking about opening the portals, the death counts, was heart-breaking. He'd known the truth, but now he was seeing the man Amiron had been.

As he watched Amiron talking about an attack in which three families had lost their lives, speaking about the necessary sacrifices in the cause of change, Gareth had understood fully how Mira could hate him. Tears flowed down Gareth's cheeks as he forced himself to see. Gareth wished for the innocence of ignorance, for that time when he'd believed Master Amiron to be the very definition of heroic.

The image stilled and sank back into the projection box, leaving blank air. It would be a simple matter to reach out and start the next log entry, but Gareth remained motionless, sitting in the very chair his mentor had once used while describing his crimes.

Amiron spoke in the records about his plans, about how he was winning the people to his side, positioning himself as the hero. He was manipulating everyone. He talked quietly about Janon and about the public opinion. Amiron had been playing the people, guessing their

193

reactions and using them to project an image of himself as flimsy as the recording hologram.

Had he done the same on Earth? Gareth had been fairly young when the first invasion had started, young enough that he hadn't started working yet and so had been able to watch the TV in the evenings. The news reports were everywhere, the kids talked about them at school. Everyone all around the world had talked about Master Amiron as a saviour, a great man with the power to stop these monsters. Gareth felt like he was the betrayer for thinking these thoughts but he couldn't help wondering. Had Amiron just decided to play the hero on another world?

Gareth had been so naïve. He'd have followed Amiron anywhere as his personal hero. Maybe that was why Amiron had chosen him. Nothing to do with the portal accident or his gifts. Maybe Amiron had chosen him as successor because Gareth was stupid enough to believe. Gareth had never questioned Amiron, not for one moment, and now he knew that he'd been as fooled as the people of Mira's world.

There was still a piece of him wanting to believe. It was getting harder each day, with each new recording, but that fragile hope was still there. A core of faith held on despite the evidence assailing it from all sides. Gareth wished Master Amiron were here. He wanted to ask, needed to know once and for all, whether he was now the man he'd been. Maybe the accident really had changed Amiron completely, made him into the man Gareth had come to know. Maybe Gareth wasn't a fool and Amiron had transformed into the great hero who had risked everything for a strange world. Maybe.

Gareth became gradually aware that he wasn't alone and reached up to dry his eyes, despite knowing it was too late. He'd been seen crying. Still, he turned to the doorway to greet Mira with a dry face. He wasn't sure how long she'd been watching him for.

"Do you understand now what he is?" she asked.

"Perhaps that's who he was," Gareth answered, trying to believe it, "not who he is."

There was a moment of silence, neither of them in a hurry to continue the argument. Instead, Mira asked him to continue teaching her to see the boundaries between worlds. She wasn't making much progress. That wasn't surprising, since most of the Defenders had been trying for years with limited success. Gareth had been able to see almost nothing before his accident. Still, they stood together as Mira slowed her breathing and Gareth tried to guide her into that state of mind where it all came clear.

He went through it himself, sinking into that state of being, trying to urge her into the same, so that she too could bathe in the golden light. They'd spent hours like this, with Mira staring at the patch of wall that glared out to Gareth with its menace. Sometimes, Gareth wondered if she only continued with the practice because she wanted an excuse to spend time with him.

On this occasion, Gareth had his hand on hers, as though he could pull her with him when she saw. Perhaps he could because, this time, she stared at the wall and announced that she thought she could see something.

Mira reached out, Gareth's hand still resting on hers, and touched the point in the centre of the web of golden light. Her hand reached that exact spot at the heart of the circle where the walls were weakest. Gareth was deep in it, barely aware of anything but the waves of gold and Mira's skin against his.

The images rushed up through his thoughts.

He saw a high, flat rooftop beneath a grey sky tinged with faint green, like an old bruise. Stretching out to the horizon was a city, skyscrapers towering above the distant ground. Wind buffeted him, carrying with it a taste of poison. There was a sword in his hand, his other clenched tightly in another's. Mira's. They stood together beneath this alien sky as Outsiders poured from a doorway in a small hatch. They kept coming in a lethal hoard, more piling up the stairway behind. His body was aching, his sword hanging from a tired arm. Yet more were coming. A single thought came, as though carried by the wind:

So this is how we die.

Mira snatched her hand away from the portal scar. The images vanished, the dimension light faded, and the pair of them were once again in the old lab. Mira was pale and trembling, looking at Gareth with wide and frightened eyes.

"I think I saw the future," she said. "I think I saw my death."

Gareth longed to comfort her, to say that these things were so easily misinterpreted, to tell her that he would never let anything happen to her. But in the memory, he'd been so certain. He was used to certainty. Living with memories of the future had taken away the element of surprise, leaving him confident of the outcome of almost anything he did. He'd glimpsed the same future Mira had and drawn the same conclusion.

All he could do was reach out a hand to her shoulder, hoping his presence would comfort her. She turned to him, flinging her arms around him and burying her face in his shoulder. He held her gently as she sobbed, one hand stroking her silky hair. He breathed the intoxication of her scent, as glad as she that he wasn't alone.

"I don't want to die," she said at last.

"At least we'll die fighting Outsiders."

She nodded and wiped her eyes with the heel of her hand.

"I don't want to see anymore," she said. She turned and walked from the room without giving him a moment to say anything else. Gareth stood a while longer, with only the ghosts of his future death and the monster Amiron had been.

He couldn't take it either.

Gareth walked out, leaving the lab behind him. He'd seen all he could cope with about what Master Amiron had done. Now he really wanted to hit something.

He found his way back to the training room, aware of the familiarity of the route. He didn't even have to try and remember; his feet found their way without thought. Surely he couldn't get so used to this palace in a month. Surely it would take longer. Surely that meant that the moment on the rooftop and the looming darkness wasn't the end for him. He wished he could convince himself of that, but with each day that passed, he was aware of the shadow growing in his mind. Sometime soon, very soon, would come a moment beyond which he couldn't remember.

He tried to believe it wasn't what he thought. Perhaps he could change things. Perhaps the rooftop wouldn't happen the way he'd remembered. But every single memory he'd experienced had occurred, even those he'd tried to fight. What had been a comfort, like believing that he'd make it back for the wedding, now became a curse. Events would lead him to the other world with Mira and together they'd make a desperate stand. And there his memories of tomorrow would stop.

Gareth stood in the training room, seeing the fighting gear that was stacked around, including pads for punching. He worked on those for a while, building up a sweat until his arms ached and his knuckles protested against the battering. It let him put his thoughts to sleep, pouring himself into the physical to set his mind at rest.

But when he stopped, gasping for air and desperate for a drink, those thoughts returned. What bothered him most of all was his own doubts. Since the accident, he'd been confident of everything. Every choice he made, he knew the consequences of. Every day, he knew how the day would end. Every moment, he knew what was coming next, the good and the bad. He might forget details, like a man misplacing his keys the moment after putting them down, and the more distant memories grew fuzzy rapidly so not many events stayed clear across time. But it was always overlaid on a background of confidence, of understanding that he didn't have to try to achieve.

Now he didn't understand. Every day, darkness crept closer. Every day, he feared how little time he might have with Mira. Every day, he became less certain how things would end.

He missed his friends. Karl had been there for him for years, helping him when things got difficult. It had been Karl who'd helped him through his doubts when he'd first become a Defender, before everything had changed. Gareth wished to have Karl beside him now, to help him through these fears.

Gareth sighed and then turned to the empty space in the middle of the room, no doubt usually employed for sparring. Now he let himself sink into the golden glow. He wasn't sure which he was reaching for, the future or the present, he just knew that he was desperately searching. He let the lines of dimension boundaries flow around him and through him, pushing deeper into the haze. Soon, the room around him was all but concealed by the flow. He guided that flow around him just as he guided himself through it, feeling the subtle differences of the worlds as he brushed by. He opened his eyes to the universe and looked through the veil of gold into the distance.

Fragments came to him, like images out of dream. He saw Karl and Lizzie in their wedding clothes. He saw Cassie in her new uniform, a dark metal sword in her hands. He tasted the sweet tenderness of Mira's lips and smelt the scent of jasmine on the night air. He saw Master Amiron, felt his mentor's strong arms around him. He even saw his sister, saw her smile a greeting at him. Memories of things yet to come, things to guide him forward. But beyond them all, he saw the emptiness. That wall of darkness barred his way but somewhere, sometime soon before he reached it, he caught the quiet memory of Amiron's fear. Gareth heard Master Amiron admit that he expected to die.

* * *

Mira couldn't shake the vision from her mind. She'd seen through her own eyes, felt her own fear like an echo bouncing back through time. No matter how many times she told herself that it was a trick or just her imagination, she couldn't be rid of it.

She had no idea where that place was but was certain that it was nowhere on her world. She didn't think it was Gareth's world either. That left one probability and the thought chilled her to the core. The Outsiders' world. She would be there with Gareth and they would fight the Outsiders to their deaths.

That was the other part of the vision that kept coming back to her, no matter how she tried to distract herself or bury her thoughts in work. In the premonition, she'd been holding Gareth's hand and it had felt natural. Maybe she should let go of her fears and let herself feel.

It was obvious he wanted her. She could see it in his eyes sometimes. She would catch him watching her and she wanted to watch him back.

It was impossible to think of him as an enemy now. After she'd caught him crying in the lab, she couldn't believe that he was some evil fiend in league with a monster. Maybe he really had been as deceived as she'd been.

They were alike in so many ways, cut off from their own people by their status, carrying responsibilities for the lives of others. But when he smiled at her, she was just a girl in the presence of a guy. She could, for a brief moment, forget about duty and rank. She could just be a person.

She wanted to feel that way. She hadn't known until she'd met Gareth how empty she'd been. Always, there had been advisors and ministers. There were people she considered friends, like Corlion who she'd always turned to for advice. But they were always separate. She always had to be aware of her position, of how things would seem. Appearance mattered so much. The queen could never be vulnerable, never relax, never just be a person.

How strange that she could find so much with a man from another world. When she was with him, there was no need for act. She could just be herself.

Yet, no matter what girlish fantasies she imagined, she was aware of the passing days and that their time was coming to a close. Corlion took pains to remind her of that fact, advising her that she shouldn't let herself grow too close to the prisoner. Corlion had been the one she'd turned to when she'd first uncovered the truth about Amiron. She'd listened to him then but she couldn't listen to him now.

Every time she thought of Gareth, she got butterflies. She craved the sight of his smile and wanted to be the one who put it on his lips. She wanted to be with him so much that she struggled to think of anything else when he wasn't there. Time spent with him just vanished, flying past so quickly that it seemed they'd barely begun to speak when it was time to part again. She wondered what he was doing whenever she wasn't with him and his face was constantly in her thoughts.

She tried to stop the flow of her thoughts, tried to shut him out of her mind. But his company was like a drug that kept drawing her in.

Twenty

Jasmine Kisses

There was always a mountain of work still to be done on Mira's desk. No matter what hours she put in, more always came to fill the gaps so it seemed she could never make a dent in the pile. For once though, she didn't mind. She could slip away from her work for a brief time and know that the world wouldn't end if she spent a few minutes doing something she wanted to do, being with someone she wanted to be with. There were moments of guilt for letting a few things slip or delegating to her ministers, but those moments were overwhelmed by the rush of joy when she got to spend time with Gareth.

In her position, romance wasn't a luxury she'd ever indulged in. She'd never imagined it could feel like this. Even as she sat at her desk working, she found herself thinking about him at random moments, smiling at the mere idea of being in his presence. He seemed like everything she could have wanted in a man, brave and kind, loyal to his friends, dedicated to protecting his world. It didn't matter if she indulged slightly; it was only for a short time.

She tried to push that thought away but it kept coming back. Just a short time until she'd promised she'd kill him.

There came a polite tap on the door to her study. At her instruction, the door opened and Corlion came in. Mira made a point of finishing reading the page she was on in the report in front of her. She didn't want Corlion to realise she'd been thinking about Gareth again. When she'd finished, scribbling a note on the bottom of the report and setting it in the completed pile, she looked up at him with a calm greeting.

"Mira, I'm concerned about you," he said. "I'm worried about you and this stranger."

"There's nothing to be concerned about."

"There's something not normal about him."

Mira couldn't deny that. There was something amazing in the way he could see into the heart of things, see the path of the portals. She'd known almost at once that he was special.

"Look, Mira, I don't like the way you're spending so much time with him. You don't act the same when you're around him and I don't trust it."

"You don't trust me?"

"No. I don't trust him. It's like he's mesmerising you or something and you don't even see it."

Mira laughed. Mesmerising was one way of putting it. She'd never had a chance for romance before. It was no wonder Corlion didn't recognise the effects on her. She dismissed his worry, smiling again at the thought of Gareth.

"I'm serious, Mira," Corlion went on. "You're normally so sensible but it's like you've forgotten all your doubts since he came here. A month ago, this boy was your enemy now... now you seem smitten with him. It's not natural. There's something about him which just isn't right."

"If I didn't know better, I'd say you were jealous."

Corlion's hesitation lasted a moment too long.

Mira looked up at Corlion, seeing the way he avoided her eyes, the nervous wringing of his hands. He was jealous. Months of past conversations flowed across her memory, words almost said and feelings nearly voiced. She wondered how she'd been so oblivious to it before. Maybe that was Gareth too; by making her think about such feelings she was able to recognise them now in her old friend. Now she could see it clearly, his distrust of Gareth was just a manifestation of his desire to be close to her.

"Corlion, I'm sorry. I just... don't see you that way."

He was older than her by several years. He'd been her teacher when she'd still been a girl, struggling under the weight of a crown. She couldn't see him in any other light.

"Mira, you need to be with someone you can trust, someone who'll look after you, help you, someone who understands the duties you must perform. I can be that someone, Mira, not this stranger who worked for your enemies. I love you, Mira."

Mira looked at Corlion's face, seeing the desperation and the desire. He was putting his whole heart out there between them and Mira felt like a monster for what she had to do next. She couldn't accept what he was offering her.

Mira stood slowly and walked around the desk. She lay a hand gently on Corlion's arm as she shook her head.

"I'm sorry. You're a good friend, Corlion, but I don't love you the way you want. I'm sorry."

It was like hitting a small kitten. The look on his face was heart-breaking and Mira felt sick for having put it there.

"I'm sorry," she said again. The words felt hollow and worthless on her tongue.

***

Days crept by in the palace. Every day, Gareth found a way to spend time with Mira, or she with him. He joined her for lunch in her study as she set aside bureaucracy for simple food and quiet jokes across the desk. Sometimes she came to the training room with him and they sparred. She was getting more used to his fighting style now, not giving him so many openings. They practiced together, testing each other's abilities and stretching them to something new. She gained some new tricks to use against him and he found himself more familiar with facing hers. Sometimes they just walked through the palace, talking of their lives and pasts.

There were other duties that Mira had to attend to. It was obvious they had a fighting force that was mobile and skilled, prepared for the instant of a portal opening. Gareth admired their efficiency as he saw the results of the team's work. Outsider attacks here were frequent, much more frequent than they were back home. Almost every day, sometimes more than once, a portal would open somewhere on this world.

Since that fight where Mira had nearly lost her arm, there hadn't been any Mira had dealt with personally, but they were still happening. Gareth saw reports, including the maps that showed where the portals had opened. The pattern was clearly centred on this city, no doubt because of the weakness beneath the palace, but the portals were still spread widely. Mira's warriors were deployed around the world, operating out of various hubs, with their territories clearly defined so that every incursion was met instantly.

Some of Mira's advisors were obviously concerned when they realised Gareth was looking at this information. So Gareth let it slide. He had no desire to make things even more difficult for himself. Besides, he wouldn't be here long.

The thought crept up on him, the realisation forcing its way into the forefront of his mind. He was nearly out of time.

Mira had given a deadline of twenty-eight days. She had given her ultimatum. If Master Amiron didn't present himself through the portal within that time, she would kill Gareth. Her followers, those that knew of Master Amiron's treason, would expect her to hold to that promise. And Gareth didn't need to imagine the preparations being made back home for the rescue mission. Both sides were aware of the looming end of this impasse, and here were Gareth and Mira, caught in the middle. Tomorrow was the final day. Tomorrow was the day she had set for his death sentence.

Gareth didn't need to ask where Mira was. He just headed for a back staircase, climbing up through the dusty upper levels of the palace until he found a doorway onto a roof garden. Flowers bloomed in pots around a small, flat area. On three sides, the sloped roofs and towers of the palace rose up into a forest of stone. On the fourth, a low balustrade offered a safe place to look down on the city below.

This was where Mira stood. She had her arms wrapped around herself against the wind, which was considerable this high on the cliff top. She wore one of the simple but elegant gowns she used for meeting with officials and dignitaries. The sun was low against the horizon, bathing her in purple and pink. Her long hair that usually flowed down her back was whipped up by the wind, flying about her in dark strands.

She seemed oblivious to her hair and to him. She lowered her arms to rest her hands on the stone of the balustrade, her head bowed low, perhaps looking down among the houses and streets that lay below them. Gareth gave himself a moment to let this sight tattoo itself into his memories. He would always be able to see her like this, his beautiful Mira, looking so frail and slightly lost above her world. He longed to take her into his arms and promise her that he would never let her go, that she would always have him to hold her and defend her against the dangers of the world.

But she'd probably hit him again if he did.

Gareth walked up to her, letting his feet sound against the stones. He saw her raise her hand to her face as he approached. He took his place beside her, looking down into the city, while she wiped away the traces of tears.

"Why couldn't you have just stayed in that cellar?" Mira asked.

"Because you released me from it," Gareth answered. "Besides, I wanted to spend this time with you."

"Why? You knew I was going to kill you."

"Because I knew you wouldn't kill me."

"So that's it? You spent the past few weeks letting me get to know you so that I wouldn't have the strength to wield the blade when it came to it?"

"No. I spent the past few weeks with you because I would spend the rest of my life with you, if I could. I love you, Mira."

"You don't really mean that." Her voice choked but she didn't let her tears fall this time.

"I've loved you since the first moment I saw you. I love you for your fire and passion. I love you for your dedication to justice. I love you for your determination to do the right thing for your people. I love you for your keen mind and for your beauty. I love you, Mira."

"I can't love you. You're the follower of my people's enemy."

"The only enemies are the Outsiders. Your world and mine can be allies, if you allow it. My friends can be your friends, my Defenders your defenders. We can stand, side by side against the Outsiders."

Gareth wondered if she too was thinking of the vision of another rooftop, where they would stand, weapons in hand, against an army. She might not believe the full truth of what she'd seen but he hoped she would. He hoped she would see the truth of his words and the conviction in his heart.

The distance between them was so small. It felt as though the air between them was tingling with promise. Gareth could just reach out and touch her but that wasn't what she needed. She needed to make this choice. She needed to choose him. He felt himself standing at a pivotal moment in his personal history, waiting for her to give him what he needed with every fibre of his being.

"This could destroy everything," Mira said.

Memories were surfacing again. Thoughts of the next few days drifting across Gareth's mind, the murky pool of future time letting him glimpse the shape of things to come. Something shimmered, a possibility shaping shape from the fog.

"Or save everything," Gareth said. "My friends have knowledge and skills to stand against the Outsiders. If we combine what we have, who knows what we could accomplish? Come with me to my world, Mira."

The silence seemed to stretch on for eternity, with the rushing wind accentuating the quiet rather than breaking it. Gareth felt the cold stone beneath his hands where he longed to feel her skin. Before them, the sun set on their final day, the sky stained pale purple with the dying light. Behind them, the wind shook the leaves and flowers of the rooftop garden, surrounding them with the scent of opening jasmine.

The words flowed from Mira's lips to the gentle melody. The song of the jasmine flower. The song they had danced to and would dance again.

"Sweetest flower that blooms by night, Gives beauty 'til return of light. My love, through gloom of deep despair, I'll hold the jasmine's flower fair."

When she finished, Gareth let his hand creep across the stone to hers, resting against the warmth of her skin. Her dark eyes sparkled with tears in the dying of the day. Still she smiled as she turned towards him.

"I will come with you, Gareth," she said. "I love you."

"You once punched me for calling you beautiful," Gareth said. "What will you do if I dare to kiss you?"

She returned his teasing smile.

"Let's find out," she said.

She tilted her head up and leaned into him, her soft lips meeting his. The final glow of sunset embraced them. Sweet jasmine mingled with Mira's own, intoxicating scent as Gareth breathed in her nearness. The fire of her passion filled him now as their lips held each other's. His hands reached around her, one sitting in the small of her back, the other resting against the back of her neck amid the silk of her hair. He was barely aware of the wind whipping up loose strands to strike against his own cheek. All he felt was the warmth of her body against his and her lips moving firmly against his own.

When they finally broke the kiss, a pale grey glow was all that remained of the sunset. Overhead, bright points of stars dotted the sky. Below, the city's lights made constellations of their own.

Gareth didn't want this moment to end. He wanted to keep Mira in his arms forever, but the rapidly growing darkness was a sign of how little time they had left. They had to be back in his world before tomorrow and she had a great deal of preparation to do before she could leave her world and its politics. Still, he kept his hand around hers as they moved back towards the stairs.

He felt the urgent stirring of a near memory. They couldn't go through without her knowing.

As they made their way down the dimly lit stairs towards the main levels, Gareth tried to find a way to frame the words for this announcement.

"He'll be there," Gareth said. "He'll arrive back on my world just before we will."

Mira turned to him, her hand snatched away, leaving the cold memory of her flesh in his empty palm. Anger burned in her eyes.

"You let me agree before telling me?"

"I didn't know until a moment ago."

She opened her mouth, perhaps to protest or argue. Then she closed it again, studying Gareth with a faintly puzzled looked. When she finally spoke, there was no trace of anger in her tone.

"I don't think I'll ever understand you," she said.

Part Three

Twenty-One

Preparing for the Test

Testing was the heart of the scientific principle. Someone worked out a proposition, devised a test with hypothesised results and then checked that their test gave the answers expected. Richard had an idea. It was an idea even he was half-convinced was nuts, but it was still an idea. Next came the experiment.

Because of the dangers involved, there were only a handful of places on the planet that were authorised for experiments with portal technology. One of them was a lab buried deep below the Defender base, capable of being sealed away tightly should the slightest thing go wrong. Richard had pleaded and eventually got authorisation from Boron to use the lab by lying and saying he was experimenting with ways to send a signal across worlds in an effort to contact Master Amiron. If he told the truth, then Boron would probably think Richard was nuts too.

So, buried beneath tons of metal and concrete, Richard tried his first test, using the principles of portal technology to create a sort of shield around a small area. He created a little bubble, ten centimetres across, cut off from the rest of the universe in a sphere of golden light.

The results were nearly perfect, the readings from his instruments the same as the ones he'd predicted down to thirty-seven decimal places. But that was the simple test, proving that he could isolate a part of the universe. The second stage was the difficult one. Could he affect time?

He calculated. He worked out equations. He weighed possibilities and checked the maths. The right energy, channelled in the right way, should be able to manipulate time within the portal bubble.

That was the second test. He created the bubble around a precise timer, channelled the power and collected the readouts. For the first time, he was actually convinced that his idea had become a solid theory. According to the timer, in the second he'd had the portal bubble activated, he'd moved time backwards inside it by almost twelve seconds.

Unfortunately, he'd blown his power supply doing so.

That proved to be the problem. Over the next few days, Richard experimented with increasing the size of the bubble and by pushing the contents back by more time. Both caused exponential increases in power requirements. Richard did the calculations and realised that creating a bubble big enough to take the Defender base back in time to before the attack would take more power than was currently being generated on Earth. Even creating a bubble big enough to take a person back any noticeable distance was unfeasible.

The initial exhilaration of discovery vanished quickly. Richard had created a form of time travel but it was utterly unworkable.

He couldn't go back and fix his mistake. He couldn't do anything that might help Gareth and he was rapidly running out of time.

They had been given twenty-eight days before Gareth was due to die and Richard had spent most of those working on an idea that was utterly useless. Richard would have been better off spending his time doing what he'd said he was and actually hunting for a way to contact Master Amiron. Now, the deadline was nearly up and Richard knew that it would be his fault if Gareth never came home.

* * *

Cassie's training continued, with the Defenders instructing her in all manner of combat. She was getting to the point where she didn't feel completely incompetent in her practice bouts, though they still ended with a breakdown of all the ways she would have been killed. She wasn't used to most of the other weapons but she was getting the hang of the sword, training with the others in the mornings and having individual sessions in the afternoons. Cassie had had doubts about her rate of progress, particularly since Karl seemed colder and more particular with each lesson. It had been Lizzie who'd calmed Cassie's worries on that account. She told her about how close Karl and Gareth had become, how Karl thought of him as a little brother. Karl's demeanour in the training sessions was related to his fear.

Because the days kept passing. Cassie had been so busy, overwhelmed with her training, that she could hardly believe it when she did the calculation of her time in the base. Twenty-six days since Gareth had made his bargain.

The tension in the base was rising to unbearable levels. Everyone snapped and griped. Cassie just got on with her practicing and tried to stay out of the way because it was obvious how scared the Defenders were. They were no closer to contacting Master Amiron than they had been when Gareth had sent Karl and the others back.

Cassie still felt disconnected from the group, more than ever now. She knew there were discussions and meetings going on. She knew that the senior Defenders gathered to debate what should be done. They had their orders, but the deadline was nearly up and they weren't just going to leave the Defence Master in the hands of an enemy. Cassie didn't know what plans there were. She just knew the fragments she picked up from overheard snatches of conversation. On the final day, the team was going to try an assault through the portal.

After group training, on the morning of the twenty-sixth day, Defender Boron came over to Cassie.

"You're going to be tested," he said. "You've learned well in practice scenarios but it's time to try your skills in the field. The next time we get a portal alert, you're going through. Until the next portal, I want you in the ready room with the first response team. When the alarm sounds, you're going through with them."

All moisture had fled Cassie's mouth but she swallowed and managed to force out a, "Yes, sir."

"Don't do anything strenuous in the meantime," Boron went on. "You need to be in fit shape to fight when the Outsiders come."

Cassie could only nod. Was she in a shape to fight? The last practice fight she'd had with multiple Defenders, one of them had grabbed her throat within the first few minutes. If that had been an Outsider, claws would have sliced open her windpipe or jugular or both. And what about the last training session with Karl? Cassie had barely managed to get her training sword anywhere near the man.

She headed up to the ready room despite the inclination to run away and hide. She found others already there, in the process of signing on for the afternoon shift as the first response team. There were four others: Lizzie, Karl, Enrico and Jerry. While there was always a senior Defender on the first response team, Cassie knew that it wasn't usual to have two seniors, the best swordsperson and the best shot on the team. Jerry had a gun strapped to his leg and that definitely wasn't standard procedure. No doubt the strong team was supposed to prevent her from getting killed. Somehow, that didn't comfort her.

Cassie hadn't spent much time in this room, though she'd seen it since her security status had been upgraded after the incursion. Now, she saw four others remaining perfectly calm and getting on with other things. Lizzie and Karl were sat at a table, paper spread between them covered in complex diagrams that they were debating quietly.

Enrico was on the sofa with a laptop in front of him. Jerry was sprawled beside him, flipping through a comic. None of them seemed the slightest bit concerned that the alarm could go off any moment and they'd be expected to risk their lives.

"Don't look so scared," Jerry said, glancing up from his pages of colourful superheroes. "Just don't drop your sword on your foot and you'll do fine."

Cassie saw Jerry's ever-present grin and tried to work out if he was being serious.

"What?"

"There was one guy, sometime back in the first invasion. Master Amiron didn't like him, but this guy begged and bullied and insisted until Master Amiron agreed to let him go through the basic training. He'd been so confident during practice, thought that he was God's gift to the multiverse. He was always showing off how well he could use a sword, boasting about all these re-enactment things he'd been on before coming here. After the basic training, me, Karl, Boron and Master Amiron took him out to a new portal to face the Outsiders for real. This guy saw the things coming. He just dropped his sword and pelted it in the opposite direction. I think he may have wet himself."

Cassie wondered if Jerry thought he was being comforting. Was he trying to tell her that she couldn't have the most embarrassing first encounter with the Outsiders? All that managed to sink into Cassie's mind from that story was that a trained and confident swordsman had run scared. What hope did she have?

She just stood in the middle of the room, looking around her. There were a few books scattered around, a magazine of sudokus on a chair, even a few newspapers in various languages. This room was designed to cope with five people getting bored for several hours of a shift. All Cassie could think was that if the alarm didn't go off, she'd have to stay here as another team came on duty, and another. There was nothing she could do but wait for the signal that would determine the course of her life. Possibly the end of her life.

Cassie wished she could go down to the training rooms and work out. All her life, whenever she'd been stressed or worried, she'd gone for a run to ease her mind. Right now though, that option was barred from her. It wasn't just that she'd be too far away from the portal. Boron was right; she needed to be ready to fight and she couldn't be that if she exhausted herself now. Without physical exertion to shut her mind up, her thoughts were running in terrified circles. Everything that might possibly go wrong played across her mind and carried her spiralling deeper into fear.

Cassie tried to tell herself that Boron wouldn't be putting her in the field if she wasn't ready, but she couldn't make herself believe that. Boron was desperate for every fighter he could get in case they needed to rescue Gareth. Cassie had even heard whispers that Boron was calling in some former Defenders, some of those who'd retired from the fight after the insanity of the first invasion was over.

Cassie kept looking across at Enrico, who was still working quietly at his laptop. His uniform hid the scars that covered large parts of his body. That weird green goop, the mirus, had done its job well, but Enrico still bore the marks. He'd nearly been killed. Enrico was a senior Defender, a skilled fighter, and he'd nearly been killed by one creature. Outsiders sometimes came through the portal in dozens or hundreds. Enrico must have caught her expression.

"Sit down," Enrico said. "Read a book or do a crossword or something. You're wearing a hole in the floor."

Cassie wondered if this was something they'd all been through. She supposed they must have. People didn't magically spring into being with years of experience fighting monsters. But during the first invasion, the portals had often opened more than once a day. They probably hadn't had to wait long. Cassie was in the conflicted state of dreading something yet wishing it here so at least the anxious uncertainty would be done.

She took one of the seats and picked up the Sudoku magazine. After about five minutes of staring blankly at the same puzzle, she stood again. She wanted to run. She wanted to punch something. She wanted to be anywhere in the universe except here, waiting to fight for her life.

"Just sit down," snapped Karl, pointing at a seat across from him and Lizzie. Cassie wasn't about to ignore a senior Defender.

"You're not the only one whose worried about something," Karl said, "but all your fidgeting's just going to make everyone else more nervous."

Cassie wanted to say that it was easy for him to say. She caught herself just in time, remembering what Lizzie had said about Gareth. Cassie was fearing for her own life; Karl was helplessly fearing for a guy who was almost a brother to him.

Now, Lizzie reached out across the table and put a hand on Cassie's arm. It was probably meant to be comforting but there wasn't a whole lot that would comfort her right now. Still, Lizzie smiled.

"You're going to do fine. This is what all the practicing has been for."

"Thanks," Cassie said. Her mouth still felt dry, her heart was racing. She wanted to stand up and start pacing again because her body was filled with energy that needed some outlet. There was also the terrified voice in the back of her mind telling her that she was crazy and that she should run into a corner and hide. Desperate to try and distract herself, she looked at the diagrams on the table, wondering if this was some battle plan or technical diagram.

"What are you working on?" she asked.

"The seating plan for the wedding," Karl answered, which earned simultaneous groans from Enrico and Jerry. "It seems there are loads of political figures who Adrian says we need to invite, which means that organising the tables badly could lead to world war three."

"You have to invite politicians?"

"World leaders, royalty, all sorts of people. It turns out that the first Defender wedding is a global affair. I'm starting to think that we should just open a portal to Vegas and be done with all this fuss."

Cassie started a smile before she realised that Karl wasn't laughing. Neither was Lizzie.

"You try that," Lizzie said, "and my mother will disown me."

The pair grinned at each other.

"Was it love at first sight?" Cassie asked.

"Not exactly," said Karl. "There were about a hundred guys for every girl on the Defenders. We were all in love with her."

Lizzie grinned, "They were all trying to woo me, or chat me up, or just gawk at me in the showers. Karl was the one who tried talking to me like a person."

A smile cracked the stern mask of Karl's face. "She says that now. The fact is, she only kissed me to get the others to leave her alone."

"Did it work?" asked Cassie.

"I had to beat up three people first."

"I'll have you know," put in Jerry, "that we weren't scared by the fact that you'd beat us up, Karl. We were scared by the fact that she would beat us up."

"Damn right," grinned Lizzie.

The attention returned to the seating plan. Cassie wondered which was more daunting, fighting creatures from another world or discovering that your romance was a subject for international politics.

As silence settled over the room again, Cassie's thoughts returned to her fears. How many Outsiders would come through the portal? Would they call in the second response team? Or would Cassie be on her own? Would they just shove her into the hoard to see if she came out alive?

Of course not. She tried to tell herself over and over that these people were trained professionals who'd see to it that she came out the other side alive. She sat there, a wall of fear building around her.

Perhaps she should just go to Defender Boron and say that she wasn't ready. But would she feel any more capable of facing this threat if she waited another week or even a month? Maybe it was better just to get it over with. Maybe she'd be hurt and would be sent home but at least she'd be able to say she tried. She couldn't bear the thought of having to go home and say that she'd been too scared. If she told Boron she couldn't face the Outsiders, that was a possibility. They might decide that they'd picked the wrong person. After all, she was only here because she'd been near Gareth when that creature had attacked the base. She wasn't going to let herself lose that easily.

Her mind was racing through visions of every possible bloody end. She wished she had an off switch for her brain. Sometimes it was days between portals. How long could she last like this? At this rate, she'd have a heart attack from the stress before the Outsiders ever got a chance at her.

The alarm blared across the base.

A portal!

Twenty-Two

Facing the Outsiders

Cassie was on her feet half a second behind the others, grabbing the sword that was ready and waiting. She was buckling it around her waist as she ran from the ready room, across the hall and into the control room.

A couple of Defenders, whose names Cassie hadn't learned yet, sat by the equipment, already firing up the portal technology. Boron was there as well.

"Where are we?" Karl asked.

"Texas. Looks pretty rural. We're in luck."

The portal devices on the wall were firing up. Karl and Lizzie were already heading through. Boron caught Cassie's eye as she hurried after them.

"Good luck," Boron said.

Enrico gave a reassuring grin and clapped a hand on Cassie's shoulder. Cassie felt the warmth of the hand like a shove towards the portal. She hurried, not quite sure how she got her legs to obey her, and let the golden light swallow her.

She stumbled from the portal to a dirt road through an expanse of farmland. It was daylight, the sun low to the horizon but all she was able to focus on was the circle of the other portal a few metres away and the Outsiders climbing out. Cassie had never seen them up close before, only ever in recordings of attacks. They seemed slightly taller than she'd expected, their apparently-frail forms reminding her of some horror movie monster. But it was their desperate, hungry gaze that shot icy terror straight through her. These things were looking at her as their next meal.

There were some Outsiders already in the surrounding area, more interested in tearing into a field of wheat, gnawing at the unripe crops. A few of the creatures noticed the arrival of the Defenders. Cassie raised her sword, her mind suddenly empty of all the things Karl and Lizzie and Boron and the others had worked so hard to teach her.

"Lizzie, Jerry, Enrico," Karl said, "you're minding the portal. Cassie and I will clean up the edges."

Clean up the edges? Cassie had spent many long hours going over the simple phrases that formed the main strategies of most encounters with the Outsiders. Cleaning up the edges meant stopping those Outsiders who'd come through first and were furthest from the portal. Fortunately for Cassie, most of those seemed more interested in tearing the wheat to chunks with their teeth than they were in the arrival of four Defenders and one trainee.

Cassie ran after Karl into the field, scrambling through a hole torn into a fence. The Outsiders were destroying the crops, both with their attempts at eating and with their movements. Cassie was treading on trampled stalks as she went to one of the nearby beasts. She slashed with her sword, slightly surprised by the lack of resistance as the blade met flesh. Dark, viscous blood splashed over the green stalks and Cassie's stomach churned again.

She didn't let herself think about it, turning to look for the next Outsider. Karl was already taking down his third but there were a few more of the beasts in the field. Cassie ran to another, astonished by the stupidity of these things as they kept on eating the plants up until the moment when the blade was almost on them.

Cassie didn't let herself pause to look at the blood she spilt or the bodies of those she left at her feet. She just kept looking around for more of the things to kill. She and Karl were moving in a wide circle around the portal, heading in opposite directions. She was still scared, but the racing adrenaline was holding it in check.

At least at first.

Then she saw several Outsiders that had somehow made it past the three at the portal. They were bearing down on Cassie, obviously deciding that she looked tastier than the unripe wheat. One that had been eating the crops, the one Cassie had meant for her next target, looked up and saw her. Cassie found herself with five of the things coming at her.

All style and training vanished. Her mind was blank of everything but the mind-numbing terror that she was about to be torn apart and eaten.

She flailed wildly with her sword, meeting their flesh only by luck.

They were all around her, teeth bared, that terrible hunger in their eyes. Cassie hacked in all directions with her dark metal blade, hardly noticing when she actually hit the things. She saw nothing but those eyes.

Then there were more blades in the air beside her.

Two of the creatures stopped their attacks, a faintly surprised looked crossing their faces before the heads toppled free of their bodies. Karl and Enrico stood there, grinning slightly as their blades finished the simultaneous slaying. Cassie looked round, seeing the bodies of the other Outsiders around her. Had she killed them? The terror had wiped the actions from her mind.

Enrico grinned at her, raising his left arm to glance at a watch on his wrist.

"Twenty-seven minutes," he said.

"What?" Cassie asked.

"Between going through the portal and starting to panic," Enrico explained.

"That's actually pretty good," Karl said.

The two Defenders turned back to the fight. The portal was shut now and just a handful of Outsiders remained. Lizzie and Jerry were several metres away, immersed in the field as they hacked down a few more. Karl and Enrico went to clear up the stragglers, leaving Cassie to stare at the dark blood that covered her sword and soaked her clothes.

Had it really been nearly half an hour since stepping through the portal? It seemed moments. The whole fight a blur of fear and blood. But she was alive. Somehow. Impossibly. Alive.

The other four walked over to her as she stood there in this daze. The hand that held the sword was shaking. Her stomach was still reeling, this time with a shock of disgust at her own state. Her whole body seemed trembling and weak. Yet she wanted to laugh at the sheer joy of living.

"Congratulations," Lizzie said, "Defender."

Cassie barely remembered what happened after that, though somehow she made it back to the base and showered away the gore of the Outsiders. She made it back to her room and collapsed on her bed, slipping instantly into dreamless darkness.

It was mid-morning when she woke. Her brain didn't seem to be fully functional yet and she couldn't understand how she had slept through the alarm but she'd obviously missed the pre-breakfast run, as well as half the group training. She found clean clothes and pulled them on with shaking hands. A large part of her wanted to just crawl under the covers and hide from the world for several hours more, but she knew she had to get going. She was probably in trouble already; the Defenders had made it clear that punctuality was vital round here.

She made it out of her room, but Richard was sat on a chair in the corridor. He had a laptop open on his knees, but he looked up and gave Cassie a smile that lacked any trace of condescension. He must have been waiting for her to emerge. There was no sign of anger or reproach for oversleeping.

"Congratulations, Defender," Richard said.

It took a surprising number of seconds for those words to pass through her ears and reach her brain. Defender. Lizzie had called her that last night after the fight. Not candidate or trainee or on probation. Simply Defender.

A small smile made its way onto Cassie's lips. She'd done it. She'd been in a battle with the Outsiders and she'd killed them. She hadn't run away or wet herself or got eaten alive. She'd passed the test. She really was a Defender now. The thrill of knowing she was one of the elite was as good as the feeling of standing on the podium at the Olympics with a medal round her neck.

"Come on," Richard said, folding the laptop. Cassie let Richard lead her to the dining room, not minding in the slightest that she wasn't going to have to walk into the training room late and be the focus on everyone's attention. She still couldn't quite believe she was alive, let alone a Defender, and she needed some time to come to terms with the shock. The terror was back now, whispering in the quiet of her mind. What if yesterday had been a fluke? What if the next time she was torn to shreds?

Richard sat Cassie down at a table and then went to gather food. Cassie stared at the pile of sandwiches and salads that was put in front of her. Then she began eating in a slightly autonomous way, no more aware of the flavour than she had been before the fight.

"There was a betting pool on, you know," Richard said.

"About what?"

"How long you'd keep your cool. Karl had you down for thirty-five minutes. That's quite a compliment."

"I didn't manage it though."

"Do you know how long Gareth lasted the first time he faced real Outsiders?"

"How long?"

"About thirty-five seconds." Richard laughed.

"But he took over from Master Amiron!"

"I know!" Richard laughed again. "I wasn't there, but the guys that were said that Gareth basically froze. Karl killed a few of the Outsiders that were trying to eat Gareth and yelled at him."

"Yelled?"

"Yep. He told Gareth that if he wasted all that time training by getting killed, he would never forgive him. Apparently Gareth was more scared of losing Karl's respect than he was of the Outsiders and so he started to fight. He never panicked again."

"Does everyone panic?"

"Not everyone. Most."

"And how many people... don't make it through the test."

"No one's ever died, if that's what you mean. The Defenders make sure that they keep an eye out. A few have flipped out straight away and been shoved back through the portal. Sometimes, they've had to call in back-up because the candidate's just standing there useless and there's a big attack coming through. Mostly, the ones that fail just run away. As long as we get the sword back, they just let them go."

Somehow it was a comforting thought that most of the Defenders had, at some point, felt that mind-numbing terror and lost control to it.

Cassie munched her way slowly through the plate of food. Physically, she was feeling much better now, the shaking banished by the sustenance. But there was still the empty ache of fear. She remembered the feeling she'd come here with. She'd been terrified of failing, that she wouldn't be up to the task of being a Defender. But behind that fear was the warm glow of success. She'd succeeded at every challenge she'd set herself; she'd succeed here too. She'd made it as a Defender and she'd make them see how great she could be.

The door to the dining room opened and a flow of people began, the Defenders coming to eat after their morning's training. Every single one of them crossed the room to Cassie first, offering congratulations, shaking her hand or clapping her on the back. Every single one of them addressed her as Defender.

The room was rapidly becoming crowded, the buzz of chatter and clatter of cutlery filling the air. Then silence fell like a rock. Cassie looked up, following the attention of the room to the doorway, where Defender Boron stood with an armful of black cloth. Boron walked across the room to where Cassie sat.

"It should be the Defence Master who presents this to you," Boron said, "but I'm afraid you'll have to do with me until we get him back. Welcome to the team, Defender."

He held out the pile of cloth, which Cassie saw now was the black uniform they all wore. She reached out to take it as thunderous applause filled the room.

Twenty-Three

Deadline

Richard had wanted to be there for Cassie's official welcome to the Defenders because there was something almost mystical about the way the team welcomed a new member into their midst. Richard had wanted to be a part of that, to feel that inclusion. He now knew that was impossible, but he could taste it slightly by being the one sitting beside her, just as he'd tasted it once when Gareth had been presented with the uniform. That momentary glimpse of family was a reminder that Richard wasn't completely and utterly alone.

He needed a reminder of that because it was hard to remember anything other than how alone he was.

They were almost at the deadline and Richard hadn't got one damn thing that could help Gareth. He was supposed to be intelligent but he was drawing only blanks.

He started heading down from the dining room back towards the lab, but an arm stuck through the lift doors as he got in them. The arm turned out to be Enrico, stepping into the lift and staring at Richard as the doors closed. Richard had already keyed in the security code for the lab's floor.

"How's the research going?" Enrico asked.

Every instinct told Richard to bluff his way through, pretending he was on the verge of a breakthrough because he couldn't stand the thought of admitting defeat. But he couldn't do that. He could look Boron in the eye but not Enrico. Not after what Enrico had sacrificed to protect him.

Richard leaned back against the wall of the lift with a sigh.

"I can't do a damn thing to get Gareth back."

"I know how you feel."

"No you don't," said Richard.

"Get it through your genius skull that no one expects you to solve all the problems of the universe."

"I expect it. At the very least, I expect not to be the one who causes them!"

"What the hell are you on about?"

Of course Enrico didn't know. Boron had agreed to keep things quiet and Meg tended to keep her head down when she wasn't yelling at Richard. No one would have wanted to admit, with all the fear going on around here, that Richard had screwed up. Boron had been relying on Richard to save the day so he wouldn't put that in jeopardy.

"I caused this," Richard admitted. "I accidentally put a hole into the security system because I was pissed at Jerry and wanted to get revenge on him. My friend is a prisoner of a monster because I was playing a prank. So, no, you don't know how I feel."

The lift ground to a halt finally and the doors slid open. Richard delivered the last words over his shoulder as he walked off. Enrico could find his own way back up.

"My friend is a prisoner of a monster," Enrico said, "because I wasn't a strong enough fighter to keep from getting captured. Yes, I do know how you feel."

Richard paused. The corridor was silent, waiting for him to answer. Richard hadn't even stopped to think about how Enrico must be feeling. This was exactly why Gareth always yelled at him about seeing things from others' perspectives. So Richard turned back to look at Enrico.

"I guess you do," Richard said.

"Now that's established, why don't you show me what you've been working on? Maybe if you use me as a sounding board, you'll have one of your brilliant flashes of inspiration."

Richard led the way into the lab. Since he'd started working in here, he'd cleared a space in the middle of the room, set with his modified portal generators and their power sources. Around the room was the various clutter of equipment and pieces of machinery that he'd either discarded or pilfered for parts. Enrico looked round at the chaos and then turned to Richard.

"What's the big project?" he asked.

"Take off your watch."

Enrico didn't bother arguing. He just handed over the watch, which Richard placed on top of the bubble generator, adapted from their standard portal equipment. It was a flat rectangle on the floor, hooked into a military-grade power generator as well as the computer on which Richard had crafted the software. Richard fired up the computer now.

As he kicked off the program, a golden light formed above the bubble generator, spreading out to form a perfect sphere just large enough to hold the watch. As Enrico stared, Richard shifted the coordinates and watched the seconds on the watch tick backwards. He tweaked the power up and watched the hand move slightly faster. The sphere took on a bluish tint as he pushed the power further, the second hand now moving backwards about four seconds for every one that was passing.

Then the power generator reached its max and the safety switch cut off. The watch sat there, ticking away in the right direction again.

"Time travel!" Enrico was grinning despite everything. "You've gone and built time travel?"

"I thought I could go back and stop myself messing with the security files or warn Gareth about the attack."

"This is..." he gave a disbelieving laugh. "This is incredible."

"It's useless. I took your watch back in time by about a minute and that blew my power. We simply can't generate enough energy to do any good."

"Maybe if we made some adjustments for efficiency," Enrico began. Richard was not about to listen to someone talking about the basics as if he were an idiot.

"I've done that! Check my calculations and see for yourself. The maths doesn't lie. It would be impossible to go back in time by a month. Even sending a note would need about as much power as the sun."

"You have just uncovered the most astonishing breakthrough in science since the portals themselves," said Enrico.

"I don't care. I just want my friend back."

* * *

Cassie would have loved some time to enjoy her accomplishment. She phoned her parents, of course, and had to endure their congratulations, as well as their fearful instructions to be careful. She dressed in her new uniform, surprised each time she caught her own reflection. The neat-cut black seemed to make her look more serious, more dangerous.

Then she was given the exciting but petrifying news that she would be added to the duty rotas. This meant she would have shifts sitting in the control room watching the machines for any sign of danger. It also meant that she would have shifts when she would be one of the first team to go through should a portal open. If a portal alarm went, she was expected to get a weapon and be ready even if she wasn't scheduled for a shift, just in case the attack turned out to be a major one and they needed extra fighters.

Her fears for her future as a Defender weren't the only ones. Everyone was acutely aware that tomorrow was the final day. The creature had given them this deadline, promising Gareth's death should Master Amiron fail to present himself through the portal. Cassie knew by now that no one had any idea how to contact the former Defence Master. Any hope they had in his intervention was gone.

So Defender Boron summoned them all to the canteen, which now had a projector shining up against one of the white walls. Cassie saw a partial plan, what little they knew of the layout of the place where Gareth was being held.

"You all know the situation we face," Boron said. "Our Defence Master is a prisoner of a creature that even dark metal weapons cannot hurt. Tomorrow, she will kill him. We're not going to let that happen."

There was a faint murmur from around the room. Cassie wasn't sure if it was agreement or dissent.

"Apart from the creature, the only people who've been seen in this place are human. Some of them are armed but not all. The humans we can fight. Tomorrow, we go through the portal and we're going to rescue Master Gareth."

"That's suicide," someone called.

"He'd do it for you," another voice responded. The speaker was across the other side of the room but Cassie thought it was Enrico.

More voices rose up but Boron held out his hands for silence.

"Gareth was the one named by Master Amiron. More than that, he has risked his life time and again for this world and for all of us. We will be going after him. There are multiple phases in this attack plan. I will be asking for volunteers for the infiltration team and the first assault. Those of you who have doubts can be in the second wave."

Boron spoke on with no more major interruptions. He outlined quite a simple plan, with a small group scouting the area and trying to identify where Gareth was held. They would signal through the first assault to fight whatever enemy soldiers they encountered or should they meet the creature. The second wave would be waiting as back up should the first wave be overwhelmed. Richard had found a way to open multiple portals at and around the location where the team had gone through before.

"These people have portal technology," Boron said, "so we have to assume that they can detect and locate our portals. We have to plan for this so, thanks to Richard, our portals will open in different locations to let through the different groups. Make sure you stay in radio contact at all times so we can co-ordinate our efforts."

Boron finished describing the plan, going into details of teams and assignments. There were so many variables. Without knowing the full layout of the building, or even if Gareth was still inside it, they couldn't be sure how long the searching would take. They couldn't know how many enemy they'd face or if there were more of the creatures. They couldn't know what weapons the enemy might have. They couldn't even know if Gareth was still alive.

When the briefing ended, most of the Defenders began heading off, perhaps to make their preparations or to call their families, just in case. A few stayed to speak with Boron. Cassie lingered with them, edging her way to where the second-in-command was still giving advice and instruction to those that wanted it.

"Erm..." Cassie said.

"You'll be staying on duty in the control room," Boron said. "We need someone to monitor the systems in case another portal opens, whether this enemy or Outsiders."

"OK." Cassie didn't ask why Richard couldn't do that duty. She was relieved not to have to go into battle so soon, particularly against humans. But that didn't mean she wanted to be told that it was because she wasn't ready yet.

* * *

There were final preparations to be made for tomorrow's rescue attempt. Karl sat in the control room with Boron, Enrico and Jerry, discussing again what they'd seen during their brief trip to the other side of the portal. Richard was sitting beside them, working on the calculations needed to get their portals to appear in the appropriate places on the other side. There were so many things they didn't know, so many pieces of information missing. Karl couldn't help feeling that Gareth had some agenda, some plan that he hadn't let them in on.

After all, he'd told them not to try and rescue him.

That didn't mean he was objecting to Boron's plan. Even if that creature kept her side of the deal and kept Gareth alive, she might be torturing him. Karl had spent the last month fretting constantly about what might be happening to the guy he cared for like a brother. Karl would attempt a rescue if it meant going through the portal alone.

Boron had the list of volunteers to go on the first wave. As the only ones who'd been there before, the three Defenders in the control room now would be going through with Boron as the infiltration team. Lizzie had also insisted on taking her place with them and Karl knew better than to try and talk her out of it. The first wave of the assault was made up of multiple teams who would go through the portals at different points, reducing the chances of the locals detecting their portals and being ready with weapons the moment they stepped through. Richard was plotting out the expected portal locations on their rough plan. That was another layer of difficulty; the plan had been drawn up from their memories, with estimates and occasional arguments on the distances. They couldn't be certain that Richard's portals would line up to where they expected the teams to emerge.

There were far too many ways that this could all go horribly wrong.

"We'll get him back," Jerry said, reading the worry on Karl's face.

Karl nodded. Gareth had promised he'd be coming home. He must have had a reason for being so confident.

Karl was still angry with Gareth about this whole situation. Gareth had called that creature by name! He'd known something about her, known some secret of Master Amiron's that was behind this assault. Whatever it was, why hadn't Gareth told them before going through the portal? Why hadn't he said that he was planning on staying behind? Why hadn't he let even Karl know what was going through his head?

For that matter, why hadn't Master Amiron warned them that this creature was out there and, for whatever reason, wanting him dead?

Karl caught himself listening to his own internal rant, rather than Boron's discussion of the attack plan. He forced himself to focus back on the present. He wouldn't do Gareth any good by being too distracted to be sure of the plan. Not that the plan was particularly firm. Because of the huge number of unknowns, all of the Defenders were expected to use their own initiative to some extent.

Boron was discussing weaponry and how to allocate the guns when the alarm signalled an opening portal. Controlled lightning surged against the wall, where their primary portal generators were placed. Karl stared at the streams of golden light forming the familiar circle, hope flaring as brightly as the light.

Richard and Enrico had made some tweaks to the security protocols since the attack on the base, Karl knew. Only a member of their team should be able to open a portal into this room and there was only one member of the team who wasn't here.

Could it be Gareth?

He tried to hold his excitement in check. After all, the creature had broken through their security once before. He laid his hand on the sword at his waist, ready should it be an enemy, but he couldn't keep the smile from his face.

The figure that stumbled from the portal wasn't Gareth, but one just as welcome.

The man who emerged was not overly tall but he portrayed an aura of authority. His once-dark hair was streaked with grey and his face bore the lines of concern that came with bearing responsibility for an entire world. He still wore the black Defender uniform he'd been wearing the last time Karl had seen him, just before he departed into the portal.

"Master Amiron!"

"I need to speak to Gareth," Amiron said. Then he toppled forwards.

The Defenders were moving in an instant, shaken from their frozen shock. Boron had crossed the room first, catching Amiron just before he hit the floor. Amiron's back showed the cause. Something had slashed through his shirt and into the flesh beneath, deep red already flowing out to stain Boron's hands and seep down to drip onto the white floor. Karl thought instantly of the creature and its claws.

He was crouched beside Master Amiron as Boron turned him over. Amiron was barely conscious, his face drained of colour.

"I can undo it," Amiron said. "Tell Gareth, I can fix it."

Twenty-Four

The Return

All this time, they'd been hunting for a trace of Master Amiron, coming up with plan after hopeless plan about how to contact him. And he'd just walked in, right when they needed him, but he was still unreachable to them. Karl had, simply by virtue of being in the control room at the time, ended up being allowed to stay by Master Amiron's bedside in the hospital wing. Boron sat at the other side, while all the medical staff on the base did their best to aid him, patching up deep cuts and scanning for internal damage. Karl couldn't follow half the discussions but they had mirus and they had the best technology on the planet at their disposal.

Karl had no doubt that Master Amiron would be perfectly fine. But in time? The minutes had ticked their way into hours. The clock on the wall was edging its way slowly towards midnight. Then it would be the final day of the deadline.

There would be no time to plan a new approach. They would have to make the call about whether or not to go through the portal after Gareth. They had their Master back, but they hadn't got the guidance they were all hoping for.

Outside, various members of the team would peer through the door, until one of the doctors yelled at them and Boron ordered them all back to their rooms to get some rest. It would be a big day tomorrow. Even if Amiron woke up in time, they still had to find Gareth and bring him home.

Alarms blared across the base again. Another portal.

Both Defenders stood. Both hesitated.

"Wait with him," Boron ordered. He headed out the door, up towards the control room to discover what the situation was. They had enough on their minds without an Outsider attack now. Or maybe it was the creature, back for Master Amiron's blood.

Karl looked back to the pale figure on the bed and saw him stir, perhaps roused by the alarms which were only now being quietened. Karl was back at his side, leaning over the bed.

"Master Amiron? Can you hear me?"

A nearby doctor heard those words and was there, checking readouts, looking into Amiron's waiting face. Even he was grinning like a loon to see the old Defence Master awake.

"Karl," Amiron waved the doctor away, "I need to speak to Gareth. Worlds depend on it."

"Gareth," Karl began. "He…"

Karl didn't know how to finish. How to explain that they'd failed him so badly? How to explain that Gareth, the Defence Master appointed his successor, was captured, perhaps dead?

"I'm here."

The words were like a jolt through Karl's brain, the familiar voice so unexpected. Karl jumped back from the bed, seeing Gareth walk through the door to the hospital wing as though he'd just been delayed by a minor inconvenience. Karl stared at the young man, who walked with assurance, and the young woman who stood behind him. This woman, this girl, was armed with dark metal but it was her face that Karl found his eyes locked on. Not because of her beauty, but because of the resemblance to the man in the bed.

Master Amiron was staring at her too and, for a long moment, silence filled the room as she stared back.

"You look like your father," Amiron said at last.

"My father is dead," she answered, her voice so empty of emotion that it could break hearts.

Gareth turned to Karl, "Please could you wait outside. We have important matters to discuss."

So calm. Karl had spent a month scared half to death that he'd never see Gareth again. He wanted to run across the room and hug the breath from him. And Gareth was just dismissing him, like he meant nothing, like his anxiety didn't matter. Karl had never been more angry with the kid than he was in that moment.

"What happened?" Karl demanded. "How did you get away? What about that beast? Are you alright? How – just how the hell are you here?"

The words flowed in a torrent that Karl couldn't have stopped if he'd wanted to. At last, he stumbled out the end of his astonished questions. Gareth gave a slight smile, almost indulgent. He closed the distance across the room and laid a hand on Karl's shoulder.

"It's OK. I'll explain everything but right now we have things we need to talk about. Please, just wait outside and make sure that we're not disturbed."

Gareth was dismissing the medical staff even as Karl turned for the door to the corridor outside. He stood there, and leaned against a wall. It felt like his brain had stopped functioning properly. Gareth was back safely, after all this concern, and he acted like it was no big deal. Karl didn't know whether to laugh or cry or punch a hole through the wall. So he just stood there and waited for his thoughts to start again.

Boron came down the corridor. His face showed the same astonishment that Karl felt.

"Is he in there?" Boron asked.

Karl nodded, "Asked to be left alone to talk with Master Amiron."

"Master Amiron's awake?"

Karl nodded again, "Just now. He said he needed to talk to Gareth."

"They just came through the portal. Gareth knew Master Amiron was here, said he needed to speak with him. Didn't say how or why."

"Who's the girl?" Karl asked.

"No idea."

"Master Amiron knew her."

"I guess we should know better than to expect answers from a Defence Master," Boron said, his voice betraying the same bitterness that Karl felt.

"Either of them."

* * *

Inside the sickroom, silence reigned for a long time. Master Amiron and Mira were staring at each other. Gareth was looking between the two, wondering who would make the first move. Gareth was still angry, still hurting, but it was hard to look at Master Amiron and not see him as the first person to take a chance on him. Master Amiron had given him everything he ever wanted and more, finding him a home and a family and a purpose. It was hard to keep that in perspective with the fact that Master Amiron was also a cold-blooded traitor who'd deliberately caused the death of hundreds of innocent people.

"I'm sorry," Amiron said at last.

Mira was across the room in a blur, her hand drawing the dagger as she reached the bed. She pressed the blade to Amiron's throat. Gareth had barely moved, knowing that his interference could cost Amiron his life. He'd had the flash of future knowledge a fraction of a second before she'd acted, which wasn't nearly long enough to actually do any good. He tried to search his memories for some clue how this could resolve, how he could keep his Master from getting killed. He stood, frozen, his heart racing with fear as he watched the girl he loved, her face blazing with unbecoming rage, threatening a man closer to him than his father.

The worse thing was that a part of him wanted her to do it. A part of him was still screaming in rage at his betrayal.

"You're sorry? Sorry! For what? For betraying my father? For causing his death and my brother's and the deaths of hundreds of others? For destroying my world? Your world! You're sorry!"

"Yes." His voice was quiet, barely more than a whisper, but Gareth heard it clearly. He wanted so desperately to believe it.

"I should slit your throat and let you bleed for your crimes!"

"You won't. You won't kill an unarmed man."

"You did! When you let those things into our world."

"I know. But you're a better person than I was."

The seconds seemed an eternity as Gareth watched them frozen in this tableau of rage.

"There is a chance I can save our world," Amiron said quietly, "and this one. There is a chance I can stop the Outsiders forever."

There was something in his voice, a certainty in his tone that was hard to deny. Gareth felt the words strike through to his gut and he saw the effect on Mira, the flicker of doubt on her face. For that moment, she believed. But her hate was enough to push through the effects of Amiron's master voice.

"Why should I believe a word out of your lying mouth?" Mira snarled.

"Ask Gareth."

Gareth's memories had become clearer the moment he'd stepped back through the portal but there was still that great darkness looming.

It was much, much closer now. Each minute brought it nearer. Gareth could see the moments leading up to it, the preparations and the plans. He could see Richard's excitement as he tried to figure out the science behind the impossible. He could see the hope for a better future and the battle that would come. He couldn't see what lay beyond.

He didn't know if the plan would work.

For all he knew, this was just another lie, just another deception. Amiron had destroyed his world because he wanted to appear a hero. What if he did the same again? He could send Gareth to his death and destroy the only person in this universe with the knowledge of his true nature. Gareth had absolutely no way to be sure that this wasn't just another plot that would allow Amiron to return home in glory, with the only obstacle to the throne gone and the Defence Master of Earth dead.

But there was a chance that what Amiron said now was the truth. There was a chance that this plan could end the war. For once, they wouldn't be just defending.

"I don't know," Gareth said. "I don't know if his plan will work or if he's lying through his teeth. I just know we have to try. This is a chance to stop the Outsiders forever and it doesn't matter how slim that chance is. Neither of us can refuse."

Mira's hand started to shake and she could almost have slit Amiron's throat by accident. She withdrew her hand, stepping back from the bed as sobs overtook her and she managed, on the third attempt, to get the dagger back into its sheath. Gareth was by her side in a heartbeat, wrapping his arms around her. Mira leaned her whole body into him, the grief flowing from her in a rain of tears that seemed unstoppable. He held her.

After a long while, the sobs slowed. Her eyes were still wet, but Gareth wiped a stray strand of hair away and kissed her forehead. He kept one arm about her shoulder as he turned them both back to the bed.

"I make no excuses for what I did," Amiron said. "I never meant for the worst of it, but it was my doing nonetheless. It was my greed and pride that caused so much pain. I can't undo all of that, but there is something I can do, something I can fix."

Gareth saw it in his memories. He saw the plan laid out like a storyboard through his mind. He saw the world filled with mighty machines, damaged by radiation, its people twisted into a new form.

Lethal and ever-hungry. He saw a world so broken that the barriers to other universes were fraying apart. He saw the terror and the horror and the death. He saw the machines that Richard would build, twisting the golden light of dimensions into a new shape, weaving them around this ruined world.

He saw the blackness in his mind. It had been looming closer for a while but now he saw its centre. Something would happen on that world and that made a wall where his memories stopped. The reflections of future time couldn't make it through that barrier.

Would he die there?

"What are you talking about?" Mira asked.

"These machines we've built can manipulate the dimensions."

"I know. That's how we create portals."

"But it's not just the spatial dimensions or the barriers between universes."

"Are you talking about time?" Mira asked.

"I've done it before, just once. I twisted the dimensions around a person, used this power to move a tiny patch of the world through time just as we use the portals to move people through space."

"When you brought me back from the dead," Gareth said. Amiron nodded.

"What are you talking about?" Mira asked.

"There were damaged portal generators," Gareth said, "about to overload and he used the power to manipulate the dimensions around my body so that I was in a sort of bubble, cut off from the rest of the world. Then he somehow made time flow backwards within that bubble. He undid my death."

"You can rewrite time? You can bring our home back!"

"You moved me by a few minutes," said Gareth. "You really think you could change history on a whole world? The power needed would be astronomical!"

"Not our world, but the world at the heart of all of this trouble. It's fracturing away from its place in the multiverse anyway. Whatever happened to damage that world broke its hold on the normal dimensions, that's why the portals from there open randomly. It would take a nudge, comparatively speaking, to move it. The reason it's such a danger is the reason we can save it. Richard has built a device that can influence time. We can expand on that around the Outsider world." Amiron turned to Mira, "I can't rewrite the years on our world. I don't know if there's enough power in the universe to do that. But I can change one world and make it so that the Outsiders are unmade. Changing time there will strengthen the walls of reality, prevent the random portals and make sure that there are no monsters to come through. I can't change the past on our world but I can preserve its future."

"You really think you can stop the Outsiders?"

"It's risky, but I believe it's possible. I have to make the attempt. It's the only way I can make amends for my crimes. Will you help me?"

Master Amiron didn't have to ask Gareth; he knew what that answer would be. Even with his own memories of the future, he still had to look into Mira's eyes and hear the words from her lips. He was offering her the chance to prevent all future attacks by Outsiders on her people. But he was the man she hated most in all of creation. She had no reason to believe him or to follow him. Her eyes were still wet from her earlier tears, but the dagger was sheathed and she made no move towards it. She leaned into the warmth of Gareth's chest as she studied the man on the bed. Her father's cousin. The man who had tried to steal a throne and ended up destroying everything they both fought to serve.

"If it will protect my people," Mira said. "I will help you. But only so that I can bring you back in chains to stand trial for your crimes."

Her voice choked with tears again and she turned away, heading for the door and the corridor outside. Gareth looked to Amiron.

"For a moment, I thought she was going to kill you," Gareth said.

"She still might. I don't have any memories beyond going to the Outsiders' world. I think I'm going to die there."

Gareth thought of the blackness in his own mind. Was that what he was feeling approaching? His death?

Twenty-Five

Reunions

Karl and Boron stood waiting outside the hospital room for some minutes. For once, Karl hated the sound construction of this place which meant he could barely hear more than a few murmurs on the other side. Occasionally, the voices would grow louder, but not loud enough for them to work out what was being said. Karl wondered what Boron would think if he stuck his ear to the crack at the edge of the door.

Then Karl looked up at Boron, pacing slightly in silent frustration, and knew that he probably felt exactly the same. Boron was supposed to be the second-in-command of the team, yet he was as much in the dark as any of the rest of them. Karl had looked out for Gareth for years, at first because Master Amiron insisted but later by choice. Karl had helped him, taught him, guided him, protected him. He'd watched Gareth grow from an awkward teenager to a strong young man. Yet now Gareth shut them out, like parents pushing children aside to discuss vital matters.

He hadn't even seemed happy to see them.

Maybe that was what hurt the most. Karl had spent the past month desperately fighting to control his fear, holding himself in check at all times because he was terrified what might be happening to his friend. Gareth had seemed barely aware of that.

Karl heard the sound of feet in the corridor. Lizzie rounded the corner, her face flushed from her brief sprint and an excited smile on her face.

"Is it true?" she asked. "Is Gareth back?"

Karl nodded, "He's in there, talking to Master Amiron."

Lizzie laughed. That sound shifted something inside Karl and let the anger melt away. Gareth was alive! He let himself feel the joy and relief at that simple fact. Surely all the irritations in the worlds didn't matter compared to that!

He grabbed Lizzie round the waist and spun her about, right there in the corridor. He returned her grin.

"He's home!"

The door to the hospital room opened and Karl turned, hoping to see Gareth emerge. It was the girl who came out first however, walking quickly past them as though she didn't see them. She stopped a few paces down the corridor, facing the white wall. Karl saw her raise a hand to her face, her shoulders shaking as she stood. Lizzie pulled away from him gently and went to her. Lizzie lay a hand on the girl's shoulder.

"Are you alright?" Lizzie asked. The girl nodded mutely, still looking away from them.

Gareth emerged from the room next, going straight to the girl. He gave Lizzie a slight smile as he passed her, then he laid a hand on the girl's other shoulder.

"Hey," he said gently.

"I couldn't do it," she said. "You were right; I couldn't."

She turned to Gareth, wrapping her arms around him, her eyes wet with tears. Gareth held her closely, letting one hand stroke her hair gently. There was something tender, almost beautiful, about the way he held her. A month had gone by but Karl was left to wonder just how much he'd missed.

"So we were here worrying about you," he said, "and you were getting a girlfriend?"

Still holding her, Gareth said, "Karl, this is Mira. Mira: Karl."

Mira slipped from Gareth's arms. She lifted one of the trailing pieces of her coat and used it to wipe her face. Then she turned to them.

"Hi," Karl said, offering his hand.

"Hello." She didn't take the hand, but Karl noticed that neither of them had denied his teasing remark about a relationship.

"This is Adrian Boron and Lizzie Bowers."

"Nice to meet you," Lizzie continued the polite formalities.

Mira looked at Lizzie for several seconds.

"I'm sorry," she said.

"For what?"

"For trying to kill you before."

There was a flicker of confusion before Lizzie asked, "You sent the beast?"

"Not exactly."

Karl noticed Gareth's hand on Mira's shoulder, tightening slightly. A warning? Or a signal that he was still there beside her?

Karl's mind went back to that huge room on the other side of the portal. He'd gone over the memory a thousand times in the days since then. That creature had spoken with a woman's voice and Gareth had talked to it, calling it by a name. Gareth had called it Mira.

"You are the beast!" Karl said.

"Yes."

Karl had a hand on the hilt of his sword without even thinking about it. He drew the blade in one smooth motion and stood there, facing Mira. This young woman, standing so casually in their base, had nearly cost him the life of the woman he loved.

Gareth stepped in between them. With one hand on the flat of the blade, he pushed the sword aside. Karl let him, reason catching up with his emotions. He shouldn't be about to kill another human being. Besides, Gareth wouldn't be treating this girl so kindly if she were an enemy.

"Mira thought we were her enemies," Gareth said. "She thought we served a man who betrayed her world and caused the death of her family."

A horrifying thought loomed in Karl's mind. Mira had wanted to kill Amiron. All she'd done to Lizzie and Enrico and Gareth was because she wanted Master Amiron dead. Karl wanted to run into that hospital room and just check his master was still alive. He ought to know better. He ought to trust that Gareth wouldn't be standing here so calmly if anything had happened. But he couldn't stop that whisper of doubt.

Gareth, still perfectly calm, turned to Lizzie, "Lizzie, Mira needs a room to stay in for the next few days. Can you find spare quarters for her?"

Lizzie hesitated for a fraction of an instant, her eyes flicking between Karl, Gareth and Mira. Then she smiled.

"This way," she gestured down the corridor.

Karl had to fight to keep himself still. He still had the urge to run this girl through. But he was calm enough to hear the beginnings of their conversation as Lizzie led her away.

"Are you alright?" Mira asked. "There's no lasting injury?"

"I'm fine," Lizzie replied.

"And the man I captured? Enrico? Is he alright?"

"He's fine."

Mira's concern sounded genuine. Then they rounded a corner and it was just the three of them left. Karl sheathed his sword.

"We've got a lot to discuss," Gareth said, turning back towards Master Amiron's hospital room.

"That's the understatement of the century," Karl muttered. But he and Boron followed, stepping quickly into the room where Amiron, still completely alive, lay waiting for them.

* * *

Gareth had summoned Richard to join them in the hospital room. They needed him for this because it was Richard who actually understood the science of what they were trying to achieve, the technology that would be required. If this was going to work, he was the one who'd make it possible.

Richard joined them quickly and then Gareth experienced the most awkward greeting he'd ever had to endure. For a moment, it seemed Richard might hug him, then he pulled back, hesitant. Richard next offered a hand to shake, only to change his mind before Gareth could take it. The whole fumbling exchange ended with Richard sort of patting Gareth on the arm. Gareth fought not to burst out laughing at Richard's embarrassment. Of every soul on this base, Richard was by far the least physically affectionate. The fact that he would attempt a greeting like this, however badly handled, was still rather touching, so Gareth smiled politely. Karl was less discrete, sniggering behind his hand as he watched the scene from the other side of Amiron's bed.

"I'm sorry," Richard said. "You were right about me not doing stupid pranks."

Gareth had a sudden insight based on a future conversation and knew exactly what Richard was apologising for. He wondered if he should be thanking Richard. Without that stupid prank, Gareth would never have met Mira.

"Don't worry about it," Gareth said instead. "Just remember that, no matter how clever you are, sometimes other people do know things you don't."

"Like the fact the portals can manipulate time," said Richard.

"Precisely."

"What?" cut in Karl and Boron at about the same time.

Gareth gestured to Amiron to speak, "It's your plan."

Gareth listened quietly while Amiron explained the principles, saying that they could use the device Richard was prototyping to influence time around the Outsiders' world.

"How do you know about the device?" Richard asked. "I've only shown it to Enrico."

"You punched a hole in the fabric of time," Gareth answered. "That's the sort of thing we're going to notice."

Amiron went on, explaining what he wanted the Defenders to do. Gareth listened to every word, straining to hear some sign of Amiron's honesty or some evidence of his lies. This plan might save everything but it could also get them all killed. Right now, Gareth had no idea which was even Amiron's goal. A month ago, Gareth would have listened to this apparently insane plan with the rapt awe of the naïve. A month ago, he would have been the first volunteer, despite the darkness looming on the horizon. A month ago, Gareth believed with all his heart in the man in front of him.

He wished he could feel that blind faith again.

When Amiron finished speaking, he looked towards Boron.

"It's an ambitious plan," Boron said, "but you're right that we have to try. Stopping the Outsiders forever is what we've wanted since the beginning. I just think we should wait. We can shore up the numbers; bring in a few more kids like Cassie so we can go in with everything we've got. Give Richard a bit more time to test his work. Not that I doubt his brilliance. I just don't think we should rush this. We've been fighting the Outsiders for ten years. Surely waiting a few more weeks can't hurt."

"Actually, they could," said Richard. "The power requirements for this are enormous. Every second's delay means we'll have to push back another second and that adds to the difficulty exponentially. Even with what Master Amiron says about less power being needed on the Outsider world, I'm still not convinced we can physically generate enough of a thrust to move an entire planet."

"It can't make that much of a difference."

"Do you want me to show you my calculations? Of course, by the time I explain the mathematics slowly enough to get the meaning through your skull, we'll have as much chance of reversing time significantly on the Outsider home world as I have of reversing the Earth's direction of rotation by pushing really hard. Just leave the thinking to me and accept that I know what I'm talking about when I say delay does make a difference."

There was something strangely comforting about the fact that, with all the strangeness and horrifying revelations lately, Richard could still be relied upon to be Richard. Gareth grinned.

"Your humility and contrition didn't last long," Gareth said.

"If you want me to redefine the laws of physics and perform a technological miracle for you, you're going to have to accept whatever I tell you and not waste my time contradicting me."

Gareth looked round at the assembled faces. He still wasn't feeling confident about this plan but at least Richard was on board. Richard, with all his genius, thought that this might work. Gareth could put his faith in that, even if he couldn't put any faith at all in Master Amiron anymore.

"We'd better get to work," he said.

* * *

Cassie had been woken by the alarms in the night but no one seemed to know what was going on. She asked the other Defenders and just got contradictory rumours: Master Amiron was back; Master Amiron was dead; the creature had attacked again; Gareth was home; a new assault of Outsiders had begun. Cassie was left bewildered and confused.

First thing in the morning, all Defenders were summoned to the canteen for a briefing. There was no hint of training today. Cassie pulled on her crisp, new uniform and made her way with the others, expecting to hear a final version of the rescue plan. Instead, she saw Gareth standing by the projector Boron had used the day before. There was an older man beside him as well, wearing the Defender uniform but completely unfamiliar. It took a moment for Cassie to work out who the man must be.

Many of the Defenders were faltering in the doorway, staring at Master Amiron. Quite a few went up to him, shaking his hand and offering words of welcome. Cassie saw many doing the same with Gareth, offering handshakes or even hugs in greeting. Cassie just stood to one side, feeling awkward and out of place.

But Gareth caught sight of her. It was Gareth who crossed the room and extended a hand. He smiled cheerfully as he said: "Congratulations, Defender. I'm sorry I missed your test."

"I... um... thank you," Cassie managed. "Welcome back."

Then Gareth was swept up by others wanting to speak to him. Cassie drifted across the room and found a spot from which she could see the rectangle of light from the projector. It didn't take long for the other Defenders to finish arriving, but getting everyone settled down was considerably more of a challenge. Gareth and Boron both made several attempts to call the room to order. In the end, Jerry climbed onto one of the tables and yelled at them all to shut up.

"Thank you, Jerry," Master Amiron said.

"I've got a mouth; I may as well use it."

"Most of you will be wondering where I have been for the past few months," Amiron went on. Cassie had been wondering a large number of things and that one had actually been pretty low on the list. "The truth is, we have spent the past ten years fighting a defensive war, reacting to attacks but never making any progress in attacks of our own. There have been reasons for this but it's still not reasonable to try and keep this up forever. We can't just keep leaping into action whenever a portal opens until all Outsiders are dead; the fact is that that could take centuries. We need to wage an assault that will stop the war once and for all."

"Are you talking about attacking the Outsiders' home world?" someone asked.

"Yes."

A wave of sound drowned the room, voices giving objections, or giving support, people yelling out their views. Cassie could barely pick out individual words for the tumult. It seemed that every single Defender had an opinion and they were determined to get it spoken regardless of whether anyone else heard. This time, even Jerry couldn't yell for silence and Master Amiron had to wait several minutes for the crowd to shout themselves out.

"I know what it is I'm asking of you," Master Amiron continued. "I know the dangers involved. But I also know the potential benefits. If this plan is successful, we can prevent any future portals. We can prevent all future Outsider attacks."

This time, it was shocked silence that met his words. Cassie was so new to this that she couldn't experience that revelation on the same level as the others here. These guys had been fighting Defenders for years, some of them since the start of the first invasion. The possibility that all of that could be stopped was just too much for them to cope with. So Master Amiron gave them a moment of quiet to let it sink it.

When he started talking again, he gave a high level description of what he proposed, talking about some machine Richard was developing that would manipulate dimensions around the Outsiders' world to stop the random portals opening. He said that he was going to be working with Richard and Enrico to build the devices that would make this possible.

"We don't have to defeat every Outsider," Master Amiron said. "We just have to position these devices around their planet and start them up. If we create a web of enough devices, we will be able to reinforce the boundaries of the Outsider world to prevent the random portal openings which are the source of the problem."

"How many is enough?" someone asked.

"Richard is in the process of doing the calculations, but I believe around twenty will be enough, if positioned correctly with enough power. If we don't get optimal positioning then it will take more so we will, of course, take more devices through to give us a safety margin."

What he didn't say was somehow louder than what he did. A safety margin. He meant in case some of the devices were never activated. He expected some of the people going through would die before ever finishing the job. Looking round the room, Cassie knew that everyone else understood this too. They'd signed up for this job knowing the risk. The Defenders had lost friends and comrades to the battle before now.

The hollow space was back in the pit of Cassie's stomach. She'd only just passed the test. She wasn't ready to go to the Outsiders' home world. She had barely learned how to use the sword. She might be wearing this uniform, but she didn't feel like a Defender yet.

A part of Cassie wanted to flee the room. She could call her parents and beg them to pick her up and take her home. Fighting a few Outsiders coming through a portal was one thing. Going to a whole planet filled with these monsters was quite another. Cassie realised she was shaking.

She wasn't up for this.

Twenty-Six

The Calm Before

Richard was currently the busiest person on the base but Gareth had managed to get him to one side briefly and ask him about the plan. He needed to know whether this could really work.

"Master Amiron thinks," Richard began. Gareth cut him off.

"I'm not interested in what Master Amiron thinks. I need to know what you think. You're the expert here, the person designing the equipment. Can it work? Can we really create a massive shift of time on the Outsiders' home planet?"

Richard hesitated a moment before uttering words Gareth didn't think he'd heard him say before.

"I don't know," Richard said. "It's all theoretical. My work in the lab implies it's possible and the mathematics is sound but no one has ever done anything like this before. It's not like we can do a controlled experiment to make sure. So much is dependent on the energy requirements. I know we couldn't do it here but the random portals imply that the dimensional barriers are less of an issue on the Outsider world and therefore the prerequisite power should be significantly less. But there's no way to test by how much. All these people are getting ready to go into battle and I don't even know if our plan is physically possible."

Gareth heard such doubts in his voice and recognised them because he felt such doubts himself. His whole life remembering the future and now, when he most needed certainty, he had nothing. He couldn't ask Amiron because he couldn't trust that whatever answer he received was the truth. He needed someone he could rely on, someone who'd never lied to him.

"Richard, do you think it can work?"

There was only the barest hesitation before Richard answered, "Yes."

And that would have to do. Gareth wished he'd sounded more confident though.

Gareth sighed and reached into a pocket, pulling out two letters, each signed and sealed. One was written by him, the other by Mira. He'd fought down an irrational surge of jealousy when he'd seen she'd addressed it to Corlion. He wasn't sure what was in hers, but his letter held instructions to Richard of what should happen if the plan were to fail as well as details of everything he now knew about Amiron's past and crimes.

"I don't know if I'll be coming back," Gareth said. "I want you to keep these safe, just in case. If Mira doesn't come back, see that this is sent through a portal to her world. The other, only read if I don't come back and Master Amiron does."

"Surely, if Master Amiron comes back, you'll want him to..."

"The letter is for you, Richard, not Master Amiron. I'm trusting you to take care of things if something goes wrong."

"Do you think it's likely that he'll come back and not you?"

"It all depends."

It all depended on whether or not Gareth was being taken in again. If Amiron was honest then this mission would be the great salvation of their worlds. If Amiron was lying, then this was all a trap, just one more ploy in his web of plots. The problem was that Gareth had no way to tell one way or the other. He just had to trust and hope that the trust wasn't misplaced.

* * *

Regular training had been cancelled. Defenders were discussing strategies or building Master Amiron's devices or calculating the optimal distribution of teams around the target planet. No one was going to spend this morning running through woods or practicing sword work. They all had duties to perform and decisions to make.

Except Cassie.

She didn't have anything really to do. Sure, she could probably go to the control room and volunteer for something, but she was more likely to get in the way of the trained professionals than she was to actually help. Particularly in her current, distracted state. Thoughts of impending death were cycling through her mind.

When she'd started the testing to become a Defender, she'd known that it was a dangerous job but the knowledge had been somehow abstract. It hadn't really sunk in until her field test and now she couldn't get it out of her mind. The next time a portal opened and Outsiders came through, she might be on the front line fighting them. If this plan went ahead, she might be heading through a portal to a world full of those creatures. If experienced Defenders were scared by the risk, what hope did she have?

Cassie stood in the small training room. She was running through training patterns with the sword because pouring herself into physical exertion was better than thinking. Besides, she needed every moment of practice she could get; she was way behind the others. Her uniform was damp with sweat and her arm beginning to ache. She had no idea how long she'd been at this but she was almost afraid to stop. If she paused to rest, her thoughts would be flowing again and she might never be able to stop the terror. So she focused every ounce of attention on her body. She didn't even notice the door open. It took her a while to realise she was being watched.

Gareth was standing by the side of the room.

"I see Karl's been working you hard," Gareth said, as Cassie came to a halt.

"Yes, sir," Cassie said.

"Please, my name's Gareth."

"Right."

Cassie thought it strange that things should be so awkward. A month ago, she would have chatted with Gareth freely. But, of course, that was before she'd learned exactly who Gareth was. How could she speak calmly to the man who was responsible for leading this team in the defence of the planet?

"You came to this base," Gareth said, "afraid of the danger of the responsibility that might be placed on you. Are you still afraid?"

"More than ever."

Gareth nodded, "That's probably sensible. You don't have to come. No one would blame you if you chose to remain behind."

"No one but me."

* * *

Gareth had become too accustomed to knowing what would happen. Now, as Master Amiron worked with Richard and Enrico to build the necessary equipment, Gareth was aware of the looming darkness up ahead. There was a shadow in his mind that he couldn't see through. Every heartbeat took him closer to that fight on the rooftop he had foreseen with Mira. The others were worried too, nervous about the dangers ahead, but they couldn't understand. They were used to uncertainty. Every time a portal opened, they would respond, never knowing if this would be the mission they didn't return from.

But Gareth knew. He always knew. Every day, every fight, every moment, Gareth knew who would live and who would die. He hadn't been conscious of how much he relied on the ability to prepare for the bad moments. Now he was struggling with the horrifying doubt. He didn't know if they would win or lose this time. All he could feel was the empty void where his future knowledge should lie.

He didn't even know if Cassie would be coming on the mission with them. He'd spoken to her about the mission, about the fact it was her choice, and all he could see was fog regarding which she'd decide. That should have been so simple. How could he trust his ability to remember anything when he couldn't even spot something that should be so obvious? It felt like he didn't know a damn thing anymore. He didn't know about Cassie. He didn't know if this was all some plot by Amiron to clear the way for him to take power. He didn't know if he'd be alive this time next week.

All that kept the soul-slaying terror from overwhelming him were the few fragments of memories that didn't belong. He knew he would dance with Mira to the music of the jasmine song. He knew he would see Karl and Lizzie in their wedding outfits. He knew he would see that child in the arms of the armoured warrior, while she had to choose which of them she could save. He clung to those fragments as a promise that something must lie beyond the darkness, but with his each moment, his doubts grew. Those fractured images were fading into the black and Gareth was left blind to the way ahead. It was getting harder and harder to bring those moments to mind and it almost felt like he'd imagined them.

He tried to distract himself with tasks, practicing in the firing range, helping Richard with his devices, or going through sword routines with Cassie. Anything to keep his mind on the present rather than the rapidly diminishing future.

He put up with Jerry insisting that Karl's stag party needed to be rearranged for before the mission.

The unspoken, "Just in case something goes horribly wrong and we all die in agony," hung in the air between them. Gareth could see the memory of Enrico that had helped him through the kidnapping rapidly approaching.

Adrian Boron pulled Gareth into the office to go over paperwork and various bits of bureaucracy that needed to be attended to, just in case none of them came back. It was hard to push the terror from his mind when everything everyone said reminded him of the uncertainty. How could he not think about dying when Boron gave him a stack of forms to sign regarding what should happen to the Defenders in the case of his death?

Gareth managed to escape both Jerry and Boron and was now on his way to Karl and Lizzie's room. They'd asked to see him and Lizzie had sounded quite urgent. He reached the room they shared and stepped into a memory.

Lizzie stood in the centre of the room, dressed in white silk. A fine veil hung over her blond hair and she clutched a bouquet of silk roses. She beamed a white smile when she saw Gareth but deep inside his hope died a little.

Karl was standing nearby, fastening the buttons on a silk waistcoat, looking rather less at ease in his finery than Lizzie. More plastic-swathed suits lay across the bed. Lizzie looked through and picked up one that had Gareth's name pinned to the cover.

"We need to check the fit," Lizzie said, "in case adjustments need to be made before the wedding. I want to do this at once, before the mission."

Gareth looked from one to the other. All his confidence had withered in an instant. He'd remembered this moment, remembered the sight of them in their wedding outfits. He'd been so certain he was going to stand at their sides as they were married. Now, all he saw ahead was blackness.

"Are you awake?" Karl asked.

"I don't know if you're going to survive this mission."

"Well, thanks for that dampener!" Lizzie said.

"No one knows what's going to happen," Karl said, "but we're not going to stop planning for the future. This way, we've got a reason to survive."

Gareth felt like the floor had vanished from under him and he was plummeting into depths of uncertainty. All he could see ahead was the shadow, looming closer with every minute. He sank down on the edge of the bed, aware of nothingness that threatened to swallow him whole.

"I remember," Lizzie said slowly, "the day the portal opened on the Norwegian coast."

"We all remember that day."

Five people had gone through as the initial response team, as per procedure. They'd emerged on rocky terrain in a pitch black night with the sea battering them. They'd called for back-up almost the moment they'd got there but, in the two minutes it took the secondary team to mobilise, the slippery rocks and the Outsiders had done their combined work. None of the first five had returned alive.

"When we brought the bodies back," Lizzie said, "you were upset but you weren't shocked. And, over the previous couple of days, you'd talked to all of them about being Defenders and how they felt about the risks involved. You knew they were going to die?"

"Before the Outsiders' portal even opened."

"You didn't try to stop them?" asked Karl.

"It doesn't work that way."

"Then how does it work?"

Gareth wondered what to say, how to say it. This was the closest he'd ever come to admitting to his ability to remember the future. A large part of him just wanted to spill everything. But Master Amiron had warned him never to tell a soul. Despite all his doubts about Amiron's motives, he'd been right about this. No one could understand what it was like to remember what would happen and know that all he could do was watch it unfold. They'd expect him to make things better and blame him for the things he couldn't change.

"I just know," Gareth replied, "before a mission, who's coming home and if they'll be hurt."

"But not this time?"

"Not even Master Amiron knows this time. I thought I knew you two would come back but I was wrong. At least, I've lost my certainty. I don't know if anyone will survive. I don't even know if I'll survive."

There was a long-drawn silence. This was the closest Gareth had come to acknowledging his terror. He'd become too used to knowing what would happen, at least as a feeling in the back of his mind. Much as he hated being different, he'd come to rely on it. He tried to tell himself that most people coped with the future as a blank unknowable. He'd managed for most of his life; he should be able to manage now.

"We all knew the risks when we signed up for this job," Karl said. "I nearly died the first time I saw Outsiders. We face death every time a portal opens. We never know if we'll be coming back."

Karl was right. Of course he was right. But Gareth couldn't shake the feeling of wrongness.

Twenty-Seven

Cassie's Choice

The design had been completed for the devices and now they were being produced in massive numbers in the labs below the base. Richard had been working through the night to make sure they would operate as expected. In the final stage, Defenders with any technical experience were pulled in to help, following his instructions with no knowledge of what it was they were doing. Enrico and Master Amiron supervised the final completion as more and more of the things were piled ready.

For those who weren't conscripted into building, Gareth announced that they had free time. A skeleton staff remained on the base, along with those on device duty. He was convinced there would be no Outsider attack before they made their assault, so everyone else had several hours in which they could leave the base and go anywhere they liked. There was a brief flurry of activity as everyone headed for the control room to give their portal destination to those who had volunteered to remain on duty there. It seemed like the whole place was in exodus. Gareth was apparently going to visit his sister and then a group of the guys were planning a trip to Las Vegas.

Jerry told Cassie that they wanted to give Karl a proper stag party before the attack and, of all the world, they were sure Vegas was the place to go. He gave his usual grin, saying with certainty that a European accent would get them some action.

"Besides," Jerry had said, "girls love a guy in uniform."

He winked at her and then wished her luck on her own trip.

Cassie took her turn and gave her coordinates, stepping through the portal that was opened for her. She emerged in a quiet side-street just off a main road. It was a tucked away spot where the portal wouldn't cause too much notice or alarm, around the corner from her parents' house. She was going home. She spent the morning with her parents, with none of them knowing quite what to say. Her mother complimented her several times on how striking she looked in her new uniform. They both said how proud they were of her and how they were sure she would do amazing things. And, naturally, her mum told her to be careful.

Cassie didn't dare tell them what was about to happen. It wasn't just that they were meant to be quiet about the nature of the mission. She knew that if she admitted that there was activity planned so much more dangerous than the norm, her parents would be terrified for her. Cassie was having a hard time keeping a grip on her own fear. If she admitted to those feelings, she wasn't sure she'd ever find the courage to go through the portal back to the base when the time came. This way, she could pretend to herself that the danger wasn't really so great. She could smile and drink her tea and imagine that she'd be coming home soon in victory.

She wasn't sure she could do this. She knew that everyone was getting ready for the biggest mission in the history of the Defenders, which made her fears seem even more selfish. She'd been told, by Boron and Gareth, that no one would blame her if she decided to stay behind. The choice was entirely up to her.

That almost made it worse.

If someone told her that she had to go through the portal, she had to take part in the mission, in some ways it would be easier. She wouldn't be caught in this cycle of her doubts and questions. What if she died? What if she was hurt? What if she froze again when faced with the Defenders? What if she screwed up and someone else got killed?

But among those circling ifs was another big one. What if she chickened out and someone died because she wasn't there?

Her mum must have sensed her fear, saying once again how proud they were of her and how brave she was. Cassie felt anything but brave.

She went upstairs in that little house, her old bedroom seeming strange and alien to her now, like it had belonged to some other person. She saw the cork board above her former bed, pinned with certificates and hung with medals. Every victory was on there: a little pin badge from a kindergarten race; the first place medal in the national championships; a certificate of completion for a charity marathon. Every goal she'd ever had was pinned to this wall, her hopes and dreams collected in one place.

They seemed so small now. All she'd wanted was to be fast.

She'd seen blood now, seen the injuries this war could cause. She'd watched the footage of bodies falling before an Outsider onslaught. The dreams hanging on this wall were the petty dreams of a child. As a Defender, she had a worthier goal, to protect, to guard, to save lives.

Cassie thought of her room on the Defender base, how empty and bare it had seemed when she'd arrived. She wanted to make it her own. That was her home now. Looking round at this room in her parents' house, that had never felt more clear.

She reached up to the board above the bed and pulled free the kindergarten badge. It was a tiny thing, a little red circle with 'first place' in white letters. She left the rest. Her parents could keep the trophies to remember the girl she'd been, just as they could keep the Olympic medal on the mantelpiece downstairs.

Cassie stared about the rest of the room, choosing small items with great care. A family photo was obvious, and a picture of herself with her coach by the podium after a race. A silver vase that had been her grandmother's. A woven bracelet she'd been given by a friend she'd parted ways with long ago. Fragments of memories to take with her, to decorate her new home. She put these trinkets into a bag to carry back to the Defender base; that little grey room was her rightful place now.

Back downstairs, with another cup of tea, Cassie talked about training and her new friends. She listened to tales of neighbours' antics and reports on former acquaintances. She found it hard to pay attention, hard to care. Her life was full of battles and danger now; how could she sit and listen to stories about who won best decorated cake in the WI fair? What she did now mattered. What she did now allowed these people to have their petty arguments over icing without fear of slaughter, without living in terror of Outsider attacks. Cassie was the sword at the gate that kept those people safe.

And that felt good.

Back on the base, she'd thought how easy it would be to ignore the return portal and stay here. She could go back to running. She could coach other athletes. Who had decided she needed to be a hero? But she could see now that wasn't an option. She wasn't that innocent girl anymore. Her life was waiting for her.

But she still wasn't sure.

She could still be a Defender without joining in this mission. It made sense that there be someone left behind, in case something went wrong or in case there was an incursion at the same time. In case everyone died and the mission failed, she thought, and someone needed to stay behind to keep up the fight. Gareth and Boron had told her she could stay behind. The choice was hers, completely hers. And that made it harder than if they'd given her an order.

The doubts were still bouncing around inside her head when it was time to leave. She hugged her parents goodbye, leaving her old life behind, still unsure of where the path ahead would take her.

Cassie was walking slowly back towards the location in which the portal was scheduled to open. As she walked, another young woman was walking towards her, a canvas shopping bag over one shoulder. This woman stared at Cassie, wide-eyed and excited. As they came close, she gave a nervous, fumbling greeting.

"You're a Defender, aren't you?" she asked, in the same tone that might be used to greet a favourite celebrity.

"Yes," Cassie said, feeling strange as she said it, feeling that it was half a lie. After all, she'd just been thinking of chickening out of the biggest mission in Defender history. But she'd passed the test and she wore the uniform.

"Oh, wow, I... Can I get your autograph?"

Cassie had been asked for her autograph before when she'd visited athletics clubs full of young hopefuls dreaming of medals of their own. Somehow it felt different to be asked because of her uniform. Still, she couldn't bring herself to refuse when faced with the excited grin of this stranger. This woman, about her own age, was staring at Cassie like she was something special and she retrieved a crumpled shopping list from the bottom of her bag and handed it over with a pen for a signature.

Cassie leaned against the rough wall of one of the terraced houses to write.

"What's your name?" she asked.

For a moment, the other woman stumbled over her words, as though forgetting something so obvious in her excitement. "Abby," she said. "I'm Abby."

Cassie signed the autograph to Abby, half-listening to the excited babble.

"I can't believe I'm meeting a Defender. You guys are, like, my heroes. Out there, protecting us, saving people. It's incredible. I wish I had half your courage. I mean, it must feel amazing to know you're out there, making a difference. Me, I just do a job. You guys save the world. To have that opportunity... I'm so jealous. I mean, you must go to bed at night feeling fantastic, knowing that the world's safer, that people are alive because you've done something. Isn't that what everyone wants? To make a difference in the world?"

Cassie smiled, "I guess so."

She handed over the autographed shopping list just as the burst of light indicated the formation of the new portal.

"Good luck," Abby said. "Save the world."

"I will."

Cassie stepped into the portal, knowing that she had no choice. The whole reason for starting on this journey was to do something important with her life and there was nothing more important right now than this mission. She couldn't turn her back on it.

* * *

On her return to base, Cassie announced her definite decision to go on the mission, receiving a nod of approval from Boron, who was on duty in the war room directing various groups. After those short hours at home, sitting in the quiet stillness of the living room, everything became a frantic rush of action. Teams were assigned and equipped. To her initial surprise, Cassie found she'd been assigned the same team as Gareth. The whole group consisted of herself, Gareth, Karl, Lizzie, Enrico and Jerry. When she thought it over, she guessed it might be because Karl and Lizzie were known as exceptional fighters and Jerry was acknowledged as the best shot. Maybe Gareth thought Cassie stood a better chance of coming out alive if she was grouped with them. Whatever the reasoning, Cassie was grateful.

Cassie joined the queue of people outside the armoury. She had her assigned sword. Now she was given bulky armour that would apparently shield somewhat against Outsiders as well as radiation. She was told that the radiation was not so severe as to cause problems with a short exposure, but she was given a mask that would fit over the lower part of her face and filter the air she breathed. Cassie felt that she'd have to be extremely lucky to live long enough to suffer from radiation poisoning.

Cassie was also issued with a gun and a spare clip loaded with dark metal bullets. As the Defender in the armoury handed it over, he issued another lecture about how valuable those bullets were. Cassie was not to waste them. She was only to use them in a life-threatening situation where she was certain she would make the shot count and using the sword wouldn't be enough. Given her status in the firing range, Cassie suspected she'd never fire this gun.

Once she was equipped, Cassie was herded into the large training room, where about a hundred anxious Defenders waited for the final order. More filed into the room over the next hour and Cassie located the others of her team. The decision had been for a large number of small teams, to increase the likelihood of enough teams activating their devices spread out across the planet, even if several groups fell to the inevitable Outsiders.

Cassie's fear was obviously written on her face, judging from the encouraging comments she was given by most of those around her, even Defenders whose names she couldn't remember and who she was fairly sure she'd never spoken to before. She was feeling as bad as she'd done before her first test, maybe worse. She'd only killed Outsiders on one occasion. She'd been rushed through her training because of Gareth's kidnap. She wasn't sure she was up for an assault into the heart of the Outsiders' own world. Maybe she should have accepted Gareth's offer to back out gracefully.

Gareth came to the group just before the order to move out. He'd apparently been in last-minute discussions with Master Amiron and Richard about the devices and the exact deployment of the teams. To Cassie's astonishment, Mira came with him. She was dressed in armour of her own, the sleek black she'd worn on her attack of their base. She had gloves tipped with claws, which had caused such devastation to Lizzie, as well as a sword hanging at her side. She'd exchanged the black beast mask for one of the air filters the rest of them would wear. She seemed utterly calm in the face of the nightmare they were about to endure. Cassie was less calm at the thought of having on their side someone who'd attacked them and nearly killed Lizzie in the process. But, since Lizzie didn't seem to be complaining about this assignment, Cassie supposed it wasn't her place to do so.

The Defenders were split between the training room and the canteen and Master Amiron went first to one then the other to give his final speech. Cassie barely heard a word. It felt like her guts were an icy knot from the fear. She couldn't stop the thought circling round her mind that she was about to die. Sweat soaked her palms and she felt moments away from screaming. She was barely aware of anything until Gareth touched a hand to her shoulder and told her that it was time to go.

Gareth was in charge of their team's device, which was strapped carefully to his back. It was astonishingly simple in appearance: a black box about twenty centimetres each side, with a silver-coloured circle taking up most of one of these. Richard had made the thing utterly idiot-proof, with just a single switch to turn it on next to the circle. Their orders were to get the device as high as possible, outside to avoid interference, and turn it on with the circle facing upwards. Richard hadn't been certain about the battery life of the devices, just as Master Amiron hadn't been certain how long it would take the various teams to reach a suitable position. So their orders were to only turn the machine on when they reached a good location for it, or as a last resort if they were pinned down and would be unable to get it anywhere better. About fifty teams were going through the portals to the Outsiders' world. They would need somewhere between twenty and forty devices to be activated, the number increasing if the positioning of those active was poor.

Cassie had overheard someone asking why they didn't just open portals to the best possible locations. She hadn't understood much of Richard's answer, but gathered the difficulty involved in sending people to a world about which they had no data. This wasn't like moving people about Earth, for which the Defenders had the best geo-spatial data in existence and could line up portals to the nearest millimetre.

Now Cassie and her team were part of the queue of people moving through the control room. As each team walked into the room, Richard entered the required settings to start the portal. The team pulled their masks over their faces and hurried through the portal, leaving the space ready for the next group. Cassie felt almost claustrophobic as she fastened her mask across her mouth and nose. For a moment, panic welled inside her and she almost yelled out that she wasn't ready, she couldn't do this. Then hands on her shoulders half-shoved her through the portal.

Cassie stepped out of the golden circle onto a grey street in the shadow of massive buildings. The only sounds were their own feet and the wind that howled between the great towers. On all sides, metal and glass towered upwards to a sky filled with greenish-grey clouds. Each building was a sky-scraper worthy of New York, but there wasn't a hint of anything growing among the paved streets and mighty structures. This place must have been impressive once, but Cassie could feel the oppressive silence weighing down on her from all sides.

"I guess we won't have difficulty finding somewhere high up," Jerry said, his voice surprisingly clear despite the mask.

"This way," Gareth said, pointing to one of the buildings that had a long line of glass windows towards them, one of which had already smashed. The windows rose from floor to a ceiling which struck Cassie as slightly too high. The room within, some sort of atrium or hall, had a few items of furniture that were obviously tables or storage. Everything was just a little too tall though, giving a strangely disorientating impression.

Gareth moved confidently through the deserted hall. Their feet seemed disturbingly loud as they walked across a floor of mirrored tiles, the shining surface obscured by dirt and age. They left a clear trail through the dust but no one seemed concerned. Cassie wondered how Gareth knew where they were going, or even if he did, but she followed along behind.

After the terror she'd been feeling back on the base, this seemed astonishingly easy. Gareth found a door, again disconcertingly tall, and opened it up to reveal a staircase of high steps, spiralling up into the building. The stairway ended after perhaps two hundred steps, something that was both frustrating and a relief. They passed through another door into a hall of machines. Huge masses of grey metal, some still whirring with hidden life, flickering with lights, others charred hulks that had obviously died from lack of maintenance, they stretched off in all directions. Their shapes reached up to the high ceiling, creating a forest of industry that prevented them from seeing clearly. The only lights were those on the still-working machines, creating a dim world of elusive shadows.

"Everyone, keep your eyes open for more stairs," Gareth instructed.

As they moved through the maze of machines, the noise grew. Cassie couldn't even guess the purpose of any of this stuff but strange clunking, faint whines and rhythmic pounding filled her nervous mind with a sense of dread. She walked along in the middle of the little group, seeing the hands of the other Defenders resting on the hilts of their swords. Cassie realised that her own right hand had found her sword without her even thinking about it. She wanted a weapon, just as they did.

A grey form leapt from the top of one of the machines.

Cassie was only aware of it as a blur in their air, launching itself towards Gareth. Gareth spun, his sword coming from its sheath to cut the thing in half mid-air. Two pieces of Outsider hit him and fell to the dusty ground on either side. The spray of dark blood covered much of Gareth and he gasped a few seconds before yanking off the mask. The gore in the filter wouldn't allow him to breathe.

Cassie just stood there. The attack had lasted less than a second, Gareth somehow knowing the Outsider was there, despite the noise of the machines. Gareth didn't seem at all phased. Cassie was fighting down the urge to either vomit or run and hide in a dark hole somewhere.

"Where there's one," Gareth said, "there will be others. Everyone stay alert."

Cassie held the hilt of her sword in a white-knuckled grip, ready to draw it at a moment's notice. The group moved faster now after this reminder that this world was filled with threats. They wound through the machinery with no clear path. The only comfort was that the dust in front seemed undisturbed, meaning that at least they weren't wandering in circles.

"Stairs," Jerry said, pointing to a metal staircase a little over a hundred metres away, rising from among the machines to a dark hole in the ceiling.

"Outsiders," said Lizzie. Sure enough, things were moving in the shadows of the machines between them and the staircase.

Cassie drew her sword, the hilt slightly slippery in her sweat-soaked palm. She didn't need it. As they reached the first of the snarling creatures, Mira moved in a dark blur. Her gloved fingers snapped out the dark metal claws that slashed through the first of the things, cutting deep strokes through its chest. Even as its claws reached for her throat, Mira raked one hand down it from head to hip. The thing fell, twitching to the ground in a puddle of thick, dark blood. Almost before the thing had hit the floor, Gareth's sword had made quick work of the second.

The thought entered Cassie's mind that this was easier than they'd anticipated. Then she reminded herself that they'd only come a short way up the building and they'd already faced three Outsiders.

Gareth was still very much in the lead, taking the stairs up to the next level, his sword out. Mira was immediately behind him, with Karl and Lizzie right behind. Enrico nodded for Cassie to go next, while he and Jerry brought up the rear.

The stairs climbed through a circular hole into a space that was almost black. Cassie could just about make out the shadowy forms of her teammates by the light that filtered up from below. As they activated the lights on their armour, Cassie became aware of more shadows moving. This room was cavernous, darkness stretching out all around them. In every direction were hungry growls, grey shapes moving towards the targets they'd just made of themselves. It was impossible to count how many Outsiders were there and Cassie didn't want to try.

She was just aware of this dark space filled with these bringers of death.

Jerry reached the top of the stairs and swore.

Twenty-Eight

Guarding the Door

"This way!" Gareth ordered. Under other circumstances, Cassie might have asked how on earth he knew. But they weren't on earth and Cassie would accept just about any orders right now in the face of such a nightmare. Cassie wondered about killing the light from her armour's torch, but the Outsiders knew they were here now. Besides, these lights were the only chance they had at staying together and avoiding killing each other by accident.

Cassie stayed close to Gareth as the team moved in a near circle of blades. Outside the circle, everything was shadow and movement. The sword work didn't require any skill now. Cassie just had to wave the sword, hacking away at the forms around them. Grasping limbs rained down and creatures fell. Cassie felt the blood, warm and thick, splattering all over her. The Defenders moved at a crawling pace, cutting their lethal path across the room. There was no time to pause or catch a breath as their swords were constantly working in the mass of flesh around them. Cassie's arm was quickly aching, but their progress seemed excruciatingly slow. They were just a circle of lights surrounded by death.

At one point, Cassie dodged a grasping claw and slipped in the trail of blood those in front were leaving. She nearly fell into Jerry, who was a step behind. Jerry's hand around Cassie's upper arm helped haul her upright and Cassie managed to gasp a thanks.

Whatever Jerry might have said in response was drowned in screams. The distraction had allowed the Outsiders to get past his defences. Jerry screamed as claws and teeth tore into his leg.

Cassie and Enrico were at his side, cutting through the sea of Outsiders, but Jerry was on the floor, his leg gushing blood and his sword barely held in a shaking hand.

Light burst in. Half-blinded, it took Cassie a moment to realise that Gareth had opened a door in a wall that was, miraculously, only a couple of metres away. Cassie and Lizzie held off the nearest Outsiders while Karl and Enrico each grabbed one of Jerry's arms. They hauled him through the door, a metal ridge at the bottom of the doorway eliciting another howl of pain as his leg was pulled over it. Jerry was still clinging to his sword despite the fact he wasn't able to stand.

The instant Cassie was through the door, it slammed shut, leaving her with just the memory of the seething mass of Outsiders on the other side, desperate for a taste of their flesh. Cassie took a breath, grateful for this reprieve, however short-lived it might prove to be. They were in another stairway, this one on the edge of the building, with massive windows overlooking the city and the street below. Cassie glanced down, seeing the ground seeming a long way below. But the skyscrapers still towered upwards. The height seemed insurmountable, given the carnage they'd just come through.

Jerry was on the ground, his trouser and the leg beneath torn to shreds. Blood was everywhere, soaking his clothes and pooling on the floor. Lizzie had pulled out a tube of mirus and was smearing the green paste across the entire lower leg, but Jerry was ghost white. His mask was gone; whether lost in the fight or clogged with blood and abandoned, Cassie didn't know.

"We've got to keep moving up," Gareth said.

"Give me a minute to get a bandage on," Lizzie said.

Cassie thought of the mass of beasts on the other side of the door and the potential numbers elsewhere in this building. Jerry was lying on the floor at the base of the stairs in a mess of his own blood and the Outsiders had torn huge chunks of muscle from his leg.

"No bandage is going to let me walk on this," Jerry said. Cassie had known that. They'd all known that. But Lizzie was still fighting the truth.

"We're not going to leave you behind," she said.

A sound of tearing metal came as answer. Cassie looked up. Terror gripped her again as she saw the door being pulled away from the doorway, the thick metal bending under the grip of grey claws. How strong were these things? How desperate were they for another taste of the humans beyond? Metal was folding in the corner of the door like someone dog-earing a page in a book. A snarling face appeared in the hole, its teeth dripping saliva from the sharp teeth.

The sudden bang made Cassie nearly drop her sword in surprise. The Outsider fell backwards, a hole in the centre of its skull. Jerry had his gun in his hand, still aimed at the hole.

"Go!" Jerry insisted. "I can hold them here for a little while. Get up to the roof!"

He fired again. An Outsider was now slumped dead halfway through the hole, blocking it temporarily, but the others were yanking the body out to clear their path through.

There was no time for argument.

How long had it been since Jerry had joked about heading out to Vegas in search of girls? Less than a day but it felt like a lifetime. Cassie wished she'd have had a little longer with the cheerful, smiling figure who had been so friendly since Cassie's first day on the Defender's base. Now there would be no more jokes, no more pieces of advice in the training room, no more sessions in the firing range.

All trace of his usual grin had disappeared from Jerry's face. Determination set his jaw and his gun remained unwaveringly towards the gap in the door. He didn't look at them. He didn't say goodbye.

No one said it to him.

Maybe they all wanted to lie to themselves, to believe that they might come back for him. There was no doubt in Cassie's mind that Jerry was sure he was staying behind to die. As the others started up the stairs, Cassie felt the gun at her side.

She'd become adequate in the firing range but never great. She stood little chance of hitting moving targets in the heat of battle.

"Come on, Cassie!" Karl ordered, hesitating on the bottom step while the others were already moving up into the tower.

Cassie pulled her gun from its holster and pressed it into Jerry's left hand. The spare clip, she dropped on the ground within easy reach.

Jerry fired again, with Cassie's gun this time, the shot no less deadly. Another Outsider clogged the hole for precious moments. Only then did Jerry's grin return. He sat on the floor at the base of the stairs, a gun in each hand and a sword by his side. Despite the pain and the oncoming death, this was what Jerry had been born for, the sharpshooter in the rush of adrenaline, fighting for his friends and his world.

Cassie turned. There wasn't a moment to lose. Most of the others were already well ahead on the stairs. Only Karl had waited. Cassie hurried now, moving up the stairs at a fast pace something between a walk and a jog. They couldn't run up these stairs, not with the great height still above them. Cassie's heart was pounding, her breath struggling in gasps through the filter mask. Cassie touched the front of the mask and felt the stickiness of Outsider blood.

She yanked it from her head and dropped it down the stairway below. Karl didn't question the action. Leaving Jerry behind was further sign of how little chance any of them had of making it out of here alive. Somehow that made things easier. Cassie could gasp the foul-smelling air without fear of poison or radiation. The panic that had been threatening since they'd stepped through the portal was gone. In the grim certainty that they were about to die, all Cassie had to worry about was doing her duty.

So she pounded her way up the stairs.

Below them came repeated bangs as Jerry did his duty. Each gunshot sounded more distant as the team hurried up the staircase. Cassie wasn't counting shots. She wondered how long it could be before those shots fell silent. How many bullets did Jerry have left? How long before the Outsiders got him and continued on after the rest of the team?

* * *

Gareth hurried up the stairs, almost grateful for his position at the front of the group because it meant none of them would see his face. He'd abandoned one of his team. Worse, he'd known he would do it since before they'd even opened the portal. He remembered Jerry, always so cheerful and friendly. He'd never see that grin again.

He could feel the future looming. Every heartbeat carried him closer to the abyss. He didn't dare look more than a few seconds ahead, just enough to guide his steps, because he was constantly aware of the darkness.

Something shifted. It was like a tremor running through his entire body, just for a moment. It was enough to make him stumble slightly on the stairs. As he hurried on again, he knew something had changed but he wasn't sure what. There was some subtle difference in the immediate future that awaited them at the top of this staircase, but he didn't have the time now to stop and analyse exactly what that change might be.

Back in the lab beneath Mira's palace, they'd glimpsed their future together. They'd glimpsed a desperate stand on the roof of a skyscraper beneath a greenish grey sky. Gareth had seen the sky when they'd arrived. He'd seen the buildings around them. He'd known his destiny was close.

He tried to tell himself that this might not be the end. After all, he still had to dance with Mira in that ballroom, to the song of the jasmine flower. He'd seen that, as clear as most of his other visions of the future. But now, that image was harder to hold onto. He felt the blackness creeping closer with every step in this staircase. It was hard to believe that dance to be anything more than fantasy.

Mira was a step behind him, close enough that he could hear her heavy breathing. Gareth thought of all the things they'd never get to say or do. He wished she were anywhere else, but he knew her well enough to be certain that she'd never have agreed to stay behind. This was the fight to save her world as well as his; she would never agree to be anywhere else right now. But Gareth still felt the guilt that he was leading her to her death.

He'd never really get the chance to love her.

* * *

There were still periodic gunshots from below as they reached the end of the stairway. Cassie was exhausted and desperate for a break, but the view out the window showed that there was still considerable height above them, even though the ground was dizzyingly far below. At least they were now higher than the tops of a small few of the other buildings.

"Aren't we high enough?" she asked.

"Too much interference," Gareth answered.

"We could break a window."

"All the buildings would still get in the way and weaken the signal. We need to get higher."

They opened the door that let back into the rest of the building. Lizzie muttered that she'd like a word with whoever had designed the stairs in this place. Cassie supposed that a desperate rush for the roof hadn't been something the architect had planned for. She was grateful at least that they got to leave behind the last, desperate sounds of Jerry's last stand below them.

The floor beyond the doorway had probably been an office once. There were chairs and tables that, like everything else, were disconcertingly tall, as though someone had stretched the room ever so slightly. A distant wall was lined with windows, letting in a grey and gloomy light, but this time they could at least see their way through the maze of furniture. Gareth paused only long enough to seal the door behind them, but that gave enough time for Cassie to take in the scuffed markings through the dust. Outsiders had been here.

She'd sheathed her sword to help in the climb up the stairs but she drew it again, ready for another assault.

She'd always prided herself on her endurance, but she was flagging now. She was a sprinter, not a marathon runner. All her limbs had a deep ache set into them. Her armour was drenched in sweat. She longed for a safe place that she could sit down and rest. Instead, they pushed on. Gareth was in the lead again; Cassie had to hope he knew something they didn't.

Across the room was another door of heavy metal. That seemed to be their destination. Cassie wondered briefly what sort of work had gone on here to require such secure doors and confusing access paths. Then she told herself to stop idle wondering and be alert for more Outsider attacks.

There was no sound but their footsteps and laboured breaths. They reached the new door without incident, Gareth turning to the control panel beside it. Cassie hadn't noticed the one by the other doors; she'd been too preoccupied by Jerry. Now, she saw Gareth peer at what was obviously a keypad for a few seconds, then calmly type in a code. The door opened. How the hell did Gareth know the proper passcode for a lock in an alien building when the keys were marked with unrecognisable symbols?

Beyond the door was another set of stairs. Cassie felt she'd barely recovered from the last lot. This stairwell was gloomy, with only small windows set in the walls at sporadic intervals.

"Everyone, stay alert," Gareth warned as he began to climb. Cassie bit back a retort that they'd of course been taking it easy until now. It wasn't Gareth she was really angry at. She just couldn't banish the thought of Jerry lying at the bottom of a set of stairs like these.

Up they went, step by leaden step. Cassie was focused on little more than putting one foot in front of the other. It was several turns of the staircase before she realised that those in front were slowing. It took another few steps for her to realise the reason. She heard movement somewhere above.

"Don't worry about stopping them all," Gareth said in a whisper. "We've just got to get past."

They paused briefly, recovering their breath and gathering strength. They waited maybe a minute, nowhere near enough for Cassie to feel at all ready. But she was aware that there were more Outsiders somewhere behind them and the other teams, spread across the planet, needing this part of the mission completed as soon as possible.

Assuming any of the others were still alive.

Cassie banished the treacherous thought and, at the nod from Gareth, resumed their progress up the stairs.

The first Outsider saw them from above, scrambled over the banister and leapt several metres down to them. Karl cut the thing in two, but was knocked backward by the creature's momentum, stumbling and nearly falling down the stairs. Lizzie half-hauled Karl back up and the group continued on.

The narrow staircase was their only advantage, reducing the impact of the Outsiders' greater numbers. Gareth and Mira started at the front, bearing the brunt of the assault, swapping places with Karl and Lizzie when they got too tired. But there was still plenty for Cassie and Enrico to do. The Outsiders were climbing over the railings up above, dropping down to where the group of humans were. Cassie hacked away at them as they jumped down.

All the while, they had to keep up their ascent. None of the training had prepared Cassie for this, fighting a foe from above while climbing up and up stairs that were high enough to be challenging at the best of times. The clutter of bodies left by the vanguard made the stairs an obstacle course. Cassie had to be careful of every step because of potential trip hazards and the slippery puddles of blood.

A few steps above her, someone was thrown off balance by the fight, stumbling on a step. Karl fell back a step into Cassie, who was dominoed down. Her foot went out from under her and she grasped at thin air for a moment before gravity took hold. The pair tumbled down a few stairs, swords clattering beside them. Her legs bashed against the edges of the steps before she slammed into the wall where the stairwell turned. Cassie's breath was knocked from her body by the impact and, a moment later, Karl landed on top of her.

She lay a moment, sore and shaken, as her body registered a dozen pains. Even in the chaos of battle the group had glanced their direction. She could see on their faces the fear that they would have to face another Jerry so soon. But the pair each managed to get to their feet. Cassie's left leg was registering a dull, throbbing ache where she'd struck the corner of a step, but she could still walk on it. Some bruises were the least of her concerns right now. Cassie grabbed her sword and hurried back up the stairs to where the rest of the group were still facing off the hoard.

They slowly forced their way up the staircase, everyone careful now of the fallen bodies. They rounded a bend, revealing a landing with another doorway, another dark hall beyond. The metal door here was twisted severely out of shape, allowing the flow of Outsiders from whatever dark space lay beyond. The stairwell continued upwards, the steps above relatively free of the things; no doubt they were too interested in the group of humans below them.

The next few metres made the earlier climb seem easy by comparison. It was such a short distance, but every step was crowded with Outsiders. They were a wall of grasping claws that had to be hacked through. Every body that fell was replaced by others and the weight of the dead pressed down above them. Cassie had to push past fallen limbs even as she battled the nightmare above. Each step was a breathless charge, each inch of space painfully bought. Cassie was shielded from the worst of it to begin with, Gareth and Mira struggling through in the front of the group.

Cassie saw Gareth falter, splatters of red joining the black blood puddling the steps. Karl forced his way, with great difficulty, past Gareth into the vanguard position. Gareth kept fighting, holding his left arm close to his body all the while. Cassie hadn't seen exactly what had happened but she knew the dangers of Outsider bites and how quickly the poison could set in. They needed to get through this mass of creatures to somewhere that they could apply the mirus. It felt like forever since this stage of the battle had begun and it showed no sign of ending.

As the group pressed forward, Gareth stayed on the same step for the minute or so needed for him to end up at the back. Gareth and

Cassie were side by side, behind the cluster of the rest of the team, inching their way up the stairs.

The moment they reached the landing, everything changed. Suddenly, Karl had access to the empty stairs above. He didn't head that way, instead pushing towards the door against the sea of enemies.

"Gareth! Lizzie! Up there and sort out a bandage!"

No one questioned the fact that Karl was giving orders. Karl, Enrico and Mira held the landing, Mira fighting like a demon now that Gareth was hurt. Lizzie and Gareth hurried up the stairs, Lizzie having to almost haul him up as the poison began to take hold. Cassie stayed with the other three, a step above them now as they began their journey up the stairwell.

Progress was better now, but still painfully slow. Each step, they had to be aware of the Outsiders that still poured through the doorway, clambering over the slaughtered bodies the Defenders left in their wake.

Mira was obviously tiring, so Cassie let her pass and she took her turn on the front line against the Outsiders. Enrico was beside her as they edged two abreast up the stairs, walking backwards and hacking away at anything that came close. If she'd felt tired before, this position was utterly exhausting. Cassie wasn't sure how the others had managed to keep it up for so long. She was constantly moving, her arm a whirl of metal without any semblance of style.

They'd only reached the next turn of the stairs when Karl took over the difficult position again. Gareth and Lizzie rejoined them. One sleeve of Gareth's shirt had been torn away and wrapped around his left forearm as a makeshift bandage. His sword arm was undamaged and he appeared ready to continue the fight.

From then on, they moved upwards in a constant cycle. A pair would hold the lowest step, then they'd move back hurriedly, past another pair who held a couple of steps above them, then the process would repeat with another pair. The movement became much faster then and it actually began to feel that they might make it up the stairs sometime this century. It was still exhausting and there seemed no end to the fountain of Outsiders surging up the stairs behind them.

Stair by stair, turn by turn, they worked their way upwards. Somewhere, during the battle for the landing, Cassie had found a new burst of energy. That seemed to be deserting her now. Her whole body was sapped of energy, the effects of adrenaline fading. How long since they'd come through the portal? It felt like an eternity. Certainly, it must have been a few hours. The morning training sessions hadn't prepared her for this level of exertion for this amount of time.

One turn and there, almost an answer to formless prayers, was another door at the top of the stairs. Cassie didn't dare wonder if there were Outsiders on the other side, in case the thought could make it so. Gareth passed the rest of the group, running up to the door and somehow finding the code to open it.

The stinking wind gusted down the stairwell, the most divine scent Cassie could have hoped for. They'd reached the roof!

Twenty-Nine

Above the World

As he searched his future memories for the code to the door, Gareth knew how little time he had left. He could see almost nothing ahead of him now except darkness. All that was left was that moment he'd witnessed with Mira and then the fight.

Gareth forced open the door to the roof and hurried through with the others. They poured out of the doorway onto the flat top of the building, Karl shoving the door closed behind them. It locked automatically, but the doors below hadn't been enough to hold back the Outsiders and Gareth didn't dare hope that this one would protect them for long. The roof was a flat expanse across the whole of the building, a rectangle of smooth greyness. Simple railings offered meagre protection at the edges. They had little cover but a few chimneys and vents along with the doorway they'd come through.

Gareth had seen this place before. He'd seen this coming and known then what it meant.

He wasn't going to make it off this roof alive.

He just hoped he'd made the right call. He was giving up his life and risking everything on the hope that Amiron really was a hero, really wanted to help. That fear was worse than the certainty of death. What if this had all been for nothing? What if all Gareth had done was lead his teammates into death so that Master Amiron could rid himself of those witnesses who knew his treason?

Gareth hoped, fiercely and desperately, that he'd been right. He'd believed Master Amiron to be a great man, his personal idol and mentor as well as the protector of his world, the one true Defender. Evidence had shattered that blind belief. All he had now was hope.

Hope that a man truly could be transformed and seek to right the wrongs he'd done.

Right or wrong, they had little time before the Outsiders would break through. They had work to do.

* * *

The city stretched away to the horizons in all directions. There were great buildings everywhere Cassie looked. Some rose a few storeys above the one on which they stood, some were considerably taller, but most reached their peak a little below the one they'd chosen. The sickly clouds overhead were so close it felt like Cassie could reach up and touch them. And, every moment, there was the wind. It whipped across the peaks of the buildings with enough force that Cassie felt like she could just spread her arms and be carried away by it. The wind brought with it the stench of chemicals, even breath disgusting. But Cassie suspected she didn't have much time to worry about the poisons it bore.

Gareth had slung the device from his back and he placed it now on the flat top of one of the vents. He flipped the switch and a tiny light indicated that the thing was working.

"Is that it?" Karl asked.

"That's it," Gareth answered. "Now we have to wait for enough other devices to be in place."

"And how will we know if it works?"

"I think we'll know. If we're still alive. And assuming enough teams manage to get their devices into position."

Not exactly encouraging. The thought crossed Cassie's mind that if Jerry were here, he'd probably crack some joke about Gareth needing to learn how to give a pep talk. But Jerry wasn't here. They were a team member short and, from the sound of tearing metal, the door was giving up the fight to the Outsiders. Any minute now, they would be overwhelmed by those creatures again.

They were all exhausted. A part of Cassie wanted to just sit down and let the Outsiders come. They'd done their duty. They'd got the machine this far. Now it would either work or it wouldn't regardless of them. It was so tempting to just give in to the creatures, or to walk over to the railings and let the wind take her. The fight would be over and she could just rest. Cassie looked around at the battered and tired figures of her fellow Defenders, covered in sweat and dirt, their neat uniforms stained with the blood of enemies and allies. If any of them suggested giving up, Cassie would agree, but she wasn't going to suggest it first. She wasn't going to be the weak link.

"This is where we make our stand," Gareth said. "Guns out, everyone. Either way, we won't need to save the bullets."

Cassie didn't have a gun anymore. It probably wouldn't have made much difference once the chaos started.

"We'll fight them until the last moment," Lizzie said. "We'll give the other teams every last second we can buy. If there's a chance in hell that we can survive this, we will. I want my wedding day."

Karl looked to her and managed a smile, "I don't regret this. Not for a moment."

They kissed, on the rooftop in an alien world. They gave themselves to each other in a moment that was both farewell and desperate hope for the next moment.

Cassie turned away from them, wanting to give them an illusion of privacy for such a personal instant. Instead, she saw Gareth and Mira. They had their hands locked together, staring at each other with a depth of gaze that carried volumes of meaning. They gave murmurs of love, then Gareth leaned down to kiss her.

Cassie looked across at Enrico, who grinned and said, "Don't expect me to kiss you."

Cassie laughed, the sound so strange amid the howling wind. It was a strange, surreal noise that seemed to be carried across the city by the gusts, letting this world know that there were people here who would fight it until the end. Despite the pain and the fear and the horror of it all, they would keep resisting. No matter what monsters came at them, they would face them. Maybe they could hold out long enough for Master Amiron's plan to work. Maybe they would all be torn to shreds and eaten alive. Cassie didn't know. She should probably regret this. She should probably be wishing she was back safe and sound, having failed in the tests, but she wasn't. She was here and she had played her part.

Win or lose today, she had done something significant with her life and she would give everything in herself to keep going.

"They're coming," Enrico said.

The group stood on the rooftop, the two couples close enough to be nearly touching, even as they prepared their weapons. Cassie shifted the grip on her sword as she watched the metal door tear away from the doorframe.

The creatures' snarls were caught by the howling wind, the Outsiders streaming through the gaping doorway. They ran across the rooftop to the waiting humans. Cassie was moving as she'd been trained, efficient strikes against those that came near her.

The deafening cracks of gunshots pierced the air above the city. Creatures fell all around, by sword and gun. Cassie saw Karl, his sword in one hand, gun in the other, tearing down the Outsiders. Lizzie's blade was a whirlwind of death as she danced through the monsters, black blood flying in all directions. Enrico was screaming a wordless cry of rage as he fought, yelling himself hoarse as he severed the Outsiders from the lives. Mira and Gareth were still side-by-side, Mira using her claws as well as her sword, Gareth reacting to attacks almost before they happened.

And there was Cassie, in the middle of it all, adrenaline fuelling this last, desperate stand. No training could have prepared her for the sheer numbers but she didn't pause. Even as one got through her guard and drove its teeth down into her left arm, Cassie didn't stop fighting. She simply sliced her sword through the creature's neck and kept fighting.

She was somehow cut off from her pain, aware of it but not really feeling it. Her left arm hung uselessly, but she still had her right. She could still defend against the onslaught. She kept moving. She kept her sword up.

There was no style now, no rhythm to her movements. She was just moving constantly, her sword a blur in the air, in the hope that she could cut through the beasts before they got to her.

She stumbled, tripping over an Outsider corpse.

She landed among the bodies of those she'd slain, losing her grip on her sword for a moment. She rolled away from a swiping claw, grasping for the hilt. Teeth and claws were at her leg, tearing through the flesh. Cassie had her sword in hand again, slicing through those that held her, giving her a moment of respite.

For an instant, she thought about trying to get back to her feet, but one glance at her mangled legs told her that wasn't going to happen. The pain was a fire so intense she could barely process it, filling her entire being. But still she held the sword, hacking away at anything that got near.

She was aware, briefly, of Enrico. The other Defender was by her side, trying to protect her from the hoard. But the numbers were too many and it was obvious to anyone that Cassie wasn't going to make it.

Teeth buried themselves into her right shoulder and Cassie lost her grip on her sword again, screaming out in pain. The Outsiders were all over her, grabbing her from all sides, tearing at her flesh like it was nothing.

Cassie collapsed back against the cold ground, seeing the faces of the monsters that would end her.

The golden light burst from all directions. A tower of fire shot into the sky, cutting through those bruised clouds. Even the Outsiders stopped, staring at this pillar of light that rose from Master Amiron's device.

Cassie stared up as golden lines were traced across the clouds. A few at first, then many, criss-crossing the sky. More and more appeared until all there was up there was this amazing radiance. The whole world shone with gold, brighter and brighter. Cassie was nearly blinded but she wouldn't have looked away even for an instant. The light filled everything overhead.

They'd done it. They'd actually done it.

Cassie smiled as the light came racing down from the sky towards them.

Thirty

The Road Ahead

Gareth stood, dazed and blinded by the sudden light. It faded quickly, leaving the little group still standing on the rooftop. The Outsiders were gone. The bodies and parts of the dead creatures had also vanished. The only blood in evidence was soaking in the clothes of the Defenders. Cassie lay on the ground, her blood spilling from a dozen different wounds. She was still staring up at the sky but her eyes weren't seeing. Lizzie dropped to her side to try and stem the bleeding, but one touch of the cold skin and she knew it was too late.

Gareth just stood there, overwhelmed by what was going on inside his own mind. One moment, he'd been feeling the shadow creeping up on him, knowing that he was only a few seconds away from the point his memories ended. One moment, he'd been expecting the emptiness of death, then the golden light had shone from the device and from the whole world.

Now his mind was full. A million memories were surging round inside his skull so that he couldn't focus on any single one. He was just intensely aware of their presence and their quantity. He had a whole life still ahead of him. His recollections were filled with agony and delight, fear and joy. A lifetime was trying to cram itself into his consciousness in the moment of golden light so that now he struggled to even remember how he'd come to be here.

"Gareth, are you OK?" Karl was at his side, touching his arm, looking with concern into his eyes.

Gareth looked at him and one memory forced itself through the mass. He saw Karl and a knife and blood on the wedding gown. Gareth blinked at Karl through his tears.

"I'll survive," he muttered.

Survive! A near memory surfaced. Gareth sheathed his bloody sword and began running, yelling at the others to hurry. He raced down the stairway, leaping several steps at a time. There were no Outsiders to face now, no blood to slip in. He pounded down floor after floor, hearing the others above him.

He reached the bottom of the stairs but didn't stop running. He crossed the office space, past people who were staring about in a dazed and dreamlike state. They seemed human, apart from their unusual tallness. They looked confused as Gareth ran past but he didn't bother to stop and explain things. He just reached the other staircase and continued his journey downwards.

He found his target still lying by the stairs in a pool of his own blood, beside a door that was in perfect condition. The guns were lying abandoned but Jerry was holding a sword. He must have been fighting the Outsiders off the whole while, fighting even as they began devouring him. His legs were a mangled mess of blood and bone, the flesh almost entirely tore off them. Gareth couldn't understand how anyone could have survived the bloodloss, much less kept fighting hard enough to keep them from eating the rest of him. But he had.

Jerry was still conscious, albeit barely, when Gareth knelt down beside him.

"Hold on," Gareth said. "We won. You'll make it, I promise."

* * *

The price of victory had been high. Some teams had been wiped out in their entirety. None had made it through completely unscathed. The hardest loss for Gareth was Cassie, who'd been right beside him and who'd been so close to making it through. He couldn't help wondering if he could have saved her life by acting just slightly differently during the battle.

There were others whose loss hit him hard. Adrian Boron hadn't made it. Only one man in his team had survived, the rest sacrificing themselves one at a time to let the device reach its destination. Adrian had died a hero. They all had.

Only four of the senior Defenders had made it through the battle alive. They sat in the war room to discuss their state afterwards, so many of the chairs empty. Gareth looked round at Karl, Enrico, Jakob and Jonny. The rest were gone. Some he'd liked; some he hadn't. It didn't seem to matter now.

There were surprisingly few injuries, beyond numerous scrapes and minor cuts. Most had made it back whole or not at all. Jerry was the exception. He'd get the best prosthetics money could buy and a nice, shiny medal, but it wouldn't make up for the loss of his legs. Gareth had told him he could stick around, stay with the Defenders for as long as he liked, but he'd refused. It hurt him too much to be around his healthy teammates and feel so helpless.

The words had turned heated, with Jerry yelling at Gareth for saving him, implying that he wished he were dead rather than a cripple. He'd elected to be shipped out to a regular hospital and Gareth had been forced to agree, even though he hated the sight of his friend so distraught. Gareth had wanted to go with Jerry to that hospital and beg the doctors to watch out for him, to make sure he didn't do anything stupid. But Gareth knew the direction Jerry's future would take. Besides, he had duties to attend to.

Gareth had to make funeral arrangements for so many dead, so many fallen heroes. He had to write the letters to families, explaining about those lost in the line of duty. He took it upon himself to visit Cassie's parents, still wondering if he could have done something differently there. Cassie had come so close to making it. If they'd been a little faster, fought a little harder, would she have made it?

Gareth had to stand in a neat hallway and explain to a supportive couple that their daughter was gone, slaughtered in battle. He endured the tears and the shouts of recrimination, the angry voices that demanded to know why he'd let her go through without more training. He accepted them all because he'd been asking himself the same things.

Then he returned to base, knowing that there were still more innocent people who would have their lives torn to shreds because of the letters he still had to write.

The base felt strange, half-empty. Those that were here were feeling a strange confliction of emotion. They were thrilled to be alive and delighted to have won, but each of them felt the agony of loss. They'd all lost friends, comrades, brothers.

He gathered them together in the large training room, lines of coffins crammed in side by side, so many that there was barely room for them. Gareth remembered a funeral, so recent but seeming like a lifetime ago. He'd thought five deaths had been a tragedy. Now he looked across line after line of bodies, knowing that he'd caused this. They'd trusted him and followed him. They'd paid the price.

He had to say something. He had to find the words to give their sacrifice meaning. He saw the faces of the surviving Defenders, expressions grave and grieving, all watching him, waiting for some insight.

"We did the impossible," Gareth said. "We ended the war that's been plaguing this world for ten years. Our friends, our brothers, laid down their lives for this victory. All we can do is thank them and honour their memories."

He thought of the words he'd spoken at that other memorial.

"The last time we gathered to grieve fallen friends, I told you what Pip once told me. That if his sacrifice meant one more person alive who would otherwise be dead, it was worthwhile. Think how many people will never die, never feel the terror of an Outsider attack, because of what we accomplished and what these people sacrificed. We will remember them and we will never let the world forget the cost of this victory."

He finished the speech but the words tasted like ash in his mouth. He knew it wasn't that easy. This victory, however significant, wouldn't stop the deaths completely. He almost wished he'd not regained his future memories. It would be easier if he didn't know what was coming. He faced recent grief in both directions.

Gareth found himself wandering through the corridors of the base, letting himself sink into future memories of a time when the pain would have subsided. It wouldn't hurt forever.

Karl and Lizzie were lost in preparations for that better future, burying themselves in wedding plans and in each other. They grieved for their friends like everyone else, but they were thrilled at the prospect of a future together, babbling about the eternal bliss they would share.

Gareth couldn't bear it. He knew their future. He knew how short their bliss would be.

Gareth's wanderings took him to the small training room. Their practice halls were almost deserted now, since the immediate threat was gone. But in this small room, Master Amiron was sitting. He'd survived, to his own surprise, but now had to deal with the certainty of what his future would contain.

"I'm sorry," Master Amiron said as Gareth sat across from him. "I'm sorry to leave you alone to face whatever is coming."

"I'm sorry too."

Master Amiron had promised Mira to return to their world to stand trial for his past deeds. He was guilty of treason and would accept the penalty without a fight. They hadn't told the other Defenders, even Mira agreeing that there was no point in destroying the faith the team had in their leader. All Master Amiron had said would that he would be going away after the wedding and that this time he wouldn't ever be coming back.

Gareth felt guilty for not believing in him almost as much as he felt guilty for the deaths. Amiron had gone through the portal expecting to die, just as Gareth had. The time shift had blocked them both from their future memories, except for the couple of moments that had somehow slipped through into Gareth's awareness. Now, Amiron was going to go through another portal, knowing that it wasn't a trick of time shutting off his future this time. Amiron would give his life in penance for his crimes.

In the end, after all the pain and deception, Gareth had his mentor back. Right now, that was what he needed more than anything because he could see the future that was looming.

"I can't stand not telling them," Gareth said. The advantage of their shared gift meant that they could skip parts of the conversation, each remembering the context from what would be said.

"Karl and Lizzie are happy."

"They're talking about their future together."

"Of course. They've just had a great victory and are planning on starting a life together in a world of peace they helped create, a world that they can bring a family into. Do you really want to shatter that happiness? Do you really want to tell Karl that he'll never see his child born?"

"Of course not. But I want to warn them."

"It won't change anything. Keep your silence and let them have this brief time of joy."

Gareth sighed, but nodded. He'd known he'd make this choice. He'd have to live with the silence for the rest of his life.

"What about you and Mira?" Master Amiron asked.

Much of those memories were still fuzzy, the future time a mystery still to be revealed. It was like Gareth was looking down a road through fog. Near events were clearer but the ones more distant were just shadows, until everything was buried in whiteness. Only a few points stood out like beacons of his future with Mira, moments of joy and passion, anger and jealousy, fear and pain. Their life would never be easy, but Gareth couldn't imagine a future without her.

"We'll dance to the song of the jasmine flower," Gareth answered, "and we'll love each other."

"Just remember that love can never be simple for you. If you have a child, he won't be like a normal baby. He will be born different. You and I were born human. We remember what it was like and so we can pretend, even to ourselves, that we still are. He will have no such luxury."

"I know that." And he knew from the distant echoes of a child in Mira's arms that would be called a mongrel. But he couldn't change the future and he wouldn't change that even if he could. He would someday hold his son in his arms.

"I'm sorry," Amiron said again, "that you must face everything alone."

Amiron's Story

Part Two

Master Amiron's plan seemed to be going perfectly. His cousin's rule was failing and the people cheered the great hero who fought the Outsiders. It was surprisingly easy to lure the creatures through the portal. Perhaps the appearance of his team was enough to associate portals with food in even their primitive minds. Perhaps they were drawn to the portals, sensing somehow the vibrant life in the world beyond. Either way, they now came automatically to his open portals, unwitting pawns that played as he wished.

Few knew that Master Amiron was behind the portals. He swore them to secrecy and, at the first whisper of doubt, arranged for quiet accidents. Now only he knew the truth of things. He hid his operations away below the palace in a disused cellar so he would not be discovered.

Victory was within his grasp when the accident occurred. He was preparing for a large incursion that would surely lead to his cousin's abdication. As he opened simultaneous portals, something tore in the walls of the worlds. He was caught in a backlash of energy powerful enough to fling him from his place in the universe.

Amiron's next awareness was confusion. His mind was a jumble of memories like puzzle pieces scattered and unable to form a whole. Fragments of facts, recollections of events, all tumbled together. All seemed familiar yet distant, new yet unknown.

Barely conscious, he was nursed to health by a young soldier. Adrian Boron, recently returned from active service, had seen him arrive in a blaze of golden light. Boron, unsure if Amiron was angel or alien, chose to help the suffering man.

Amiron recognised Boron as a friend, forming a thread of memories out of shared experiences. Weaving into that thread came other memories, faces and events slotting into a tapestry that stretched away in both directions.

He recalled the future as if it were past.

He saw the suffering he had caused.

All his good intensions left a trail of destruction across multiple worlds. His shattered mind had reformed into something new, a wiser person than the one who'd begun this war. He wished to atone for his crimes, to make amends.

He told Boron where he came from and of the creatures who would follow and of the war to come. He was astonished how quickly Boron believed. Amiron had always been persuasive but this ability to sway others was something new, another gift of the portals.

Boron led him to places of science and Amiron talked his way in, his new-found gift persuading others to give him what he needed to rebuild his portal technology. He spoke to those Boron had served in war and tried to reach figures of power with his warnings, struggling through layers of bureaucracy to find those in charge. Where Amiron was able to speak directly, he convinced, but still it was a battle to find those who could make decisions and authorise the organisation that was required.

Amiron could see it in his memories, the Defenders who would stand against the enemy. Through them, Amiron could prevent further harm, but undoing the harm already done would be harder.

A face lingered in Amiron's memory as a distant promise, a man who might hold the key to Amiron's atonement. This man might be the leader Amiron only pretended to be. As he built the Defenders up from nothing, he waited for that young man to cross his path.

He waited for Gareth.

Thirty-One

Blood on the Wedding Gown

Gareth had so much to do in the aftermath that he'd barely seen Richard. It was two days after they'd returned from their mission that Gareth had a few minutes to spare and went to the computer lab to find him. Richard was typing away at his computer, the tracker bracelet still on his wrist. Gareth would have to see about getting that removed. After what Richard had just done, he'd repaid his debt to society and then some. He looked up at Gareth's entrance with an expression that was equal parts joy and guilt.

"I'm glad you made it back," Richard said.

"I know you read the letter," Gareth replied. It was inevitable, he supposed. Richard hated not knowing anything. Sometime during the mission, Richard had got sick of waiting to find out whether they'd win and he opened the letter Gareth had given him before the fight. In it, Gareth had explained everything about his own abilities, his doubts, and the truth he'd learned about Master Amiron.

"You really know what's going to happen?" Richard asked. Gareth nodded. "That's awesome!"

"Not today," Gareth replied. "I know something terrible is going to happen and I can't stop it. I can remember it and so I know it's going to happen, however much I might wish it otherwise."

"The tragedy of Laplace's demon."

"Huh?"

"It's the thought experiment on the subject of hard determinism," Richard said, "which implies that free will is merely an illusion and—" Richard must have caught Gareth's confused expression because he trailed off.

"Sorry," Richard said. "I guess I don't have anything helpful I can say."

"It's OK," Gareth said, feeling anything but OK. "I thought I was going to die on the Outsider world and I didn't. Maybe this will turn out alright in some way I can't see yet."

They sat together for a while in silence. Gareth was grateful for the company and for the fact that there was at least one person on the planet who wouldn't hate him for what was about to happen.

* * *

The world was celebrating. Today, they'd officially announced the success of their mission to the Outsiders' home world. It seemed that everyone on the planet was involved in the party, a great rejoicing across the face of the Earth.

Richard was the hero of the hour. The official reports, of course, explained who it was who had developed the theory and the technology that had been responsible for their great success. So Richard found himself suddenly in demand, called in for interviews and appearances by people wanting to hear the side of the great genius. Gareth saw a clip of one interview, with Richard giving long answers that were probably incomprehensible to most of the audience and devoid of any form of humility. From the way he spoke, it sounded as though Richard was single-handedly responsible for saving the world.

But Gareth couldn't begrudge him his moment of glory. They'd done a great thing and someone deserved to enjoy it.

Gareth was working like mad on his best man speech. He hadn't worried about it before because he'd been so uncertain about his odds of surviving the mission. Now, he glared over his drafts, crossing bits out and fretting over the jokes, worrying that they were too rude or not funny enough. He spent hours sitting over his notes, researching websites that gave tips on a good speech. He spent so long on trying to get the perfect balance between humour and sap, knowing that this would be his final farewell to a friend.

At last, the big day came and Gareth had his notes in the pocket of his suit. He stood at the front of the church, feeling utterly unlike himself in the grey suit and silk waistcoat. Karl stood beside him, again looking unlike his usual self. For one thing, he was constantly grinning and yet fidgeting with anything in sight. Usually so stern and confident, this cheerful, nervous man was a bizarre change.

The church was huge and packed full. All the surviving Defenders were there, mostly dressed in their uniforms. Even Jerry was there, sat at the back in a wheelchair with a nurse in attendance. Karl and Lizzie's parents were there, along with various cousins and old school friends. Then there were the political figures whose lack of invitation could have been cause for a war. There were even a couple of heavy-duty cameras, ready to stream the footage onto TV screens around the world.

The organ music struck up and Lizzie glided along the aisle, a young cousin walking behind as bridesmaid. Karl managed to stop fidgeting but his grin remained in place.

The ceremony was beautiful. They gave their vows. Gareth offered the rings at the right time, managing not to drop them, and they each slid one onto the other's finger, both smiling constantly. There were cheers when Karl kissed Lizzie at the announcement they were man and wife. Gareth almost managed to get caught up in the atmosphere of joy. But all the while, he was aware of the future edging closer.

Somehow, he managed to smile through the mass of photos that were demanded outside the church. He tossed his handful of rose petals and even laughed as Enrico grabbed Karl's collar and poured a box of confetti down his back. Gareth was going through every moment, remembering what Master Amiron had said about joy. They would have so little time together; Gareth wouldn't ruin this moment.

Master Amiron had decided that the happy couple should go to their reception in style, so he had Richard open a portal between the church and the hall. Karl and Lizzie led a procession through. The hall was decorated with flowers and balloons, the tables laid with finest porcelain. Gareth took his seat beside Karl at the head table and tried to smile through the fine dinner, though he barely tasted a mouthful of his roast duck and the strawberry shortbread heart. It felt as though time was racing to the final moment.

Lizzie's father stood to give his speech, talking with pride about the courage of his daughter and the man she loved. It was short and fairly sappy. Lizzie wiped away tears at the end and hugged her father when he'd finished speaking. Around the room, people were both awing and laughing. Then Karl stood, making his speech about fighting alongside Lizzie and, of course, fighting with her. Gareth listened in a detached fashion. He wished for a moment that there was something he could do to pause time, to hold the world frozen with this smile on his friend's face.

But the treacherous hands of the clock moved round and it was Gareth's turn to stand. He made his speech as prepared, reading from notes held in trembling hands. He made the obligatory joke about Karl finally acknowledging which of them was best, which earned a playful punch on the arm from Karl. He kept his smile locked on his face and his tears locked away deep inside. Karl and Lizzie would have their happy moment.

By some miracle, he reached the end of his speech without breaking down. He picked up his champagne glass and saw the others around the room raise theirs. He started the words of the final toast.

Then blue light shot from a point in the middle of the hall, a circle forming rapidly. It glowed in the air, a portal unlike any they'd seen before. Everyone paused for a moment, staring, as a figure all in black leapt from the portal to land among the confused wedding guests. The man stood, his face a mask of resolution as he raised the long knife.

"Death to the abomination!"

The blade whirled across the room. Karl reacted on instinct, shoving himself in front of Lizzie. Then they fell together, Karl landing on top of her and Lizzie desperately calling his name the instant they hit the floor. Gareth was on his knees beside his friends, knowing that the attacker would be dead from self-inflicted poison before the other Defenders could even reach him. All Gareth cared about now was the fact that his friend was lying on the floor, blood spilling out from where the knife pierced his chest.

"At least I got to be your husband," Karl muttered. Then he was gone.

Lizzie was still holding him, hugging his body close to her. The white silk of her dress was crimson with Karl's blood.

Most of the room was still in shock but Gareth knew what this meant. His future was barren of his best friend. He sat beside the unhappy couple and almost wished that he had died on that rooftop.

* * *

Gareth knew that Lizzie would come to speak with him and he knew what she'd say. But he'd have to let her say it. Telling her that he

287

already knew would mean admitting what he could do. It would mean admitting that he'd walked into that wedding reception knowing that Karl wouldn't be walking out again. He'd have to admit that he'd known how Karl would die and why. He'd have to admit that he was the reason Karl was dead. He could never do that, which meant he'd be carrying this secret to his grave.

He had to let Lizzie come to him and tell him her secret. And he had to face the consequences without any guidance.

Master Amiron, his mentor and teacher and the man who'd been more of a father than his dad, had gone back to his home world and wouldn't be stepping through the portal again. Adrian Boron, who had acted as second-in-command and council had been eaten by the Outsiders in the great mission. And now Karl, who had been friend and teammate and brother, was dead, killed in defence of the one he loved.

Gareth waited alone for Lizzie to come to his bedroom, peering through the clouds of grief for those memories of a happier time, a future time. He could picture her smiling and knew that those memories were still to come. The secret that was tearing her apart now would be a source of joy in the days ahead, a bright beacon of light amid the darkness of her grief.

She sat in silence on the edge of Gareth's bed for a long time, gathering the strength for the confession. Gareth just sat beside her, letting her do this in her own time.

When she spoke, it was barely a whisper, as though she was afraid of her own words:

"I think I'm pregnant."